Clare Connelly was raised in a small town in Australia among a family of avid readers. She spent much of her childhood up a tree, Mills & Boon book in hand. She is married to her own real-life hero in a bungalow near the sea with their two children. She is frequently found staring into space – a surefire sign she is in the world of her characters. Writing for Mills & Boon is a long-held dream. Clare can be contacted via clareconnelly.com or on her Facebook page.

Ellie Darkins spent her formative years devouring romance novels, and after completing her English degree, she decided to make a living from her love of books. As a writer and editor, her work now entails dreaming up romantic proposals, hot dates with alpha males and trips to the past with dashing heroes. When she's not working, she can usually be found at her local library or out for a run. You can visit her blog at elliedarkins.com

Sophie Pembroke has been dreaming, reading and writing romance ever since she read her first Mills & Boon novel as a teen, so getting to write romance fiction for a living is a dream come true! Born in Abu Dhabi, Sophie grew up in Wales and now lives in Hertfordshire with her scientist husband, her incredibly imaginative daughter and her adventurous, adorable little boy. In Sophie's world, happy is for ever after, everything stops for tea, and there's always time for one more page.

In The Spotlight

In The Spotlight:
Chasing Stars

CLARE CONNELLY

ELLIE DARKINS

SOPHIE PEMBROKE

MILLS & BOON

First Published in Great Britain 2025
by Mills & Boon, an imprint of HarperCollins*Publishers* Ltd
1 London Bridge Street, London, SE1 9GF

www.harpercollins.co.uk

HarperCollins*Publishers*
Macken House, 39/40 Mayor Street Upper,
Dublin 1, D01 C9W8, Ireland

In The Spotlight: Chasing Stars © 2025 Harlequin Enterprises ULC.

Burn Me Once © 2018 Clare Connelly
Falling for the Rebel Princess © 2017 Ellie Darkins
Island Fling to Forever © 2018 Sophie Pembroke

ISBN: 978-0-263-42079-1

BURN ME ONCE

CLARE CONNELLY

For anyone who's ever fallen hard for a muso.

And for Isaac Hanson, who was my first rockstar crush. We'll always have *MMMBop*.

PROLOGUE

In what distant deeps or skies
Burnt the fire of thine eyes?
On what wings dare he aspire?
What the hand, dare seize the fire?

—*William Blake*

SHE HAS GOT to be kidding me.

I stare at the screen one last time, checking that the Tweet actually exists. And there it is. One hundred and forty characters reaching through time and space to slam me hard over the head.

I'm getting married! @_TheRealTomBanks asked and obv I said yes!!! Couldn't be happier! #soinlove #dreamsdocometrue #happyeverafter

I curl my fingers around my phone, tempted to pitch the damned thing into the street. Only the thought of the personal information I keep stored in it stops me from being so reckless. The press would have a field-day if they found my phone lying in the gutter.

How can she still screw with me even now, three months after we 'took a break'?

Then again, isn't this so like Sienna? Sienna who's had six years of my life. Sienna whom I thought I loved. Sienna who is now engaged to another man.

Fractured memories of our last months together assault me from all angles; they are blades of mirrored glass, shards through my mind, tormenting me every which way, pricking me with exquisite ecstasy.

It was a nightmare.

And yet it was my life.

The nightmare has ended and I don't know if I remember how to live.

I need a drink. And I need to get Sienna the hell out of my head once and for all. And I can think of a really good way to kill two birds with one stone.

The bar is hardly my usual scene. It's retro, but in an authentic way, which I guess means the décor hasn't been updated since the early nineties. There's peeling linoleum in the corner of the bar, where I prop my arms and hunch down, not wanting to attract attention to myself.

#happyeverafter, my ass.

I order a beer, barely noticing the recognition that flickers across the guy's face. I'm used to being recognised. So is Sienna. Which makes it even harder to believe she's been able to keep this relationship secret. Not just from me, but the world.

A frown gravels across my jaw. No, she didn't keep the whole thing secret. They're *friends. Just friends.* She's told me that a dozen times. And I bought it.

Was she fucking him at the same time she was me? Jesus. Was that why she ended it? She told me she needed space to figure herself out and I bought it. Space? *Space?*

After six years together she doesn't even have the

fucking decency to give me a heads-up that she's with someone else?

Nausea rolls in my gut.

I don't particularly ascribe to the rock and roll lifestyle, but tonight I want to write myself off. I want to get hammered. I want to get drunk. I want to get fall-down pissed.

I need to forget about Sienna somehow.

CHAPTER ONE

'COME ON! IT'S the perfect opportunity to put Jeremy behind you.'

I send Eliza a look of impatience but can't fight the ever-present swoop of shame that accompanies any mention of his name. 'He *is* behind me.'

'If that were true you wouldn't have spent the past eight months wallowing!'

'I am *not* wallowing,' I deny, turning to Cassie pleadingly.

'I can see why you think I'd back you up, but seriously, Ally, you *have* to get back out there.'

My stomach flops and my gaze wanders towards the man at the bar.

Ethan 'rock star' Ash. And so much hotter in real life than I could ever have imagined.

I shake my head. 'No way. I'm not going to talk to him.'

'Why not?' Cassie throws a look over her shoulder, and when she looks back at us she has a pretty flush in her cheeks.

'*Because.*' I shoot them both a look they know better than to argue with. 'Now, can we please talk about something else?'

I sip my drink, crossing my legs in the other direction, and most definitely *not* looking towards the bar again.

'What's new?'

I listen to their responses, relieved as all hell that they've let the matter of the smoking hot rock god drop. At least for now...

'Drinks are empty. It's your turn, Ally.'

I blink, drawn back into the conversation by Eliza, who is handing her glass to me. I frown. 'Isn't it table service?'

'Nah. Not on a Friday.'

I grimace. 'Remind me why we chose this place again?'

Cassie points to the sign overhead and I know what it says without even reading it: *Happy Hour—9-9!*

As the only one of our little trio who can afford full-price drinks in decent bars with professional wait staff, I resist the urge to complain. Besides, the place is obviously good enough for Ethan Ash. Which begs the question: *what's he doing here?* He's alone, and has been since I got here an hour earlier. Is he waiting for someone? Has he been stood up? That doesn't make sense. Who'd stand *him* up?

I'm two cocktails in, so I know I have a bit of an alcohol-confident swagger as I make my way to the bar. But I'm immune to tall, dark and handsome men now—Jeremy cured me of that habit for life—so I determinedly move past him—*way* past, like other-planet past—choosing to prop my elbows on a spot that's practically in the kitchen it's so far away from him.

Despite the fact there are at least seven people serving behind the bar, I'm kept waiting for several minutes. Slowing down is probably a good thing, so I don't make a fuss. I pull my phone out instead, flicking through Instagram and checking my emails, humming along without realising to the song overhead. It's only when the song begins to surround, envelop and roll over me, with an oddly perfect surround-sound quality, that I look up and realise he's right beside me.

He.

He of the thick brown hair and ocean-green eyes. He of the tanned skin and gazillion-pack abs. He of the torn jeans and loose grey shirt—designer dishevelled. And the way he smells—delicious. My gut twists in enthusiastic acknowledgement of all of the above and my knees tremble as if they're conspiring to pull me closer to him.

But my face is still following orders and thankfully stays resolutely unimpressed.

A smile flicks his lips as he continues to croon—yes, he's actually *crooning*—the words to a pop song, for God's sake—and I desperately don't want him to stop.

'How's it going?'

It's so completely *not* what I expect he of the stubbled jaw to say that I laugh softly. 'How's *what* going?'

His grin is disarming and he obviously knows it. How could he not? His accent is huskier in real life—broad British that is more Midlands than Eton. It's sexy AF.

'Life. The universe. Your place in it.'

'Ah. That sounds like a conversation more suited to Neil deGrasse Tyson's living room.'

'Want me to give him a call? See if he's free?'

I roll my eyes. 'Sure. You got him on speed dial or something?'

He lifts his phone out of his pocket. It's an iPhone, I think, but it looks to be pure gold. Catching me looking, he seems almost embarrassed as he clarifies, 'I get given them.'

At that moment, thank God, a waiter appears behind the bar. 'What'll it be?'

'Vodka gimlet, gin and tonic and Prosecco.'

He nods and moves away, picking up where he of the smooth as caramel voice left off, singing the song softly as he mixes our drinks.

'See?'

Ethan calls me back to him and he's holding his phone so I can see the world's most famous astrophysicist staring back at me.

'You seriously know him?'

'Sure. We did a charity thing together a year ago. Nice guy.'

I arch a brow. Am I *really* standing in a bar in SoHo talking to a veritable rock god superstar about a world-famous scientist?

'I'm impressed.'

'So am I. I think you're the first girl I've met in a bar who outed herself as a science nerd.'

'Your implication being that knowing who one of the most pre-eminent astrophysicists of our time is makes me a nerd? I would think that's kind of mainstream knowledge.'

He shrugs. 'Not in my experience.'

'Ah. So maybe your experience is just…limited.'

The bartender returns with our drinks, and before I can hand my credit card over Ethan Sexier-than-Thou Ash slides his own across the bar.

'Maybe it is.'

His eyes hold mine and my tummy lurches as though

I've just driven at speed over the crest of a hill. I'm in free fall.

'Don't use his card,' I say, my voice croaky as I drag my attention to the waiter behind the bar. 'It's my shout.'

'You can get the next round.' Ethan's voice brooks no opposition and the bartender taps his card on the machine.

'Next round?' I arch a brow. 'Meaning…?'

He leans closer. He smells amazing. Like salt and sand and sunshine all rolled into one.

'Meaning these drinks are on me.'

He pulls back just far enough to grin at me while his eyes meet mine, green versus blue, and I am losing whatever battle it is we're waging. Then his fingers lift up and press lightly to the back of my hand. Just for a second, but it's enough. Heat spirals up my arm spreading goosebumps on my flesh and, mortifyingly, tensing my nipples. His eyes catch the reaction and my cheeks flush bright pink.

'It was nice to meet you…?'

His question hangs in the air but I'm flummoxed. The way my body has reacted is strange. Unexpected.

'You too.'

I deliberately don't give him my name. Names are where the problems start.

I'm over Jeremy. I am.

If I ever see him again I think I could seriously find myself in a federal prison for life.

But the ghost of what we were…what he turned me into…is thick inside me. *Always.* I don't remember the last time I looked in the mirror and didn't see *her. That* woman. The woman he made me. The woman I came to loathe.

I fight the shudder. I'm not her any more. But it's taken eight long months to claw my way back, and names are the beginning of forgetting that.

No names.

I lift the three drinks easily between my hands and give him one last smile without meeting his eyes before making my way back to the table.

Eliza and Cassie are staring at me, the former with a knowing smile and the latter with a dropped jaw.

'You *talked* to him?' Cassie squeaks in obvious disbelief.

'He talked to me,' I mumble, sliding their drinks across the table and looking guiltily towards the bar. He's talking to someone else now. A guy. Is that who he came to meet? My heart drops. Does that mean he'll be going soon?

'He's *hot*,' Eliza pronounces. 'Why the hell are you still sitting with *us*?'

I change the subject back to Cassie's work situation, ignoring Eliza's pointed stares and occasional jab beneath the table. But I drink quickly. Because I want to go back to the bar? Or because I need something to cool down my fevered blood?

Only it's not working. My body is vibrating with a sensual need I haven't felt in a long time. Heat is forming between my legs and I am so tempted to do something really stupid. Something I haven't done in a long time.

Of their own accord, and definitely without my permission, my eyes shift towards him. He's propped against the bar with glorious nonchalance, and he's still chatting to the same guy, but his eyes are locked on me. He doesn't try to hide it when I look up.

A thrill of something runs down my spine.

I'm so close to giving in to temptation, and that would be bad. Oh, it would be really good in some ways but… no. *Bad.* Definitely bad.

'Okay, ladies,' I murmur, pushing my almost finished drink aside and standing in one movement. 'I'm going to head home.'

'What?' Eliza pulls a face. 'Alone? *Now?* It's so early!'

'I know.' I shrug. 'But if I don't go I think I'll live to regret it.'

I wink at them, so that they can't help but understand my meaning, and then blow each an air-kiss. There's a slight tremble in my legs as I cut my way through the bar. Despite the fact we're past the cut-off for free drinks it's heaving busy now.

My body seems to be in silent rebellion of the decision I've made and is trying to make me change my mind. I don't, though.

When I emerge from the bar's air-conditioned comfort the night's humidity crashes at me like a wave. But it's nothing compared to the fever in my blood. I lift my hand, calling for a taxi, but it sails past.

'Damn it.'

I begin to walk further down the sidewalk, my eyes scanning the street in both directions.

'Hey.'

Though we've only spoken perhaps ten lines of dialogue to one another, his voice is imprinted in my mind. I recognise it instantly, even before I turn around.

'Oh, hey.' My heart is determinedly hammering against my chest.

'You're leaving already?'

When I frown my eyebrows draw together and I get a little line between them. I feel it form now.

'Um… I've left, technically.'

'Right. Where are you headed?'

'Home,' I say firmly, but my body rolls with the potential there. 'Alone.'

It's a defiant stop-sign and he laughs.

'How about one last drink?'

One last drink. With Ethan all-your-dreams-come-true Ash. And then what? I'm already in serious danger of begging him to come home with me. And I suspect he would be incredible in bed. A good lover is one thing, but chemistry can't be faked—and right now the chemistry bubbling between us is practically giving me an orgasm on the spot.

And don't I want that?

Don't I *deserve* that?

There's been no one since Jeremy and I ache for what I think Ethan Ash could do to me. But then what? Am I really ready? How do you know when you are?

I shake my head slowly, not quite meeting his eyes. 'I think that would be a bad idea.' The words are thick, as though my mouth is coated in honey.

'Go on. Live dangerously.'

His wink is the last word in delicious desire.

'*Are* you dangerous?' I ask.

'I think I could be around you.'

There are cars zipping past and people moving quickly around us, and yet it is just him and me, and the air around us seems to throb with awareness and the heaviness of need.

A shiver runs down my spine, but it's not a shiver of darkness or danger so much as one of anticipation. *Oh, God. I'm done for.*

'Isn't that a good reason to stay away?' I say. My

brain makes a valiant last-ditch effort to keep my decision in place.

'Depends.'

He moves infinitesimally closer and I breathe in
deeply, tasting his masculine fragrance and letting it
roll through my blood.

'On what?'

And then he does it again. Just the lightest touch on
the back of my hand, but for longer this time, so that I
have time to register the contact and enjoy the sensation
of desire that resonates through my body.

'On whether you like to live dangerously.'

'Not generally,' I respond quickly, my lips flicking
with a tight smile.

'That surprises me.'

'Why? You don't know anything about me.'

He drops his hand away. The absence of touch leaves
me feeling bereft.

'Don't I?'

'How could you? We just met.'

'Mmm…'

God, just that single throaty sound of acknowledgement sends a riot tumbling through my veins.

'I know you have the most beautiful hair I've ever
seen.'

I've heard that line before. Why do men feel the need
to compliment hair? Mine is striking more than beautiful, but I've long ago given up feeling self-conscious
about the thick rust-coloured mane that was the bane
of my middle school existence, when my white skin,
freckled nose and fire-engine-red hair led to almost
daily teasing.

Yes, I've heard the line before, but it's never made my stomach flip like this. I've never *believed* the line.

Thanks to the pioneering efforts of Christina Hendricks, right around the time I was hitting college, I made a kind of peace with my peaches and cream complexion, voluptuous figure and rusty hair, but I still never bought the pick-up lines. The guys who told me they loved my curves and dimples.

How easy it is to ignore flattery! But there's something in his eyes, his face and his voice that renders me incapable of being dismissive now.

'I know that your eyes show me everything you're feeling and that your skin is like salt-water pearls.'

My laugh is a hoarse sound in the swirling atmosphere of need. 'That's all *very* cheesy.'

It's not. It's really not. Maybe it's the fact he writes and sings some of the most famous love songs of all time, but he can totally pull this off. This guy, and this guy alone, can make those lines sound like they're being spoken for the first time ever.

His laugh answers mine, and I'm smiling even as I want to acquiesce to his flirtation and do as he bids— live dangerously.

'Even if it's true?'

My breath catches in my throat and I look away— straight into the curious eyes of a woman a few feet away. She's studying us and her cell phone is in her hand.

Strange how quickly I have forgotten that Ethan Ash is a celebrity. Heat spreads through my cheeks and he follows my gaze, quickly assessing the reason for it. Now he touches me with more urgency, placing a hand in the small of my back and leading me further down the street.

'So?'

'So what?'

I toss a look over my shoulder. The woman is still there, cell phone still in hand. Busybody! I guess this is par for the course for him, but I can't imagine that. Being watched and observed all the time. Having people think they have a right to pry into your life, crack the lid off it whenever it suits them. *No thanks.*

'Want to take a walk on the wild side?'

'I…' My footing stumbles a little as my eyes skid to his and all sense of gravity and order tips off balance. 'I'm not sure.'

I look away.

'How about we start with your name and you can make your mind up over a quiet drink?'

'I…'

I'm struck dumb. I don't think that's ever happened to me in my whole life. Acknowledging that brings a smile to my face.

'I think I'd like that.'

His smile shines bright light and heat into every microscopic corner of my world.

'Then let's get going.'

CHAPTER TWO

WE'RE SHEPHERDED INTO the obviously incredibly exclusive bar with a degree of fanfare that might make even the Queen of England envious. At the bar around the corner from our flat, with its neon lights and pumping songs, it was easy to miss the degree of Ethan Ash's celebrity. Not to ignore the fact that he's unique and different and special, but that these are qualities he has independent of his fame.

Here the deference is marked and reverent, his celebrity obvious and noteworthy. He is treated like the Second Coming, and some of that glory deflects nicely on to me, as his obvious companion.

And it *is* obvious. He kept his hand in the small of my back the whole way here, and he stays close by me as we weave our way through the establishment. I like him being close.

Close enough that I can smell his fragrance and enjoy his warmth.

Close enough that I can slip into the fantasy of what it would be like—*will* be like?—to touch his body all over. To kiss him. To taste him.

I stifle a groan, dipping my head forward to hide the liquid desire that is taking over my body. Desire is unexpected and yet it is welcome. After Jeremy I wasn't sure I'd ever feel it again.

'Here?'

He nods towards a cosy booth seat and every cell in my body ratchets up with awareness. Of him, of me, of the intimacy of that booth.

I nod slowly, then slide in ahead of him. 'Do you come here often?'

He shakes his head. 'Nah, not really my scene.'

'That's interesting. It's very much *my* scene.' I wink at him. 'At least more so than the place we were in before.'

'Yeah, you were a bit of a fish out of water there.'

'Really?' I wrinkle my nose. 'Why do you say that?'

He shrugs. 'Gin and tonic?'

It takes me a second to realise he's asking me a question—what kind of drink I want. A second longer to realise that he knows my regular drink.

'How did you…?'

'You ordered it right in front of me.'

'I also ordered a Prosecco and a vodka gimlet.'

'But you gave those to your friends.'

The certainty that he's been watching me oozes pleasure over my skin. I think he knows, because his smile hints at the same kind of pleasure reverberating inside him. Heat is a burst between us.

'So I did.' I lean forward conspiratorially. 'You're not some kind of stalker, are you?'

His laugh is heaven. 'Not until the last hour or so.'

More pleasure. His compliments are doing everything they should, and even though I'd like to think I'm genuinely hard to impress—thank you, Jeremy—I feel myself soften towards him.

Curiosity is as rampant in my body as desire. 'So,' I say, leaning in closer towards him. 'What's your name?'

For a second I have him fooled. Surprise etches across his face and then he bursts out laughing.

'What?' I continue the charade, my eyes wide, expression droll. 'Why is that funny?'

He sobers. 'It's not.' He clears his throat. 'I'm... Christopher Smith.'

A smile tickles my lips. 'Pleased to meet you, Christopher Smith.'

I wonder how often Ethan Ash gets hit on by girls who are more drawn in by his rock god status than anything else? I wonder if that makes him cynical about women? Or if it makes him think he's God's gift? In my case, I'm definitely not doing anything to disabuse him of that notion. In fact I seriously suspect that if God *did* gift women a man purely for pleasure it would be this guy.

But, hang on. He's hot, sure, and he has the voice of a husky alpha-angel—but he could be *awful* in bed, right?

The thought brings a frown to my face. Isn't there some rule of thumb about that? The really gorgeous guys don't have to work for it so they never learn to be good? Am I going to test that theory with Ethan one-look-will-melt-your-panties-off Ash?

I shift a little in the seat. Our knees brush beneath the table and I suck in a sharp breath. Apparently I am.

He catches the involuntary gesture and his smile is sensual. 'You're nervous?'

I don't know if I'm nervous or surprised. This juggernaut has picked me up and it's dragging me along with it, and I feel a strange disconnect with my own autonomy. 'Maybe.'

He lifts a hand in the air without taking his attention from my face. 'Because of me?'

I shake my head, biting down on my lip. His eyes roam my face like it's a continent he must conquer. He sees everything.

The sense of familiarity is as overwhelming as it is bizarre. I'm sitting in a booth with a bona fide rock star. I should feel strange, but I don't. It all feels so *right*.

'What's your name?'

'Ally.'

'Ally.'

He rolls it around his mouth as if tasting the two symbols. His accent is even hotter when he's saying my name. He makes the A sound like a sigh…'Ah'.

'Is that short for something?'

I nod.

'Gonna make me guess?'

I grin, and my eyes lift as a waitress approaches, her pale blonde hair pulled into a braid that wraps around her head like a crown.

'Good evening. Here are some menus.' She places two dark books on the tabletop. 'Can I get you a drink to start?'

Ethan turns away to address the waitress. He orders a beer and a gin and tonic, then adds some onion rings for good measure. In profile, he's fascinating. I hadn't noticed until then the bump halfway down his nose that speaks, presumably, of it having been broken at some point in his life. In an accident? Or a fight?

Goosebumps dance down my spine as I imagine the rather sexy image of Ethan Ash in a fist-fight with someone. He'd be a good fighter. Not prone to aggression, I'd bet, but definitely able to take care of himself.

Wow. I didn't even know that I found that kind of thing attractive.

'Alexandra?' he says as he spins back to me.

I don't instantly understand what he's saying, and then I realise. He's guessing my full name.

'No.'

'Hmm…' A low, gruff growl.

Help me, Jesus, I am about to sin.

Beneath the table his fingers find my knee and he strums it like a guitar, gently lashing his fingers over my flesh so that my breath is raspy.

'Do I get a penalty?'

'Definitely.'

'And what would that be?'

I tilt my head to the side, my eyes dancing with amusement even as desire makes my lids heavy.

'Every time you get it wrong,' I say, after a long beat of silence has stretched between us, 'I get to ask you anything I want.'

He lifts his brows skyward. 'Sure. Sounds fair. So, what do you want to know?'

Great question. What *do* I want to know? 'How does *everything* sound?'

He laughs. '"Everything" could take a while. There's twenty-eight years to cover.'

'Let's start with what brings you to the Big Old Apple?'

'A gig. And recording.'

'An album?'

He shakes his head and leans closer, so that his words whisper gently across my cheek.

'That's a separate question.'

'No fair!'

I lift a hand to playfully push at his chest, except the moment my fingers connect with his warm strength no pushing occurs. I hold my hand against him, my eyes meet his, and I feel like I'm sinking hard and fast, with no hope of saving myself.

'Alita?'

I shake my head and dredge up a smile, but it feels heavy on my face because it has to wade through all the desire that's chewing my insides up.

'You're recording an album?'

'Sorta.'

'What does "sorta" mean?'

He shifts his body a little, bringing himself closer to me. 'I'm tinkering. Sketching.'

'Sketching?'

'You know… Getting a feel for some new stuff. Working on pieces.'

'You do that in a recording studio?'

'Sometimes.' He shrugs.

My hand feels the ripple of his muscles and my gut clenches correspondingly.

'And you snuck an extra question in there. Don't think I didn't notice.'

'Uh-huh. I'm very sneaky.'

'I like sneaky.'

His head dips closer. My breath is burning through me.

'Alena?'

When I shake my head this time it brings me closer. Our lips are barely an inch apart and my hand is still on his chest, my fingertips teasing the soft fabric of his shirt. Up close, his scent is intoxicating.

'What's your question?'

My brain is thick and woolly. I want to kiss him. I want to kiss him so badly that I can phantom-feel his lips on mine already.

What if he's a terrible kisser?

My eyes drop to his lips, assessing the possibility of that.

No.

He won't be.

I'm sure of it.

'Don't have one, huh?' he teases.

A noise cracks us apart. I blink, like I'm waking from a dream. The waitress has placed our drinks on the tabletop and then a basket of onion rings. It's surprisingly sweet that he ordered something so pedestrian. Had I expected he'd ask for caviar-dressed lobster?

'What's it like? Being famous?'

His expression shows surprise. He wasn't expecting that.

'You're the first person to ask me that,' he muses, drawing the foam top off his beer in a way that is so absolutely masculine my knees knock with feminine heat.

'Really?' I sound normal. That's good. 'You weren't born famous. It must be a bit weird.'

'Weird's a good word for it.' He shrugs. 'I don't notice so much now. But at first…'

'You were…how old? When your first record came out?'

'I didn't release a record at first. I was big on YouTube before any of the labels came knocking.'

'So you've been doing this a really long time?'

He reaches for an onion ring, crunches it. 'I was sixteen when I topped the UK charts.'

I'm impressed—obviously. All the more so because

he says it without a hint of arrogance. It's just a fact, one he's accepted as a part of the fabric of his story, so that he says it without realising what a huge deal it is.

'Do you like it?'

'Music?'

'Fame,' I correct, sipping my drink.

'Nah. It's shit.'

I laugh—it's not what I was expecting him to say at all. 'Really?'

'Really.' He grins. 'You get used to it, but at first it's like being on a different planet. I'll never forget the first time I opened my front door to a throng of paparazzi. It was madness. I was still living at home—we had to move to a gated community with security fences and cameras. I can't get over how fascinated people are by the minutiae of my life. Of anyone else's life. I once had a busboy sell the cutlery I'd used for lunch on eBay.'

I pull a face, barely able to imagine the invasiveness of that.

'But the music…'

He grins and my heart flops.

'I live for it, you know? Always have.'

And he begins to hum, something low and deep, and he moves closer to me again, propping an elbow on the table to form a sort of cage around me. He is big and I'm not. I've always been little, but in the circle created by his arms I feel something I've never felt before. I feel safe.

Safe?

From what?

It's a stupid, errant thought. After all, whatever's happening between us is possibly the most danger I've been in. Even with the guys I was with before Jeremy it was never like this. I was in control. Always.

Ethan when-is-he-going-to-kiss-me? Ash is definitely *not* eating out of the palm of my hands. *Yet.*

A need to grasp control out of his hands spins through me. I reach up and curl my fingers around his shirt, so that I can pull him closer still, and then I brush my lips to his so that I feel the notes rather than just hear them. If possible, his voice tastes even better than it sounds.

'Alison?' he says against my lips.

I shake my head.

'Do you have a question for me?'

I'm at a crossroad. Past, future and present swirl around me. Need, want, right and wrong. These are all voices and forces throbbing in my head. But one voice is loudest of all.

Desire shouts through me.

'Can we go yet?'

Every time I question the wisdom of this I think of the freaking Tweet. *#soinlove*

Sienna's moved on. Why the hell shouldn't I have some fun too?

Something squeezes inside me and my past with Sienna flashes before me. The years we spent together. The way we came through the industry together. I get her and she gets me. It damned near killed me when we broke up. Only her promise that it was temporary eased that pain.

And now she's fucking engaged to another guy.

A new sense of urgency powers my intent.

'Hell, yeah. Let's get out of here.'

I drain my beer, noticing she's hardly touched her drink. I nod towards it but she shakes her head.

'I'm okay.'

She's better than okay. Briefly I feel a wave of guilt. To Sienna. To Ally. There's no doubt in my mind that I'm not thinking one hundred percent clearly, but my instincts are telling me to go with this—or is that my cock?—and I'm not going to ignore them.

'Let's go.'

I hold my hand out and she places her palm in mind. Her hand's small, and yet it fits into mine perfectly. I stand and pull her closer to me as I do. She smells like vanilla and moonlight.

Someone's tipped the press off as to my whereabouts, so that when we step out of the club there's flashes everywhere. Ally's surprised. She's not used to fame and its pointed intrusion. I pull her closer to my chest. The desire to protect her is instinctive. I don't want her being collateral damage in all of this.

I hail a cab and it stops instantly. I hold the door open for her and she slips inside, a blur of pale skin, bright blue eyes and long red hair. I follow, moving close to her in the back of the cab.

I hear every single one of Ally's rushed breaths echo inside my soul.

I give the driver my hotel address and then I turn to Ally. I don't know what I'm going to say to her. Thoughts fly from my head at the sight of her huge wide eyes and parted lips.

Fuck it.

I want her.

I kiss her as though my life depends on it. I kiss her

with an aching hunger and desperation that surprises us both.

Or maybe it doesn't—because it's exactly how she kisses me back.

CHAPTER THREE

Is IT POSSIBLE to pass out from pleasure? I know that's generally the body's response to painful stimuli, but is it possible to be so turned on that the pleasure almost becomes pain? I've never had sex in a cab, but if this drive takes any longer I'm going to do just that.

His hand is on my thigh and his tongue is tangled with mine, his lips move over mine and I am melting into the leather of the seat. Desire is like a volcano in my core, bursting with lava-like heat. He runs his fingers higher, confidently, firmly, until he reaches the lace of my thong. He pads his fingertips across me there and I groan into his mouth, my fingers lifting to knot into his thick hair, my body weak and strong all at once.

He removes his hand from between my legs and his desertion is a wave that flushes me with ice. I grind my hips impatiently and make a whimpering sound as his flat palm drags up my body, over the softness of my clothes to the curves of my breast. He rolls his hand across me as though I am an object and he its owner. His touch sends spirals of fire deep into my body, affecting me on a cellular level.

I make a gurgling sound and laugh, pushing up to kiss him harder, to let my breasts flatten his hand between us. We are wedged together and my hands are curled around his neck and, God, he tastes and feels amazing. Better than amazing.

Finally the cab pulls to a stop and I am flushed with relief—until I realise it's a stop sign.

'You've gotta be fucking kidding me,' he snaps, his brow furrowed as he shoots an impatient look through the glass of his windscreen.

He feels it too, then. This need that is reverberating through the back of the cab somewhere in the middle of Park Avenue. It makes me feel inexplicably relieved, knowing that I'm not the only one out here on this limb.

He turns to look at me and I laugh at the bewilderment on his features.

'I swear to God, if this takes much longer…'

I totally get it. Hadn't I just been thinking the same thing?

I swallow, trying to bring moisture back into my parched mouth. My hand is still on his chest; I can feel the rapid beating of his heart. *Thump, thump, thump.*

Craning my head around, I can just make out the street sign that shows we're on the corner of Park Avenue and East Twenty-Second. 'You said the Gramercy?'

'Yeah.'

'It's like a block away. Let's walk.'

He arches a brow, and heat simmers through me as he reaches forward and taps on the glass.

'We'll get out here.'

He tosses some money through the window and winks at me, opening the door and stepping out so that he can hold it wide for me. I follow, my foot landing on the pavement for the briefest moment before his arm wraps around my waist and draws me to him.

I don't think the cab has even driven off before his lips are back on mine, with renewed intensity and urgency. His body is strong and he pushes me easily, guiding me to the sandstone wall of some building. It's cold and hard behind me, and he's hard and hot against me, his body all angles and planes and thick strong legs surrounding me, holding me still as he grinds against me. His arms are my cage and, *oh*, the sweetness of being trapped by him!

His mouth holds my head to the wall and I devour him as he devours me, my hands curling around his back to find the waistband of his jeans. I slide my fingers beneath his shirt, groaning as warm skin rewards my seeking. It's so soft and smooth beneath me. I draw my fingertips on a slow exploration higher, along the ridges of his spine and then to his sides, to hips that are carved and firm.

'*Fuuuuck...*'

He groans into my mouth, wrenching his head away—and it is a wrench. Every line of his body speaks to that. It is as though he's had to fight his way through quicksand just to find space between us.

Maybe it's the whole rock star thing. Maybe it makes him sexier than mortals. I don't know. This is so not normal, though. Is it for him?

'I need to get you to my hotel. *Now.*'

I nod, not even bothering to argue with him. But there's a frown between his eyes, just like I always get.

I lift my finger to it, absentmindedly exploring the groove. 'What's wrong?'

The line deepens. He has a dimple in his cheek and when he frowns it's deliciously seductive.

'Nothing. I…' And then he shakes his head, steps back, reaches for my hand.

We've just been simulating sex with our clothes on, and yet there is something bizarrely intimate about the simple act of lacing our fingers together. His, mine, his, mine, his, mine—in and out, they are woven together, and it's a new kind of coming together.

'Let's go.'

I nod, not sure I'm capable of speech anyway.

After a few paces he looks at me with an almost embarrassed grin. 'You look like you've been thoroughly felt up.'

'Felt up?' I laugh. 'I guess I have been, now that you mention it.'

He squeezes my hand and I lift my other hand to run it over my hair. Always difficult to contain, it is beyond wild now. His fingers have done that. The knowledge makes my tummy flip.

'Sooo…' he says on a laugh. A husky laugh. 'This isn't how I thought my night would be going down.'

I don't know if it's an intentional *double entendre* but I have an instant image of him doing just that—going down on me—in my mind, and my face heats up.

Unknowingly, I quicken my step. 'You and me both,' I hear myself respond, hugely impressed at my ability to sound almost normal.

'What were your plans tonight?'

'Drinks with the girls.' I shrug. 'Then home by ten to catch up on *Poldark* and do a face mask.'

He pulls a face.

'What? You don't approve?'

'Of *Poldark*? It's something my mother watches.'

'Mmm… Her and every other red-blooded woman on the planet.'

'Seriously?'

He squeezes my hand again. I love the way that feels. Like he's reaching right into my heart and giving it a little paddle with electricity.

'Uh, *yeah*. *Poldark* is awesome. Hot, hot, *hot*. You should watch it.'

'After that recommendation? How could I not?'

We stop at an intersection and traffic moves through it, too thick for us to go against the lights. And so we wait.

The night is balmy—I love New York nights like this.

'Yeah. Summer's got something going for it.'

I hadn't realised I'd spoken aloud until he answered my observation. He pulls my hand, so that I bump closer to him. I love the way he smells. The way he feels. A shiver of something a bit like apprehension runs down my spine but I refuse to analyse it. The problem is, though, I'm really not *this* girl any more. I used to be able to just roll with the night…have fun without taking a second to think about the consequences.

When, exactly, did I grow out of that?

I remember learning to drive and my dad telling me that young people always think they're invincible. I guess it's true. It's so easy to believe that nothing will happen—nothing will go wrong.

And nothing *has* gone wrong for me, yet caution has set into my bones along with age. At twenty-five I am less able to ignore the paths before me, and I wonder which this night will lead to.

After we've slept together—then what? Do I stay the

night? Or creep out while he sleeps? If I stay, do we have breakfast together?

And then...?

Do I give him my number and wonder if Ethan I-have-won-a-million-Grammys Ash will call me? Worse, do I take *his* number and then call him? Agonising over what to say and whether he wants to see me again?

'So, Alesandre, when you're not being impossibly sexy in tacky bars what do you do with yourself?'

'Alesandre is just the Italian version of Alexandra, you know.'

'Mmm. So that's a no. Altona?'

I laugh and shake my head. The lights switch to green and we move across the street, each as swiftly as the other, our mutual anxiety to be in privacy barrelling towards us.

'My flatmates chose the venue.' I wrinkle my nose. 'They like it.'

They like the prices, really, but loyalty keeps me quiet on that score. Cassie's a Broadway actress, but roles are few and far between and she's forever auditioning and waiting for her big break. She's an incredible performer, though—I have no doubt she'll hit it big. Eliza is a primary school teacher, and while she works hard she seems to spend almost her entire salary on stuff for her students. New supplies, craft projects, science experiments...

Maybe if she didn't insist on doing that we'd be able to drink in slightly more salubrious accommodations.

'You're not from New York?'

'How can you tell?' I look up at him, surprise obvious on my face.

He draws us to a slow stop just before moving down East Twenty-Second. 'Your accent.'

'You can pick up on that?'

He grins. 'Is that weird?'

I bite down on my lip to stop myself groaning at how damned sexy the twist of his lips is. Ahead of us, the retro light installation above the Gramercy Park Hotel leads a path to our immediate future. Beneath it there's a huddle of people. I'm not sure, at first, why they're just standing there—and then I make out the shape of a long-lens camera.

'There's paparazzi at your hotel.' My eyes lift to his face.

A muscle throbs against his jaw, like he's clenching his teeth or thinking dark thoughts. My insides clench.

'You go ahead of me,' he says.

'Will that work?'

He looks at me for a long moment and then nods. 'Yeah. Wait for me at the lifts inside.'

It's easy enough for me to slip past the paparazzi. One photographer lifts his camera and holds it poised at my face. But then, when he sees through the lens that I am nobody, he drops it once more.

I am glad I am nobody.

I am glad I am not *her*.

The woman who ruined a family.

Guilt sledges through me.

Ethan Ash isn't Jeremy, and this isn't a big deal.

It's just…sex. Fun. Easy. Nothing serious.

Nonetheless, my heart palpitates furiously as I turn and look over my shoulder, catching sight of him as he saunters—yes, *saunters*—across the street, hands in the pockets of his well-worn jeans, head tilted at an angle that shows the hard lines of his face.

Desire whips me.

I move quickly across the foyer, wanting to be well beyond the paparazzi's point of interest by the time Ethan joins me. I catch a brief impression of sumptuous red carpet, black and white tiles, enormous crystal chandeliers, animal skins and a fire that would, in winter, create warmth and cosiness with stunning ease.

The elevators are simply shining doors submerged behind wood panelling. I wait beside them, staring straight ahead. I hear the rush of lenses clicking and buttons being pressed and I don't look. There's the rustle of a doorman moving outside, and then he is beside me, his finger jabbing at the button of the lift with obvious impatience. We don't look at one another.

After only a few seconds, the doors ping open. It's empty.

We step in and Ethan swipes a key card before pressing one of the old-fashioned radio buttons on the panel. It whooshes upwards and my tummy whooshes with it.

I have *never* wanted a guy this badly.

The atmosphere is heavy with that feeling, that need. It practically hums around us, so that it takes every ounce of my willpower not to press the stop button and beg him to fuck me then and there.

I dig my nails into my palms as extra insurance.

The doors ping open—finally—and even as we step out of the lift he's reaching for me. Now, in the privacy of the hotel corridor, he lifts me off the ground, his arms tight around my waist as his mouth moves over mine, and he walks like I weigh nothing, and carrying me is nothing more than a minor inconvenience. His lips are punishing and I am submissive, taking the kiss, begging for more even as my legs lift, needing greater purchase, more intimacy, closeness—everything.

I wrap them around him and groan as I hear the unmistakable tearing of my skirt—which was definitely *not* designed to be spread-eagled around a rock star's waist. *Whoops.* Somewhere in my mind I discover another consequential path of this coming together—some makeshift outfit assembly will be required in order for me to get home, whenever it is I *do* go home.

Without releasing his grip, without lifting his lips, he fumbles the key card against the door. The first time is unsuccessful and he swears into my mouth as the door remains resolutely closed. Second time it springs open and we burst through it. The door slams shut and Ethan drops the key card to the floor like litter, striding deeper into the suite.

I have a brief impression of more luxury, more red, more chandeliers made of beaded crystal—and an enormous bed that is like an oasis in the midst of a never-ending desert. But he turns sharply, propping me against a table instead.

The second my butt connects with the tabletop his hands reach for my blouse and he pulls at it, ripping every single button so that they pop and fly across the room like angry little witnesses to my thwarted needs.

It's a damned nice blouse—one of my favourites—but I don't bemoan its demise. I am as eager as he is to be naked and touching all over. I arch my back as he pushes the fabric down my arms, his fingers tracing my flesh as he frees me of the garment before they lift higher, finding my bra. He traces a thumb over the lace and I swear I whimper as though I'm about to come. I think I *am* about to come.

My eyes skittle to his face, shock in all my features. He understands. I know he does. He curves his hands around my butt and drags me to the edge of the table, so that I can feel the hard, aching heat of his cock through the fabric of his jeans, straining at it, practically breaking it. My fingers seek it—seek *him*. They fumble at his button and then a noise of triumph erupts from my lips as I find the zip and push it downwards.

But he's moving, pushing at my bra, freeing my breasts in one moment and claiming them with his mouth the next. His tongue lashes my nipple as his fingers roll the other, and his dick grinds against me through the fabric of our clothes.

Perspiration sheens my skin. I lift my fingers from his jeans, from their futile mission of cock-hunting, and curl them around his hips instead, digging my nails into him, lifting my feet to the edges of the table and crying out as his teeth press into my nipple with enough pressure to make me see stars.

I'm at the edge of the world. Ethan's there too, but I'm the one who's stepping off...who's being flung off! I dig my nails in harder and he rolls his mouth to my other breast, bringing his fingers to tease where his teeth have just been. It's too much. The sensations and juxtapositions. The heat of his mouth and the coldness of the air-conditioned hotel room. The softness of his fingertips and the hurt of his teeth.

I cry out loudly as an orgasm crashes over me, sucking me under, rendering me the opposite of mute. I am loud and I am desperate and I have no grasp of control. No grasp of time, space or date either, to be honest. If you'd asked me where I was, I would have needed a shot of black coffee to wake up and remember.

I am doused in more sensations than I was even aware existed and yet I'm not done. *He's* not done. This is just the beginning.

'I want to fuck you.'

'Isn't that what you're doing?' I smile up at him, my body singing.

'Hell, yeah.'

He pulls at my butt, jerking me closer to him, and then he rolls his cock against me so that I cry out again.

'Please, Ethan…' I groan hungrily.

Apparently he doesn't need to be asked twice. He reaches into his pocket and pulls out his wallet, then slides a condom from within its folds.

There is a small part of me that is consciously cheering what is about to happen—unlike my body, which is so in the moment. This isn't just sex. It isn't just relief. It's release—it's an exorcism. I am going to fuck another man, and with every moment and motion I am going to blot Jeremy further from my mind.

I am going to reduce his importance in my life.

With sex.

'I've never been happier to see a little foil square.' I grin, reaching for it. 'Now. Let me see what I'm dealing with here.'

His grin is like warm treacle on a hot day. 'You're mighty impatient… Alicia.'

Hearing him say my real name is the biggest turn-on yet. And that's saying something.

My eyes meet his and he knows.

'Alicia.'

Even better than Ally. My name tastes wonderful on

his mouth. He pushes at his jeans and I take over, sliding my hands into his grey cotton boxers, feeling the curve of his ass—of course it's a fantastic ass. I hold his eyes as I bring my hands to the front, feeling for his long, hard dick. As I enclose it in my fist, wrapping my hand around it hungrily, he lets out a hoarse groan.

'How do you feel about being fucked fast?'

His laugh is borderline apologetic, and there's a vulnerability that makes me ache for more than just this. But only for a moment.

'I feel really, really good about that.'

I rip the top off the condom with my teeth and then slide it over him as he steps out of his jeans. For a moment I wonder at his size—I haven't slept with anyone in a really long time. Is it possible I've forgotten that dicks do this when they're hard? But it's big. Really big. And beautiful.

A shiver swirls through me. He pushes his shirt off impatiently and then he's lifting me up once more, carrying me against his chest, cradling me, into the bedroom. He throws me on the bed and reaches for the remains of my skirt, tearing it off me and then pulling my thong down my legs.

It's not slow, like he was with the bra. His hands graze my legs, my calves, my thighs, but that's accidental. He needs me now as much as I need him. There's no sense denying it. No sense in pretending.

As he brings himself over me I push my palm against his chest, knocking him so that he is on his side, next to me, and we're face to face. I kiss him as I hitch my leg over his hip, and then push up on my knee so that I'm straddling him.

I don't know why having control is important to me,

but I suppose if I had to analyse it I would probably say that I feel so utterly out of my depth in what I'm feeling that I need *something* to make me have a sense of agency.

Choice is my agency, though, and I choose *this*. I choose to move on. I choose to forget. I choose not to let Jeremy make me cower any more. I choose all of what we're doing.

And my choice has nothing to do with anything other than desire and need and everything to do with Ethan Ash and me—Alicia Douglas.

We are two chemicals, mixing together, swirling, swarming and about to explode.

'Fuck me,' I whisper as I lift up and lower myself over him, taking his length deep inside me slowly, letting my muscles adjust to this strange newness. To his size and his needs.

I almost can't bear the perfection of that moment. The haunting rightness.

He lets out a long, slow grunt and his fingers dig into my hips. He holds me down, low on his length, and he throbs, pulses. I feel every jerk of his desire deep inside me. I hold my breath, chewing on my lip as my nerve-endings quiver in response. His cock is whispering secrets within me and my body is listening intently.

It's but a moment. A magical moment. And then he's moving, holding my hips low as he thrusts, his abs rippling with each movement. I drop lower, my mouth chasing each ridge of his chest, my tongue flicking his hair-roughened nipples, my body pressed against his.

His fingers roam my flesh again, like an object, like he owns me, and I love the feeling of being owned by him. I roll my hips and he swears, moving his hands to hold my face, dragging me up to his mouth, to kiss me. And he pushes up, flipping me onto my back while barely breaking the kiss.

Oh, God. It's bone-meltingly perfect. Like this, he is deep, so deep, and he thrusts harder and faster and his tongue echoes the movements. I lift my legs and his hands grab my ankles, pushing them higher, moving them over his shoulders so that he has complete access to me. It breaks the kiss but I don't care, because now his lips are moving over my leg, and every thrust is waving me on, nearer to explosive release.

I dig my fingers into his shoulders and there it is!

I cry out as the orgasm shreds me, my hand lifting to his chest to still him, to implore him to wait, so that I am able to feel every tremor of the earthquake he's created. He knows. He waits. He is patient. The only sound in the room is that of his breathing, loud and hoarse, his control almost at breaking point. But he watches me, watches the effect of pleasure on my face, my skin, and then, when he knows—because he *knows* me—that I can take it again, he moves once more, slowly at first, letting new sensations build up, before he drops my legs back to the bed and brings his mouth to my mouth, kissing me, making me groan under the weight of the rightness of that moment.

The next time I come it's with him. We are both on the edge of the cliff, stepping off it together. My fingers seek his and I lace them together again, and that act of intimacy means everything and nothing as our bodies sing in unison.

We are entwined. Him, me, and the luxury of the Park View Suite. I fear that I am lost. Or is that I'm found?

CHAPTER FOUR

IN AND OUT. In and out. I breathe slowly, trying to calm my racing pulse, my raging nervous system, but still my body is part electrical current, part hurricane.

'Okay,' I murmur softly, more to myself than anything else. I'm processing it. Or trying to.

What just happened?

He pushes up onto one elbow so that he can look down into my eyes and I spy the galaxy in his.

'Okay.' He grins. 'That was…'

'Perfect,' I supply, lazily tracing a drop of sweat as it runs down his chest. He leans forward to kiss my fingertip and his dick, still strong inside me, makes me groan anew.

So far as exorcisms go, I think we might have nailed it.

'Yeah.' He nods. 'It was.'

He kisses me again, but this time it's slow. Gentle. A kiss of curiosity that I welcome. *Damn it.* I'm back at those paths, looking at each of them, wondering, wondering, and uncertainty is making my knees weak.

Do I want his curiosity? Do I welcome it? Or does it speak too strongly of wanting other things than this bed, this man, this night?

'Are you hungry?'

'Hungry?' I blink, the question not at all what I expected.

He nods against my lips, then braces his forehead against mine. 'Yeah. You know, that thing people get? It generally involves needing food. Eating. Maybe conversation.'

'I'm familiar with the concept.'

My own little divot forges between my brows and his eyes lift to it. His grins, and that makes me smile, erasing the similarity.

He rolls his hips luxuriantly, slowly throbbing warmth through me, and desire surges like a wave at high tide, rolling inwards towards the shore. I lift my hips to meet it, to welcome it.

'Room Service,' he murmurs. 'Definitely Room Service.'

Still inside me, he stretches, reaching for the phone on the bedside table, and my whole body stretches with his, reluctant to relinquish even a hint of connection.

He brings his mouth back to mine, the phone hooked casually under one ear.

'Ethan Ash,' he says, and my eyes lift to his, surprised until I realise he's speaking to someone else.

That surprise, though, is nothing compared to what shoots through me when he pulls out of me, leaving me instantly bereft, before inserting a finger deep into my core. I can't help the moan that escapes my mouth. It falls out like a waterfall, slumberous and urgent at the same time.

His finger swirls around already-over-sensitised nerve-endings and I arch my back as he brings his mouth to my breast at the same time.

'Two crab linguine. Some fruit.'

'A peach,' I whisper.

'A peach,' he repeats, then drags his mouth across my chest, his stubbled jaw making the raw, aching, sensitive flesh tremble beneath him.

His mouth is an instant relief. And as he rolls my nipple with his tongue he speaks into the phone. The words are husky against me. I feel his voice a baritone on my skin. And he feels me inside.feels my heart and my core.

'Definitely champagne. Lots of champagne.' He draws his lips lower, to my navel, and then, still with the phone under his chin, to my clit.

'Oh, my God!' I squawk as his tongue finds the cluster of nerves and flicks it punishingly.

'Ice cream,' he adds, his fingers curling around my ankles and pushing my legs apart on the bed.

There is a tiny part of me that is embarrassed by this intimacy—but only a tiny part. The rest of me is way up on cloud nine, wondering if any woman has ever felt this good. If any person has ever known this pleasure.

I presume he's done ordering, because he drops the phone to the ground. The cord is still stretched across the bed but I don't ask him to hang up. Nor do I attempt to do so. I'm not moving, and I'm not going to encourage him to do anything that might bring an end to this sweet, sensual invasion.

'A peach, huh?' he murmurs against me.

I dig my nails into the bed, trying to breathe, trying not to fall apart.

'Yeah.'

'A favourite?'

'Mmm, yes…' I don't think I'm talking about fruit any more.

'You taste fucking amazing.'

Even that doesn't embarrass me. I groan in response, reaching above me for a pillow, which I drag down, holding it over my face as I cry out and he continues to run his tongue over me with the kind of skill that should win him a gold medal. Seriously. If oral sex were a competitive sport then this guy could hang up his microphone. He's *that* good.

His hands lift up, finding my breasts, and he knows what I love already. He's learned fast. He tweaks my nipples and palms the roundness of my flesh, and his mouth lifts me up and carries me away until I can stand it no longer, and I give in to the euphoric relief that has been building and bursting.

I feel it drop over me and whimper into the pillow. Which is no help, actually, because it smells intoxicatingly like him. So like him that I want to take it with me. *Uh-oh.* Another road opens up before me. I resolutely shut all paths out and surrender to the sensations of *this*. This very, very, *very* delightful everything.

He slows down as he feels me come apart, still touching me, tasting me, but no longer driving me to insane heights. I have exploded and now I am recovering. I am trying to catch my breath. He stays close and I'm comforted by his closeness—until he pulls back and stands in one fluid moment.

He's still wearing the condom—but not for long. He rolls it off and wraps it in a tissue, tossing it carelessly into a wastepaper basket before reaching for the phone and replacing it on the cradle. Then, hands on hips, gloriously naked, he stares down at me, where I'm hiding behind an organic Italian cotton pillow.

'Alicia?'

I can't speak. Maybe not ever again. It is quite possible that he's erased my voice, like some kind of kinky *Little Mermaid* scenario.

'Come here.'

I can't speak, but I can move, and I *will* move as he demands because he's offering me a whole new world of pleasure and I am anxious to enjoy it, and with it to erase Jeremy's significance in my life.

I stand. My legs shake and my skin is raw—pale pink, I see, as I look down at my breasts. The sight of his marks on my body makes me soar. An ancient feminine power rocks me to the core. *He* did this to me. His passion did it to both of us. And the passion was bigger than either of us could control.

'You never answered my question.'

'What question?'

He links his fingers through mine and pulls me gently away from the bed. For the first moment since entering the suite I notice the view.

'Holy shit.' I stand completely still—naked, uncaring. 'Wow...'

Manhattan glistens before me. It is high-rises and high dreams, lights and lives, lows and loves.

'Yeah.'

His voice is hoarse and it draws my attention. I stare at his profile again, and it's so different now. I see all his lines and marks and strengths, and somehow I feel that I know him so much better than even an hour ago.

'I've always loved the contradictions of New York,' I say.

I am drawn to the view and step towards the window, relinquishing his hand without realising it. I press my palm to the glass. It is darkly tinted and I am confident in the privacy it affords.

'So much beauty…so much despair.' My smile is crooked as our eyes latch on to each other in the reflection. 'Nowhere in the world can you find such wealth and poverty in the same city block.'

'It's a unique place,' he agrees. 'Where are you from?'

'Wisconsin, originally. I moved here five years ago—right out of college.'

'What did you study?'

'Fine art and art history.'

I've surprised him. I see the way he nods, but it's speculative. Funny, because I'm well-known and well-respected in my field, and it's been a long time since I've met anyone who doesn't know what I do.

'You're an artist?'

'I wish…' I sigh wistfully, turning to face him with mock sadness on my face. 'I always wanted to be. My mom says I spent so much time clutching paintbrushes I practically deformed my fingers.'

I lift my hand up and we both stare at it in the silence of the room. They're normal to look at now, but I remember the claw-like grip they manifested after days and days spent hunched at a canvas.

'But…?'

'Can't paint to save my life.' I grimace. 'I'm a buyer now. And an appraiser by appointment.'

'So you take other people's cash to choose fashionable art?'

I shrug. 'Fashionable, abstract, classic. I spend a lot of time with my clients and in the spaces the art will inhabit, making sure it's going to work.'

'That's a *job*?'

'Hell, yeah.' I gesture to the room we're standing in. 'This whole hotel is fitted with contemporary American masterpieces—testaments to the modernist movement. You look around and you see the art and maybe you don't realise the effect it creates. But we're standing in a *movement*, Ethan!'

I hear the enthusiasm and passion in my own voice and wince. I adore my job. That's a good thing, but it can be a bit bizarre to people who don't feel the same way.

'I know what you mean.'

I exhale. 'You do?'

'Well, not exactly...'

He turns and cuts through the suite, disappearing through a door. I follow.

'But the first time I recorded at Abbey Road I just about shit myself. I mean...' He shakes his head as he reaches for the faucet and turns on the water. The bath is around the corner, half hidden by a dark wood-panelled wall. 'The history is thick in the air at that place. The microphones, the carpet, the pictures. Legends—so many, a list as long as my arm. Not just the Beatles—though that's *everything*. But all the bands, musicians, songwriters. It's impossible to explain—except I guess it's like you just said. I was in the middle of something so much bigger than me. It took me three tracks to get the jitters out of my voice.'

'The jitters?'

Oh, no. There goes my heart, flopping just like my tummy has been all night, squeezing with something a lot like affection at the sweetness of that word. *Jitters*. Twenty-eight, sexy as sin, and a gold medallist at pleasure-giving and he uses words like 'jitters'. He gives *me* the jitters.

'Yeah. You know. The heebie-jeebies.'

'Stop.' I burst out laughing and hold a hand up at the same time. 'You need to stop using language like that.'

'Like heebie-jeebies?'

'Yeah. It's too…' *Cute. Adorable. Sweet. Lovely.*

'I'm sorry, Ally, there's no other word for it. I had medically diagnosed heebie-jeebies.'

But he grabs the hand I've held out and pulls it— and me—towards him. Our bodies meld together and his eyes lock to mine. Breath snags in my throat like a piece of thread that won't give. I stare up at him, waiting, transfixed, my heart throbbing.

He kisses my forehead lightly, softly, gently, and a moan is trapped in my throat. *Yes. This. All of this.* The paths are back in my mind, opening up and inviting me to choose one.

There's a sound from outside and he reaches for a towel, breaking the sense of magic that was enveloping me. 'Hop in. I'll join you in a minute.'

'The bath?'

'Why not?'

He wraps a towel around his waist, low-slung so that—if it's possible—he looks even sexier than when he was all gloriously golden and butt-naked.

'You got somewhere else you need to be?'

The paths look at me.

He looks at me.

I expel a long, slow sigh as I shake my head. 'Not right now, I don't.'

'Good. Then you're all mine.' He kisses me quickly on the cheek. 'And I'm going to make the most of it. I'll be right back.'

He disappears from the bathroom but I move to the

door and watch him. I watch him because I seem unable to help it. Because I am pulled to him like a bee to honey.

Her eyes are shut when I step back into the bathroom, bowl in hand. The water swirls around her, and her breasts are two perfect peaks floating on the surface. She's added some of the shower lotion, and the bubbled top creates a frustrating visual barrier to the rest of her body.

A body I now yearn to see again.

To make completely my own.

It is a primal need to possess her, and I'm more surprised by that than I should be. It's been a long time since I've been with a woman. And things between Sienna and me were shit at the end. For a long time *before* the end, actually.

But I don't want to think about her now.

I don't want Sienna in my head, ruining this for me.

'You look good enough to eat.'

Her eyes ping open, searing me with awareness. 'You should know.'

'Uh-huh.'

I grin as I step into the bath, relieved as all fuck when my legs brush against hers. I like touching her. I like it *a lot*.

Maybe it's just the newness of this. The freshness of being with a woman I barely know.

'Definitely something I want seconds of.'

Her cheeks flush bright pink—God, I love how she blushes, and I can't resist teasing her more.

'And thirds…and fourths.'

Darker pink glistens on her cheeks. I settle myself against the head of the bath and scoop some ice cream onto a spoon, holding it out to her. She keeps her eyes locked to mine as she takes a bite. A dribble of vanilla escapes down one side of her chin and I watch its progress. She makes no effort to check it, and after a moment it falls to her décolletage and slips down to where her breast meets the water.

Shit.

She's perfection.

'You know…' I continue, hell-bent now on my mission to make her whole body glow red with knowledge and awareness. 'You make the sweetest noises when you're coming.'

Mission accomplished. She lights up like a Christmas tree, her eyes not meeting mine.

'Why are we eating ice cream?'

It is the most goddamned clunky conversation-change I've ever heard—and I'm often around women who are nervous as all hell.

I laugh, the noise soft in the quietness of the bathroom, and I lift a spoonful of the confection out of the bowl. 'I'll show you.'

I place it in my mouth and then move through the water, finding one of her breasts, which I'm already thinking of as *my* breasts. I know how she loves them to be played with—how much it drives her crazy.

For the smallest moment Sienna is in my head again. And she's pissed off as all hell at what I'm doing.

Anger briefly flares in my gut, followed by satisfaction. I'm glad she's pissed off. She can join the club.

Sienna always was jealous. Jealous of the women who'd get backstage at my concerts. Women the band would introduce me to. Women who'd find out where I was staying and make their way to the hotel and wait outside my room. Women who emailed and Tweeted me their most obscene fantasies in the hopes I'd turn them into lyrics…or reality.

Well, no sense crying over spilled milk or unsown oats. Here, in this enormous bath with Ally, I've got every opportunity to make up for lost time. And I intend to use it.

She's so hot. Like the sex gods recognised my deprivation and decided to reward me with an actual bona fide angel.

I slide the ice cream over her perfect peach nipple, my hands braced on her hips beneath the water so I feel the way she sucks in a hard breath of surprise at the ice-cold invasion. The frozen heat—such a contradiction.

She shifts underwater, dragging her breath lower. I make a 'tsking' sound of disapproval. 'You don't like it?'

'Oh, I like it,' she mutters, without meeting my eyes. 'What I *don't* like is how easily you can drive me crazy. It's not fair.'

'Not fair?' I shake my head. 'Believe me, I get as much out of your pleasure as you do.'

And to prove my point I nudge my dick against her, so she can feel how hard I am for her already. How no relief could erase the need I feel for her.

'That's reassuring,' she murmurs.

I laugh. 'I'm glad you're reassured, Alicia.'

Something serious flickers in her eyes and she moves forward in the bath, making a small wave that ripples around me and crashes to the edges. She reaches for the ice cream spoon and takes a bite before bringing her mouth to mine. The kiss is hot and cold and I groan into her mouth, my hands seeking first her hair, tangling in its lengths, before dragging themselves down to her hips and squeezing her flesh, loving the feeling of her as she moves over me.

She's so close I want to take her then and there.

Thank God she's still got room for thought. She shakes her head, keeping herself just far enough away from me to inspire a sort of madness. 'No condom,' she murmurs.

I swear, if it hadn't been for that I'd be taking her now, driving into her again.

She kisses me and I move closer and closer to bursting. She rolls her hips against my waist, teasing me, inviting me, even when we both know we can't do this. She's tilting her pelvis, simulating sex, and my temperature is skyrocketing. I'm harder than granite and there's only one cure.

While I want *her*, I want more of this, too. More of feeling like I'm about to explode, like I'm close but far away. I wanted to get blind drunk tonight, but instead I met Ally and I'm drunk on something besides alcohol. Is this just deprivation talking? Just the fact I haven't been able to do this for a really long time?

Flesh on flesh…her under my fingertips.

Fuuuuck.

'What would you say about getting out of the bath?' All I can think about is taking her again. Driving into her like she's my new home.

'Can we bring the ice cream?'

'Hell, *yeah*, we can bring the ice cream.'

She's so graceful. Even as she pushes up to standing and moves out of the bath it's like a ballet performance. She's lithe and lean and, though I'm aching to follow, I take a moment just to watch her. To watch as she pulls her wet hair over her shoulder and squeezes

it into a towel, her eyes fixed straight ahead. She drops
the towel to her body and pats herself dry in what is my
new definition of sexiness. Then she turns back to me
and she looks like Mona Lisa might have if she'd just
rolled out of bed.

Enigmatic. Hot. Desirable.

'Ready?'

'Yeah.' Is that my voice? So gruff and hoarse?

She reaches for the ice cream and once more spoons
it into her mouth, but she holds the spoon there, her eyes
holding mine. Just for a second. A beat. But it's enough.
Enough for me to imagine it's me in her mouth.

I would be some kind of animal if I didn't feel guilty
for what I'm doing. Four months ago I thought Sienna
and I would work through our shit and probably one day
get married. Four months ago I wouldn't have dreamed
of being with someone else.

And now I'm fucking this beautiful, sexy Ally.

Am I doing it to hurt Sienna?

Am I doing it to fuck Sienna right out of my head?

Am I doing it because Sienna deserves that?

Hell, yeah. But I'm also doing it because Ally seems
to have robbed me of any ability to walk away. She has
drawn me into something I cannot fight.

And I don't want to fight it anyway.

CHAPTER FIVE

THE SUN IS WEAK, straining to break through the sensuality that has formed a deep fog in his room. I squint and stifle a yawn, arching my back until I ram against him. A feline smile curves slowly over my lips. I reach for him on autopilot, turning at the same time as his lips seek mine, crushing against them.

I haven't spent the night in a stranger's bed in a long time, and whenever I have in the past there has been the inevitable dawning of awkwardness the next morning. A raising of self-consciousness along with the new day. A desire to begin the forgetting—forgetting what I've done and with whom.

I do not feel that now.

I lose myself in the kiss and my body seeks his, hungrily, urgently, naturally. He groans into my mouth and it is an answer to my feral needs, my wildness and abandon. For a brief second he is distant, turning away from me, and then I roll with him, straddling him even as he laughs and extends an arm to the side table. He knocks a glass of water to the carpeted floor but doesn't react.

Nor do I. I'm already seeking him, wanting to take him deep inside again. I need him more than I can express.

He laughs. A throaty sound of agreement. And then he swears. 'Hang on.'

I don't want to hang on, yet I pause, just long enough to frown and follow his fumbling hand. *Oh, shit.* A condom—of course. Had I really almost forgotten? Colour flushes my cheeks, but embarrassment is quickly swallowed by something else. Something far more primal.

Even before he's ripped the packet open I'm bending my head forward and my mouth is taking him in the way the rest of me wants to. I curve my lips around him until he reaches the back of my throat and he swears again. I feel the curse reverberate through his body and into mine.

I don't stop.

His fingers push through my hair, tangling in its length, and I move my mouth upwards, then take him all the way in again, over and over.

'Fuuuck.'

He drops his fingers to my shoulders and pushes me up. I stare past his cock, beautiful as it is, up his toned chest, to a face that really is the stuff of dreams. God, he's hot. Seriously hot.

The kind of guy a girl could lose her mind for.

And her heart too?

Not me—not my heart. My heart is staying boxed in my chest, right where it belongs. But my mind…? Yes, I'd happily be mindless for this rock god.

'I want you.' He rips the condom out and slides it over his dick.

'Tell me something I *don't* know.' I laugh, and then his hands are beneath my arms, pulling me up even as

I crawl higher over his body and straddle him, taking him and moaning as he thrusts into me.

I tilt backwards and stare at the ceiling as all the walls of my world implode.

I am lost.

'You know…' He runs a fingertip down my spine and I shiver, my body still in paroxysms of desire even now, ten minutes after we've both crested that glorious wave and felt the complete delight that follows absolute surrender to pleasure. 'You're very good for my ego.'

I smile against his chest, listening to his heart thumping solidly. 'Shouldn't that be the other way around? It's not every day I get seduced by a superstar.'

He runs his finger lower, curving it over the roundness of my ass.

'Is that what I am?'

'Uh-huh. Apparently.'

'I'm not sure I seduced you, though.'

I laugh. 'Seriously?'

'You were staring at me all night…'

'Was not!'

I push up onto my elbows and my hair falls over his chest, tumbling across his tanned skin. I drop my lips to the ridge between his pecs and kiss him slowly, tasting the tang of his sweat and the masculinity of his body.

My insides clench. He is warm; he is hot. I could stay here all day.

The very thought is a dangerous electrical current I must immediately subdue.

I don't do that. I *won't* do that. Sex is fine, but anything more is where things get tricky. I swallow, pretty sure confusion is in my smile as I pull away from him.

'Anyway, Mr Rock Star, I think this is where our time must end.' I sigh dramatically, doing my best impersonation of a Shakespearean actress, and stand up.

My clothes are spread like confetti over the carpet. I feel his eyes on me as I move through the room, watching me scoop the garments off the floor.

'Mind if I grab a quick shower?'

He doesn't answer straight away. His expression is vague, like he's not concentrating, or perhaps he hasn't even heard.

'Ethan?'

'Sorry—yeah. Right. Go ahead.' He nods towards the bathroom.

My body feels like it's been stripped raw. Every nerve-ending vibrates as I rub myself with a loofah, spreading suds across my skin and rinsing them away. In the past, whenever I had one-night stands, I used to feel the after-shower was almost ceremonial. A wiping away of what I'd done.

I don't feel that now.

Or, if I do, I feel it with regret.

I don't want to walk away from him. And that's a serious problem. I've only ever felt that one time in my life and it led to a verified disaster.

Jeremy almost broke me. *Almost?* I forgot how to function for *months* after it ended.

Following desire to the point of stupidity was almost the end of me.

I will never make that mistake again.

I flick the taps off and stand in the steamy cubicle for a moment, steadying myself for what comes next.

Goodbyes are never nice, are they?

I brace myself for the inevitable swapping of numbers as I dress. The promise to call. The certainty that neither of us will.

When I step out into the lounge area he's dressed in a pair of low-slung jeans and nothing else. His chest is a piece of art—and I should know, given what I do!—but it's his bare feet that I find strangely erotic. There's something so confident about the way he stands, legs wide, arms crossed—seriously gorgeous arms—his eyes fixed on the bathroom door as though he's been waiting for me to emerge. He's like a caged lion, and yet there's something inherently laid-back about him.

The second I step out heat erupts, like wildfire spreading across a desert. It burns all of me, all the way through. I smile brightly, pretending I'm fine. Pretending hard that I don't feel it.

'Sooo…' I move towards him, reaching for my purse. 'This has been fun.'

'Fun…yeah.' He nods, still with that same sense of distraction on his handsome face.

I lift up on tiptoes and kiss his stubbled cheek, then step back.

Goodbyes are *never* nice.

I fight an urge to say any of the things that people might say in this situation. *I'll call you…* Or *Let's do this again sometime…* Or, *If you're ever in town let me know…*

'Listen, Ally…'

He drags a hand through his hair and I catch a hint of his beautiful fragrance and almost groan.

How can I want him again?

No, it's not that I want him *again*. I *still* want him. I want to stay curled up in bed, my body wrapped around his. I want to eat ice cream off him until I can't eat any more.

Every thought like that is a brick against my side. I've been stupid before. I've lost my heart before. I've lost it in a way that taught me the most important lessons about myself and my life. My heart has been broken and I doubt it will ever fit back together again.

He's searching for words, searching my face too. Looking for a way to tell me what he needs to say.

'It's okay.' I rush the words out, my smile over-bright. 'Seriously, Ethan, it's okay. You don't need to say anything.' I reach for his hand and squeeze it. 'I'm not looking for anything more than last night. It was…perfect. Let's not do the whole swapping numbers thing, okay?'

Still his eyes roam my face, intuiting more from me than I want to share. My cheeks heat and I turn away, scooping up my bag and tucking it under my arm.

Props are a funny thing, aren't they? Just the simple act of putting my purse in place gives me an added layer of confidence, tethering me to myself and my feelings, reminding me of who I was before this night reached into my soul and swished everything up.

'Thank you,' he says, and I acknowledge the incongruity of that polite remark.

I spin and kiss him on his cheek once more. 'You're welcome.'

In the end I didn't say goodbye. I just walked away as though I was heading to the shops or out to get coffee. No biggie.

I walked away and didn't look back.

I couldn't. I fear one last peek might have killed my will-power.

* * *

She is everywhere I look in the room. I smell her on the pillow as I press my head into it, and when I close my eyes I see her.

Ally.

Ally naked, glorious, owning me, burning me.

Ally.

My gut twists as though I've cheated on my girlfriend. My *ex*-girlfriend, who is now the fiancée of someone else.

It doesn't change the way something strange is shooting through me. Emotions that are hard to interpret. Anger. Jealousy. Resentment.

Relief.

And something I have to own as sinister.

Sienna would hate it that I fucked Ally.

And I think I kind of like that.

I check the details of my appointment once more, wishing my assistant Lesley would proofread her emails before sending them.

Two p.m. appuntment with Grayson Heynes. 44 West Eleventh, The Vilage. Complete renovashun. Meet at address.

Her spelling is so bad that I've often wondered how the hell she graduated from high school. But what she lacks in her ability with the written word she makes up for in every other way. Lesley is my organisational guru, and she works harder than anyone I've ever known. No matter when I email her, she writes back within minutes. She is calm and strangely unflappable.

God knows I need her stability.

More now than usual.

I have to admit that since the weekend I've been in a weird headspace. I went running twice—morning and night, both days. That's not completely out of the ordinary, but it's been a long time since I've pushed myself that hard.

Only I've found myself with an odd surplus of energy since that night with *him*.

I shy away from using his name.

It's as though my blood has been supercharged and I am a different person altogether. I look the same, but I'm not. It's really weird. And I don't welcome the feeling— not one little bit.

Jeremy taught me everything I need to know about relationships. I will never again let a man change who I am. I will never again let a man make me doubt myself.

I shiver. I've been thinking of Jeremy more lately than usual. That's Ethan's fault too… Maybe Eliza was wrong. I'm not ready for this. What's wrong with being celibate and alone anyway? I'm pretty sure I can get all my kicks from *Game of Thrones*.

Mmm… Jon Snow…

I feel nothing.

God, what kind of sexual spell has Ethan Ash cast over me that even invoking Jon Snow doesn't dull the memories of our night together?

I turn my head, scanning the street in one direction. Nothing. Just the buzz of normal West Village life. A woman with two small children and a Golden Retriever on one side of the street and a tourist couple on the other.

Neither of those looks like my new client.

I turn in the opposite direction just in time to see a

man step out of a black limousine. He wears a suit but it barely contains his strength. He's short and broad, with close-cut blond hair, a golden tan, and he wears sunglasses despite the fact the day is bleak.

He moves towards me purposefully so I smile, glad I applied an extra layer of my favourite bright red lipstick.

'Miss Douglas?'

'Ally, please,' I say, extending my hand, trying to place his accent. Australian?

He nods in answer. 'This way.' He gestures to the door of the townhouse behind me and I have to fight my smile.

I *love* these brownstones. Like every woman my age, I grew up on *Friends* and *Sex and the City* repeats, and these buildings exemplify New York to me. It's why I love where *I* live, around the corner from here. Because I feel like I've walked onto the set of my favourite TV show and it's every bit as amazing as I thought it would be.

But a whole townhouse—no, *two*? He pushes the door open and we're right in a construction site. There are tins of paint, ladders, and yellow tape, presumably indicating 'no-go' areas.

'You're joining the two together?'

Excitement swarms through me. The cost of the real estate alone, and then these extensive renovations, indicate that Mr. Heynes has considerable finances at his disposal.

I take on many projects, for clients with varying degrees of wealth, but by far the most fun to work with are the couples or clients who are seriously loaded. Who let me go to town on assembling an art collection worthy of a world-class gallery. I suspect Mr. Heynes might just be one of them.

'This way, please.'

I fall into step beside him, breathing in the architectural beauty of the building as we go. I note with pleasure that someone has chosen to keep all the original features. Deco ceiling roses are in a state of restoration, so too the fancy balustrade that borders the stairs. We move deeper into the townhouse and the natural light that floods in from the back garden is exquisite. A grey day it might be, but this garden is both a sun-catcher and a green oasis in the middle of New York City.

A movement in the corner catches my eye and I'm drawn to it instinctively. Another man, sitting in a folding director's chair, stands up.

It takes my mind longer than my body to recognise who it is.

My body knows straight away, of course, as proved by the way my nipples strain against the fabric of my shirt, and the way all of me pulses with need. Memories of our night together flood my brain and desire is instantly, obviously heavy in the room.

Ethan Ash stares back at me, a sexy smile on his face, like he's waiting for me to speak. Or to jump him.

CHAPTER SIX

'ETHAN…?' THE WORD is an exhalation. A query, yes, but also a soft, muted groan.

He's wearing jeans again. The same ones he was wearing the day I left? Saturday? Four days ago? Is that all? But he's teamed them with a simple blue and white button-down shirt, the sleeves pushed up to reveal his tanned forearms, and he's got simple Nikes on his feet—nice shoes, but I miss his sexy bare feet instantly. His hair is in disarray, reminding me forcibly of how it looked after I'd run my fingers through it.

'Thank you, Grayson.'

The man I met outside nods. 'I'll be out front.'

I turn to face Mr. Heynes, but he's already disappearing back down the hallway we walked together.

'My bodyguard,' Ethan says, with a grin that is instantly disarming.

Usually I'd have something pithy to say in response to that, but I'm blindsided. Blindsided by the fact that I'm staring at the man I had the best sex of my life with—whom I thought I'd never see again. I thank the fashion gods that I chose to wear my favourite black jersey dress today, teamed with sky-high Louboutins and a chunky gold necklace. It's an outfit that always leaves me feeling confident.

I haven't said anything in a really long time, and his smile has turned into a frown. A little line has dug its way between his thick brows.

I look away quickly, needing to gather my wits—urgently. 'What are you doing here?'

'It's my place,' he says simply, as though that explains everything.

I expel a sigh of frustration. 'That's not what I mean.'

'I know.' He moves towards me and the vibrations that are affecting me on a cellular level intensify sharply. My stomach swoops.

Great.

'How did you get my number?'

He doesn't look the slightest bit ashamed. 'I looked on the internet for art advisors with long red hair and hypnotic eyes. You were right there.'

I cross my arms over my chest, tapping my fingers at my elbows disapprovingly.

'You have an excellent reputation, Alicia.'

I arch a brow, ignoring the way his praise makes something pleasant spread through me. 'Why am I here?'

He stops right in front of me, so close that I can see all the flecks of black in his ocean-green eyes. 'I have a proposition for you. Two, actually.'

'A proposition?'

'Two.' He nods towards the garden, and for the first time I see a little table has been set up there. 'Have lunch with me.'

Swoop. Swoop. I'm on a rollercoaster of emotions. I tighten my seatbelt mentally, donning my best hyper-professional voice. 'There's really no need...'

His eyes pierce me all the way to my core. 'Lunch.'

He speaks so authoritatively his strength and dominant confidence slam into me, and I am completely powerless to resist his request.

I *shouldn't* stay. I know that. I should go. No, I should run. Because I'm looking at him, and what I really want to do is collapse against him, against his strong chest, press my ear to his heart and listen to its shudderingly wonderful rasp. What I really want to do is strip his clothes off his rock star body and touch him all over.

But I can't. I don't. That would be madness.

What was so natural and easy that night is now just out of my reach. We are not a couple. We are not even friends. We are strangers who fucked. Once.

No, not once, my memory hastens to correct me. We fucked the hell out of each other. But it was just *one* night. One glorious night.

I don't even realise I'm chewing on my lower lip until he reaches down and smudges his finger across it, pushing my hand away. Heat sears me and my eyes lock to his. I feel the earth shift beneath our feet. Does he as well?

'Lunch?'

I realise I haven't answered. Slowly, I nod my head— so slowly that it's as though I've been drugged. And I kind of have been. *He* is a drug. And exposure is fast turning me into an addict.

'Okay.' I sound pissed off, and I am. I have dealt with my desire for him and I have boxed away what we were that night. Now I am looking at him again, and possibilities I dare not explore are twisting and turning inside me.

I have to be strong.

I can manage this.

I can control it.

It is a balmy day. The low cloud cover has layered humidity over the city and I'm pleased to see that he hasn't organised anything hot to eat. The table has some kind of yam salad on it, with what looks like feta cheese and herbs, and another salad. Kale?

And in the middle, so beautiful and attention-grabbing: a single peach.

'I remember what you like,' he says with a wink, and my blood boils. It's intentionally ambiguous, but I imagine he's not talking about the peach. I don't think I'll ever be able to look at a peach without remembering the way Ethan Ash went down on me.

Against my will, my eyes run down his body, landing on his crotch. I'm not imagining the way he's straining against his pants, and I'm glad. Immediately glad.

If I'm going to be wading through sensual heat then he'd better damned well be doing the same.

'Good to know.'

His smile is droll as he pulls the chair out for me. As I sit his hands brush my shoulders and my stomach lurches.

He pours us a couple of glasses of sparkling mineral water and I watch him. I watch everything about him. The way his thick hair flops forward over his brow a little, the way his fingers are firm and commanding as they wrap around the bottle. The way he is strong and confident and sexy even while undertaking such a mundane task. The way his eyelashes, long and thick, clump together.

It was like this with Jeremy, I remind myself. Desire made me dumb. It made me incapable of feeling anything else.

He looks up and smiles—a smile which drops slightly when he sees the look on my face. I imagine I look a little bit the way a wolf might stare at a lamb. I am hungry; he is my meal.

Or is it the other way around? Beneath the table he kicks out his legs and his foot brushes against my ankle. I can't tell if it's intentional or not, and it hardly matters. The effect is the same. The heat of the sun rampages through my system.

'So…' I say, desperate to regain some control of the situation. 'Why don't we cut to the chase?'

His eyes narrow, regarding me thoughtfully. As if he's trying to read my mood. 'I had fun the other night.'

I swallow, but it's no good. The beauty of that night burns me with its heat. 'Me too.' It's a raspy, cautiously given admission.

'I want to do it again.'

Alarm bells are screeching through me. *Again?* 'Why?'

His laugh is soft and he leans forward, his eyes hooked to mine. 'Seriously? You want a reminder?'

Heat flames my cheeks. 'It was a one-night-stand, Ethan. By definition, we're done.'

He nods thoughtfully. 'And that's what you want?'

'Get out of my house, you little whore!'

The way she spun around, her face puce, her hair black.

'Did you think you could bring her here and I wouldn't know? Jesus, Jeremy. Did you think I didn't smell her on the sheets? Our children will be home in ten minutes! Get her out of my house!'

I feel like I'm going to vomit. The horror of that lazy afternoon, of being woken up by my fiancé's wife, by the realisation that I'd bought his story hook, line and sink-me-sinker, tears through me. I'd looked at Jeremy and seen all my dreams, and he was actually a walking nightmare.

How easy it had been to believe his lies!

'I'm staying with my brother's family while my place is being renovated.'

It had been *his* family! *His* kids' drawings all over the fridge. *His* wife's photo on the landing. How foolish I was.

I told myself I'd never be so stupid again. That I would never be so caught up in a man that I forgot common sense and rational thought.

I don't want a relationship.

I don't even want sex.

It was only Ethan too-good-to-resist Ash that made me forget that.

For one night.

'Yeah.' I nod, but it's weak with uncertainty. 'Look, Ethan…' I sigh almost apologetically and a small part of my brain wonders how often Ethan Ash gets rejected. 'I'm not looking for a relationship. The other night was great, but it was just sex. Really, *really* good sex…'

He nods, a droll expression on his face. 'That's why this is perfect.'

'Why? What?'

'I don't want a relationship either.'

He sips his drink, keeping his eyes latched to mine the whole time. He replaces it on the table without breaking eye contact.

'I just want to fuck you.'

A lightning bolt of anticipation flashes down my spine. It is so tempting. And, hell, I want what he says *he* wants. I want to rip my clothes off and beg him to take me right there, on the manicured lawn and beneath the sultry grey sky.

But can we do that? Can we really just fuck without getting our emotions, all of ourselves, involved? I don't know if I have what it takes for that.

'It's too complicated.' I hear the prim rejection, and somewhere a part of me is glad that I have at least a degree of common sense.

'There's nothing complicated about what we feel,' he contradicts.

I shake my head. 'I can't get involved.'

'Why not?' His eyes narrow speculatively and he's tense suddenly. 'Are you with someone else?'

My heart turns over at the very idea. I shake my head, but the memories of my affair are too strong inside me. Being cast as 'the other woman' without my knowledge and without my consent. It is a wound I will probably always carry. It doesn't matter to Jeremy's wife that I had no fucking clue he was married. That he was a dad. I *slept* with her husband. I got *engaged* to the father of her children.

I broke up a family.

Guilt colours my cheeks and I feel the warning sting of tears out of nowhere. I push them back.

'Look…' He sighs again. 'I don't know if you heard about it—I mean, it was all over the news at the time. I broke up with my girlfriend a few months back.'

His eyes show torment when they meet mine: a torment that is matched by my swirling gut.

I tilt my head to the side, trying to remember. My Poldark knowledge is exceptional, so too my knowledge of Westeros family trees, but real-world drama…?

'It was completely messed up.' He shakes his head, as if dismissing tormenting thoughts of his own. 'The night I met you I'd just found out she got engaged.'

'And you were pissed?' I murmur.

It's not a question, but he answers anyway. 'That's an understatement. I wanted to tear the world apart.'

Something strange shifts inside me. 'How long were you together?'

He is quiet, and my experience with Jeremy reminds me that this is a sign of secrecy. That he's hiding something from me.

'Forget it,' I say sharply. 'It doesn't matter. I'm not getting in the middle of it.'

'She's engaged to someone else,' he says throatily, and I hear the emotional rawness in the words. 'There is no middle.'

'But you're still in love with her?'

The question catches him off-guard. It's as if he realises the inappropriateness of talking to *me*, the woman he's most recently-fucked, about the woman he loves.

'Hell, no. Right now I think hate would be a better word to describe what I feel for her.'

I discount that. I know that pain. I've felt it. 'You can love at the same time as you hate.'

'Speaking from experience?' he prompts.

'Yes.' It's both an admission and a warning. I'm shutting the conversation down.

He seems to understand that. 'Not with Sienna. Not after this.'

Sienna?

'Sienna Di Giorgio?'

Now I remember. It *was* in the papers at the time, and on news websites, and people were gossiping about it.

It was a big deal to people who cared about that kind of thing—which was almost everyone.

'Have you spoken to her?'

'Nah.'

Jealousy curdles inside me. 'Maybe that's what you need? To get some closure?'

He laughs. 'Talking to Sienna isn't going to give me "closure".' And he stands up, his manner completely animalistic, wild, untamed, as he prowls to my side of the table. 'I want to fuck you.'

I startle at the bald-faced honesty of the statement.

'Rebound sex?' I prompt, some sense of self-preservation forcing me to face up to what he wants before this goes any further.

His eyes glint and I feel the determination of his heartbreak. I recognise it.

'Something like that.'

And I want to agree. To acquiesce. To give him all of myself.

But is there danger here? Am I being foolish?

'Just sex?'

'Just sex.' He nods, reaching for me and pulling me to stand.

We are body to body…so close. I hesitate and he strikes, moving even closer, speaking low and throaty.

'I…'

He brings his mouth to my ear.

'Want…'

He sucks my lobe between his teeth and then bites down on it. I pull in a breath.

'To…'

His fingers find the bottom of my dress and push it up my thighs until it's at my hips.

'Fuck…'

His hands curl around my ass and thrust me forward, holding me tight to his arousal. He grinds his hips and I groan as I remember how good he feels inside me.

'You.'

He hasn't even said the last word before my fingers are searching for the buckle of his belt and pushing it open. I want that too.

His ex. My ex. They cease to exist.

There is no one in my mind but Ethan Ash as I push at his jeans until they're open and then reach in and wrap my fingers around his cock.

'Shit…' he groans.

'This is crazy.'

'No,' he grunts. 'This is a proposition. You. Me. Sex. It's easy.'

He rubs his cheek against mine, his stubble coarse, and then he kisses me—hard, achingly, his tongue punishing mine, as though our four days apart were my fault. It is crazy and it is reckless and I know I might regret it, but I will regret stopping even more.

He pulls me as we kiss, in through the doors, but we've barely made it inside before we tumble to the hardwood floors, a tangle of clothes and hormones, of need and lust. He pushes me onto my back and I'm shaking as he slides a condom in place. I'm pushing at his jeans and he's sliding out of them, and all the while I'm chasing his mouth, not wanting our kiss to end.

He doesn't remove my underwear—who has time for that? He pushes the flimsy lace aside and thrusts into me hard and fast, with all the desperation in the world, as though he knows how ready I am for him. And I am.

So ready, so wet, so hungry. I cry out at his possession and arch my back, inviting him to touch me.

He doesn't need the invitation.

His hands are under my dress and he finds my breasts, rolling my nipples as he drives into me, and I am moving higher and higher above the earth with every touch, morphing out of this very plain of existence. I am all his…all this…all need.

It is a primal coming together. There is nothing slow or seductive about it. But I have never been more aroused. Even as I come I feel another orgasm building immediately afterwards, intense and powerful. I dig my nails into his hips, feeling his warm, smooth flesh and wanting to mark it with my possession of him.

I wrap my legs around his waist and he drops his hands to my ass, curving his hands beneath me and kneading my flesh until I groan into his mouth.

I am incapable of thought. I am incapable of anything but feeling. And I feel him everywhere. Each thrust drives him deeper into my body until I am existing purely for this. All for him.

And I'm just sensible enough to be afraid of that.

'You said two propositions?'

Our breathing is returning to normal. His body is a weight on me that I crave.

'Right.'

He grins slowly, sensually. My stomach flops.

'Do I take it that means you accept the first?'

I pull a face. 'I'm thinking about it.'

He nods thoughtfully. 'Might you need more convincing?'

My body trembles. 'I might.'

I don't. I want to sleep with him again and again—
which should in and of itself warn me off.

Ethan shifts a little; my body responds instantly.

'I have a designer for the interior. But I want your artistic input. I want you to wave your magic wand over
this place. Think you can do that? For me?'

The way he says that should warn me, but I am not
afraid. We have been honest—we have immunised ourselves against emotional fallout. Flirting with him is fine
because we both know what we want.

And what's at stake if we don't.

'You're asking me to work for you?'

He nods. 'Yes. What d'you say?'

I say *yes*, don't I?

'Why don't you show me the place while I make up
my mind?'

'I guess this will be a kind of entertaining area.' He gestures around the large open space on the top floor of the
townhouse. It's huge. Cavernous, even. I instantly see
it as it could be. Neutral décor. Cream walls, polished
floorboards and a single feature wall of a dark, earthy
grey colour. Modern lighting, like round floor lamps
and curved wall lamps, and perhaps a shag pile rug in
the middle.

And contemporary art. Abstract without being corporate.

There's a Hirst I know Christie's has coming up for
auction and mentally I picture it on the wall. I can't recall the exact dimensions off the top of my head, so I
reach into my bag and pull out my iPad mini.

'What about something like this?' I load up the painting and hold the iPad closer to him. Not too close. Not so close that I can breathe him in or risk touching him.

What happened downstairs is still playing on the edges of my mind, and I don't know if I should run and hide or pretend it's business as usual. I've opted for the latter, but every movement he makes reminds me passionately of what we've done. What I want.

I struggle to make sense of it.

'I love it.'

He smiles as he meets my eyes. He's so straightforward and simple…it's hard to believe he feels anything like my inner-turmoil.

Why am I complicating things? We're two adults who want to have a no-strings-attached sex-fest. What danger is there in that?

I quickly spin away from him, not wanting him to see even a hint of my thought processes on my face.

The business with Jeremy scared me. For life, possibly. Well, Eliza says it fucked me up good, and I've always kind of agreed with her.

I fell in love with him hard and fast. And I thought it was mutual. I believed everything he told me. Six months into our relationship I should have seen the signs. The way he would often not answer my calls. The way he'd have weird explanations for what he'd been doing, and the way he'd change plans at a moment's notice. The way we once went to a restaurant and a couple came over to speak to him and the woman kept looking at me with obvious confusion.

And then, yes… The way his wife walked in on us *in flagrante*.

God, what an idiot I'd been.

So? Was I being an idiot now?

'How come you have such a huge place when you don't even live in the States?'

His shrug is non-committal, as though we're talking about a studio apartment rather than two brownstones joined at the seams.

'I like it here. And there are times when I do American tours and it would make sense to have a bit of a home away from home. You know? Plus, it's a good investment.'

I nod thoughtfully. 'Do you get sick of the travelling?'

'I try not to do too much of it.'

'But you tour…?'

'Yeah, I tour.' His smile is so sexy. 'But I get my agent to build in weeks of time when I get back home. To sleep in my own bed.'

To see Sienna?

I push the other woman aside. She's engaged. They broke up months ago. This isn't like Jeremy and Fiona.

'I'd hate it,' I say thoughtfully.

Moving carefully, I step over a large gap in the floorboards into the other side of the room and towards the floor-to-ceiling windows that overlook the garden. Our lunch is still down there. My poor fork stabbed into a slice of yam, indignantly waiting to be wielded.

'Yeah?'

'Oh, yeah. I'm such a homebody.'

'I wouldn't have guessed that.'

'No?'

'No.'

He comes to stand beside me and I'm aware of all the things I don't want to be.

'I can't get involved with you,' I say, without meeting his eyes.

'Can't? Or don't want to?'

It's a distinction I hadn't even realised I'd made. I side-step it deliberately. 'I think you're trouble.' Now I force myself to look his way. 'And I'm not into that.'

He studies me without speaking. Then…

'But you used to be?'

I'm startled, blinking away my surprise. How can he tell?

I twist my lips to the side and shrug, just a little. 'Trouble used to be into *me*.' It's a subtle correction. 'I've learned to spot it.'

He doesn't say anything. We stare down at the garden— it really is very beautiful. My body is still tingling from the way we came together. We are dynamite and flame. On our own, innocuous enough. But together…?

We have no hope.

'And yet the idea of sleeping with you holds definite appeal.' I run my eyes across his handsome face, over his lips that drive me wild.

'*Sleeping* isn't part of the equation.' He winks and, heaven help me, my body—*all* of it—groans.

'Right.' I smile. 'And, you know, I wonder if we shouldn't just…have fun together.'

He expels a sigh of relief. 'Thank God for that.'

But I'm still not convinced this is a good idea. I'm still terrified of everything that could go wrong.

'How would this work? I mean, I really…*it* really has to be just sex. No strings.'

'Yeah…' He grins, scanning my face. 'We can do that.'

'But what if we can't? What if one of us wants more?'

He arches a brow. 'We won't.'

'How do you know?'

He shrugs. 'If it makes you feel any better, we'll put some ground rules in place.'

'Ground rules?' I nod slowly. It's a good idea, but I can't resist teasing him. 'You're disappointingly conservative for a rock star, aren't you, Mr Ash?'

'I'm afraid I might be,' he says, with a wink that makes my tummy roll and my body vibrate.

Nothing, I repeat, *nothing* about him is disappointing.

'Would you find the conversation more acceptable if I do this?'

And he kisses my neck, sending shoots of awareness through me. I nod, but coherent thought is becoming difficult. It's worse when he drops his hand beneath my skirt and finds my heated core, sliding his fingers deep inside me. I throb around him, groaning at the sweetness of the invasion.

'You were saying…' I whimper as pleasure builds, need intensifies.

'Ground rules…' The words are throaty.

'Right.'

I tilt my head back until it connects with the glass of the window. I am lost to pleasure once more. How can he do this to me? I read a *Cosmo* article years ago about the number of calories a woman burns when she comes. Was it sixty? A hundred? I'm going to need to up my carb intake while I'm fucking Ethan, that's for sure.

'What do you want from me?' he asks, his lips brushing the words into my mouth.

I shiver; it's so sensual.

'Fun,' I grunt back as pleasure intensifies and thickens around me. 'Just fun.'

'No flowers? No sleepovers? No expectations beyond satisfaction?' he teases. 'Nothing serious?'

'God, no. *Fun.*' I dig my fingers into his hips. 'Fuck, Ethan, I'm…'

He withdraws and my eyes fly open, finding his. Outrage trembles inside me, but only for a moment—because then he's crouching on his haunches and his mouth is against me, his tongue demanding that my pleasure continues.

'Oh, God…' My fingers dig into his shoulders now and all my weight is against the window.

Please, don't let it break.

But would I even care? What a blissful way to go.

'What else?' he asks my clit, so that I can't help but laugh.

It's quickly subdued by a keening cry of need. He's *so* good at this. *So* good at everything.

'It's just temporary…' I can hardly speak now. I don't want to talk. I don't want to think. Feelings are carrying me away. 'How long are you…' I pause, trying to catch my breath '…in the States for?'

'Two weeks.'

'Okay.' I nod, but I am losing my mind with pleasure. 'That's our end-date.'

And that's it. That's all she wrote.

I cannot form more words or thoughts or objections. I vibrate against the window and against him and he holds me tight, kisses me until the wave has calmed. He knows what I need; he expresses that knowledge with every movement of his body and his mouth.

I am afraid and yet I am fearless. I am a contradiction in his arms, against his wall, in his house.

And then he stands.

'You've got yourself a deal.'

CHAPTER SEVEN

'WHO THE FUCK is she?'

I'm groggy, and it takes me a second even to recognise it's Sienna's voice coming from my phone.

'Who is who?' I rub a hand over my eyes and then flop back on the bed. 'Sienna, it's five o'clock in the morning.'

'Who is the woman you're with?'

I think of Ally instantly and flip over, reaching for her on autopilot. She's not there. Of course she isn't.

No sleepovers.

'What woman?'

'Oh, I'm sure there's a billion. I'm talking about the one on all the gossip sites today. With the red hair.'

The photo. Taken the night we hooked up. It's online?

Curiosity has me putting my phone on speaker, so that I can load up a browser without cutting Sienna off.

'Are you *kidding* me? You're engaged. Why the hell do you care who I'm fucking?'

Sienna's sharp intake of breath is audible. 'So you *are* fucking her?'

Bingo. My gut clenches. You can't see Ally's face but it's obviously her. There's something so elegant about her, even in the paparazzi shot. Her long hair is tossed over one shoulder and her face is averted. My hand is clutched possessively around her.

My eyes narrow. 'Yeah. You'd better believe I am.'

'Jeez, Ash. *Classy.*'

'*You* can talk! You didn't think you owed me a heads-up before you Tweeted the whole goddamned world with your engagement news?'

She's quiet. I wonder if she's feeling guilty and then discount it. Sienna is selfish. Singularly so.

'I shouldn't have done that.'

It's something. But it's not enough. This typifies our relationship. Her spectacularly bad behaviour followed by an almost-apology. Always insufficient, and yet I always let her get away with that.

Not any more.

'Damn straight. What were you *thinking*?'

'We'd had a few bottles of Bolly,' she murmurs. 'I don't think I really *was* thinking. Anyway, you're no better.'

'Because I'm sleeping with someone else? In the privacy of my hotel?'

'Oh, don't expect me to believe it's just *one* girl. I've seen the way they chase after you. I imagine you're engaged in nightly orgies by now.'

I laugh. 'If that's what you want to imagine me doing, go right ahead.'

An orgy would have nothing on what Ally offers.

I lie back against the pillows and close my eyes. I remember the way she went down on me, her huge eyes looking up at me. My dick clenches.

'You're such a bastard…' Sienna sniffs.

'Yeah, well, just as well you don't have to put up with me any more.'

I disconnect the call and toss my phone aside. It's far more fun to imagine Ally's lips around my cock than it is to argue with Sienna.

But the conversation has unsettled me. Our break-up was bad. No—it was so much worse than that.

I have vague recollections of Sienna pitching a crystal vase at me as she shouted, and I remember saying awful things to her. Things I regret.

We were both so angry.

We were both aware that we'd been holding on to something that had at one time been good, but that had soured slowly. As if poison had been dripping into our relationship for years and we didn't want to acknowledge it.

Our final fight was proof of that.

There had been no love left.

I regret the way we ended it. Most of the time we were together it was okay, even good, and we knew each other in a unique way, both having gone from normality to immense fame almost overnight.

Which means we should have known better than to take our fight into the street. Well, that was Sienna, actually, storming out in the middle of the afternoon, mascara running down her cheeks, bare feet, shouting at me as though the world needed to know our issues.

Yeah, the break-up had been shit.

I get up and pull on some boxers, moving to my guitar on autopilot and staring out at Manhattan.

Things with Sienna are messed up, but that's okay. Because what I've got going with Ally is just perfect for where I'm at. Fucking someone normal and undemanding. Someone who seems even less interested in the whole romantic dating bullshit than I am.

No flowers.
No dating.
Just sex.
With a reassuring end-date that takes all the *Where are we going?* crap out of the equation.
Suddenly I'm as impatient as all hell to see her.

So, I've been thinking…

I send the text to Ally with a smile on my face, not expecting to hear back. It's so early she's probably still fast asleep.

The idea fills my imagination very pleasantly.

I place my phone down on the coffee table, beside my bare feet, and reach for my guitar. It's never far from me when I'm working on new songs, and I've been doing that for a month in earnest.

I begin to strum, and all I can think of is her smile. *Ally.*

Her name whooshes out of me. I lean forward and scrawl lyrics in my own particular brand of can't-be-fucked shorthand that will only ever be decipherable to me, note the chords, then lean back and stare out of the window, singing the lines over and again.

My phone buzzes.

Just in general? Or about something specific. Because I think you should be worried if you're ever *not* thinking.

She puts a little kiss emoji at the end and it reminds me so much of her that my grin threatens to split my face.

Oh, my thoughts are very, very specific.

Three little dots appear, to show that she's typing back, but then they disappear again. I grin, put the phone down and return to my guitar, continue playing. But after ten minutes, when she hasn't replied, I'm impatient to hear from her.

I pick the phone up and am about to start typing when a message swishes onto the screen.

Specifically…?

I laugh.

Ten minutes for one word? Seriously?

Her dots move frantically.

Are you literally standing by your phone waiting for me to reply?

Everything inside me tightens. This is *fun*. The kind of fun I haven't had in…years?

I think of Sienna with guilt. When did I stop finding her fun? Or is that normal after you've known someone a really long time?

Yep. Aren't you?

I stare out of the window, waiting for her to reply. It doesn't take long.

My prayers are answered. She's sent a photo of herself, a smiling photo taken as she…*runs*? Is she *running*? I pinch the picture. It looks to be a park somewhere. She has earphones in and a cap pulled low.

Even like this, with no make-up, her face pink from exertion, she is so beautiful. I ache for her.

Nice. How about you run my way next?

I briefly question the wisdom of such an obvious bootie call but her response is immediate.

I'll be there in ten.

Thank fuck.

Ethan Ash doesn't walk. He saunters. He saunters like the rock 'n' roll sex god he truly is.

I watch him from my vantage point on the other side of the foyer of the Gramercy Park Hotel, and every sauntering sexy step he takes makes my temperature heat and my blood boil, so that by the time he stops in front of me I am a hot puddle of lava on the expensive leather seat.

'Hey, you.'

'*Jesus.* It should be illegal to be that sexy.'

He bursts out laughing and I fear I'm crab-pink all over, colour heating my cheeks all the way to my hairline as I realise I've said the words out loud. I briefly question the sense in coming to him like this—straight from a run. Should I have gone home and showered first? Done my hair and make-up?

He sobers, taking pity on me. And he leans down. 'Right back atcha.'

The kiss he presses against my cheek is chaste. My body doesn't get the memo, though, and every single cell inside me seems to vibrate and tremble and squeal in anticipation. With his lips beside my ear he whispers, the words husky, 'You in Lycra is something I'm never gonna forget.'

Desire pitches through me, rolling my stomach. I stand up on legs that are somewhat wobbly and almost collide with him. Almost? I *want* to collide with him. It's only his quick movement that saves us from bumping together, and he puts a hand in the small of my back. It is a touch of possession and it sparks my blood.

My eyes lift to his; in his face is the same heat as fills my body.

'Shall we?'

I nod, not sure I can speak in that moment.

His grin is my further undoing. It spreads across his face and all the while his eyes hold mine and I am sinking, incapable of staying afloat.

Another couple is waiting for the lift and they obviously recognise Ethan don't-forget-I'm-a-celebrity Ash. I step away, my smile tight, my body language instantly businesslike.

His teasing grin is all the indication I need that he has noticed.

I stare straight ahead, ignoring the obvious looks of appraisal from the other woman. When the elevator doors open they move in ahead of us. I step to the back of the lift and stay there, while Ethan leans nonchalantly against the panel of buttons, a hint of amusement obvious in every single one of his features.

'What?' I say, as soon as they step out and we are alone.

'You're embarrassed to be seen with me?'

'No.' I force a smile. 'There was a photo of us in the papers this morning.'

'The papers?' He frowns. 'I knew it was online.'

'It's *online*?'

My heart thumps. It's okay. *It's okay.* The woman in the picture doesn't look like me. Only it's not okay, because I can't bear putting my mom and dad through yet another scandal.

They're definitely not over the whole Jeremy thing. I think they took it harder than I did. Not just that I'd been 'the other woman' but that I'd been a homewrecker too. He had *kids*, for Chrissakes.

If they find out I'm in a purely sexual fling with a superstar like Ethan Ash they'll actually disown me.

'Mmm.'

He closes the space between us and I stay where I am, my back to the wall. My breath feels heavy somehow, weighted in such a way that it's dragged down instead of pushed out. His body presses against mine, but he doesn't touch me with his hands. Those he uses to brace himself against the wall of the lift, one on either side of me. He is the cage but my desire is untameable. It fills the cube we are in, surrounding us completely like a dense fog.

The doors open and he steps back from me, reaching for my hand and pulling me after him, out into the carpeted hallway. It's deserted, thank God, because I don't want to pull away from him again. We move quickly, the same silent force motivating our movements, making us step in haste.

He slips the key into the door and then pushes it wide. 'After you, Miss Douglas.'

'Thank you, Mr Ash.'

I step into the room and the table we first made love on—no, *fucked* on—is right in front of me. I walk towards it on autopilot, propping my hips against its edge, trailing my fingertips over the glass. Memories spike my blood. He's watching me, and that knowledge makes me smile.

He prowls towards me and lifts my baseball cap off my head. I briefly wonder how badly my hair is plastered to my head—particularly when his eyes continue their mapping of my features.

He lifts both hands and cups my cheeks, then runs his hands back to the elastic band holding my thick mane in a ponytail. He pulls at it determinedly, his eyes focused on the job so that I am able to focus on him. On the thumb-print-sized divot in his chin. The little score between his brows. The colours in his eyes that have mesmerised me from the first moment I saw him.

My breath escapes as a sigh and his lips twist in acknowledgement of the noise.

His fingers find the hem at the bottom of my shirt and push it up, just enough for his fingertips to glance my flesh. His touch is strangely reverent, as though he is worshipping at the altar of *me*. It has to be said that if I were ever granted deity status I would totally spend my time doing this.

His eyes roam my face, but he says nothing. He just stares at me for a long, cold second, and then his fingers find me again, and this time they lift my shirt all the way up, over my face, discarding it on the table top.

I'm wearing a neon green sports bra and it's glued to my skin. He slides his fingers under the elastic at the back and loosens it, but before he attempts to remove it he kisses me. It is a kiss of such depth and need that my gut twists. It is a kiss of ownership, of punishment, of anger and of conquest. Oh, and passion, too. So much passion.

I wrap my legs around his waist, holding him tight. His cock is hard. I feel him through my clothes and I moan into his mouth…a moan that must convey everything I want, because he picks me up, holding me to him, carrying me through the suite towards the bedroom.

He eases me to the ground and removes my bra at the same time, sliding it over my head. I laugh as it catches my hair.

He doesn't.

His mood is serious.

Focused.

A stone drops through me.

Is this about wanting me? Or wanting *her*? The night we met, he was furious with her. And he wanted me. For *me*? For myself? Or was it payback? Did he want to hurt her by fucking me?

So what? I remind myself. This is exactly what I want. Sex. Hot sex. No-strings sex.

It is a swift coming together. We fuck like two people who have been kept apart for months. There is a furious hunger in our movements that burns brightly and explodes swiftly.

He holds me tight afterwards, holds me against his chest, kisses the top of my head and strokes my hair.

'So, break it down for me. What's all the fuss about?'

He slides another piece of peach between my lips. I take it, savouring the juicy sweetness without looking at him.

'We've watched two episodes. How can you not *get* it?'

'Maybe I've been a bit distracted.'

He reaches over and catches a dribble of peach juice that's running down my chin. My cheeks flush.

I sigh with mock exasperation. 'It's just so *angsty*. I mean, he's been away at war, and everyone thought he was dead. His poor fiancé has had to grieve his loss and move on with her life—which she's done, by deciding to marry, let's face it, an obviously very poor second choice. Then he comes *back to town*!'

He's staring at me as though I've begun to talk in a foreign language.

'It's essentially a fight between good and evil! It's a drama, and, yes, there's romance, but it's *so*... Oh, forget it.'

He shrugs. 'It's just kind of boring.'

'How can you not *get* it?' I'm outraged. It is *so* not boring.

He slices another piece of peach, and though I'm facing forward I can see him in the periphery of my vision, his fingers lean and insistent, the paring knife wielded expertly.

I turn to him as he lifts the fruit, my lips parted. He slides it in but I wrap my lips around his finger, holding it in my mouth a moment while my eyes meet his.

'Plus,' I say quietly, pulling away, 'Aidan Turner is seriously hot.'

His brows shoot upwards. '*This* guy?'

'Uh, *yeah*.'

I turn back to the screen, smiling to myself as I hear the cogs turning.

'I mean, sure...if brooding and honourable is your thing.'

'I think it's kind of *every* woman's thing,' I say without looking at him.

'Careful, Alicia.'

My expression is one of innocence. 'What's wrong?'

He straddles me quickly, surprising me, and holds the last piece of peach to my mouth. I bite around it, but he pulls his fingers away this time, disposing of the stone and then reaching for the remote. He silences *Poldark* as he crushes his lips to mine. I taste peach and imagine he does too.

'Nothing's wrong.' He drags my lower lip between his teeth. 'I just don't want to share you with Poldark.'

I grin against his mouth even as a warning bell bleats in my brain. He's just joking. Being silly. Distracting me from a show he doesn't like. And I'm more than willing to be distracted.

'Stay the night.'

I'm on the brink of sleep.

Time has ceased to have meaning. We have been in his bed for hours. Talking. Dozing. Kissing. My body is an odd mix of weightlessness and heaviness. I am satiated and needy.

'What day is it?'

I'm only half joking. The week has passed so quickly that I can barely remember where I'm at.

'Saturday. Tomorrow's Sunday.'

He traces a finger down my nose, following the curve, lifting it over the small jump at its tip and then pressing it to my lips. I kiss it and he smiles beside me, then runs his finger onwards, over my chin to the cleft between my breasts.

Goosebumps scatter across my flesh.

'Ally?'

'Mmm?' I rouse myself to pay better attention.

'Stay tonight.'

'No sleepovers, remember?'

'Mmm… But you feel so *good*.'

He roves his hand over my naked breast, finding my nipple and circling it until I suck in a shuddering breath.

There is danger in spending the night. I know I must go. And I will. Soon.

I am no longer capable of thought, speech or staving off exhaustion. My eyes sweep shut.

I fall asleep with his hand on my breast and memories of him in my mind.

CHAPTER EIGHT

Where are you?

I PUSH MY phone back into my bag without answering, determinedly turning my attention to the flowers before me.

Stalls line the footpath, but I have my favourite, and I am nothing if not faithful. I select two bunches of tulips—yellow and pink—and hand over some cash from my back pocket. I cradle them against my chest as I weave through the markets, pausing to buy a pretzel and a coffee which I must juggle in one hand.

It's worth it. The pretzel is warm and soft, the dough salty on the outside and almost sweet within. The pretzel is a perfect metaphor for New York, this city that I found so impenetrable at first and which I now adore.

I have been wandering the streets for over an hour, wondering that same thing. I feel my phone buzz, but have no choice but to ignore it. My hands are now full.

It will wait.

Just sex.

No flowers.

No sleepovers.

No romance, no commitment.

No hassles.

No potential for heartbreak.

I smile resolutely and weave my way through people and stalls, puppies and children, and turn into my own street. Familiarity makes my heart skip a beat or two. I tell myself I am happy to be here, that I want to be in my own home rather than in his hotel room.

Yesterday was fun, but staying there again today would be habit-forming, and I'm not prepared to do that. I tell myself it was *smart* to sneak out while he was asleep, without so much as kissing his cheek for fear that it would wake him, and he would kiss me back, and then all my good intentions would be scarpered.

I reach the front door at the same time as Kelvin Monteith from the upstairs apartment is leaving; he holds it open and offers to carry the flowers up for me. I shake my head and climb the stairs, jiggling my key into the slot and pushing the door inwards.

Eliza's still asleep, but Cassie is in the kitchen, fixing breakfast. I can smell the bacon the second I step inside.

'Morning!' I call cheerfully, waving the tulips in her face. 'Aren't these beautiful?'

She arches a brow and taps her foot pointedly.

'What?'

'Well?'

'Well, what?'

'Have you been with *him* again?'

I shake my head. And then I shrug. 'Yeah.'

'That's three times this week?'

Heat suffuses my cheeks. 'Who's counting?'

She watches me for a long moment and then expels a sigh. 'Ally…'

'I know.'

I lay the flowers down on the bench and stretch on my tiptoes to rescue a glass jar from above the fridge. I half-fill it with water, and am about to stuff the flowers in when Cassie retrieves the jar and tips the water out. As she begins to wipe the inside of it I note the visible watermark with a wry smile. Trust Cassie to see such a small detail.

Cassie and Eliza were with me at my lowest ebb. Their concern is natural. But I am not going to be hurt again.

'This is different.'

'Yeah, well...*duh*. There can't be *two* men in the world as misogynistic and narcissistic as Jeremy.'

We all read a lot of psychology self-help books after the Jeremy incident. He stood as a cautionary tale for all of us. I have no doubt he will move into urban myth in time. *Bastard.*

And yet, despite all the metaphorical wounds he inflicted, I still rail against an instinct to defend him. Such was his power over me, I suppose, that even now I am somewhat in his thrall. How can I hate him but not want others to do so?

'Ethan's nice,' I say instead, definitely not adding that I'm pretty sure he's using me to get over Sienna Di Giorgio.

'Uh-huh.' Cassie's caution is understandable. 'Just... be careful.'

I nod, and my eyes meet hers reassuringly. I can't begrudge her concern. Cassie and Eliza had to scrape me up off the floor after Jeremy—they had to wipe my broken heart from the walls of our lives.

'I really, really am fine, Cass.'

After all, what could be more cautious than contrac-

tually agreeing to the terms of our arrangement prior to
undertaking an affair?

'Okay.'

She reaches forward and bites my pretzel. Such is our
friendship that I don't complain, even though I live for
these damned things. I hand it to her and sip my coffee,
and when I think she's distracted by turning the bacon
I fish my phone from my pocket and swipe it open.

Be still my beating heart.

It's a photo of him. He's wearing a simple white singlet and it looks like that favourite pair of jeans. He's
pulling a confused face and the rumpled bed is behind
him. In his hand he's holding a peach. My gut clenches.

Come back?

I stare at the photo for several more seconds. The
slick of desire is unmistakable. I enjoy its possession of
my body because I feel it with the certainty that I will
be with him again. *Soon.*

When I have proved to myself that I can stay away.

Being cat-called on the streets of New York is frustrat-
ingly common. So when I step out of work Tuesday
evening and hear a wolf-whistle I straighten my spine
and keep going.

'Hey, sexy!'

The voice is familiar. I stop walking and turn slowly,
my eyes catching the limousine and Grayson immediately. The window is down just far enough for me to
make out Ethan's hair and eyes and it's all I need. My
tummy flops.

I pull on my handbag strap and walk towards the car. 'Hey.'

'Your chariot awaits, m'lady.'

I arch a brow. Emotions war inside me. Pleasure at seeing him, sure. But also worry. Worry that this isn't part of our deal.

'My chariot can go on its way,' I say. 'I like to walk.'

'Ah.' He nods slowly. 'But I have a surprise.'

I roll my eyes. 'I don't like surprises.'

'I think you'll like this one.'

He pushes the door open an inch. I'm tempted to walk away, but I've stayed away from him for two nights, so I've sort of proved myself capable of handling this… haven't I?

'What's the surprise?'

I slide into the limousine and instantly I'm overpowered by his proximity. The smell of him, the possibility that I'll soon be touching him.

I buckle up in the seat beside him. 'Ethan?'

'You'll see.' He grins cryptically, then leans closer. 'You look good enough to eat.'

Grayson is behind the wheel. He starts the engine and then pulls out into the traffic. I watch the buildings pass in a blur, curiosity as to where we're going lasting the entire drive.

Well, almost the entire drive. I recognise the approach to the MoMA a few blocks out. I have spent so much of my time here since arriving in NYC that it is almost like a second home.

I love it.

But I do not love the idea of being here *now*.

Not when Ethan Ash hasn't kissed me in days. Not when Ethan Ash hasn't fucked me in days. Not when we could be back in his hotel, doing all the things I've been fantasising about all afternoon.

'Well?'

I step out of the car, staring up at the building with grudging admiration. From this vantage point it is modern and it is beautiful, but my favourite place to admire it from is two blocks away, from where you can see the higgledy-piggledy arrangement of the various levels, all precariously balanced on top of one another. Like a three-year-old might build a high-rise.

I could write a thesis on what that incautious, irreverent juxtaposition means. The balancing of lines and order with chaos and random-seeming placement. The way it makes sense even when it shouldn't.

'You look at this place like I'm looking at you,' he observes with sensual heat.

'Like I'm a mix of order and disarray?'

'Something like that.' His wink is a flirtatious whip across my spine. 'Shall we…?'

Desire to be alone with him is fighting a battle—and losing—with my love for this place. I nod and move towards the entrance, the pull of the gallery strengthening with every step.

Grayson has procured us some kind of special entry. We don't queue, and a museum staffer greets us. She is a stunning young woman, with caramel skin and chestnut hair, enormous brown eyes and an impressive cleavage barely contained by her museum uniform. Her eyes cleave to Ethan in a way that makes me think she wishes it were her body, not just her gaze.

An unpleasant tang of adrenalin flavours my mouth. My sense of anticipation is somewhat dimmed by the prospect of being accompanied by *anyone* other than Ethan but that's not why I stiffen.

Ethan Ash is seriously hot.

Hot in that way that is unusual and distracting. Hypnotic. He is also hugely famous. And he's here with me. But in the space of a little over a week he won't be. In a little over a week he'll be with someone else. Making love to someone else. Charming the pants off them with his husky voice and smile. Someone like this obviously very willing museum staffer.

My jealousy is misplaced, and yet it's real.

When he dismisses the woman with, 'Miss Douglas is an art expert. I'll be fine in her capable hands,' I am childishly relieved.

'Oh, sure, no problem. But you just shout out if you need anything at all, okay?'

'So, is this how it is for you?' I ask as we walk away. 'All special entry and people tripping over themselves to serve you?'

He grins at me and reaches for my hand, squeezing it in a way that speaks once more of intimacy and closeness. I squeeze back.

He grins. 'Nah.'

'Nah?'

'Where to?'

We pause outside the sculpture garden and I nod towards the stairs. 'Contemporary, of course.'

'Why *of course*?' he asks, taking my lead and walking with me.

'I like to start at the end and work my way backwards.'

I smile up at him and I'm shy suddenly. It's inexplicable; I don't like it. I look away, focusing on the wall ahead. This isn't a first date. It's an aberration. A distraction.

'It's easier to make sense of contemporary art in some ways. It speaks to people because it fits within the sphere of our current tastes and wants.'

'Not me,' he says with a shake of his head. 'Give me the Impressionists any day.'

My lips twist in acknowledgement but I try to hide my cynicism.

He sees it regardless. 'What? You don't approve?'

I select my words with care. 'The Impressionist movement is probably the most adored of all.'

'So I can't like it because everyone else does?'

'You can like whatever you like,' I demur. 'I'm just saying that its accessibility gives it a head start. Sunflowers. Lily pads. They're borrowed from so heavily in popular culture. You can see Monet splashed through airport advertising. People don't necessarily *like* the Impressionists so much as recognise them.'

He clutches a hand to his chest in mock pain and stops walking.

'What?'

I look around. Luckily no one is watching us.

'You *wound* me,' he says with exaggerated complaint.

'I'm sorry.' I grin, showing I feel no such thing. 'I'm always unstintingly honest.'

'You're wrong.' He sobers almost instantly and catches my hand. 'Let me show you.'

I resist the urge to point out *I'm* supposed to be giving *him* the tour, and willingly go with him, up several more flights of stairs, until a sign points us towards the Impressionists wing.

Despite everything I have just said I pause as we step into the hall, instantly overpowered by the beauty and profound uniqueness of each and every piece before us.

Ethan looks at me, and then continues to move slowly, skimming his eyes over each piece of art until finally he stops in front of a lesser-known Matisse.

Woman Reading, the caption proclaims.

'This was the first painting I ever loved.'

I look from him to the painting in surprise. 'Why?'

'There's something about it that speaks to me. Perhaps it's the way her back is turned. The whole painting is almost disdainful. The composition confusing. And yet the way I'm kind of…*excluded* makes me *want* to intrude. To tap her on the shoulder; make her look at me.'

He is describing a sense that is so perfectly what I think Matisse was aiming for that I want to kiss him.

Art-speak is not something everyone is comfortable with, and the fact that Ethan über-sexy Ash can do it so well is incredibly desirable.

'That's good,' I say, wondering at the catch of feeling in my voice. 'Art *should* create that kind of emotion in you. An emotional response is all that matters—no matter what inspires it.'

'So I'm allowed to like the Impressionists again?' he teases, all cerebral philosophising over and done with.

'I suppose so.'

And so, amongst the Van Goghs, Mondrians, Monets and Seurats, we begin our tour of the MoMa…

'Okay,' he says after we've finished two full floors. 'I showed you mine. What's yours?'

'My what?' I'm genuinely confused.

'Your favourite piece in here?'

* * *

Holy crap, she's hotter than Hades when she's talking about art.

I thought I might have lost her with my waffling on about *Woman Reading*, but if anything it spurred her on. As though she thought she was speaking to a kindred spirit—someone who understands her love of art.

And, Jesus, listening to her, I think I might.

Ally Douglas could explain *anything* to me and I'd be somewhat spellbound. I stare at her as she discusses the way light and shade have been used to create an apparent three-dimensionality to the simple painting, but all I can think about is the light and shade in her face, and the multi-dimensionality in her eyes as the late-afternoon sun cuts through the glass and settles freely on her face.

I think about the light and shade in her voice, too—the way it pitches and rolls with emotion as she moves along the exhibit, teaching me effortlessly. Not because she wants me to learn, or because she thinks I should know this stuff, but because she can't help herself.

Art is her passion.

And she feels passionately.

I listen to her patiently even as I am burning up. We reach the end of the display and there is only a red fire alarm on the wall. I want to tell her how beautiful she is. I want to tell her she's the most beautiful woman I've ever seen.

It's not just that. I want to do more of *this*. I like being out with her. Holding her hand. I like the idea of taking her to dinner. I want her to come to my concert and to be waiting backstage for me.

The arbitrary boundaries we've insisted on are annoying me now, and I know why.

I don't like it that Ally is making an art form out of pushing me away, walking away from me when it suits her. I have an insatiable need to unsettle the ease with which she does that. To unsettle her a little bit. Why? To make her forget about our rules? Just for a while?

Stuff it.

I lean closer and murmur, 'You're beautiful.'

Her head whips up to mine so fast I briefly worry she might have dislocated something. She stares at me but says nothing. I could get lost in those damned eyes of hers.

Then, as if reading my mind, she blinks and looks away, withdrawing herself from me.

'That's it.' Her voice is gravelled.

I can't take my eyes off her face immediately, but she lifts a finger and points and I am drawn to the gesture. I follow the direction until my eyes land on a portrait across the room.

It is of a woman with pale skin and rust-coloured hair. It's painted in profile and there's an enigmatic twist to her lips that prompts curiosity. I reach for Ally's hand, still outstretched, and move us towards the picture.

'Your favourite?'

'Yeah.' The admission is softly spoken.

I look down at her; she's blushing. Is she annoyed with me?

Objectively, Ally is stunning. *Always.* But when her face flushes with colour she glows with all the warmth in the world and she is unlike anything I've ever seen. Even in the midst of this art she is…*intriguing.* A mix of intelligence, maturity and vulnerability.

An ache spreads through me, pervasive and hungry. There are too many people around for me to do what I want—to wrap her in my arms and kiss her as though my literal survival depends upon it.

'Why?'

She bites down on her lip and her eyes flick first to me and then away. 'Oh, I just really like it.'

She pushes the conversation away with tangible determination.

'They're going to be closing soon. We should go.'

CHAPTER NINE

I FEEL AS THOUGH the lift isn't moving.

Ethan is beside me, and we are being pulled upwards by cables and knots, but I *need* him. I need him to fuck me. Not to tell me I'm beautiful. Not to wander through the MoMA with me, looking at pictures and listening to me explain them.

That's breaking the rules!

What the hell were we thinking?

We have to fuck, and now, to remind us both of all the things we want from this—and all the things we *don't*.

When the doors finally open I can't help but groan my relief. He grins at me and wraps an arm around my waist, pulling me into his side, leading me down the corridor towards his room. The second we are inside I launch myself at him, holding him tighter, seeking his mouth.

He seeks mine back. Our need is mutual. Urgent. Inflammatory.

'Fuuuuck.' He rips himself away and stares at me like he's trying to make sense of this, of me, of our need. 'Fuck.' He shakes his head. 'What the hell are you doing to me?'

I don't want to talk. Even about sex and our insatiable need for it. I push myself against him, kissing him, pushing at his shirt, and he answers in kind, lifting my dress over my ass, higher, breaking the kiss just enough to undress me completely.

His fingers are demanding as they slide into the waistband of my underpants, pushing down, curving around my ass, and then he lifts me easily, as though I weigh nothing. He lifts me, and I wrap my legs around his waist, and his kiss is warming me up from inside. He lies me on the sofa but stays on top of me, and his kiss, the weight of his body, the roll of his hips—it is everything.

I arch my back, seeking him, needing him, but there are too many clothes in the way.

'Need…' I whimper, snapping his belt open and pulling it out of his jeans.

He reaches down and undoes his button and zip and kicks his legs out of the pants, barely breaking our kiss. His lips move over mine. His tongue is daring me, daring mine, taunting me, making me forget all my reasons for keeping this light. Making me want more, want to beg him to stay in my life in some capacity even when I know that temporary is all we are—all that makes sense.

Also all I should want.

I run my fingers up his back and he grunts; I think he swears but the ringing bell of desire is all I can hear. And our own urgent breaths, tangling together, the sound of the impatient passion that defines us.

He hums in my ear, and I make a sound a bit like a moan. He is so sexy—his voice so beautiful, so raw, so famous. It hits me then, for the first time, that I'm sleeping with a celebrity. Someone so famous that everyone in the world must know who he is.

And I pull back a little—just enough to see his face, to look into his eyes.

Fuck. What am I doing?

My heart trips over a little, thumping hard against my ribs, and my stomach swirls with emotions I don't even want to think about analysing. Recognition pulses through me. Why has it taken me so long to realise that he's not just Ethan? To remember that he's Ethan Ash, superstar?

'What is it?'

His gravelly voice travels through me, finding every space inside me and warming it up. Superheating me from the inside out.

I shake my head, but a frown lingers on my lips. I kiss him to chase it away, losing myself once more in the sensual charge that besieges us both.

'Are you okay?'

I nod, jerkily. 'Fuck me.'

His laugh is without humour. 'Alicia…?'

Oh, great. *Now* he goes and brings my real name into it.

'I'm fine,' I say, digging my fingers into his hips, dragging him down against me, lifting myself up in a wordless invitation.

But he breaks away from me and for a second I think he's not going to give me what I need. I am empty and bereft. But he returns a short moment later, a condom in his hand and a smile on his lips.

'You, Alicia Douglas, are a mystery.'

My heart twists. 'A good mystery?'

'A fantastic one.'

He winks and my throat is dry suddenly.

Keep it light. Keep it fun.

I reach up and lace my fingers behind his head, pulling him down, greedily seeking his mouth, taking everything he offers and still demanding more. There is nothing light about this, even while it is the most fun I've ever had.

My need for him—and I'm not blind or stupid enough to pretend I *don't* need him—is all-consuming. If I'm not careful it is going to take over, and I will no longer have autonomy.

I have to fuck him and go.

I push him angrily, needily, desperately, and together we roll off the couch onto the carpeted floor. He laughs, but I'm ripping the condom out of his hands and tearing it open, sliding it from its packet and pushing it onto him. His eyes are watching me, and it makes my fingers shake. I remove my own underwear quickly, then straddle him, leaning forward to kiss him at the same time I take him deep inside me.

Passion tears through us and we are fast, we are hungry, we are desperate. I move my hips, but he makes a growl of frustration and rolls us so that he is on top of me, the weight of his body a heavenly pleasure. I wrap my legs around his waist but he catches my calves and lifts them higher. I can't contain the furious pleasure that is taking over me. I lie back, my eyes squeezed shut as flames lick my nerves, making me tremble and sweat.

He stills and I groan, twisting my hips.

'Look at me.'

The command is husky, and he accompanies it with fingers that press under my chin, pulling my face towards him, angling me so that I am facing him.

'Look at me,' he says again, and I realise my eyes are still squeezed shut.

I blink them open and regret it immediately. It is as though I have been stabbed. Something unpleasant and sharp thrusts into my chest—something I don't recognise yet but know I don't want. I look over his shoulder but he shakes his head.

'I want to see you come.'

'You will,' I whisper, knowing that the wave is about to crash. Any minute.

He pushes deeper and I draw in an unsteady breath, digging my fingernails into my palms.

'Let me see you.'

I don't know what he means. I look to him for clarification and our eyes lock. He moves inside me, not looking away, and I don't look away either because suddenly I can't. There are invisible forces at work and they compel me to be brave even when I'm running from this feeling.

This perfect, perfect torment.

Inexplicably, tears threaten to moisten my eyes. I blink, but still I look at him. And I fall. I fall off the edge. There is nothing to hold, nothing to save my fall. I am weightless in the air—just me, my pleasure, no gravity, nothing.

I'm sure he sees this, because he's watching me so closely, and because he kisses me differently as I tremble in his arms. A kiss of warmth rather than heat. Of understanding and acceptance. I kiss him back.

What else can I do?

He moves inside me slowly, letting muscles that are squeezing him frantically return to their normal state, and then he thrusts hard, so that I cry out, and we are falling together this time, holding hands, riding the same wave of pleasure at the same time. I cry his name into his mouth over and over again. Not Ethan Ash, because he is just Ethan again. Ethan who makes me feel as I never knew I could.

Ethan who is mine. Not the world's.

Though he is. I know that.

But like this, right here, he is mine.

And I am his.

The thought rattles through me as though I am an empty barn and it is tumbleweed. It rocks me to my core.

I am no one's.

I stiffen beneath him and press my fingers into his chest. I angle my head away.

'You are fucking amazing,' he says. '*This* is amazing.'

'It's not me,' I say seriously.

'I think it must be.'

He kisses the tip of my nose and my gut twists. I must flee from this tempting perfection before it sucks me under and robs me of breath and sanity altogether.

'I should go.'

His laugh is husky. 'I'm still inside you.'

He throbs and my breath catches in my throat. Heat suffuses my cheeks.

'I know.' With great effort I make my voice light. Amused.

'You're not going anywhere.'

He pulls away from me, though, straightening and then standing, striding through the hotel room towards the bathroom. I watch him go, my eyes hungrily devouring this aspect of him—his beautiful, naked body.

He emerges a minute later, a towel wrapped low around his waist. He strides to the phone and picks it up. 'Ethan Ash. Give me Room Service.'

I prop myself on my elbows, knowing I should make

an effort to get dressed, but enjoying watching him too much. I'll move soon, I tell myself.

He turns to face me; our eyes lock. I am lost once more. I can feel him inside me even though he is across the room. The phantom of his being with me is a powerful, beautiful thing.

'Fillet steak. Fries. Onion rings. A salad.' He lifts a brow questioningly and covers the receiver. 'Anything else?'

I shake my head.

'Ice cream. Some oysters. Maybe some garlic bread. A peach.'

He winks at me, then hangs up as he strides over to me. He stares at me for a heart-thumping second, his expression unreadable, and then he drops his hands down, inviting me to grab them.

I know it's not wise, but I put my hands in his as if on autopilot and he pulls me up to stand. Our bodies press to one another. My breath catches.

'I've missed you.'

My heart drops.

He can't have missed me. It's not what we are.

I smile, but I know it's only half a smile. I'm too perturbed, confused, concerned, to be properly amused.

'I want to ask you something.'

I don't think my look is encouraging, but apparently he doesn't notice. He begins to sing again. His latest song. The one that is on all the radio stations—everywhere. His latest song that is a number one hit.

God, he's so famous.

And yet we speak as though it doesn't matter.

'Yeah?' It's a hoarse prompt.

'I'm doing a gig Friday night. Wanna come?'

It takes several seconds for me to connect the words with the truth. The fact that by 'doing a gig' he means performing at a concert. And not a little local town hall concert either.

'Where?' I ask with a sinking heart.

'The Garden.'

'Madison Square Garden?'

He nods.

He'll be performing for tens of thousands of people. On Friday night. When I would usually be at happy hour with my two best friends.

'That's okay,' I say, not quite sure how to reply properly. 'I'm good.'

'I *know* you're good,' he responds with a wry twist of his lips. 'I'm asking if you want to come to the concert.'

I bite down on my lip and decide honesty is the best policy. 'Will you be offended if I say no?'

He laughs. 'No. My ego isn't *that* fragile. I'm curious, though.'

Naturally. 'It's just...' How can I put into words what I don't fully understand myself?

'You don't like my music?' he teases.

'Can't stand it,' I quip back.

His smile makes my stomach lurch. 'I just...'

'Yes?'

His lips are twitching at the corners, showing his amusement even as he tries to listen seriously to whatever wisdom I'm about to share.

'I don't know. I mean... I just... First of all, I don't see you like that. I know you're some superstar, but I like it that this feels so normal.' I pause. 'I mean apart from the luxurious apartment, the mega-mansion at the heart of the village and your penchant for ordering everything off the room service menu.'

He laughs.

'And we both know this isn't a relationship.' I force myself to meet his eyes. 'We're two people who have agreed to…to sleep together. To fuck. That's our thing.' I sigh. 'I had fun today. At the MoMA with you. But we shouldn't do that again.'

'We can do the Staten Island Ferry next time,' he teases.

'I'm serious, Ethan.' I need him to understand. 'We've both said what we want from this. The MoMA, your concert… Those things aren't on my list.'

He stares at me long and hard for a few seconds. 'I thought we said we'd have fun?'

'Yeah. *Sexy* fun.'

He laughs. 'I found you *very* sexy at the MoMA. Think of it as foreplay, baby. It was just one afternoon.'

'No.' I shake my head quickly. 'It's more complicated than that.'

His eyes crinkle at the corners, as if he's trying really hard not to laugh. 'Has anyone ever told you that you have a tendency to overthink shit?'

'Not so eloquently,' I mumble.

His laugh is short. 'Well, you do.'

'There's danger in this,' I say seriously, softly, pulling him back to the heart of my worries. 'Danger for *me*.'

His eyes throb with mine. He is reading me. Studying me. Analysing me. I keep my expression blank of emotion with an enormous effort.

'Who hurt you?'

The question knocks me sideways. I drop his hand and take a step backwards.

'No one.'

I move towards the window. I'm awkward. My body is hot and cold.

'Who hurt you?'

'No one.' I say it more emphatically now. 'You think that the only reason a person can not want to be in a relationship with you is that she's running from a past trauma, or something? Talk about egomaniacal.'

The charge is completely unreasonable—particularly given that he's right.

'I think there's more to this than you're telling me,' he insists quietly.

My eyes lift to his in the reflection of the window. There is strength in his stance and I feel it push against me. I suck in a breath; it barely reaches my lungs.

'So?' I'm on the defensive. I make a point to lower my voice. 'Have you told me everything about you and Sienna?'

I see his frown in the reflection. 'No.'

'But you think I should be an open book to *you*?'

'Hey.'

He walks behind me slowly, but his hands on my shoulders are firm. Demanding. He turns me around, then presses his thumb beneath my chin, holding my face towards his.

'You're the one who's acting like I've just fucking proposed. Why?'

'I'm not.' I bite down on my lip and jerk away from him. 'I just don't want you to go shifting the goalposts.'

I sink my teeth into my lip harder. His eyes drop to the gesture.

My heart twists painfully. Far worse than his desire to negotiate our…whatever this is…is his quick acceptance of my position. I know it's for the best, but it hurts that he doesn't fight harder.

What am I wanting? Him to prove that he wants more from me than I'm willing to give? What kind of emotional sadist am I becoming?

'So, a concert, huh?' I say, the words so over-bright they are brittle, like wood that's been left in the sun for days on end. Paint peels away my confidence. 'You nervous?'

His own smile is dismissive, distracted. 'No. It's not my first time.'

'No, of course.'

We're on safer ground, and I'm grateful, but the awkwardness of our conversation is still between us, lumpy and insistent. I hate it. I hate it that we've argued. I hate it that he probably thinks I'm either completely crazy or completely weird.

'You've been doing this a long time, I guess?'

He sighs. Wearily.

Weary of me?

Warning bells flash.

I'm messing everything up.

Isn't that the point? Isn't that why I'm fighting to keep my emotions out of this?

'Yeah.'

I sidestep his touch. Our intimacy is gone. We're just two strangers in a cold room full of misunderstanding. My dress is by the door. I move towards it on legs that are shaking, lift it up with the tips of my fingers and pull it on. When I turn around he's watching me, with that same look of confusion on his handsome face.

God, he deserves better than this.

I swallow, looking towards the window, uneasy and uncertain.

'You're not wrong.'

The words are so soft they're almost a whisper; I don't even realise I'm going to say them until I hear the way they float across the room towards him.

'About what?'

I clear my throat. 'Before you, I hadn't... It had been a while since I'd been with anyone else.'

'But there was someone important before me?' he prompts.

I nod, my eyes locking to his, showing the depth of my emotion and the ache of my pain. 'Yes.'

'And it didn't work out?'

He says it gently, like teasing a knot out of a rope.

I shake my head and those stupid, *stupid* tears are back, hot in my eyes. I blink furiously, wiping them away without touching my face.

'What happened?'

He asks the question with such kindness that I think I could collapse.

I don't.

I'm not going to be weakened by Jeremy any more. I'm stronger now. Stronger than when I first met him and I believed in fairy tales and happily-ever-after and soulmates. *What a load of nonsense.*

Ethan takes my silence for an unwillingness to discuss it.

'Look...' He shifts his weight from one foot to the other. 'You don't have to talk about it. But don't run away from me, Alicia. Just...stay and have more fun.'

My body jerks at the prospect. It's what I need and want. More than anything.

'Why don't you have a bath? Relax. I'll call you when dinner gets here.'

He's being so kind and it's hurting my heart to experience that, knowing the limitations of what we are.

I nod, though, and move towards the enormous bathroom before he can see the emotions on my face. And before I can make sense of them.

Because they're scaring me half to death.

We have devoured almost the whole tray of room service food. Despite the fact I said I wasn't hungry, it turns out that incredible, mind-blowing, multiple orgasm sex is enough to give anyone an appetite.

'Things with me and Sienna hadn't been working for a long time…'

I am torn. Morbid curiosity is at the forefront of my mind, but so too is the knowledge that this discussion is dangerous.

'Why not?'

Curiosity, apparently, wins.

He reaches for a chip and eats it thoughtfully. 'I don't know.' His smile is disarming. 'Maybe we were never right together. But, man, we hated each other by the end. Still, for her to be engaged to someone else months later…'

I wince at his description and again I think of Jeremy. Of that afternoon.

'Is this what you do? You farm me off to my mother's, with our *kids, so you can screw* her?'

'Come on, Fiona! Why wouldn't *I be fucking around behind your back? You're as cold as ice and I'm bored. We never see each other any more. I don't remember the last time we actually fucked.'*

The memory makes my heart hurt.

'I guess relationships change. People change. Love is complicated,' I say with a shrug. 'Do you know the guy?'

'Tom Banks?' He grimaces. 'Yeah.'

'That's so much worse,' I say softly. 'Do you like him?'

Ethan shrugs. 'The thing is, I kind of thought something was going on between them. She told me I was imagining it.'

My stomach twists. Lies. Love and lies. How common—and complex—it is.

'How long were you guys together?'

'On and off around six years,' he says.

As though that's nothing. As though that doesn't change everything. Honestly, if he'd told me they'd had twins together I'd have been less shocked.

That's a hell of a long time. He's only twenty-eight. So they started dating when he was in his early twenties. I blink at him, but he doesn't seem to realise how spun out I am.

'We were friends for another six or so years before that.'

It's Jeremy and Fiona all over again. A shiver runs down my spine—that same trickling sense of being an outsider, running over me like a rash. But for some reason this almost seems worse, and I can't say why.

'All this...the fame thing...it's a tricky son of a bitch. I guess because I knew Sienna *before*. Before I made it...before she made it... I thought that somehow future-proofed us. I thought that made us more real.'

Does he know how hard this is to hear? Of course not. I've told him I want nothing from him. So we're people who fuck...and apparently now I'm his therapist as well.

I'm tempted to establish some kind of barrier here. A line in the sand meaning we don't talk about Sienna *or* Jeremy. But my morbid curiosity is still thick inside me and I find it impossible to ignore.

'Do you miss her?'

His eyes latch to mine and his smile spreads across his face slowly. But there is resignation in that look, too. 'I seem to have found the perfect Band-Aid.'

CHAPTER TEN

'LOOKING FOR SOMEONE?'

I tweak the E-string, play a chord, closing my eyes as I find every single note. They are floating through space and I am able to see them from every angle—but, more than that, they reverberate in my blood, hitting a frequency that I know intimately.

Then I hear the question. Carl has toured with me for years; he knows me well. In that moment, I think he knows me better than I would like.

'Nah.'

It's a lie. I keep wondering if she'll come. Thinking how annoying it is that she hasn't.

Why does it piss me off so much? Hard to say.

'Sienna here?'

Sienna? Is that who he thinks I'm scouring the audience for? 'Nah. We broke up, remember?'

'Fuck. Sorry, mate.'

I grimace, turning back to the guitar. I play the beginning of 'Wild Silver', sing a few lines into the mic and then stop abruptly. I wrote this song for Sienna. *With* Sienna. The memory is like a ball, bobbing on the horizon of a stormy ocean. I can see it, but it keeps fading away and there's no way I can reach it.

How many of my memories will be like this? Inextricably linked to her but no longer tangible?

'Did you hear about the tickets?'

I blink, focusing my attention back on Carl. On the now. Only there's a different mirage on the horizon now. One that makes me smile rather than frown.

If Ally's not here, where *is* she?

I picture her naked in my suite. In the shower, lathered up, slippery and sweet, singing in that sweet off-key way she has. All of me is pulled. I want to be with her. Fuck the concert.

'Nah. What about them?'

'Someone's scalping seats for a thousand bucks.'

I arch a brow, yet I'm not totally surprised. The concert was booked out in under thirty minutes. My management refused a second show.

'Jesus…'

'Yeah.'

Carl hands me another of my guitars. I pass the Fender over and begin to tune the Gibson.

'You all good for drinks after?'

Shit. I'd forgotten about that. Our tradition. I always take the crew out for a post-concert wind-down.

But… *Ally.* Naked in my shower. In my bed.

I'm saved from needing to answer by the arrival of Grayson and my manager, Paul. I smile at them, but in my mind I'm already back at the hotel, and Ally's eating out of the palm of my hand…

I tell myself I made the right decision. I'm not a groupie and I think it would be weird to see Ethan up on stage, larger than life, as Ethan Rock God Ash.

So why am I sitting glued to my phone, stalking the

Twitter hashtag *#ethanashNYC*? Which is trending—of course.

There are videos of the concert being uploaded and I watch them almost faster than they can appear.

There's his beautiful acoustic cover of 'Hallelujah,' which sends goosebumps into every part of my body, like shooting stars chasing their natural end. Then there are his faster, earlier songs, full of youth and enthusiasm. There's a few ballads. He performs a song with Hunter Smith and Esther Scott, of Scott Smith—only my favourite band *ever*.

He looks amazing.

I mean, *amazing*.

And like himself as well.

Only it's so hard to reconcile Ethan—*my* Ethan—with this guy. This guy who's performing in front of tens of thousands of screaming fans. Women who are passing out. Who are shouting his name, waving their hands, holding posters that cry out their love for him. And he's so…*cool*. So effortless. He waves. He sings. He wanders from one side of the stage to the other, sauntering with his trademark nonchalance, and my pulse is raging.

My God.

He is so hot.

And he is mine.

Shh! I silence the grumpy part of my mind that constantly wants to remind me not to get too possessive or invested.

I seem to have found the perfect Band-Aid.

Those words have chased themselves around my head, and finally I can admit that they spark relief in me. They free me. Because they show me that he is indeed using me as a crutch. On the rebound while he gets over Sienna. And that means I can relax. This isn't serious for him.

Which means this is okay.

It's okay that I am waiting for him.

That I am in his hotel room and that he knows I am here, that he has promised to hurry back. That he told me he'd be counting the minutes.

Because I'm just a Band-Aid. And he's just hot sex. It's simple. Easy. I'm in control. Our boundaries are established and we are staying firmly within them.

Anticipation rolls through me. I look around his suite, checking all the details with a small smile. Candles. Music. Dinner.

Me in a slinky black negligee and nothing underneath.

I curl up on the sofa, dragging my finger down my phone obsessively, refreshing my feed as though my life depends on it.

And finally the concert is over.

It can't be long now, right?

How long?

I stare at my phone, contemplate messaging him but decide not to. *I* know that I'm desperate to see him; *he* doesn't need to.

It's almost an hour later when I hear noises outside the hotel room. And with the moment upon me I am nervous suddenly! I stand up uneasily, running my hands down the front of my lingerie, my eyes fixed to the door. I fan my hair from my face quickly, just to give it body, and then I wait.

Seconds.

Just seconds.

But long enough for my heart to flutter and my stomach to twist and my brow to sweat and my mouth to dry out.

I wait, and I stare, and finally he pushes the door inwards.

I'm not sure what I'm expecting. For him to step inside, shut the door, and look around?

He doesn't. He opens the door and looks right at me. As though he knew exactly where I'd be, exactly how I'd be standing, waiting. Our eyes lock and time ceases to exist. There is a void. A black hole with just us at its cosmic heart.

Who moves first? I can't say. I know only that we are both moving, and we are both urgent, our arms wrapping around one another, our mouths seeking, our bodies melding. His shirt is wet with perspiration. I wrap my arms around him and seek his mouth. I kiss him and he kisses me, pushing me through the room while his hands roam my back.

I grip his shirt, lifting it, finding his beautiful flesh, his chest, and I drop kisses along the ridge of his neck, down to his pecs. I taste his salty perfection and he laughs, lifting his hands to my wrists and holding me still, holding me back.

My eyes fly to his; hunger must be visible in them. It is almost burning me alive.

'Not like this.'

'Like what?'

'I need to shower. I'm all sweaty.'

I laugh. 'I don't care.' I push his pants down, finding his ass and cupping it in the palms of my hands.

He swears, fisting my hair and pressing his forehead to mine. His eyes are shut, his face scrunched up.

'*Fuck*, Alicia.'

'Shower later.'

I tilt my head, chasing his lips with mine, kissing him, inviting him. Begging him. I drag my mouth lower, nipping his shoulder with my teeth, laughing when he growls in reply.

'Fuck me now.'

I bite him again and he makes a guttural noise.

He acquiesces, stepping backwards, pulling me with him, so that we are kissing, walking in a tangle of limbs and lust and discarded clothes towards the bedroom.

'This is nice,' he grunts, pushing my negligee down, sliding it over my body quickly, desperately. The silk slides across my skin like liquid as it reaches my hips and then falls to the floor. I step out of it at the same time as he pulls me to the bed.

He is on top of me and I don't question it. I don't question the fact that he is making love to me and I am not in control. I don't question the fact that I'm staring up at him, my heart thumping, my body alive with needs that only he can address.

He remembers protection—thank God. It's nowhere near my mind. He slides it down his cock and then his hands are on my inner thighs, separating my legs, his eyes hooked to mine as he pushes into me.

The ownership is immediate and intense.

He is just Ethan. *My* Ethan. And he is fucking fantastic.

But tonight he is also Ethan Ash, superstar rock god, and I am his.

I press my fingers into his hips and he rolls low, reaching deep inside me. His fingers run over my bare chest, finding my breasts, holding them, cupping them, and his fingers flick my nipples. I cry out; he smiles.

He drops his mouth, taking one with his tongue, kissing it, rolling it, teasing it. I am panting with pleasure just beyond my reach. He thrusts hard at the same time as his mouth clamps down on my nipple and I am done. I cry out as I begin to fall apart and yet he doesn't stop. Even as my body explodes at its zenith of ecstasy he is driving me to new heights of awareness and need, to new pleasures and sensations.

I dig my heels into the bed and push up, keeping us close, connected, making sure he stays right where I need him. But Ethan is the master of my body. He knows without being told. He is still when I need him to be, knowing that I'm at my limit, and he watches me.

I watch him back.

He does not need to ask me to look into his eyes this time. I cannot look away. I don't want to. I am helpless, though. In the depths of his eyes there is something that calls to me, and I answer it without even knowing what it is.

I answer it with *all* of me. Every single piece of me is like a puzzle and it slides into place.

He thrusts again and I moan, riding the wave he is creating, being pulled under by it. His hands lift higher, finding my hair, and he runs his fingers through its length, worshipping it as his body owns mine.

He moves faster and brings his mouth to mine, kissing me hard, pushing my head as his hands thread through my hair and his body controls mine. I cry out into his mouth as my orgasm explodes and he answers with his own throaty oath, pushing himself into me and tipping us both over the edge. His body shakes on top of mine and I brace him with my legs, wrapping them around his waist, kissing him even as we are both disintegrating.

My heart.

My heart is all I am aware of.

It is thumping heavily, hard and fast, demanding I listen to it. I am, but I don't know what it is saying.

I know only that I have never, ever, in all my life, known the pleasure that Ethan Ash can create.

It is wrapping around me, tighter than rope, holding me prisoner, making me ache and fly all at the same time.

He shifts a little. Our eyes lock. I smile.

All of me smiles.

From the inside out.

'Hi.'

'Hey.' It's a gravelled admission.

'How was your concert?'

His eyes roam my face with a lazy interest that turns me on in different ways. His confidence is a thing of beauty, because it is natural and so different from egotism. I have learned the difference—before Jeremy I thought they were one and the same thing.

'Good.'

'You've taken over the Twitterverse.'

He arches a thick, dark brow. 'Yeah?'

'Uh-huh. You're a top-trending hashtag.'

His face flashes with something I don't recognise. 'That's normal.'

I laugh. 'For *you*, maybe.'

'For anyone performing at the Garden.'

His finger finds my breast and he traces a circle around my nipple, making my breath husky. I watch him watch me and my hunger intensifies. My need for him is unending.

'Tell me something…' I murmur.

'Something.'

His grin flips my stomach.

My smile is just a whisper on my lips. He swaps his hand to my other breast and I breathe in sharply.

'You were saying...?' he prompts.

'I forget.'

He laughs and removes his hand. I make a noise of complaint and reach for his wrist, dragging him back. I like it when he touches me. No, I love it. I love *everything* about being with him.

Wait. Where the hell did *that* come from?

I love *fucking* him. That's it.

Goosebumps run over my flesh.

I flip up onto my side but he keeps his hand where it is. For a moment. Then he drags it down my side, resting it on my hip. For a moment. Before yanking me closer, so our bodies are touching. I feel his hardness against me and my eyes flicker half-shut.

'If you hadn't become a world-famous superstar—'

'As opposed to one of the non-famous superstars?' he interrupts with a lazy grin.

'Right.' I nod importantly. 'If you hadn't become a world-famous, super-interrupting superstar, what would you have been?'

'A gigolo?'

I giggle. 'I'm serious.'

'Right.'

He moves his hand again, curling it around my ass, his fingers drumming against my flesh, stirring new heat.

'The thing is, Ally...'

God, the way he says my name is *so* amazing.

'It's not about the fame. That's incidental. If I'd only

been able to be a busk on a corner, playing my songs, I'd have done that. It's always been about the music.'

His passion—oh, how can I *not* respond to his passion? It is *so* sexy.

He leans over and kisses me, his fingers still pressing against my ass, our naked bodies hard against one another. But he separates from me suddenly and without warning, so the impact is intense and immediate.

'I'm going to grab a quick shower.'

He stands, sexy and naked, and I watch him disappear through the door, sauntering through the lounge area of the suite. He bends and reaches for his jeans, lifting his phone out of the pocket.

He does something with it. I watch curiously. But it is the work of a moment. A quick text? A check on Twitter? Whatever... He is gone again, and a second later I hear the shower running.

I push back against the bed, breathing in the smell of him that still hangs in the air.

My fingertips run over my body without my knowledge, touching the skin that he has sensitised, that his lips have kissed, that his body has possessed.

I listen to the shower and impatience zips through me.

Impatience to see him again.

I push up, my body sore in the best possible way, and stroll through the hotel room. I pick up our clothes as I go, used to this now. Used to removing the signs of our passion almost as quickly as they appeared. I lay his jeans over the back of the sofa and place my negligee on top, then pad naked into the bathroom.

He's humming, his body covered in shower gel foam, hot water steaming the glass, so that I see him without seeing all the glorious details of his body.

Hungrily, I move closer, listening, smiling, admiring.

His eyes are shut, and I can just make out his spiky lashes, all clumped and wet.

'Hi.' I prop my hip against the vanity unit, my smile widening as he opens his eyes and looks towards me.

'Hey…'

'Don't stop.'

He arches a brow. 'If you wanted to hear me sing you should have come tonight.'

'Didn't I just come?' I tease.

He laughs, but starts singing again—louder, so beautiful. His voice is like warm caramel and sunshine, but it's dusty too, with a depth and husk that makes my knees weak. There is no one like him. He channels the best of Bruno Mars, Ed Sheeran, Jason Mraz, and yet he is singularly unique.

'I could listen to you sing all day.'

He pushes the glass shower door open and holds a hand out without breaking off the song. *Thank God.* I step in and he pulls me close, moving his hips as he sings. I can see the passion on his face. A passion for music. He creates worlds with his voice—the same way I do when I put pieces of art together. When I create a room. A feeling. A mood.

He sings on, holding me close. He's looking straight at but I know that he's seeing the song, feeling the words. It is beautiful, magical. Water streams over us. I don't want to say or do anything that will break the moment. I watch him closely and my heart thumps hard against my ribs, my stomach swirls.

At the end of the song I lift up on tiptoes and kiss him.

Gently.

Gratefully.

His music is a gift and he gave that song to me.

Just me.

It is so much more special than if I'd seen him at the concert.

'Now, why would I go stand with a heap of screaming fans when I get to listen to you in the shower?'

His grin is beautiful. 'The acoustics in here are actually pretty fantastic.'

'I'll say…'

His fingers wander over my skin, and I sigh.

'Okay, Ethan Ash. Dinner's ready.'

He groans, rolling his hips. 'But it's so *good* in here…'

He's right. Being in the shower with him, I am in a blissed-out state of nirvana. I cup his cheeks.

'That's true.' I reach behind him and flick the taps off. 'But I've cooked, and I never do that, so you kind of *have* to eat it.'

'You've *cooked*?' He's fascinated by that. *'Where?'*

'At my place.'

He's frowning. Thinking. Instinctively I shy away from his thoughts, despite having no clue what they are.

'You live with those two women?'

'Eliza and Cassie? Yeah.'

'How'd you meet them?'

I step out of the shower and he's right behind me. He reaches for a towel and hands it to me. I know it's a small, inconsequential gesture, but there's something in the tiny little act of thoughtfulness that pokes holes in my resolution to keep him at arm's length.

I harden my heart as I dry my arms. Easier said than done. Because he's watching me, smiling.

And then he sings again. Only it's a song with my name in it.

Hair like flame, I turn to fire
Sky-blue eyes, you're my bad liar
Can't hide secrets you try to keep
Truth seems to make you weep, Ally... Ally...

My smile is heavy. As if resin has been poured over my face, casting me in a mask that will be an approximation of how I really look for ever.

'Is that about me?'

'Nah.' He reaches for a second towel and rubs it through his hair. 'It's for another girl I know. Alisandre.'

I roll my eyes. '*You're* the bad liar.'

He laughs. 'I don't think so.'

I wrap the towel around me, tucking it under my arms. The song echoes through me. 'What do you think I'm lying about?'

'It's lyrical,' he says with a shrug, but then he looks at me curiously, his expression watchful. 'I don't think you're lying. I think you're...closed off.'

'Closed off?' I arch my brows and think my expression must show how unimpressed I am. 'Seriously? I have been more intimate with you than...than anyone in a really long time.'

'*That.* Right there. *That's* what you do. You catch yourself before you can say *anything* about yourself.'

'That's not true!'

'Okay. Why do you love that painting at the MoMA so much?'

My cheeks flush pink. 'I told you...'

'You *"just do"*.' He imitates my voice and rolls his eyes, but his lips are twitching into a smile. 'See? Vague, vague, vague.'

'Well, no… I just…' I huff an indignant breath. 'It's kind of embarrassing.'

'Yeah?'

He crosses his arms over his naked chest and my eyes drop lower. Man, it's so much easier when we're having sex. There are no barriers then.

I grimace at the secret I'm about to share. Something I've never told anyone.

'When I was in middle school I really hated the way I looked. You know—bright white skin, orange hair…'

'It's not orange,' he murmurs.

'It felt like it. Everyone else was blonde and tanned and I was all…*me*.' I shrug. 'My mom wouldn't let me dye my hair, even though I desperately wanted highlights.' I sigh dramatically. 'And then I saw that painting. And…and she was so beautiful and mysterious and she kind of looked like me. Don't you think?'

'No one looks like you,' he says, wrapping his arms around me.

His voice is thick and so full of sincerity that it reaches right into my heart and curls around it.

'You are completely unique.'

The atmosphere between us is a net, tangling me in its midst. I stare at him, and everything is quiet but the beating of my heart and the gushing of the super-charged blood through my veins.

It's too much.

I smile awkwardly and step away from him, moving out of the bathroom, my heart still racing, my body aching for him.

'So…' He follows me, all casual nonchalance because he knows it's what I need. 'What'd you cook?'

'Ah!' Safer ground. 'Lasagne.'

'My favourite.'

I'm rewarded with a grin. A grin that curls my toes. Apparently *not* safer ground.

I move on to business, seeking something that will suck the sparkle out of the air around us.

The lasagne is burned on top.

It almost does the trick.

His kisses run like raindrops down my skin. They are soft and sweet and I shift a little.

'Was I asleep?' I stretch in the bed, lifting a hand to capture his cheek. My heart twists.

'Yeah. Did I wake you?'

'Uh-huh.' I blink. My mind is groggy. 'What time is it?'

'Four.'

'Four a.m.?'

I frown. *Shit.* I planned to go after we'd eaten. Why am I still here?

'Why are you awake?'

He lifts his mouth higher, finding my breast and kissing the underside before reaching a nipple and wrapping his lips around it. It is bliss, but too short. He moves higher, pressing his lips against a pulse point at the base of my throat, and then he samples my lips.

But it's a kiss that lacks our usual desperation and urgency. I am tired and he is probing me. Curiosity is at the fore of this exploration.

I sigh softly.

'I never sleep after a concert.'

'Really?' I lift a hand up and stroke his hair. 'Why not?'

He shrugs. 'Too wired.'

'Let me teach you a trick.'

'What is it?'

'Lie down.'

He does, on his back, beside me. I rearrange myself so that my head is on his chest, listening to his heart, and search for his hand, lacing our fingers together and resting them on his chest.

'What do you usually do instead?'

'Of this?'

'No. Instead of sleeping.'

'Oh.' His fingers wander over my hair distractedly. 'I go out with my crew.'

'Your crew?'

'Yeah. Like technical crew. Not gangsta.'

'But not tonight?'

His fingers still for a moment. 'No. Not tonight.'

Because of me.

The implication is so beautiful. And so problematic.

'What's the trick?'

'Oh. This. Is it not working?'

He breathes in deeply. I feel his chest move and smile.

'Kind of.' He yawns. 'How could you have ever hated your hair?' He murmurs. 'I have dreams about it.'

'My hair?'

'Yeah.'

'Really?'

'Of course. Your hair. Your body. Your smile.' He yawns again. 'Your eyes. Your body.'

'You said that one already.'

'It's worth an extra credit.'

I smile. My fingers, still held by his, stroke his chest beneath them. I touch him rhythmically, enjoying the feel of his body, the way it is so vibrant and alive, warm and smooth.

I shift a little, burrowing against him.

'Thanks for staying tonight.'

I don't respond. I don't plan to stay. It would be really, really stupid. But I'm tired, and he is asleep before I can think of the words. I don't want to risk waking him up. And besides…

There's nowhere else I'd rather be.

I can say it to myself. There's no harm in that, is there?

I am falling asleep. Ally is against me, our breath-sounds matching. We are our own music: a song of our bodies' making. I stroke her in time to the lyric-less song and it is perfect. A slice of time that belongs with the stars for its beauty.

But the stars are so far away. Beautiful, yes, but distant—and I don't want to make that comparison with Ally.

Nor do I want to think about how good she is at *this*. How right it feels.

I don't want to wonder about who else she has held so close, breathing in sync with him, helping him to fall asleep as she is me.

CHAPTER ELEVEN

IT IS LATE when I stir, and Ethan is no longer in bed. I blink, a little disorientated, a lot satisfied, and stretch my arms over my head, smothering a yawn. Then I am still. I listen. I hear music.

I push the duvet back and step out of bed, padding into the lounge. He has his back to me, sitting in the wing-back armchair, looking out of the window at Manhattan. It occurs to me that no one out there has any idea that Ethan *trending-on-Twitter* Ash is right here, high above them like some beautiful, sexy sky-angel.

I know the song he's playing. It's not his. I think it's Bob Dylan's. I listen, trying to catch the words, but he's humming them quietly, as though he's not even aware he's singing.

Is this what it's like for him? Does the need to make music simply overtake him? Beyond his control, his realisation, his intention?

Much like the way I am moving towards him, which is also beyond my intention. I have sometimes felt that there is a sort of magnetism between us. I don't really go in for all that woo-woo universal energy stuff. Or, I didn't, at least.

'Hey. Sleeping Beauty's up.'

He smiles at me at the exact moment the sun beams from behind a cloud and his face glows gold. He places the guitar down as he stands and moves towards me.

He's wearing his favourite jeans—and now, let's face it, *my* favourite jeans—low on his hips. His feet are bare. So is his chest.

And suddenly my breath is lost. My throat is dry.

He wraps his arms around my waist, pulling me to him. 'How'd you sleep?'

'I think I passed out.' I smile up at him. 'That is one comfy bed.'

'You should stay over more,' he says with a grin.

It's just a throwaway comment, yet prickles of danger flush my spine. I ignore the suggestion.

'Coffee?'

'Yeah.' He nods towards the machine. 'You don't like the idea?'

'Of coffee?' I wilfully misunderstand. 'Of course I do. I live for the stuff.'

'Of staying over.'

I meet his eyes and I know my expression holds a warning. 'Ethan…'

His phone rings, interrupting whatever the hell I had been going to say.

He shoots me a look that speaks volumes. *This isn't over.*

I gnaw at my lip, half watching as he moves across the room and lifts his phone off the coffee table, where he left it the night before. Something crosses his face—an emotion I don't comprehend—and then he drops the phone again.

'Dodging someone?'

His eyes meet mine. He's distracted. 'No.'

I remember the message he sent the night before. Or whatever it was he did. Was it to a friend? Or another woman? Or Sienna?

Something like alarm bells sound in my mind. I have to silence them. Not care. Because it's not what we are. And he's not Jeremy.

'You were saying?'

I push a pod into thecoffee machine and wait for the light to show that it's ready to wor.

'I had fun last night. But I think it's really important to remember—'

'That we're just fucking,' he interrupts. Tersely.

I am irrationally emotional in the face of his obvious annoyance. 'Well, yeah. I wasn't going to put it quite so crudely. I just mean that we should remember what we're doing here.'

'Right. The *rules*.' He nods.

He is keeping a grip on his temper but I know him better than that. I know he is tense and cross.

'And what are they again?'

I force a light smile. 'Fun! No-strings!'

'Right. And we can't do that if you stay over with me?'

'*You're* the one who said no sleepovers.'

He laughs—a harsh sound of disbelief—then drags his fingers through his hair. Of all the tools in his arsenal, this and this alone has the power to weaken the last threads of my resolve. He looks impossibly, edibly hot, his chest rippling, his hair spiking, and yet there is such an air of sweet helplessness in the gesture that I ache to go to him and properly explain. To tell him everything.

His eyes lock to mine and it's almost as though I have.

'Who hurt you?'

The machine whirls into life, pushing coffee through with its reliable hum. I drop my attention to it, pretending fascination with the dark brown liquid that is running into the bone-china cup. But my chest is moving too fast as each breath struggles for release.

'Alicia?'

God. Hearing my full name is such a weakness. When he says it I melt.

'I…'

He thrusts his hands on his hips, staring at me, and I blink my eyes shut.

'This isn't a request for state secrets. It's not that hard.'

I bite down on my lip. 'Yeah, it is.'

I swallow and force myself to look at him. I see the interest. The speculation. The sympathy.

'It was serious with you and him?'

My nod is barely a tick. A slow lift of my head. Yet it's all the confirmation he needs.

'Yeah. We were… It was.'

'And it ended badly?'

I nod again.

He moves towards me and runs his thumb over my cheek. 'What kind of asshole would ever hurt you?'

My heart jumps. My body throbs. I don't know what to say.

'*I'm* not going to hurt you.'

'God! Don't do that, please.' I pull away from him. 'Don't be so perfect. We both know you *will* hurt me, unless I'm very careful. Don't…don't make promises you can't keep.'

'I'm not.'

'We both agreed. We want the same thing here.'

'And what if that's changing?'

'*No.*' My denial is sharp, and panic is obvious in my voice. 'It can't.'

'Why not?'

'For many, many reasons.'

'Such as?'

'Well… You're not in any kind of place to be getting serious with anyone. And I've just… I've done that. I've done the whole falling in love thing. Getting to know someone. Swapping secrets. Planning a future.'

My voice cracks and I think of my engagement ring for the first time in months. Unconsciously I rub my finger, trying to focus my thoughts. Ethan is watching me, though, and I am distracted by him.

'I'm not… I'm barely myself again. *Eight months.*' My eyes feel hollowed out. 'For eight months I have tried to make sense of how terribly things went wrong. I have tried to move on. To forget. To look in the mirror and see myself as someone other than *that* woman. It almost killed me when it ended.'

I stare at him, willing him to understand.

'I'm still so…so broken. *So* broken. If I let myself… If I let you in and you hurt me… God, Ethan. I wouldn't do so well.'

He pulls me close roughly, urgently, and he wraps his arms around me so tight, as though he can put me back together again.

'I'm not going to hurt you.'

'That's exactly what *he* would have said.'

He doesn't let go. And I really, *really* don't want him to.

'Okay,' he murmurs against my hair. 'I promise I'm not going to push this. We can do it your way.'

Relief—or I think that's what it is—moves through me.

'I'm not going to hurt you,' he says again. 'But I want to see more of you. I want to see as much of you as I can before I go.'

Hurt. Pain. It lashes through me.

Just contemplating his absence from my life, the finality of his departure, fills me with an ache I didn't to expect.

And I know then that we have to shift the rules slightly. Because I don't want him to go from my life and for me to realise I didn't see as much of him as I could. I want to grab him with both hands while I have him, so long as my heart isn't in play.

I nod slowly. 'More is fine. Just so long as we both remember what we want here.'

'You know what *I* want?' he says seriously, his expression impossible to interpret.

'What's that?'

'I want a burger.'

'A burger?' I think for a second I've misheard.

'Yeah.' A sexy grin. 'A burger. Whaddya say, Miss Douglas? Brave the streets of New York with me once more?'

I have become used to indecision. I think one thing and want another. And then I question what I want and what I think until they become tangled together. But I am glad for this change in conversation topic and tempo. It is a relief not to be thinking about defining what we are, nor the rules we have already agreed *do* define us. I try not to think of them as limiting us, because that has negative connotations and our boundaries are definitely a *good* thing.

'A burger sounds good.'

It does. My stomach is prepared to answer that question.

'I know just the place. How quickly can you get ready?'

The promise of food motivates me.

I shower in record time, pulling on what I arrived in the day before—a pair of jeans and an oversized shirt. I have just a few cosmetic basics in my handbag. I wipe some concealer underneath my eyes and some rouge on my cheeks, tap a little gloss over my lips. But I've forgotten a hairbrush, meaning my hair is wild and sex-styled. I comb it with my fingers and pull it over one shoulder.

He whistles when I step out of the bathroom, low and soft, but it makes my tummy flip-flop.

'Same to you.'

He's wearing jeans and a black shirt, with the sleeves rolled up to the elbows. He's got a black baseball cap on his head. *Groan*. He's *hot*.

He puts a hand in the small of my back as we leave the hotel. The contact is nice. No, it's better than nice.

The elevator doors swish open and we move inside, but the second we're in he pushes me against the back wall and kisses me, his mouth on mine demanding. It is a kiss that drugs me with its intensity and changes the parameters of my existence.

He doesn't break it until the elevator touches down with a gentle thud on the ground floor of the hotel.

'Wait a sec.'

I am not even sure my legs can carry me, so it's easy to do as he suggests. He lifts a spare baseball cap off his head—I didn't even realise he was carrying it—and places it on mine, then reaches for my hand, pulling me out of the lift.

The foyer is as usual. There are a couple of guards

by the doors. But when we step out it's like the whole world erupts.

Flashes go off in my face and Ethan, beside me, swears. He squeezes my hand and suddenly Grayson is there, pushing people back, cutting a path for us through the crowds. But they move with us, following, and I am afraid.

Beside me, Ethan tosses a look over his shoulder. 'Wankers.'

There's a car waiting. Grayson shepherds us into it. Ethan steps back to let me in first and I don't hesitate. I slide in, keeping my head down, grateful for the protection offered by the cap, which shields at least some of my face.

My breath is fierce.

Ethan moves in beside me. He stares at me for a long second and then shakes his head.

'I'm sorry about that.'

I don't know what to say. Questions and doubts run through me. He must have known that would happen?

But I've left his hotel lots of times and not seen anything like that.

'It's the concert,' he explains, reaching for my hand again and lifting it to his lips. He presses a kiss against the racing pulse point.

I nod, but only because he seems to be waiting for me to say something. I'm full of doubts.

'That's... I can't believe you live like that.'

'Yeah.' His lips compress. 'It takes a bit of getting used to.'

'I could *never* get used to it.' I shudder in revulsion. It is yet another reason to be grateful for the fact that this is going nowhere.

'It's not all the time. In fact when I'm out on my own I can usually do most stuff. I should have checked the foyer before bringing you down. That won't happen again.'

I shrug, staring out of the window. 'It's only one more week,' I point out. 'We can keep a low profile after this.'

He doesn't say anything. What is there to say?

Grayson takes us a few blocks south and pulls up outside a diner. I've never heard of it, but when we step inside the guy behind the counter comes over and wraps Ethan in a bear hug. I stand back and watch curiously.

'How you going, mate?'

'Not bad.'

'See you lit up Manhattan last night.' The man, who's wearing chef's pants and a white T-shirt, punches Ethan jokingly on the chest. 'Surprised your head still fits through the door.'

Ethan laughs. 'Benji, this is Alicia. My cousin Benji, here, happens to make the best burgers in town.'

'Think you might be biased there.' Benji grins, but reaches across and shakes my hand. 'Though they *are* pretty damned good. Nice to meet you, Alicia.'

'Likewise.'

Benji nods towards a table at the back. 'You want coffee? Beer?'

'Coffee.' Ethan nods. 'Ally?'

'Same. Thank you.'

He nods and moves through the restaurant, talking to a waitress as he goes. Our coffee appears almost instantly and I curl my hands around the cup.

'Your cousin seems nice,' I say, with my head tilted to one side. 'This is his place?'

'Yeah.'

'It's *our* place.'

Benji is back, handing menus over. Ethan makes no effort to pick his up. I don't either.

'Your place?' I prompt, studying Ethan.

'Yeah. Ash bought it years ago. Got me in to run it.'

'Huh. So you're a restaurateur-cum-rock-star, huh? Is there no end to your talents?'

Benji laughs. 'I like her. She's got your measure.'

'She has that,' Ethan agrees.

'Okay, what'll you two have?'

'The usual,' Ethan says.

'I'll have whatever you recommend.'

'Great.'

Benji winks and moves away, leaving us alone once more.

Something heavy lodges in my chest. I can't explain it, but then I realise. Ethan is renovating a house in New York. He owns this restaurant and his cousin works here. He's not leaving in a week—not really. Not for good.

He'll be back again soon and then what?

Will he call me?

What will I say?

Would I see him again?

I stare out of the window.

Worse. What if he doesn't? What if I find out through Twitter that he's here and he hasn't thought to get in touch?

And that second option is far more likely, isn't it?

It doesn't matter. Because this is what I want.

This is all we are.

And so long as I remember that I'll be fine. He can call. Or he can not call. It changes nothing about what we are. *Nothing*.

* * *

Hours later, back in his hotel suite, I look at him and feel myself smile. Without my consent. He's reading.

Yes. Ethan panty-melting-superstar Ash *reads*—and not just anything. It's *Les Misérables*, by Victor Hugo.

'Good book?'

He presses a finger into the page and looks up at me, his own smile crooked in response. 'It's one of my favourites.'

'Really?'

'Sure. Why not?'

'I just… I don't know.'

'Oh, I see.' He grins, putting the book down and moving closer. 'You're surprised I can actually read, right?'

'No!' I deny, my cheeks burning. 'It's just not very… rock and roll.'

'So what do you *think* I do with my spare time? Snort cocaine and trash hotel rooms?'

I wrinkle my nose. If anything, he's a complete neat freak. Oh, he's sexily dishevelled in his personal appearance, but he makes his own bed each morning and tidies up after himself.

'I don't really like the whole housekeeping thing,' he said, when I asked him about it.

'Yeah. Sleep with supermodels—that kind of thing.'

He laughs. 'How boring the reality must seem.'

I grin. 'You're not boring, Mr Ash.'

'I'm glad to hear it, Miss Douglas.'

He moves closer and so do I, drawn as ever by that inevitable pull. He smells insanely good. It is dark outside now, and his hotel room is warm. I know I will need to leave soon, get home and get ready for work the next day, but I am reluctant to bring our weekend to an end.

I should be worried by that, but I cling to our agreement and trust in my own strength. He'll go, and I'll be fine.

I ignore the strange presentiment of emptiness that fills me.

'I have a question for you.'

I lift myself up and straddle him, smiling at his immediate look of desire. At the way I feel him harden beneath me.

'I'm yours. Ask me anything.'

My laugh is soft and husky. 'Anything? Hmm… Maybe I don't want to waste that on this question.'

'You can ask me anything. Again and again.'

His generosity, sweetness and openness are beautiful. But didn't I feel that about Jeremy?

'You're amazing. I can't believe I got so lucky as to have you in my life. Ally, marry me. Please. I want to spend every morning waking up beside you…'

God!

An acidic taste permeates my mouth. I focus on Ethan beneath me. Ethan who's holding my hands. Ethan who's pulling me into his world with no expectations or strings.

'Where does Grayson go when you're up here?'

'Grayson?' He pulls a face. 'I don't know if I want to think about him right now.'

I grin. 'Sorry. I was just wondering if he's, like, sitting outside the door, waiting for you to call.'

'He has a room on the same floor,' Ethan says after a small beat of time.

'And how does it work? If you go out you text him and he has to stop whatever he's doing…?'

'I try to give him notice if I'm changing the schedule.'

'And he's your bodyguard?'

'Yeah. Technically he's my driver, but he's ex-military, ex-cop, a martial arts expert. You wouldn't want to be on his bad side.'

'Wow. I had no idea.'

'Plus, I trust him completely. He's been with me for over seven years.'

'He doesn't have family?'

Ethan shakes his head slowly. 'He was married once.'

'It didn't work out?'

Ethan looks over my shoulder. And despite the fact that he said I could ask him anything I sense that he's feeling awkward about betraying his friend's trust.

I lean forward and hover my lips just above his. Close enough that I can feel his breath but not touching him. 'It doesn't matter. It's not my business.'

'It's no secret,' he murmurs, not attempting to bring himself closer.

But then he shifts his hips a little, so I feel his hard cock between my legs. Desire shreds me. How can I want him again? All we have done today is touch, kiss, feel, make love, doze, eat and repeat. Suddenly the thought of going days without being able to have him whenever I want is anathema.

All the more reason for me to get the hell out of Dodge and prove to myself that I can live without the wonder that is Ethan Ash.

'She died.'

It's ice water on my flaming needs. 'What? Who?'

'Grayson's wife. Matilda. A car crash.'

'Oh, God. That's awful.'

'Yeah. It was years ago. Before I knew him. But so far as I know he hasn't dated since.'

'That's *so* sad,' I murmur, thinking of Grayson's faithfulness to his wife.

'There's no guarantees in life, right? You just have to make the most of what you've got. Every day.'

He buzzes his lips over mine, lightly, sweetly, just so I get the faintest hint of him before he pulls away.

'Speaking of Grayson—are we going to be needing him tonight?'

I arch a brow. 'Threesomes aren't really my thing.'

'Then you're missing out,' he teases. 'I meant do we need him to take you home?'

I draw my brows together and his finger lifts to the little divot between my eyes.

'I want you to stay,' he pushes on, the words roughened, 'but I presume you're going to do your disappearing act sometime soon?'

'Right.'

I nod, but my body is screaming at me to stop being so stupid. What harm will it cause if I'm late in tomorrow? I can stay here. Spend the night in his bed and then cab it home early. It's no biggie, right?

But then what? Two nights in a row is habit-forming, and I will *not* let this become a habit. Even if Ethan Ash *is* more addictive than any substance on earth.

'I'll get a cab,' I murmur.

'Stay.' He pushes his fingers into my hair and draws my mouth to his, his kiss one of promise and pleasure.

I surrender to it on a sigh. 'A little longer.'

A little longer...

I fall into his kiss. I have been wearing a shirt of his all day. He pushes at the fabric, lifting it up, and I obligingly raise my arms, making it easier, so that I am straddling him wearing only a flimsy pair of lace panties. His mouth drops to my breasts and I cry out as his tongue rolls over the flesh that is already so sensitive. His fingers run down my back and there is something so reverential in his touch, as though I am an object he was born to worship, that I feel a strange emotion lurch inside me.

His hands slip beneath the elastic of my underwear and he cups my ass, pulling me closer to him. I press myself down. Were it not for the barrier of clothing we would be together, and I want that.

I want everything.

It is never enough.

Should I have known that from the beginning?

Should I have understood how dangerous it is to play with fire?

Probably.

Would it have stopped me?

I doubt it.

This is as inevitable as day following night, autumn embracing winter. I want him, but I want more than that. I want to make him lose his mind as much as I am losing mine.

I pull away from him with regret, and he makes a sound of frustrated confusion. I drop to the floor between his legs and loosen his belt, my eyes holding his as I pull it from his jeans and then unclasp his button and zip.

He knows what's about to happen and he doesn't move. He stares at me, as lost in the moment as I am.

He is rock-hard and I bring my mouth to his tip first, encircling him with my tongue, my eyes locked to his as I tease him with what's to follow.

He keeps his hands by his sides, balled into fists, his expression one of determination.

'Something wrong?' I smile as I take him deeper, rolling my tongue over him as I guide him to the back of my mouth.

'Fuck…' He shakes his head.

But as I move my mouth up and down, he moans my real name, low in his throat.

'Alicia… You are perfect.'

I'm not.

We're not.

But this is.

Our bodies might well have been forged with this in mind. They are perfectly designed to please one another. It has never been like this for me. Not with anyone before Jeremy, and not even with Jeremy.

What we shared was good once. But it was borne of love and friendship and knowing one another.

This is different.

It's indefinable.

At least for me.

I wonder if it has ever been like this for him. If it was like this with Sienna. Or anyone else. *Has* there been anyone else for him?

I know they were together a long time…

These are questions I want answered, but not now. Now I want to experience this moment to the full.

I bring one hand to cup him around his base and I roll him further back in my mouth. He lifts his hands over his head and slides lower on the sofa, giving me more access, and I taste a hint of him in my mouth.

He drops a hand to my hair, and another to my shoulder, and I know why. He wants me to stop before he finishes.

But the power is thrilling. I take him deeper and he lets out a groan. And then he moves, sliding across the sofa, out of my grip. He moves quickly, dropping onto the floor beside me at first, and then he is behind me. He straddles me, his chest to my back, the weight of his body bending me over the sofa so that my face is flat against the cushions. He's so deep, and my body welcomes him as its master returning.

His fingers find my nipples and he teases them, pulling at them, cupping my breasts, his fingers callused against my smooth skin.

I swear low in my throat as he pushes into me again, harder, faster, and then he drops one hand to my clit and moves his fingers over me. I explode. It is fast, it is intense, and I am loud. I cry out with no care for who hears me. Pleasure rips through me like a hurricane.

I kneel straight up, arching my back, but that just gives him better access. To my breasts, to my body, and then his mouth is on my throat, kissing me as his harder-than-granite dick controls me.

I am his.

I am completely his.

'Your mouth on me is the fucking hottest thing ever.'

'No…' I shake my head, trying to find his lips. It's too awkward the way I'm positioned. '*This* is.'

He laughs—a sound of dangerous desire. He brings his hand around to my ass and then to the small of my back. He presses down with enough strength to bend me over the sofa again. I do not even dream of resisting. I am on a ride of his creation and it is a *good* ride.

The best.

He holds my hips, his fingers digging into my flesh in a way that is deliciously painful, and he drives into me, thrusting and finding every single nerve inside me. My body is melting. His fingers run over my flesh, across the curves of my ass, and I moan as he moves inside me.

Heaven is a place and it's right here—in the middle of the Gramercy Park Hotel.

It is midnight when I surface from the haze of our sensual exploration. My body is heavy with lust and liquid heat. Ethan is asleep beside me. I roll over, staring at him, watching the rhythmic intake of his breath, the gentle exhalations, and I smile at his beauty in repose. At the way he looks younger somehow. And so handsome.

I don't want to go. Which is all the more reason why I must.

I slide sideways slowly, pulling myself out from under his arm. I'm almost there. But when I'm right at the edge of the bed his fingers clamp around my upper arm and he pulls himself closer to me.

'Stay, baby,' he murmurs, the words husky and coated in sleep and dreams.

'I can't.' *I shouldn't.*

'Stay.' His eyes blink open groggily and land on my face.

And I weaken completely. I nod, smile and wriggle a little closer.

One more night won't hurt.

CHAPTER TWELVE

'IS THAT YOUR PHONE?'

I barely hear him through the haze of sleep. I am naked in his bed, my limbs heavy, my hair a tangle across my back. I push up onto my elbows and look at him quizzically, before realising that, yes, my phone is ringing.

'Oh. Sorry.' I reach for it and cringe when I see my mother's face.

I swipe it to answer at the same time as I push out of his bed, grabbing one of the hotel bathrobes and wrapping it around me, cinching it in at the waist.

'Hi, Mom.'

I move out of his bedroom and into the lounge, slipping a pod into the machine on autopilot.

'Alicia Jane Douglas. Would you mind telling me what the *hector* you're doing?'

'I'm making coffee,' I say only half-jokingly. 'Where's the outrage in that?'

'Young lady, I'm serious.'

Young lady? Uh-oh. In my mom's native tongue that's really, really serious. It sobers me.

'What about? What's happened?

"'Ethan Ash isn't wasting any time moving on from

Sienna Di Giorgio after her shock engagement to Tom Banks. The Grammy award-winning star was seen leaving his hotel with the same mystery woman he was spotted out and about with in SoHo last week. Could romance be on the cards for the heartbroken singer?"'

I grab the coffee cup out of the machine and stare at it, my heart racing. 'What *is* that?'

'It's in the *papers*,' she hisses. 'I've had a photographer come to my house. This *morning*!'

Worse and worse. My mother believes calling on someone before midday is just plain rude. I grimace.

'I'm sorry, Mom. It's… It's not like it sounds.'

'Alicia, your father and I have barely recovered from your last run-in with poor decision-making. We've hardly lived down the reputation of what you did then. And now this article? Your father is the minister of this town, missy. How the hector is he going to explain *this* to his congregation?'

Colour flames my cheeks and a noise behind me alerts me to Ethan's presence.

'The same way he did last time,' I say, not caring that Ethan's there. 'What I do has nothing to do with you or him. You can say what you want. Disown me.'

'It's not that simple. You *are*, in fact, our daughter. You moved to Manhattan and assured us you wouldn't be changed by it. That you'd be the same good girl we raised. And now you're sleeping with married men and *celebrities*?'

Pain lashes through me. Because even my mother can see that being with Ethan falls into the same category of foolhardy as my relationship with Jeremy.

'It's okay, Mom. This isn't a big deal.'

'It's a big deal to *me*! *And* to your father!'

Invoking Daddy is another sign that she's seriously pissed off.

'So? Who *is* this man? Did you *really* spend the night in his hotel?'

Argh! Possibly the least comfortable conversation of my life and Ethan Ash is watching me, one shoulder propped against the doorframe, his eyes resting on me with undisguised interest.

'It's not serious,' I say slowly, and then wince.

'Not *serious*? You're giving your body to a man and it's *not serious*? Good Lord, who *are* you? I think it's time for you to come home. Spend some time with your father and me, remember how we raised you.'

'Mom...' I shake my head. 'It's okay. My immortal moral soul is not in jeopardy.'

Ethan laughs—just a soft sound, but it pulls at me. It pulls at me in a way that makes me need him. Not sexually, though. I need him to hug me.

Everything is spinning out of control—and the irony is that it's because of him yet I want *him* to fix it.

'You're laughing at me.' My mother sniffs.

'I'm not, Mom, I'm really not. But I'm twenty-five years old. I think I can be trusted to handle my own life.'

'You had an affair with a *married man*!' she exclaims, and I cringe, squeezing my eyes shut. 'You brought him home to us. You clearly *aren't* handling your life.'

'I had no way of knowing that,' I remind her softly. Her outrage hurts. The facts of my situation were all she cared about, and not the extenuating circumstances— like Jeremy's psychopathy. Nor the fact that there was no way for me to know that my 'fiancé' was a married father of two!

'I want you to come home.'

'No.' I square my shoulders. 'I know you're worried about me, Mom. But I'm fine. I'll… I'll come for Christmas, okay?'

I instantly regret the promise, but it does its job and mollifies her.

'And, please, Alicia. No more photographs in the national papers. Your daddy has a reputation to think of.'

I disconnect the call and then hurl my phone onto the sofa, wishing I could throw something else.

'Trouble?'

'Yeah!' I snap, sipping my coffee.

My fingers are shaking. With exasperation, I place the cup down on the coffee table and move towards the window, staring out at Manhattan.

'Your mom doesn't approve of me?'

'She doesn't approve of *me*,' I correct softly.

He wraps his arms around my waist and I close my eyes, leaning back against him, taking strength from his proximity, allowing myself to surrender to this.

'Because of him?'

'Jeremy.'

I say his name and it is as though I am invoking his spirit. I shiver at the fact that I've done that—that I've brought him into this room by speaking his name.

'They didn't like him?'

My lips twist in disagreement. 'Oh, they liked him fine.'

My voice is hoarse. It isn't the past I fear. It's confessing to the part I played. Guilt at what I did, even when I know that I didn't knowingly enter into an affair, colours me. I don't want Ethan to see me as I see myself.

I don't want him to know what I've done.

And yet the burden of this guilt is a weighty confession that will only be lightened by speaking.

He seems to understand. He is quiet, waiting, giving me a chance to speak.

'They thought he was a good, sensible choice.' I sigh. 'He was a banker. Educated. Wealthy. Conservative. Everything they wanted for their little girl.'

Ethan's lips buzz my cheek and a heavy smile passes over my lips.

'But it didn't work out?' he prompts after a moment.

'No.'

It's a whisper. He spins me around to face him, keeping his hands on my waist, his eyes locked to mine.

'Why not?'

I'm back in the past. 'The first time I met him I was just…just blown away.'

A muscle jerks in Ethan's jaw but I barely notice it.

'We were at an art auction and we were bidding on the same piece.' My face is shadowed with the memories I have suppressed for so long. 'I won the piece. He won the prize.' A pause. 'That's what he used to say. And you know what the worst thing is?'

'What, Ally?'

'He was trying to buy the painting for *her.*'

'Who?'

'His wife.'

The words are torn from me and I close my eyes for a long moment, not wanting to see what I know must be on his face. Judgement. Surprise. Pity.

None of those emotions are good.

'He was married?'

I nod slowly. 'I didn't know.'

'Hell, of *course* you didn't. You think I believe you'd get involved in something like that?'

His instant understanding is the last thing I expected and it's everything I need.

'You're not that kind of person.'

'I'm *not* that kind of person,' I agree urgently. 'He never told me. He didn't wear a ring. And he was so available. I mean, I saw a *lot* of him. His wife travelled a heap for work, and his kids were at her mom's a heap of the time.' I shake my head. 'It doesn't change the fact that I broke up a family...'

Ethan lifts his hands to my face, cupping it and making me face him. 'You didn't break up a family. *He* did. And he broke your heart in the process.'

I nod softly. 'And not just because I loved him—I did, Ethan.' Colour floods my cheeks. 'But he made me into something I despise and that took away every good memory. I have no right to look back on any of the fun we had and smile because it was all wrong. *All* of it.'

'I'm sorry,' he murmurs.

And then he kisses me. It's a soft kiss, gentle and slow. An apology and an explanation and it's everything I need. I surrender to it, and in that moment I am weak, because my heart surrenders too.

Later that day my assistant Lesley pops her head into my office. 'Ally?'

I put aside the Christie's brochure I'm leafing through and give her my attention. She's holding a huge bunch of tulips—huge. At least one hundred flowers crammed together and wrapped in brown paper. They are my favourites.

They can't be from Ethan, can they?

The very idea makes adrenalin course in my veins and flavour my mouth. I hope—and I know I shouldn't—that he *has* sent them to me. And yet if he has? I'm scared of that possibility too.

'What are those?' Suspicion is obvious in my tone, my inner conflict apparent in the question.

'Flowers. For you.'

'Who are they from?'

She shoots me a quizzical look. 'I didn't open the card. Do you want me to?'

'No, no, that's okay. I'll do it.'

I take the flowers from her with a dismissive smile and place them on the edge of my desk as if they might burn me.

Lesley is hovering inside the door. I understand her curiosity. Occasionally I get gifts from clients—bottles of whisky or champagne, the odd paperweight.

Never flowers.

And these are my *favourite* flowers.

My heart accelerates as I finger the card. Surely they're not from him? Then again, how can they *not* be?

'Are they from *him*?' Lesley prompts breathily and I realise she's seen it.

She's read the papers. She knows about me and Ethan.

'Thank you,' I say dismissively, sitting down without opening the card.

And, though she's probably still dying to know if they're from him or not, she steps out of my office and closes the door behind her.

I cannot rip the envelope open fast enough. I tear the triangular back and lift the card out, my eyes running over the neat florist's typeface.

Your immortal moral soul is not in danger.

I groan, dropping my head forward. My soul might not be but I think *I* am.

All my good intentions, all my boundaries, are crumbling.

He's leaving soon.

Less than a week.

I need to be strong and then I need to move on.

That's all.

But... Ethan Ash is in my blood, my bones. I see him when I blink and I inhale him with every breath I take. He has become a part of me—and not just of me, but of all that surrounds me.

I reach for my phone on autopilot.

How did you know tulips are my favourite?

I can practically feel him grinning through the phone.

Lucky guess. What time am I seeing you tonight?

I smile as I shake my head. I should say no, but the reminder that he is leaving soon fills me with something like panic.

I finish around six.

His response is swift.

Great. Let's do dinner. I'll pick you up.

My heart races. Dinner? And he'll pick me up? From work?

He texts back before I can respond, before I can demur. After all, dinner is not in our rules. And now, more than ever, I think we need to stick to them.

Don't worry. It doesn't mean anything. It's just more foreplay...

I put my phone into my top desk drawer as though it's a lit stick of dynamite, slamming it emphatically shut. I should be glad.

It doesn't mean anything.

Those words are important. Those words show that he and I are still focused on keeping our boundaries in place. It shows that we can engage in 'high-risk' activities like dinner and flirting and flower-sending-and-receiving and not run the risk of forgetting.

Because it doesn't mean anything. None of this *means* anything. It's just fun.

Panic is what I feel instead of gladness.

I do my best to concentrate on work, but every time I pause my mind wanders to Ethan. To his body. His kisses. To the way he held me all night. To the way he made love to me, hard against the sofa, taking me from behind and playing me more expertly than he does his Fender.

To the way he listened to my heaviest confession and held me tight. Better—to the way he saw past the facts and *understood*. He absolved me of all guilt with one simple smile.

It wasn't my fault.

I couldn't have known.

I reach for my phone almost guiltily and load up Twitter.

He's still trending. My cheeks flush as I click guiltily into the hashtag. The concert videos are still going strong, being re-Tweeted and liked ad nauseam. But there are new photographs as well. Photographs of *us*.

I stare at them and read a few comments, smiling—until I find the comments that are calling me a whore and other less nice things. Someone called *@DreamingOfAsh* really has got a thing against me.

I push out of the thread. It's a timely reminder of why I would never choose to be involved with a man like Ethan. The paparazzi. The fans. The pressure. The constant fear that he'd actually go for one of those groupies after a concert one night.

@SiennaandEthanforever has commented on the pic: *Rebound Fuck*. I smile, pleased on some level that an outsider can identify us for what we are. Yet the smile is brittle, and I find that not *all* of me is pleased by the description, even though it's accurate.

Like watching a train wreck happening before my eyes, I click back into the comments. There are one thousand and twenty-three.

He'll never stay with her. He's always loved Sienna.

Dude, Sienna's engaged to @TheRealTomBanks didn't you see?

Engaged...whatever. This is just to promote her album.

Sienna and Ethan are made for each other. Always have been, always will be.

I can't look away. I click out of Twitter and load up a browser, and before I know what I'm doing my fingers corrupt my intent to remain uninvolved.

Ethan Ash + Sienna Di Giorgio.

I only have to type the 'S' of Sienna's name before I'm prompted with the full name. I click and wait.

In seconds my screen is populated with articles, blogs and pictures. I click hungrily into the first blog. It's by a popular blogger who runs a mostly benign site with occasionally mean-spirited posts about celebrities he's taken it into his head to hate.

Apparently he hates Sienna. And loves Ethan. Which makes me smile again—more naturally this time. The photo on my screen was taken in broad daylight. They're obviously fighting. She's crying, but still looking like a beautiful porcelain doll, and Ethan is looking pissed off.

And sexy.

For a moment I let myself wonder what they were saying, what their fight was about. I can see that Ethan is tired and angry and frustrated and annoyed. I can imagine the roll of his voice as he implores her to be reasonable. I can hear him as though he were standing in front of me.

He looks exhausted, and I want to reach into the photo and smooth away his worries. It's a silly fantasy—one that is out of place in our arrangement.

A shudder runs down my spine, reminding me of the way he dragged his lips down my back, nipping me at the base of my spine before rolling his tongue over the bite mark.

There are new photos of just Ethan, too. From today?

Ethan stepping out of the hotel, baseball cap tugged low, covering his eyes. Head bent. Even in the still images I can see the swagger in his step.

Desire throbs in my gut.

I scroll to a concert video and tap to watch it without realising.

It goes full-screen and I press the volume higher, then lean back in my chair to watch. It's from the start of a concert. He's walking on stage and the crowd is going wild. The noise is deafening. He raises his hands in the air in greeting and whoever is filming lifts the camera to the big screen, so that I can see his smile as he lifts his guitar.

He slips the strap over his head, turns to face someone just off stage and nods, then strums the guitar. Once. Loudly.

The crowd erupts.

'How you doing, New York?' he calls, and the crowd's screaming is louder. 'We're gonna have some fun tonight.'

He launches into a song—one of his earlier hits. I am mesmerised. I watch the whole thing twice, my heart throbbing, my body craving, and then my eyes lift to the tulips.

Tonight can't come soon enough.

'I'm impressed your attention span's lasted this long. She must be *really* in good in bed.'

I stare at the screen in frustration.

'Is there a reason you're Face Timing me, Sienna? Other than to show more than a natural interest in my sex life?'

She swishes her hair over one shoulder—a gesture

that used to drive me crazy. I can imagine the way it will smell, like flowers and vanilla. You know that weird way smells have of binding themselves to your core memories and triggering them whenever prompted?

'We were together a lifetime, Ash. Am I not allowed to care about who you're with now?'

I laugh. An instant dismissal. 'Not really.'

I unbutton my shirt, my eyes on hers mockingly. There is a part of me that knows how fucked up this is—that acknowledges I'm playing with fire and that someone's going to get badly burned.

But it won't be me. And I won't let it be Ally.

'So?' Sienna slowly runs her eyes down my body, her admiration something she doesn't bother to hide. 'Is it serious?'

'No.' I grin, but something like pain clutches inside me. 'It's fun. A whole lotta fun.'

'What's *that* supposed to mean?'

I lean closer, so that my face is all she can see. 'It means that Ally and I are having a whole lotta fun. And that's it.'

Tears sparkle in Sienna's eyes and my reaction is instantaneous. *Guilt.*

What am I *doing*? I'm not this guy. I'm not going to flaunt it over my ex that I'm fucking someone beautiful and hot and sexy and distracting. What Sienna did is beyond forgiving, but that doesn't give me a free pass to be an A-grade dick.

Besides, whatever satisfaction I thought I'd get from rubbing my sex-life in Sienna's face is non-existent. What I'm doing is about Ally and me and the way she makes me feel. Sienna is incidental.

'You're engaged,' I say slowly. 'None of this matters.'

'I just…' She wipes away the tears and her lower lip pouts. 'I miss you.'

Fuck.

The words hit me square in the chest—like little missiles that pull me apart from the inside out.

'You miss me?' I repeat, pulling away from my phone and reaching for a fresh shirt.

It is everything I needed to hear a month ago, and yet now those three little words fill me with a chasm of unease. I pull the shirt over my head and come back to the camera. Then I change my mind and pour a measure of Scotch. It's two in the afternoon, but I don't give a shit. In that moment I need something to straighten my head—or to un-straighten it. I need something to calm me down.

'You don't get to call me out of nowhere and say you *miss* me.'

'Don't be angry with me.'

'*Angry* with you?' Incredulity makes my voice sound amused when I'm anything but. 'Are you *kidding* me?'

'I was under so much pressure at the end, you know. The tour and the album… I think I might have…' She shakes her head and leans closer.

I don't know if she deliberately pans the camera down but I can see she's only wearing a bra and lace panties. I look away, the feeling guilt and betrayal of Ally making my breath short.

'I took it out on you. I was such a bitch.'

Yeah. She was. She was a nightmare. But that doesn't change the fact we were together for six years, that I shared twelve years of my life with her—six of them as her lover.

'We'd been growing apart for a long time,' I say, trying to take my share of the blame. 'We spent so much time apart. The end was inevitable.'

'Was it?'

It's a sad question. One full of heartache and hurt.

'*You* ended this. You ended *us*.' I throw the whisky back and place the glass down a little more heavily than I should. 'And you got engaged to Tom.'

'That was a mistake,' she says, and then she sobs.

And those six years spent caring about Sienna, wanting her to be happy, damned well *loving* her, make me forget the hurt she's inflicted.

'Can we go back in time and fix it, Ash?'

I feel a tiny bit like royalty as I step out of my office onto the busy twilight streets of Manhattan and see a sleek black car waiting for me. Grayson is beside it, dressed in a suit. I flick a smile at him but then I look lower instantly, towards the heavily tinted window of the car, behind which I know Ethan will be sitting.

Just like last time.

My pulse is thready and I feel sensual tension running through me like a powerful car idling at the lights. One hint of green and I will pounce.

I walk slowly, glad I made the effort to slip home at lunch and change into something fresh. I've gone with a black jersey dress that falls to my ankles, with sleeves which bell to my wrists. The neckline is demure, but it hugs me like a second skin.

I love this dress.

Small fact: I destroyed every piece of clothing I owned after Jeremy. Everything. Anything he had seen me in, and obviously anything he'd given me or touched me in—which was pretty much everything. I could no longer bear to associate who I was with who I'd been, and every time I put an outfit on I heard his voice. I felt his hands.

It was, perhaps, the first stage of my eight-month-exorcism—the first step in preparation for this. The final erasing of the man I once loved.

It's silly, I suppose, but I like feeling that no other guy has touched me in this dress.

I like it that it's all for Ethan.

That thought is running dangerously close to breaking our rules, so I fold it away and push a bright smile to my face. It doesn't falter when Grayson opens the door.

I move into the car and Ethan is there, overpowering me with his presence, all that I need, all that I can sense, and he's just sitting there, staring at me.

'Hey.'

He holds a hand out and I reach for it as I step in, sitting beside me. Am I imagining it or is he frowning?

I must be imagining it, because within a minute he smiles at me, and pleasure reaches right down to the bottom of my toes.

'How was your day?' I ask.

He leans forward, brushing his lips to mine. 'Better now.'

'I have a bone to pick with you,' I murmur.

'Yes? What's that?'

'Flowers.' I lift a finger in mock admonishment. 'Flowers are expressly prohibited in our terms of engagement. Clause One, Part A.'

'Ah.' He grins as he catches my finger and brings it to his lips. 'I remember. I'm revising that clause.'

His eyes hold mine and my heart thumps, and I am

grateful that Grayson chooses that moment to slide into the driver's seat.

'Where to?' Grayson tosses over his shoulder.

'The hotel?' I whisper in Ethan's ear, smiling conspiratorially.

He laughs, wrapping an arm around me and holding me close to him, keeping me cradled to his side.

'Belle Nuit,' Ethan contradicts, naming one of the hottest eateries in New York.

I've heard of it, of course. It's just over the bridge, hooked into Brooklyn, with a stunning view of the Manhattan skyline—and Brooklyn Bridge.

'Ethan,' I say softly. This is another rule that's being flaunted. 'Why don't we just grab takeout and go back to yours? Or go to Benji's diner…?'

'Because.' His eyes glint as they meet mine. 'This place is nice.'

'Nice?' I roll my eyes. 'It's better than that.'

'Have you been there?'

'Well, no, but I mean it's *the* place…'

'Right.'

'Don't you think it's breaking even more rules?' I push, concern obvious in my question.

'I'm leaving in a few days, Ally. Does it really matter?'

My heart stammers in my chest. *Jesus Christ.* A few days. Something about the finality of that pushes all my stupid objections aside. What can go wrong in a few days?

'I guess not.'

I'm still torn.

His eyes hold mine and my temperature shoots up. Suddenly every touch, every word, is a prelude of what

I know will come, and it is hyper-charged with awareness and need. There is a heat between us that is threatening to explode.

Traffic is unusually light, and we cruise over the
bridge easily. I look out at the water as we go, admiring the view, thinking what a unique place in the world
this is.

The restaurant is as glorious as I imagined. Grayson pulls up right at the front and though it's discreetly
decorated, the prestige of the place is marked. There are
two waiters standing by the doors, dressed in tuxedos.

One pulls the restaurant door inwards at the same moment Grayson opens the car door, so that it's easy for us
to navigate our way in. There are paparazzi—I suspect
they're almost permanently camped out at a place like
this. Is it stupid to come here?

'My mom's going to have kittens,' I whisper under
my breath as we move inside and another waiter appears
to lead us to a table.

The place is packed, and I see two newscasters, an
actress, and a famous-for-all-the-wrong-reasons Hollywood director and his twenty-something wife tucked
away in a corner. We're led to a booth near the windows.
It has the advantage of being private and offering an un-
rivalled outlook of the twinkling lights of Manhattan.

'This is beautiful.'

He nods, but he's distracted. *Again.*

'Does that bother you?' he asks after several long seconds. It takes me a moment to recall what I have said.

'Kind of. Not really.' I shrug. 'She'll get over it.
What's one more crime to my name?'

His smile is tight. 'I guess it shows how much she
loves you.'

I don't want to talk about my family, though. They're their own unique brand of messed-up. I'll deal with them later. After. Once all this over and I have breathing space to be me again.

'Where do you go after this?'

I ask the question almost as though talking about it will desensitise me to the fact he is leaving. As though it will make the reality more pronounced.

'London.'

'For how long?' *Shit*. Wrong question. It sounds needy.

'A couple of weeks.'

He shrugs and my gut clenches. The idea of a couple of weeks without him is bad enough. Thank God we had the foresight to put limits on this when we did. I imagine being with him for any longer—for another month. Two. Three. And then having to end it. My heart shrivels.

I was supposed to be engaged to Jeremy, and yet I suspect leaving Ethan Ash would be a million times harder and worse. Strange, given how much I loved Jeremy.

Is it just the sex?

I don't know, but I *do* know this is for best. It will still be hard. But it's right to end it now, before we get too attached. Before we do anything stupid like fall in love.

Nothing good can come of love. One day, when I meet a guy I think I can settle down with, he will be my safe haven, not my storm.

Jeremy was a storm, and Ethan Ash is a cyclone...

CHAPTER THIRTEEN

THIS IS WORK. This is work.

I remind myself of this fact over and over and over again as I head towards Ethan's townhouse. I tell myself to stop remembering the way he made love to me all night.

I mean *all* night. I think I probably got an hour's sleep all in. We didn't leave the restaurant until late. That surprised me. I was so full of need for him, and yet staring across at him, hearing his beautiful husky accent as he talked about his childhood, his family, his *life*, I was mesmerised by the details. I was mesmerised by *him*.

We were the last guests in the restaurant.

I had a glass of Prosecco when we arrived and nothing else, but I felt *drunk* as we left. No, not drunk. High. And so happy.

The second we got back to his hotel we were ripping one another's clothes off.

And I slept over again.

Which makes the trifecta of rule-breaking complete.

But with three days to go—three more days of possible Ethan Ash consumption—I don't much care. I don't even care that yet another photo of us was running on the gossip sites this morning.

Nor that two of my clients emailed me to ask about my 'relationship' with him.

Nothing can dent my mood. And now I'm here, meeting with Ethan to discuss his art selection, and I'm determined to get through the meeting without doing anything inappropriate. Step one: prove that I can separate sex-life from work-life.

Grayson is waiting out front at Ethan's place. I see him as soon as my cab pulls up.

'Hey.' I smile as I tap up the stairs.

'Miss Douglas.'

'Please, call me Ally.'

He nods. 'Mr Ash is waiting for you.'

Yeah, that's mutual.

'It's cold today, huh?'

His smile is tight. 'Sure is.'

He pushes the door inwards and I move inside, my desire to befriend Grayson instantly consumed by a greater, stronger need to see Ethan. I stride down the hallway and pause just inside the living area.

What the hell…?

First of all, there's furniture. And that's fine. It's great. It's a welcome addition, in fact. But Ethan's interior designer Natasha is also there, smiling at Ethan, nodding as he speaks.

I am mentally removing his clothes, and mine—good intentions be damned—and now we have a lovely third wheel to contend with?

'Ah, Alicia. Wonderful.' She clips towards me with an authoritative air, as though this was her idea—as though I'm meeting her, and Ethan being here is just a happy coincidence.

'Natasha.' I nod, accepting her air kisses even as my

eyes lock accusingly with Ethan's. His expression shows bemusement.

'You'll be thrilled to see my progress. Come—have a look,' she invites.

I tamp down on my resentment. She's the designer. She obviously feels a sense of ownership over the project. Her behaviour isn't untoward. It's only my expectations— first of being alone with Ethan and second of being given the tour by *him*, preferably naked and with his hands on my body.

'Great,' I say through gritted teeth.

'You guys get started. I have a few calls to make,' Ethan says.

A few calls to make? *Does* he, indeed?

Natasha shows me the whole downstairs area—and she has done an incredible job. It's beautiful. Artistic while still achieving a degree of homely comfort. The fittings are classic and top-quality and I can see Ethan living here. Relaxing here. It suits him.

My gut twists at the very idea of his inhabiting this space full-time. We move upstairs into another living room, then into a guest room. A bed! *Hallelujah.* Perhaps he'll start spending more time here, rather than at the hotel? He'd be so close to me…

My phone rings and I pause our tour.

'Sorry,' I say, lifting it from my bag, about to decline the call when I see Ethan's name on the screen. 'I'll just be a minute.'

'Take your time. I need to measure the windows again for the drapes,' Natasha answers.

I step out of the room, into the hallway, and swipe to answer.

'Yes?' I snap, conscious that Natasha can probably still hear my end of the conversation.

'You look amazing.'

I turn away, pace a little further down the hallway and lower my voice. 'Thank you. I didn't realise you'd assembled the whole team.'

His laugh is like melted caramel. 'What's the matter? Aren't you having fun?'

'I had a different kind of fun in mind,' I say honestly.

He laughs again. 'Soon. Remember? Foreplay...'

'You're enjoying this.'

'Not as much as I'll be enjoying you, believe me. Have you reached my bedroom yet?'

I lift my head and look down the hallway. 'No. It's next.'

'When you get there I want you to imagine yourself naked in the middle of the bed. Arms outstretched. Fingers curled around the bedposts as I return the favour you gave me at the hotel. I want you to look at that bed and imagine me going down on you until you can barely speak.'

My breath is rushed and I know my cheeks are bright pink. A noise—a creaking floorboard—draws my attention to the stairs. He is walking up them, phone clasped under his ear.

'Think you can do that for me?' he murmurs, his eyes locked to mine.

A slick of need pools between my legs.

Natasha or not, I want to run to him, launch myself at him and strip him naked.

I disconnect the call and slide my phone into my bag, using the act to hide my face and eyes from him.

'Everything okay, Miss Douglas?' he asks as he approaches.

My eyes are wide in my face as I force myself to look at him. 'Oh, perfectly,' I respond, with obvious annoyance.

Except it's not annoyance with him; it's annoyance at not being able to have him. It's desire and white-hot need. It's fierce and uncontrollable and it's consuming me, despite the fact I have not long left his bed.

'Are you sure?'

He brings his body close to mine and pushes me backwards, so that I connect with the wall. We are only metres from the guest room, but he braces himself beside me, partially blocking me from Natasha's view. His fingers move straight to me, touching my most sensitive cluster of nerves through the fabric of my pants.

Did I really think Natasha's being here would stop him—stop this—the inevitability of what we are? He holds my eyes as he moves his fingers in a circular motion, and when I suck in a breath he lifts a finger to my lips.

'Shh,' he says, with a smile on his face.

I don't know if I can be quiet.

I don't know if I can stop this.

I know I should. I know this is unprofessional and that I have a reputation to think about. But I also have a body that is starving for its next fix, and he's offering it to me on a silver platter.

'Come for me, baby. Come without making a sound.'

He moves faster and I press myself down, rolling my hips, begging him with my body to make love to me.

I can feel the orgasm building. I dig my fingernails

into my palms to stop myself screaming out, but my silence makes the sensation all the more intense.

Heat is burning me—I am turning to ash.

He sees the moment I explode and he brings his mouth to my ear, buzzing his lips over my earlobe and whispering against me.

'You are perfect.'

I can't catch my breath. I hear Natasha's clip-clopping heels and I step aside from him even as my blood rages like a fever. I suck in air and I spin away, moving towards the window at the end of the corridor, needing a moment to straighten my hair, to collect myself, to calm my body.

'Oh! Ethan.'

It's Natasha.

'Come and have a look at the window treatment options.'

'Nothing I'd like better.'

I hear the grin in his voice and can picture his face even though I'm not looking at him.

It takes me several minutes to calm myself, to begin to feel like I am in control once more. When I'm ready, I move back through the house.

I find them in the master bedroom. Ethan watches me as I walk in, so I know he sees the way my eyes drop to the bed. Immediately. The way colour blooms in my cheeks.

We are both picturing the same thing.

Damn him.

Damn him for knowing how to push my buttons so well.

'What do you think?' Natasha asks excitedly. 'I've gone for a dark oak, because I think it's masculine and classic without being too heavy. Don't you agree?'

'It's perfect,' I murmur, thinking of the art I've selected for this room.

It took me a long time to come up with pieces that I think will suit Ethan. The pieces that I want him to wake up to each morning.

I meet Ethan's eyes for a moment; electricity charges between us.

'I like the bed. Is it a king?'

Natasha takes over. 'Yes. And it's a memory foam mattress. Super-comfortable.'

'Lie down,' Ethan invites, his gaze simmering as it locks to mine. 'See for yourself.'

'That's okay,' I say, a tad more sharply than necessary. 'I've felt mattresses before.'

'Not *this* mattress,' he points out smoothly.

'It really is the best on the market,' Natasha interjects, apparently oblivious to our flirtatious undercurrent.

'How lovely for you,' I murmur, turning to Ethan in time to see him wink at me.

My blood simmers. I think I'm going to turn into a puddle of lava if I don't get out of here.

I reach into my handbag and pull out a printed booklet. 'This is the proposal I mentioned.' I hand it to him. 'Why don't I leave it with the two of you to discuss and I'll follow up with you, Natasha, next week?'

'Excellent,' she agrees, before Ethan can speak, leaving me wondering briefly what he might have said.

'You've done a great job,' I say with an over-bright smile. 'I'll finish the tour another time. Nice to see you both again.'

'You too, Ally.' Natasha reaches across and takes the book from Ethan. 'May I?'

'Sure. Be my guest. I'll walk Miss Douglas out.'

'Please, call me Alicia,' I invite, swaying my hips as I move ahead of him.

He is behind me the whole way. Along the corridor, down the stairs, and then through the hall that leads to his front door. I press my hand around the doorknob, knowing I should say something but not knowing what.

I turn around slowly, but there's nothing slow about the way Ethan moves. He swoops down and kisses me, his whole body pushing mine against the door, trapping me. The weight of him is immovable, his mouth demanding, the intensity of his kiss pressing my head against the door. He grinds his hips and I feel his arousal through our clothes. He kisses me as he holds me captive with his hips, his dick, his very self.

I am powerless to move. I don't want to anyway. I want to do this for ever.

'I'll come to the hotel when I finish work,' I say into his mouth, conscious that we could be interrupted at any point and wanting privacy.

'I won't be there.'

The words don't compute at first.

'Huh?'

'I have a thing,' he says. 'With my manager.'

He runs his tongue along my lower lip and I moan.

'Wait for me there.'

I don't think that's a good idea. But before I can say so, he speaks.

'When I come back, I plan to fuck you senseless.'

A shiver runs through me. A frisson of anticipation and need.

Challenge accepted.

'And I'm going to fuck you right back.'

* * *

I have no idea what I'm doing.

Ally left an hour ago and I finally got rid of Natasha. Now, ensconced in my basement recording studio, which is coming together slowly, I need to be writing and instead I'm thinking.

About Ally.

About Sienna.

About what the hell I'm doing.

I'm thinking about the fact that I lied to her just now. I have no meeting with my manager. I just wanted to give her a taste of her own medicine. Why is *she* the only one who gets to decide when we see each other?

I'm thinking about the fact that I'm flying out of the States in a matter of days and that if I stick to the rules we agreed to I'm never going to see Ally again. That I was stupid to waste an evening just because I'm pissed off with our boundaries.

I'm thinking about the fact that I hate the thought of not seeing her after I leave. In fact the idea of not seeing Ally makes my skin crawl, and that, in turn, really pisses me off. Because Sienna and I broke up three months ago and, let's face it, it was hardly a clean break. By rights, I shouldn't be obsessing over someone new already, should I? Isn't that disloyal to Sienna and what we were? Maybe. But I'm not sure I have much say in it.

I'm furious at Sienna. No, I hate her. But I loved her once—or thought I did.

And Ally? Where does she fit in to all this? When did convenient sex with no strings start bothering me more than the break-up with the supposed love of my life?

I can't say. I have no idea what I feel for Ally.

But I know that I want her. And that three more days, three more nights with her, is not going to be enough.

I know that I wish we hadn't made those damned rules.

And I know that I'm a rule-breaker from way back. It's time I remembered that.

It's after eleven before I go to the hotel. It's childish, but I feel like it's important to make her wait. Just a bit.

When I step into the suite all thought rattles through me, threatening to drop right out of my head.

Ally is lying on the sofa, wearing a silky negligee, with a book in her hands. *My* book.

'I thought I'd see what all the fuss is about,' she says, and smiles, lifting *Les Misérables* up for me to see.

I had a speech worked out. A plan. I was going to seduce her and then, when she was weakened by desire, I was going to start a conversation. But I've seen her now and I blurt out, 'I'm coming back in a month or so.'

She stands up quickly, her eyes locked to mine.

'What?'

The word is not screeched, and yet it bounces around the room as though it were.

'To New York?' she says after a moment.

'No, to Earth,' I mutter sarcastically. 'Yes. To New York.'

I move further into the apartment. Here it comes. The sentence I've spent days formulating.

'I'd like to see you again.'

Abject fear crosses her face. It is unmistakable.

'What?'

'I'd like to see you again.' I shrug. 'I'll be in London a few weeks. Maybe less. And then I'll fly back here.'

'Why?'

My eyes don't lie. I'm not going to pretend any more. 'Because I'm going to be missing the hell out of you by then.'

She practically jack-knifes across the room, the book in her hand as though it's a lifeline, her tension a palpable force. Silence hangs between us.

'No.'

It's a softly spoken word. It's a plea. And yet it's emphatic.

I brace myself for her argument.

I brace myself for her doubts.

What I don't brace myself for is the fury and rage which is obvious when she spins around a moment later, her eyes pinning me to the spot, burning me with irate contempt.

'How *dare* you?'

It's not what I expect. Did I think she'd be glad? Thrilled? That she's been feeling the same growing sense of disbelief that our arbitrary deadline is drawing closer?

It takes me a moment to shake myself into responding. 'I *dare*—' my words sound coloured with anger '—because I don't want this to end. I'm not ready.'

'Oh, you're not *ready*,' she says sarcastically, slapping her palm to her forehead in an exaggerated and sarcastic gesture of sudden comprehension. '*You're* not ready! How did I dare think you'd do the right thing and stick to our deal?'

'Come on…' I growl the words. 'Be reasonable. We made this deal when we hardly knew each other. Are you telling me nothing's changed for you in the last two weeks?'

Her eyes flash with more anger and her cheeks drain

of colour. 'Of *course* things have changed! I'm not an idiot! But nothing *important* has changed. What I want is still the same.'

'And that's for this to end when I leave?'

'Yeah.'

'So if I'm back in New York you really don't want me to call you?'

She frowns, and that little divot forms between her brows. I ache to lift a finger to it and touch it, touch her. But I don't.

'No.'

A laugh escapes my mouth. A sound of disbelief. 'I'm not ready to walk away from you.'

'This isn't about you.'

Her eyes hold mine for a moment and then drop.

'What is it about, then?'

'It's about knowing we need to let this go.'

'Why? You don't think there's something here worth keeping hold of?'

She sniffs.

Hell, is she *crying*? I can handle almost anything, but not Ally's tears. I feel like my chest has been ripped open and someone is reaching in and squeezing my organs in a fist.

I wait for her to answer, my question sitting between us like an enormous, impossible-to-navigate boulder.

'Ally?' I prompt gruffly when she doesn't answer.

'I'll admit,' she says shakily, 'that things between us are kind of amazing—'

'"Kind of amazing"?' I interrupt, running a hand through my hair.

'But it doesn't change the fact that I don't want to be

in a relationship. I don't want a boyfriend. I don't want to live with the risks that are bound up in loving someone.'

'So you're—what? Going to stay single for ever? Run through a succession of fuck buddies for the rest of your life?'

The very idea is curdling my blood.

She looks away from me and my stomach drops. *Good job, jackass.* Bully and berate her into a relationship. That's a *great* idea.

'I don't know.'

Her whisper is a plaintive cry. I can't help it. I cover the distance between us, my stride long. I press my body to hers, trapping her with my legs as my hands reach up and lock her face between them. I drag her up as I push my head down, finding her lips as though the survival of humanity will be ensured by this kiss.

'I *know* enough for both of us.'

She shakes her head, and I can taste her tears, and it makes me want to fuck her so much more. It's the only way we can communicate without doubts.

I push at her negligee, my hands demanding, my need raw. I rip it from her body and she moans into my mouth. I drop my lips to her shoulder and taste her flesh with my tongue, then press my teeth into her. She arches her back and, fuck, I need her more than I ever have.

I push at her bra—it's just a scrap of lace that barely holds her in place. I drop it with an equal mix of contempt and admiration, and then I take a breast into my mouth with a primal moan of need.

I cannot function without her.

I lift her, wrapping her legs around me, and she is running her hands through my hair, tasting me, kissing my cheek, my jaw, her hands touching every square inch of me as she goes. I ache to possess her, but this torturous lead-up is heaven on earth.

I drop her onto the bed. I'm not gentle. She bounces as she lands and her eyes contain the same rush of fury as they meet mine.

I don't care.

I'm furious as well. I'm furious with her for sticking to some stupid rules we agreed to way back when we hardly knew each other. But her crying… Her crying damned near breaks my heart.

I don't think she even realises she's doing it, but I run my tongue along her cheek, catching a tear, tasting her salt and her sadness, and then I kiss her.

I drop my mouth to her chest, running my tongue over her, and my fingers brush her sides, pausing at her hips to hold her as I take my tongue to her clit and torment her in the way I know she loves. Her fingers are tearing through my hair. She lifts her legs and I grip her ankles, holding her there, making her fall apart.

And she does.

She cries out as the rapture of her orgasm drops over us both and then I move, stepping out of my jeans, hovering over her. I stretch across and grab a condom from my side of the bed. My fingers are shaking as I stretch it over me. Need is like a spring, coiled tight in my chest.

I stare at her and, fuck it, I know I need to roll the dice.

I gamble. I gamble in the only way I can think of because I'm all in.

CHAPTER FOURTEEN

'I love you.'

The words drop over me as he thrusts into me, his possession complete. I reject the words at the same time as I welcome him. I am fevered and frantic, afraid and so aware of every pulsing need inside my body.

He grabs my hands, lacing his fingers through mine and pinning them wide on either side of my head. His eyes stare down at me.

He thrusts again, harder, deeper, and he says it again.

'I love you.'

He drops his mouth and kisses the words into me, swirling them into me, pushing them through me as he moves, each three-word bomb detonating in time with his body's possession, so that I am being stirred to the height of desire even as I want to scream and push him away. Even as I am terrified and innately rejecting his sentiment.

'Don't!' I say, sobbing, and he pauses, his body still, as if I'm rejecting the sex.

I'm not. The sex is what I want.

'Don't say that.'

'I love you,' he challenges, his eyes locked to mine. Something inside me flutters. Hope? Pleasure? Relief?

But I shake my head. 'This isn't love.'

He thrusts into me again. 'It is for me.'

I shouldn't be able to function in the midst of this, and yet I'm climbing higher and higher. My body is so sensitive that even the air around me is making me shiver with awareness. I can feel it waving over my body. I arch my back, tilting my hips, and he moves inside me again.

'I love you.'

I don't fight it. I don't reject the words. I let them fill me up. I let them curl around my heart and for a moment I pretend they're what I want. Just for a moment.

It is a coming together ruled by animalistic passion, and yet there is a raw emotionalism to it as well. His fingers squeeze mine as we come together, and he kisses me, and I know what he's thinking without him saying it.

He loves me.

Words that so many people find joyous and welcome fill me with dread. They are tainted by past misuse and all its negative associations. Ethan tells me he loves me but I hear Jeremy, and I instantly recall the disaster that followed.

I lie beneath Ethan, his weight on me, his body beautiful and warm, strong and hard. I feel his warmth and strength and I wish it would bleed into me. I am going to need to be strong.

'Excuse me.'

The words come out cold and crisp. He's still inside me and suddenly I need space and I need it now.

All I can think, as his words hover in the air like deceptive little bullets, is what an asshole he is. Why would he *do* this? Love is not why I'm here! Love is not what I want!

I pull my hands; he doesn't argue. I push at his chest

and roll him away from me, out of me, and then I stand up in one movement. I am shaking with desire and with anger. My negligee is ripped so I grab one of his shirts. It smells like him and my chest groans under the weight of certainty that soon it will be all I have of him.

'What are you doing?' he asks, watching me as I step into my jeans without bothering to put my undies back on. I tuck them into the back pocket and then run my hands through my hair.

'What do you think?' I respond with the same arctic chill.

'Listen.' He stands, the word soothing and gentle. 'Don't run off.'

I glare at him. 'Does it *look* like I'm running off?'

'Yeah.'

'I'm not,' I snap back, storming into the lounge area and scooping up my bag.

I'm struck by the similarities to that first morning when I said goodbye to him—when I thought it would be the last goodbye.

I push my clutch under my arm and am instantly steadied by its presence. 'I'm walking away.'

'Alicia…' he groans, and when I spin back to him I see he's pulled a pair of low-slung jeans on. They sit on his hips, so I can see the protrusion of where his bones meet the sinew and strength of his shape.

It dries my mouth.

I have kissed every part of him. And I'll never touch him again.

'Don't.' It's a shaky, hollow plea. 'Don't say it again. If it's really how you feel, then please respect that I don't want to hear it.'

'You love me too,' he says, prowling towards me.

'No!' I deny it on every level except one. Deep in my heart I wearily admit the truth of what he's said.

He kisses me gently. 'Yes.'

And, infuriatingly, I feel him smile against my mouth. I stamp my foot down on his. 'No.'

He rips his mouth away in surprise, his eyes laughing when they meet mine. 'What the hell...?'

But then he's back, kissing me again, holding me to him, holding me tight.

'You love me. And I know that you're not ready to see that, or to say it. But I think you feel it. I'm not going to walk away from this.'

I make a shuddering noise, as though I'm hyperventilating.

'I'm not going to crowd you either. I'm just going to be in your life until you're ready.'

That same little kernel in my heart is jumping up and down. I ignore it.

'Why?' It's a question loaded with suspicion.

'Because this is special. I know that you've been hurt and that you're shit-scared to trust someone again. But I'm not Jeremy. And I love you.'

'He—'

'Didn't love you,' Ethan murmurs. 'No guy who really loved someone could do what he did.'

He shrugs, and the simple truth is sitting between us like a diamond I never noticed before.

It makes so much sense.

Jeremy *never* loved me.

It is so simple and so immediately freeing.

Except there's nothing simple about the tangle of what I'm feeling now.

I'm still so angry. I'm angry at Jeremy and at Ethan, and I'm angry at myself for letting it get this far.

'I need to go,' I say.

'Alicia,' he says grimly. 'Don't walk away from this.'

I storm towards the door and wrench it inwards. I have no concept of what I feel, nor of what I want. I know only that I need to get away from Ethan before I start actual ugly crying.

'I have to go.' I force myself to meet his eyes. 'I'm sorry.'

I don't sleep. I brood. Ally has left me after I put everything on the line. Ally has left me after I did everything I could to help her see why she should stay.

She is everywhere I look in the hotel room. The bed smells of her, of me, of us. It is rumpled from where we lay. My towels have been used by her. We have made love on just about every surface of this damned hotel room.

I pace through it as the minutes of the night groan heavily, sombrely past. I am at the funeral of our relationship and I don't know if I should rip my hair out or... *I don't know.* I press my hands into my eyes, hard, and then I blink, staring out at the city as dawn slowly spreads like the yolk of an egg being cracked into a pan.

I stare at New York and I imagine I'm not here. That I'm back in London.

I try to picture my life BA—Before Ally—and I can't.

I know I have a heap on in the next year, but suddenly it's all so pointless.

Is she thinking of me? Is she missing me?

A little before six o'clock there is a knock at my door, and every part of me responds with a surge of relief. I

wrench it inwards, a smile on my face as I prepare to
pull Ally into my arms and do whatever it takes to keep
her in my life.

My smile drops.

It's not Ally.

I am in agony.

I am in pain.

I am alone.

I stare up at the ceiling, the incessant ticking of my
clock like a sombre marching band. It is a noise that I
used to find hypnotic and reassuring but that now makes
me want to stab my ears.

Or is that just my general mood?

Everything seemed so easy two weeks ago. It all
made so much sense.

We were fucking.

And having fun.

We both knew what was at stake if we fell in love.
We both knew why we couldn't.

And yet we did it anyway.

But love terrifies me. Loving Ethan even more so.

He's not just a normal guy—someone I can trust to
look after my heart and keep it safe with his. He is a
rock star. A celebrity. He has the adoration of the world.

I would worry all the time that some other woman
was going to usurp me.

It would be so much worse even than with Jeremy.

I give up on sleep. I'm exhausted, but the relief of
dreams will not come. I am still wearing what I came
home in yesterday. His shirt is soft against my skin. I
breathe it in and I cry more tears. I sob into the darkness of my room. I pull my blinds aside a little and stare

out at New York. A lamp from overhead casts a perfect cone of light into the street.

I rip the shirt off impatiently and pull one of my own from the drawer, not bothering with a bra. It's a simple floaty black blouse with dark grey beading stitched across the front. I rake my hair over one shoulder.

He will leave in two days and then my city will be my own. I won't have to wonder if I'll run into him. He'll be gone. In London.

Until he's not.

Until he's back in New York and I know about it from Twitter or the newspapers.

I close my eyes, anguish heavy upon me. I can hardly breathe.

I can't lose him.

I can't.

Maybe that's just inviting pain. Maybe I'll be hurt one day and it will be ten thousand times worse than what I went through with Jeremy because these feelings I have for Ethan are so different, so raw and powerful and pure. But I can't walk away from what we share just because one day it might end. It would be like never going to school because one day you might lose your dream job.

What's that expression about loving and losing? It's better to have loved and lost than never to have loved at all? Something like that.

I tiptoe out of my room and lift my keys silently from the nightstand. My clutch purse is there too. I remove my bank card and his key card and check my reflection— and thank Christ I had the foresight to do so when I see that yesterday's mascara is now two sludgy racetracks along my cheeks.

I slip into the bathroom and lather my cheeks, washing away all of yesterday except the pieces I want to keep.

His kisses.

His touch.

His words.

I love you.

I smile at my reflection. I clean my teeth, brush my hair, and then I sneak out of the apartment, making sure the door clicks softly behind me so as not to wake Cassie or Eliza.

I catch a cab but get it to pull over a block from the Gramercy. I stop for breakfast burritos and coffee. His love for fried food was a constant in our brief, blinding relationship. Besides, once I see him again I have no plans to leave his bed for the foreseeable future—arming myself with sustenance seems wise.

The waiting is soul-destroying. I glare at the burger flipper until finally he places the food into a brown paper bag and hands me the coffee cups in a recycled card tray.

'Thanks,' I mumble, pressing my card to the machine and then moving towards the Gramercy with my head bent.

The whole time I imagine what I'll say to him.

How can I convey to him that I'm willing to risk everything—even my heart, even knowing what heartache feels like? How can I apologise for letting him down last night? For not being brave when he was so far out on a limb?

I keep my head down as I glide into the Gramercy, wincing as a flash goes off in my face. I'll get better at that. I'll learn to live with the paparazzi and the other women who want Ethan I-love-you Ash.

Because he *does* love me.

Believing that takes a leap of faith, but I've already leapt. For him. And for myself.

For *us*.

Because it's what my own heart demands of me.

I jam my finger against the button for the lift impatiently, turning my back on the curious stares of a couple of women across the lobby. But heat spreads through my cheeks. They obviously know who I am, and can probably guess where I'm on my way to.

So what?

The lift whooshes open and I step inside, waving Ethan's key over the panel and pressing the number for his floor. It climbs up quickly and smoothly—and, oh, my heart.

How it pounds and races and flips and flops.

I stare straight ahead, trying to look outwardly calm when I am an absolute mess.

What if he's angry?

What if I hurt him too much?

Well, then, I'll fix it. I'll make him see that I was just scared.

And he'll understand. Because he loves me.

I hold that thought to my chest like a talisman as I reach his door. I think about knocking. I lift my hand but something stops me. I smile slowly, imagining him asleep in bed, naked. I think of the best way to wake him up. The most meaningful apology.

I slip the key card from my back pocket and slide it in the door, then push the door inwards, juggling the coffee cups in one hand with the bag of burritos dangling from the same fingertips. I'm purposely slow because I don't want to wake him prematurely.

But I needn't have worried.

He's awake.

Sitting at the table we first made love on the night we met.

And he's not alone.

I recognise her instantly. Dark hair like glossy black opal, shimmering over impossibly slender shoulders. A face without even a hint of make-up still looking *Vogue*-cover worthy. Skimpy singlet top barely concealing her tiny breasts. And she's clearly not wearing a bra—and pulling it off without a hint of cleavage sweat.

It isn't just Sienna Di Giorgio. It's all my fears—everything I've worried about—staring right back at me.

I don't know who's more shocked.

Me. Ethan. Or Sienna.

Memories of Jeremy and Fiona barrel towards me—it is just the same, but so much worse. I am the outsider again. The interloper. The home-wrecker. I look at them together and they make so much sense. They are perfect together. Two gloriously perfect celebrities.

'Ally—' He stands so abruptly he knocks over a glass of water. It seems to fall in slow motion, cascading through the air and landing with a thump, spreading liquid over the tabletop.

He's fully dressed. He looks good. And he looks bad. Like he hasn't done a heap of sleeping.

Jealousy unfurls inside me. No, it doesn't *unfurl*. That sounds too gentle and progressive. It explodes like a nuclear detonation, singeing every single nerve ending in my body.

'Wait a second.'

He surprises us all with the firmness of his command. I stare at him, and then at her, and finally, after

long seconds which feel like minutes, I shake my head
as if to wake myself up.

'I…'

I stare at him. He's moving around the table, and if
I don't act fast he's going to come up to me. He's going
to touch me.

I swallow and shake my head again, my eyes locked
on his pleadingly. It is a silent plea, but he hears it loud
and clear. He stops moving and I place the key card I'm
still holding in my fingertips onto the side table.

'I just wanted to bring this back,' I say.

I can't look at him any more. I turn around and walk
quickly out through the door, bumping my elbow on
the way out so that coffee spills down my front. I swear
between my teeth but don't stop. I pick up speed as I
get closer to the lift, dumping the coffee and the bag of
food in an aluminium rubbish bin. I press the lift button.

But it doesn't open straight away, and Ethan is behind
me. I feel him before I see his wobbly reflection in the
scrubbed metal surface of the lift doors.

'Don't touch me,' I say urgently.

'Ally, that looked bad. The timing was fucking awful.
But it's not what you think.'

I shut my eyes and drop my head forward, pressing
my heated forehead against the lift.

'What *do* I think?' I whisper.

The lift doors whoosh open and I step in gratefully.
He follows.

'Get out,' I say mutinously, staring straight ahead.

'No.' He presses the button for the ground floor.

'Ethan…' It's a whispered plea. 'Leave me the hell
alone.'

'Why did you come back?'

Tears sting my eyes. The hopes I'd cherished only minutes earlier are lined up in my head, pointing at me and laughing, mocking me. The lift begins to suck us downwards. It can't move fast enough for me. Soon I'll be out. Soon I'll be able to breathe.

He moves quickly, reaching across and slamming his hand onto the emergency stop button, his body caging mine. His hands are on either side of me, trapping me in the frame of his beautiful body.

My eyes jerk to his. 'Restart the elevator.'

'Not until you hear me out,' he says with raw emotion in his words. 'Sienna arrived thirty minutes before you did. She came to talk. That's *all*.'

I shake my head, emotions, feelings, thoughts, doubts and fears bubbling through me. I don't know what to say, and I certainly don't know how to say it. But I have to say something. He's staring at me and the silence pounds between us expectantly, angrily, needily.

'Does she want to get back with you?' It's a whisper.

He doesn't answer immediately and my heart cracks, my blood freezes. It's Jeremy all over again. The lying. The uncertainty.

'That's not what I want,' he says.

I shake my eyes. It's all the confirmation I need.

Is this my fault? Do I have some gene that leads me to seek out unavailable bastards?

'But that's why she's here?'

I lift a hand to his chest and then instantly regret it when I feel his heart beating beneath my palm as though it's talking to me. It's racing.

'Don't lie to me.'

His eyes lock to mine. 'Yes.'

I suck in a breath. It gets nowhere near my lungs.

'Do you know how often I've thought of Sienna since meeting you?'

I glare at him.

'Barely at all. Even when I've spoken to her I've been thinking of you.'

'You've *spoken* to her?' I flush hot and cold all over. It's history repeating itself and I cannot bear it.

He has the decency to look somewhat apologetic. 'She's called me a couple of times.'

'Of course she has!' I say, with an angry shake of my head. 'I told you from the beginning—I'm not going to get in the middle of this. I'm not! I *won't*.'

'I told her it's over. It *is* over between her and me.'

He presses a kiss against my hair and I shake my head in instant visceral rejection of the intimacy.

'You have to believe me.'

'I can't.'

I want to. I want to so badly.

'I'm your Sienna Band-Aid, remember?'

For a second he looks vague, as if he doesn't even remember that he said that. Then, 'Jesus. That was a stupid throwaway comment.'

'Like when you told me you loved me?' I retort, my heart boxing itself away with every moment that passes.

A disembodied voice comes into the lift. 'This carriage will be restarted in fifteen seconds. Safety checks confirm operation.'

'Christ.'

He moves his hands to my cheeks, holding me still as he does so often, trying to forge a line of trust and reliance between us.

'This changes nothing.'

My heart is wrapping itself up, determined not to crack any further.

'Don't you *get* what a big deal this was for me?' I stare at him, honesty in my face. 'I am terrified of what I feel for you and yet I came here anyway. I decided to trust you, and that was one of the hardest decisions I've ever made.'

'I'm not Jeremy,' he says softly. 'Most guys aren't. In six years I never once thought about cheating on Sienna—and, believe me, I had plenty of opportunities. That's not who I am.'

I squeeze my eyes shut at the sense of his words, and at the temptation to believe him. Because deep down I do, and pushing him away makes not a skerrick of sense.

'The problem is, Jeremy didn't just cheat on his wife and on me. He made me question *everything*. He made me question what I think and feel so that I can't say if I'm misreading you or myself right now.'

'I know. I get it. I begged you to trust me and you did—and then you found my ex in my hotel room. *Any* woman would find that hard, let alone after what you've been through.'

His understanding should mollify me, but it doesn't. 'I don't remember how to trust. I thought I could... I came here... I don't know what I was expecting when I came here. It was wrong.'

'But you did want us to give this a shot?'

I shake my head and then nod, and then the elevator moves and I suck in another breath, trying to equalise.

'Then let's try. Please.'

'No.' A short, emphatic word. 'No.' Louder. I lift my hands and push at his chest. 'You can burn me once, Ethan. But not again. Not again.'

The lift doors open. There's a team of technicians there. I step out and, sensing that he might follow me, spin around.

'Don't.'

I lift a hand, staring at him, and I walk away backwards for a few steps, pinning him with my eyes, making sure he doesn't step off the lift.

He doesn't. But he watches me the whole way across the foyer.

I feel his eyes on me and I know it's for the last time.

CHAPTER FIFTEEN

DAY FOLLOWS NIGHT, follows day, follows night, and I bear witness to it all. I'm aware of the rotation of the earth around the sun but I am weary.

I see Eliza and Cassie and I hate it that they are worried about me. *Again.* I see the concern etched on their faces and try to smile, but I have forgotten how. I am learning the hardest lesson of all.

Good intentions be damned.

You cannot immunise yourself against some things, and all-consuming love appears to be one of them. How stupid I was to believe I could control it. How awful the pain at realising my mistake.

Did he sleep with her?

I dismiss the idea instantly. Of course he didn't.

Ethan isn't Jeremy. He wouldn't do that.

Would he?

That's the problem. Just like I said to him over a week ago, when we argued. I've forgotten how to trust, and that includes my instincts. I don't know if I believe him to be good because I want to or because I should. I cannot see clearly any longer.

Jeremy took that away from me.

I'm not ignoring Ethan because I believe him to be a

cheat. I'm ignoring him because I believe he is a pathway to unimaginable pain. I know that I'm not strong enough to weather the demise of what we are. It is almost killing me now, and we have only been sleeping together for two weeks. What if I let myself admit how much I love him? What if I let him into my life? And after six months…two years…five years…two kids? What if it ends then?

I see the future and I see those paths before me, just like on that first night, and every single path leads to hurt and lost hope.

Unless I stay right where I am, pretending that I'm glad we've ended it.

I stare at the images on my screen and rouse myself. Ethan's brownstone. The proposal is complete. I have arranged two options for him, and yet I know which he will choose. I have selected pieces that inherently reflect the essence of who he is. On that score I have no doubts.

I have chickened out of presenting them to him, though. Natasha can do that. I can't see him again. I can't see him in the house that I have come to love. I can't see him there and imagine him living in those rooms, only a few blocks away from me. I can't.

'Your four o'clock is here.'

Lesley's voice comes through the intercom, about a thousand degrees too cheery for my current mood.

'Great,' I say through gritted teeth, clicking into my calendar to see just what appointment I've got. I can't see an entry but I stand, a perplexed look on my face.

The door swings open and there he is.

Ethan tormenting-my-dreams Ash—all sexy, dishevelled, good-enough-to-eat handsome, watching me as though I'm a bomb that might detonate.

I have no time to gather my wits. He moves into the room and shuts the door behind himself and then he comes right up to me, so close that I can feel his warmth and smell his adrenaline and I want to kiss him. I want to kiss him all over.

The knowledge of that makes me push back. I'm *not* that woman. I have a brain and I have a decision-making process and, damn it, I'm going to use both.

'What are you doing here?'

The question comes out in a rush, but I am pleased with how defiant I sound. How pissed off, when actually I'm part-way to melting.

'Well, you haven't been returning my calls or responding to my texts, so what choice did I have?'

I glare at him, all the angrier at the effect his accent has on me. At the way my body is sensitised, my stomach churns and my mind almost goes blank.

'You had the choice to take the hint,' I snap, moving away from him, seeking sanity in the distance. 'You had the choice to let me go.'

'No.'

His eyes glint as they meet mine and I feel like I've slammed into a brick wall. His determination is mighty.

'No?' I repeat sarcastically, even as my heart is shredding me from the inside out.

'No.'

He crosses his arms over his broad, muscular chest. He's wearing a leather jacket over a grey T-shirt and a pair of faded jeans. They're low on his hips and I know that if I lifted his shirt an inch I'd see his hipbone. I remember running my tongue over the blade of his waist, but it's wrong to remember something so personal.

I take another step back, swallowing. 'We had a deal.'

His lips flick with amusement.

'Don't you dare laugh at me.'

'Believe me, I'm not laughing.' He drags a hand through his hair, his eyes probing me thoughtfully.

'So?' My breath hitches in my throat. I almost choke on it. 'What *are* you doing here?'

'I'm here to broker a new deal.'

Danger, danger.

My eyes narrow; my heart races. 'Because our last one was such a success?'

'Yeah, actually, I think it was.'

I make a snort of derision. Yes. I snort—in front of Ethan sex-god Ash. For Christ's sake. I think I've reached pretty much the lowest ebb of my life.

'It was a spectacular failure?'

'Why? Because we exceeded expectations?' He arches a brow. 'I wanted to fuck you and instead I fell in love. You don't think that's commendable?'

'Commendable?' I repeat, my jaw dropping. 'This isn't a grade school assignment, for God's sake, Ethan!'

'Yeah, well, obviously… I think the school board would have a thing or two to say about it.'

Again he smiles, and I feel like he's laughing at me.

I square my shoulders, staring at him with what I hope comes over as distaste. 'I want you to get out. This is bordering on stalking, you know.'

'Not until you've heard what I came here to say.'

He's not joking now. His expression is hardened by intent and his eyes dare me to challenge him.

I don't.

But mentally I brace myself for the inevitable. I will walk away from him. I will draw new boundaries. I will run from this as fast as I can.

Panic fills me.

'Fine. Say what you want and then leave me alone.'

She's still pissed off. Any hope I had that she might have mellowed over the last week has evaporated. Everything I planned to say, the arguments I wanted to level, the jokes I wanted to make about planting a peach orchard at my home disappear. I stare at her and I am lost. I am lost in the sea of what we were, and what we could be, and everything I am hinges on how I do this.

'You're scared of how much you love me. I understand that.'

She makes a scoffing sound of disbelief. 'You're *so* arrogant! I walked away from you, remember? And you're standing there telling me I'm in love with you?'

'Damn straight.'

She glares at me.

'Tell me you're not,' I challenge. 'Say that you don't love me and I'll go. Right now. If that's what you want, say it and I'll walk out that door.'

Her eyes sparkle and then drop lower, mutiny in every line of her body. I hold my breath without realising it, but then I relax. Because she *does* love me. And she's not a liar.

'It was two weeks,' she says angrily, as though the shortness of time we've known each other makes a damned bit of difference.

'So?'

'So you hardly *know* me!'

My temper rises and I want to shake her. No—scratch that. I want to kiss her and I want to fuck her. I want to rip that dress up around her waist and push her against her desk and do the only thing I can do to make her understand how perfect we are.

'You think I don't know you?'

Again she doesn't meet my eyes.

Challenge accepted, Miss Douglas.

I pace towards her, so close that we are almost but not quite touching.

'I know that you love to go running in a way that I will never understand but will try to come to terms with. I know that you love Neil deGrasse Tyson. I know that you drink gin and tonic and live with Eliza and Cassie and that you think of them as sisters.'

I've got her attention—if only because I'm moving infinitesimally closer with each sentence, closing what little gap remains between us.

'I know that your parents are conservative and that you don't want to disappoint them. I know that you feel about art the way I do about music. I know that you are brilliant and respected and intelligent, and as rare as any of my favourite Impressionist masterpieces.'

She sucks in a breath and my eyes drop to her lips, to the way they're parted, revealing her white teeth and warm mouth. But I cannot be derailed from my argument. Not yet.

'I know that you always eat your burger before you touch your fries—that you never eat them both at the same time—and I know that you like coffee first thing in the morning, even before I've spoken to you. I know that watching you eat a peach is the sexiest damn thing in the world. I know that you sing in the shower and, I'm sorry to say it, that you have one of the worst singing voices I've ever heard. Seriously…you couldn't find the right key even if it landed on your head.'

'Insulting me probably *isn't* what you want to do right now,' she mutters belligerently.

Her eyes jerk to mine angrily and I lift a hand to calm her, press it lightly to her arm. 'I know that, regardless of that, hearing you sing is still one of the things that makes me the happiest man in the world.'

Her eyes scrunch closed and I recognise the anguish on her features.

'Yellow tulips are your favourite flower and you love New York. I know that the first words I spoke to you were a pop bloody song, and I remember everything about you from that night—what you were wearing, what we talked about—everything. Because that was the night that changed my life.'

She makes a strangled noise of pain…or recognition. Something I take as encouragement.

'I know that you're a homebody, and that I'm asking you to sacrifice that to be with me—because I'm going to want you with me all the time.'

Her brows draw together and I rush on.

'But I'll do anything to make you happy—which means cutting back on my commitments.'

Her eyes widen with surprise.

'I know every single thing about your body—your birthmarks, your freckles, and the ways I can touch you that drive you wild. I know that you've been hurt and that you're scared out of your mind by what you feel for me.'

She drops her eyes to the ground, and in that moment I am so angry at what that bastard did to her.

But she doesn't deny it now. Her shoulders slump as she accepts everything I'm saying. It's a silent admission and it means everything to me. I begin to breathe again.

I speak more quietly, like I'm taming a skittish horse.

'I know you're worried that I'm on the rebound, and that I'm going to wake up one morning and realise I'm still in love with my ex. And I know that I'm not. I know this because I know everything about you and I still want to know more. I know this because I was asleep my whole life until meeting you. I love you—I love you in the way that all those songs have been written about. I love you in the I-want-to-get-married-and-have-babies-and-be-with-you-for-ever-and-ever kind of way.'

I can't read her face. I don't know what she's thinking. All I know is that I hurt her and I have to fix it. I have to make her understand that I'm not Jeremy and that Sienna's not a problem for us.

I'm afraid again—afraid that she's going to reject me and that this really will be it. I can't keep forcing her to face up to what we are. If she doesn't want this then I have to let her go.

The future looks unimaginably odd without Ally in it. I can't even contemplate that I might fail here.

I try again, with desperation and need, and I lean closer, my lips almost buzzing hers.

'I write songs about love and I still can't find the right way to say this. To do this. Because it matters too much. There's no euphemism or comparison I can make that does justice to how you make me feel. You give *all* my songs meaning.'

Still she looks at me without giving anything away, so I move closer and link my fingers with hers, squeezing them.

'I spent six years with Sienna and I never knew her like I know you. Time doesn't matter. Nothing really does except the way we feel. I *know* this is it. The real deal. The thing you wait for and hope you're going to be lucky enough to find. I love you.'

She sobs and shakes her head, and her eyes look at me accusingly.

'How *dare* you?'

It's not what I expect. Panic surges through me. But then she lifts up on tiptoe and mashes her lips against mine, anger in every movement of her mouth.

'How dare you come here and be so perfect when all I want is to forget about you?'

Hope flares.

'Don't forget about me.'

'I can't,' she says.

'Because you love me.'

I know it, but more than I've ever needed anything I need to hear her say it.

She lifts her hands and pushes at my chest. I think she's going to shout at me, or push me away, but then she runs at me and takes me with her, back to the wall. She is kissing me and pushing at my jacket so that I laugh into her mouth.

I want this. I want to fuck her.

But it's just another form of hiding.

Fighting this with the sex thing is pointless. We *know* that works.

I hold her at arm's length.

'You love me, right?'

'Yeah. I love you.'

She sounds so angry I can't help but laugh.

'Good.' I nod. 'Prove it.'

She moves closer to kiss me, but I shake my head. 'No.' My eyes are determined. But every single nerve inside me is groaning and protesting my honourable intentions. 'First we have dinner. We date.'

'I don't want to date,' she says in disbelief—a disbelief I completely understand.

'Yeah, well, we're going to.' I lean in and kiss her lightly. 'I'm never going to give you a reason to doubt what you mean to me. That's our new deal. Okay by you?'

She stares at me, her eyes huge, her lips parted, her breath audible. A pulse point is jerking in the base of her throat and, damn it, good intentions or not, I want to reach over and run my teeth over it.

She moves forward, pressing her hips to me so that I'm sure she can feel my rock-hard cock through the fabric of our clothes.

I am desperate to drag her into my bed, but if I play my cards right I'll have the rest of my life for that. Now is for sealing the deal. Now is for making sure she knows how much I love her and how much she loves me back, so that she can forget about that asswipe Jeremy and begin to see herself like I do.

Brave. Smart. Kind. Good. One of a kind.

'Deal,' she purrs. 'But don't think I'm going to make it easy for you…'

I relax. I smile at her and she smiles at me and we understand one another. Love is a gamble, but so is life, and my life has new meaning because I have found—unexpectedly, unquestionably—never-ending love.

* * * * *

FALLING FOR
THE REBEL PRINCESS

ELLIE DARKINS

For Mike and Matilda.

CHAPTER ONE

'NOT YET!' CHARLIE GASPED, willing herself to be dragged back under.

In her dream her skin was hot and damp, on fire from his touch.

Awake, her tongue felt furry.

In her dream her body hummed, desperate for the feel of him.

Awake, her eyes stung as she peeled them open.

In her dream she begged for more, and got everything she didn't even know she needed.

Awake, she needed to pee.

She admitted defeat and stretched herself properly alive, wincing at the harsh Nevada sunlight assaulting her in the hotel room. As her toes encountered skin she flinched back, realising that she did have this one, small reminder of her dream. The man who'd taken the starring role was beside her on the mattress, his face turned away from her, his arms and legs sprawled and caught in the sheets. She looked away. She couldn't think about him. Not yet.

Easing herself out of bed, she willed him not to wake. And worked her thumb into her waistband, rubbing at her skin where her jeans had left a tight red line. The T-shirt she'd slept in was twisted and creased, and she glanced around the room, wondering whether her luggage had been transferred when the hotel had upgraded them to a luxury suite. She shuddered when she caught sight of herself in the mirror and tried to pull her hair up into some sort of order.

It had started out backcombed and messy, and her eyeliner had never been subtle in her life—but a couple of hours' sleep had taken the look from grunge to tragic. She wiped under her eyes with a finger, and the tacky drag of her skin made her shudder. And desperate to shower.

A glint of gold caught her eye and stopped her dead.

No. That had been the dream. It had to be.

She went over her memories, rooted to the spot, staring at the ring, trying to pull apart what was dream and what was real. After eighteen hours travelling and many more without sleep, the past twenty-four hours barely felt real, images and memories played through her mind as if they had happened to somebody else.

The thrumming, heaving energy of the gig last night. That was real. The music capturing her senses, hijacking her emotions and pumping her full of adrenaline. Real.

Hot and sweaty caresses just before dawn. Dream.

Dancing with Joe in the club, trying to talk business, shouting in his ear. Moving so closely with him that they felt like one body. Feeling the music play between them like a language only they spoke. Maybe that was real.

The slide of his bare skin against hers. So, so dreamy.

Him talking softly as they lay on the bed, trading playlists on their phones, sharing a pair of headphones, until one and then both of them fell asleep. God, she wished she knew.

But as she raised her left hand and examined the demure gold band on her third finger, she was certain of one thing.

Vegas chapel wedding. Real.

She banged her head back against the wall. Why did she always do this? She was losing count of the number of times she'd looked over the wreckage of her life after one stupid, impulsive move after another and wished that she could turn back time. If she had the balls to go home and tell her parents that she didn't want their royal way of life and everything that came with it, maybe she'd stop hitting the self-destruct button. But starting that conversation would lead to questions that she'd never be prepared to answer.

Thinking back to the night before, she tried to remember what had triggered her reaction. And then she caught sight of the newspaper, abandoned beside the bed. The slip of the paper under her fingertips made her shiver with the memory of being handed one like it backstage in the club last night, and she let out a low groan. It had been the headline on the front page: Duke Philippe bragging about his forthcoming engagement to Princess Caroline Mary Beatrice of Afland, otherwise known as Charlie. It was the sort of match her parents had been not so subtly pushing on her for years, the one she was hoping that would go away if she ignored it for long enough. She knew unequivocally that she would never marry, and especially not someone like Duke Philippe.

She'd left the cold, rocky, North Sea island of Afland nearly ten years ago, when she'd headed to London determined to make her own way in the music business. Her parents had given her ten years to pursue her rebellion—as they put it. But they all knew what was expected after that: a return to Afland, official royal duties, and a practical and sensible engagement to a practical, sensible aristocrat.

So there was nothing but disappointment in store for her family, and for her.

She shrank into the bathroom and hid the newspaper as she heard stirring from the bed. Perhaps if she hid for long enough it just wouldn't be true—Joe Kavanagh and their marriage would fade away as the figment of her imagination that she knew they must be.

Marriage. She scoffed. This wasn't a marriage. It was a mistake.

But it seemed as if her body didn't care which bits of last night were real and which were imagined. The hair on her arms was standing on end, her heart had started to race, and she felt a yearning deep in her stomach that seemed somehow familiar.

'Morning,' she heard Joe call from the bedroom, and she wondered if he'd guessed that she was hiding out in there. 'I know you're in there.'

The sound of his voice sent another shiver of recognition. British, and educated. But there was also a burr of something rugged about it, part of his northern upbringing that felt exotically 'authentic', when compared to the marble halls and polished accents of her childhood.

She risked peeking round the bathroom door and mumbled a good morning, wondering why she hadn't just left the minute that she'd woken up—running had always worked for her before. She'd been running from one catastrophe to another for as long as she could remember. Because this was her suite, she reminded herself. They'd been upgraded when the manager of the hotel had heard about their impromptu wedding, and realised that he had royalty and music royalty spending their wedding night in his hotel.

The only constant in her life since she'd left the palace in Afland had been her job. She'd worked from the bottom of the career ladder up to her position as an A&R executive, signing bands for an independent record label, Avalon. And that was the reason she had to get herself out of this room and face her new husband. Because not only was he a veritable rock god, he was also the artist that she'd been flown out here to charm, persuade and impress with her consummate professionalism in a last-ditch bid to get him to sign with her company.

She held her head high as she walked back into the bedroom, determined not to show him her feelings. The sun was coming in strong through the windows, and the backlighting meant that she couldn't quite see his expression.

'How's the head?' he asked, his expression changing to concerned.

She wondered whether she should tell him that she'd only had a couple of beers at most last night. That her recklessness hadn't come from alcohol, it had been fuelled by adrenaline and something more dangerous—the destructive path she found herself on all too often whenever marriage and family and the future entered the conversation.

Had Joe been drunk last night? She didn't think so. He'd seemed high when he'd come off stage, but she had been at enough gigs to know the difference between adrenaline and something less legal. She remembered him necking a beer, but that was it. So he didn't have that excuse either.

Why in God's name had this ever seemed like a good idea—to either of them?

'I've felt better,' she admitted, crossing the room to perch on the edge of the bed.

Up close, she decided that it really wasn't fair that he looked like this. His hair was artfully mussed by the pillows, his shirt was rumpled, and his tiny hint of eyeliner had smudged, but the whole look was so unforgivably sexy she almost forgot that whatever had happened the night before had been a huge mistake.

But sexy wasn't why she'd married him. Or maybe it was. When she went into reckless self-destruction mode, who was to say why she did anything?

Even in this oasis in the middle of the desert, she hadn't been able to escape the baggage that came with being a member of the royal family. The media obsession with royal women marrying and reproducing. Someone had raised a toast when they had seen her, to her impending marriage, asked her if she was up the duff and handed her a bottle of champagne. She'd been tempted to down the whole thing without taking a breath, determined to silence the voices in her head.

'So,' she said. 'I guess we're in trouble.'

Trouble? She was right about that. Everything about this woman said trouble. He had known it the minute that he had set eyes on her, all attitude and eyeliner.

He had known it for sure when they'd started dancing, her body moving in time with his. So at what point last night had trouble seemed like such a good idea?

When they'd left the dance floor, in that last club, their bodies hot and sticky. When she'd been trying to talk business but he'd been distracted by the humming of his skin and the sparks that leapt from his body to hers whenever she was near. When Ricky, the drummer in his band, had joked that he needed to show some real rock-star behaviour if they were going to sell the new album, and Joe had dropped to one knee and proposed.

He hadn't thought for a second that she would go along with it.

But Charlie had stopped for a moment as their eyes had met, and as everyone had laughed around them he had been able to see that she wasn't laughing, and neither was he. The club had stilled and quietened, or maybe it was just his mind that had, but suddenly there had been just the two of them, connected through something bigger than either of their bodies could contain. Something he couldn't pretend to comprehend, but that he knew meant that they understood each other.

And then she had nodded, thrown back her head and laughed along with everyone else, and they had been carried on a wave of adrenaline, bonhomie and contagious intoxication into a cab and up the steps of the courthouse. Somehow, still high from their performance and bewitched by the Princess, he hadn't stepped out of their fantasy and broken the spell.

They'd been cocooned in that buzz, carrying them straight through the ceremony. Such a laugh as they'd toppled out of the chapel. Right up until that kiss. Then it had all felt very real.

Did she remember that feeling as they had kissed for the first time? He knew in his bones that he could never forget it, as they were pronounced husband and wife.

'Are you going to hide in there all morning?' he asked.

In the daylight, she didn't look like a princess any more than she had the night before. Maybe that was how he'd found himself here. He'd expected to be on edge around her, but as soon as he had met her... Not that he was relaxed—no, there was too much going on, too much churning and yearning and *desire* to call it relaxed. But he'd been... He wasn't sure of the word. Her boss had sent her out here to convince him that their label was a good fit—and he'd been right. They had... Maybe fit was the right world. They'd just understood each other. She understood the music. Understood him. And when they had started dancing, there had been no question in his mind that this was important. He didn't know what it was, but he knew that he wanted more.

And marrying her—it had been a good move for the band. You couldn't buy publicity like that. He must have been thinking about that, must have calculated this as a business move. It was the only thing that made sense.

But was she expecting a marriage?

Because she came with a hell of a lot of baggage. Oh, he knew which fork to use, and how to spot the nasty ones in a room of over-privileged Henrys. He'd learned that much at his exclusive public school, where his music scholarship had taken him fee-free. But the most important part of his education had been the invaluable lesson he'd got in his last year—everyone was out to get something, so you'd better work out what you wanted in return.

The only place he felt relaxed these days was on the road, with his band. They moved from city to city, sometimes settling for a few weeks if they could hire some studio space, otherwise going from gig to gig, and woman to woman, without looking back. Everyone knowing exactly what they wanted, and taking what was on offer with no strings attached.

'Come on,' he said, reaching for her hand. As his fingertips touched hers he had another flash of that feeling from last night. The electric current that had joined them together as they had danced; that had woven such a spell around them that even a visit to a courthouse hadn't broken it.

'I can't believe we got married. This was your fault. Your idea.'

Was she for real? He shrugged and reminded her of the details. 'No one forced you. You seemed to think it was a great idea last night.'

So why was she looking at her ring as if it were burning her?

'Wh…?'

He waited to see which question was burning uppermost in her mind.

'Why? Why in God's name did I think it was a great idea?'

'How am I supposed to know if you don't? Maybe

you were thinking it would be good publicity for the album.'

He looked at her carefully. Yes, that was why they had done it. But also…no. There was more to it. He couldn't believe that she was such a stranger this morning. When they'd laughed about this last night, it hadn't just been a publicity stunt—that sounded too cold. It had been a joke, a deal, between friends. A publicity stunt was business, but last night, as they'd laughed together on the way to the courthouse, it had been more than that.

And maybe that was where he had gone wrong, because he knew how this worked. He knew that all relationships were deals, with each partner out to get what they wanted. He had no reason to be offended that she was acting like that this morning.

'I'm not sure why you're mad at me. You thought it was a great idea last night.'

'I hadn't slept for thirty-six hours, Joe. I think we can say that I wasn't doing my best reasoning. We have to undo this. What are my parents going to say?'

Her parents, the Queen of Afland and her husband. He groaned inwardly.

'Last night you said, and I quote, "They're going to go mental." As far as I could work out, that was a point in the plan's favour.'

In the cold light of morning—not such a good idea. Bad, in fact. Very bad.

He had married a princess—an actual blue-blooded, heir-to-the-throne, her-mother's-a-queen *princess*.

He was royally screwed.

'Look,' Joe said. 'I'm hungry, too hungry to talk

about this now. How about we go out for breakfast and discuss this with coffee and as much protein as they can cram on a plate?'

CHAPTER TWO

CHARLIE GAZED INTO her black coffee, hoping that it would supply answers. Her memories had started to filter back in as she'd sipped her first cup; shame had started creeping in with her second. She hoped that this cup, her third, would be the one that made her feel human again.

'So how do we undo this?' she said bluntly. 'This is Vegas. They must annul almost as many marriages as they make here. Do we need to go back to the courthouse?'

She looked up and met Joe's eye. He was watching her intently as he took a bite of another slice of toast. 'We could,' he said. 'If we want an annulment, I guess that's how we go about it.'

'If?' She nearly spat out her coffee. 'I don't think you understand, Joe. We got *married*.'

'I know: I was there.'

'Am I missing something? The way I see things, we were joking around, we thought it would be hil*ar*ious to have a Vegas wedding, and we've woken up this morning to a major disaster. Aren't you interested in damage limitation?'

'Of course I am, but, unlike you, I think the reasons we got married were sound. Not necessarily the *best* reasons to enter into a legally binding personal commitment, but sound nonetheless.'

She raised her eyebrows. 'Remind me.'

'Okay, obvious ones first. Publicity. The band needs it. The album is almost finished, we're looking for a new label, and there is no such thing as bad publicity, right?'

'Mercenary much?'

'Look, this isn't my fault. You were good with mercenary last night.'

She snorted. 'Fine, publicity is one reason. Give me another.'

'It shows you're serious about the band.'

She crossed her arms and sat back in her seat, fixing him with a glare. 'I've signed plenty of bands before without marrying the lead singer. They signed with me because they trust that I'm bloody good at my job. Are you seriously telling me that whether or not I would marry you was going to be a deal-breaker?'

He leaned forward, not put off by her death stare. In fact, his eyes softened as he reached for her hand, pulling her back towards him. She went with it, not wanting to look childish by batting him away.

'Of course it wasn't,' he said gently. 'But breaking the marriage now? I'm not sure how that's going to play out. I'm not sure what our working relationship could look like with that all over the papers.'

She shook her head, looking back into the depths of her coffee, still begging it for answers.

'All of which I have to weigh against the heartbreak of my family if we don't bury this right now.'

She avoided eye contact as she tried to stop the

tears from escaping. But she took a deep breath and when she looked up they were gone. 'Do you think anyone knows already? The press?'

'We weren't exactly discreet,' he said, with a sympathetic smile. 'I'd think it's likely.'

'And that can't be undone, annulment or not.'

He leaned back and took a long drink of his orange juice. 'So let's control the narrative.'

'What do you mean?'

'What story would hurt your family more—a whirlwind romance and hasty Vegas marriage, or a drunken publicity stunt to further your career? Because that's how the tabloids are going to want to spin it.'

'What's your point, Joe?' She'd taken her hand back and crossed her arms again, sure that this conversation was taking a turn that she wasn't going to like.

'All I'm saying is that we can't go back in time. We can't get unmarried, whether we get an annulment or not. So we either dissolve the marriage today and deal with the fallout to our reputations…'

'Or…?'

'Or we stay married.'

Her breathing caught as just for a second she considered what that might mean, to be this man's wife.

'But we're not in love. Anyone's going to be able to see that.'

He scrutinised her from under his lashes, which were truly longer and thicker than any man's had a right to be. 'So we're going to have to work hard to convince them. You can't deny that it's a better story.'

'And you can't deny that it means lying to my family. Ruining all the plans they were making for my life.

I don't know what your relationship with your family is like, but I'm not sure that I can pull it off. I'm not sure that I want to. Things are diffi—'

She stopped before she revealed too much. Joe raised an eyebrow, obviously curious about why she had cut herself off, but he didn't push her on it.

'Would you rather they knew the truth?'

Of course not. She had been hiding the truth from them for years, ever since she'd found out that she could never be the daughter or the Princess that they needed her to be.

'Are we seriously having this conversation? You want to stay married? You do know that you're a rock star, right? If you were that desperate for publicity you could have found a hundred girls who actually *wanted* to be your wife.'

'Wow, you're quite something for a guy's ego. For the record, this isn't some elaborate ruse to get myself a woman. I don't have any problems on that score. All I'm doing is making the best of a situation. That's all.'

Charlie took a big bite of pie, hoping that the sugar would succeed where the coffee hadn't. 'Well, I'm glad to hear that you're not remotely interested in me as a woman.'

He fixed her with a meaningful stare, the intensity of his expression making it impossible for her to look away.

'I never said that.'

Heat rose in her belly as he held the eye contact, leaving her in no doubt about how he thought of her. She shook her head as he finally broke the contact. 'I can't believe that I'm even considering this. You're crazy. There's no way we can keep this up. What happens if we slip? What happens when someone finds out it's not for real? What happens when one of us meets someone and this marriage of convenience isn't so convenient any more?'

He reached for her hand across the table, and once again there was that crackle, that spark that she remembered from the night before. She saw him in the chapel, eyes creased in laughter, as he leaned in to kiss her. Those eyes were still in front of her, concerned now though, rather than amused.

'It doesn't have to be for ever. Just long enough that it doesn't look like a stunt when we split. You weren't planning on marrying someone else any time soon, were you?'

'Never.' Her coffee cup rattled onto the saucer with a clash, liquid spilling over the top.

'Wow—that really was a no.'

She locked her gaze on his—he had to understand this if they were going to go on. 'I mean it, Joe. I didn't want to get married. Ever. I'm not wife material.'

'And yet here I am, married to you.'

He held her gaze and there was something familiar there. Something that made her stomach tighten in a knot and her skin prickle in awareness. With all the unexpected drama of finding themselves married, it seemed as if they'd both temporarily forgotten that they had also found themselves in bed together that morning.

Perhaps he was remembering something similar, because all of a sudden there was a new fire in his eyes, a new heat in the way that he was looking at her.

Her memory might be a bit ropey, but between the caffeine and the sugar her brain had been pretty much put back together, and there was one image of the night before that she couldn't get from her mind.

You may now kiss the bride.

They'd all burst out laughing, finding the whole thing hilarious. But as soon as Joe's hand had brushed against her cheek, cupping her jaw to turn her face up to him, the laughs had died in her throat. He'd been looking down at her as if he were only just seeing her for the first time, as if she had been made to look different by their marriage. His lush eyelashes had swept shut as he'd leaned towards her, and she'd had just a second to catch her breath before his lips had touched hers. They had been impossibly soft, and to start with had just pressed dry and chaste against hers. She'd reached up as he had and touched his cheek, just a gentle, friendly caress of her finger against his stubbled skin. But it had seemed to snap something within him; a gasp had escaped his lips, been swallowed by hers. His mouth had parted, and heat had flared between them.

She'd closed her eyes, understood that she was giving herself up to something more powerful than the simple actions of two individuals. As her eyes had shut her mouth had opened and her body had bowed towards her husband. Her hips had met his, and instantly sparks had crackled. His hands had left her face to lock around her waist, dragging her in tight and holding her against him. His tongue had been hot and hungry in her mouth; her hands frenzied, exploring the contours of his chest, his back, his butt.

And then the applause of their audience had broken into her consciousness, and she'd remembered where they were. What they were doing.

Blood had rushed to her cheeks and she could feel them glow as she'd broken away from Joe, acknowledging the whoops with an ironic wave.

'All right, all right,' she'd said, a sip of champagne helping with the brazen nonchalance; she'd hoped that she was successfully hiding the shake in her voice. 'Hope you enjoyed the show, people.'

She'd looked up at Joe to see whether she had imagined the connection between them, whether he'd still felt it buzzing and humming and trying to pull their bodies back together. By the heated, haunted look in his eyes, she wasn't alone in this.

He was worried, and he should be, because this marriage of convenience had just got a whole lot more complicated, for both of them. It had been a laugh, a joke, until their lips had met and they had both realised, simultaneously, that the flirting and banter that had provided an edge of excitement to their dancing that night would be a dangerous force unless they got a lid on it.

In the cold light of the morning after, she knew that they needed to face the problem head-on. She broke her gaze away from him, trying to cover what they had both clearly been remembering.

'Ground rules,' she said firmly, distracting herself by taking another bite of pie. 'If we do this, there have to be ground rules to stop it getting complicated.' He nodded in agreement, and she kept talking. 'First of all, we keep this strictly business. We both need to keep our heads and be able to walk away when the time is right. Let's acknowledge that there is chemistry between us, but if we let that lead us, we're not going to be objective and make smart decisions. And I think we both agree that we need to be smart.'

'People will talk if we don't make this look good. It has to be convincing.'

'Well, duh.' She waved to the waitress for a coffee refill. 'You're really trying to teach me how to handle the press? Obviously, in public we behave as if we're so madly in love that we couldn't wait a single minute longer to get married. We sell the hell out of it and make sure that no one has a choice *but* to believe us. But that's in public. In private, we're respectful colleagues.'

He snorted. 'Colleagues? You think we can do that? You were there, weren't you, last night? You do remember?'

Did she remember the kiss? The shivers? The way that she could still feel the imprint of his mouth on hers, as if the touch of skin on skin had permanently altered the cells? Yeah, she remembered, but that wasn't what was important here.

'And that's why we need the rules, Joe. If you want to stay married to me, you'd better listen up and pay attention.'

'Oh, I'm listening, and you're very clear. In public, I'm madly in love with you. Behind closed doors I'm at arm's length. Got it. So what are your other rules?'

She resurrected the death stare. 'No cheating. Ever. If we're going to make people believe this, they have to really believe it. We can't risk the story being hijacked. Doesn't matter how discreet you think you're being, it's never enough.'

'I get it. You don't share. Goes without saying.'

She dropped her cup back onto her saucer a little

heavier than she had planned, and the hot, bitter liquid slopped over the side again. 'This isn't about me, Joe. Don't pretend to know me. This is about appearances. I've already told you, this isn't personal.'

'Fine, well, if you're all done then I've got a rule of my own.'

'Go on, then.' She raised an eyebrow in anticipation.

'You move in with me.'

This time, the whole cup went over, coffee sloshing over the side of the table and onto her faded black jeans. At least she'd managed to miss her white shirt, she thought, thanking whoever was responsible for small mercies. She mopped hastily with a handful of napkins, buying her precious moments to regain her composure and think about what he had said. Of course she understood deep down that they would have to live together. But somehow, until he'd said it out loud, she hadn't believed it.

They would be alone together. *Living* alone together. No one to chaperone or keep them to their 'this is just business' word. Watching him across a diner table this morning, it wasn't exactly easy to keep her hands off him, so how were they meant to do that living alone together?

But she knew better than anyone that they had to make this look good. If her parents knew that she'd only done this to get out of the marriage to Philippe they would be so disappointed, and she didn't know that she could take doing that to them again.

Separate flats weren't going to cut it. By the time she looked back up, she knew that she seemed calm, regardless of what was going on underneath.

'Of course, that makes sense. Are you going to insist on your place rather than mine?'

'I'll need my recording studio.'

She nodded. 'Fine. So that's it, then? Three ground rules and we're just going to do this?'

'Well, if you're going to chicken out, you need to do it now.'

'I'm not eight years old, Joe. I'm not going to go through with this because you call me chicken.'

'Fine, why *are* you going to do it?' Nice use of psychology there, she thought. Act as though I've already agreed. He really did want this publicity. But it didn't matter, because she'd already made up her mind.

'I'm doing it because I don't want to hurt my family any more than I have to, and because I think it'll be good for my career.' And because it would save her from being talked into a real marriage, one which she knew she could never deserve.

'As long as you're doing it, your reasons are your own business,' Joe replied. She felt a little sting at that, like a brush of nettles against bare skin. Her own business. Damn right it was, but the way he said it, as if there really were nothing more than that between them… It didn't make sense. She didn't want it to make sense. She just knew that she didn't want it to hurt.

'So what are we going to tell people?' she asked after a long, awkward silence. 'I guess we need to get our stories straight.'

He nodded, and sipped at his coffee. 'We just keep it simple. We were swept away when we met each other yesterday, knew right away that it was love and decided we needed to be married. The guys in the

band will go along with it. You don't have to worry
about that.' Somehow she'd forgotten that they'd been
there, egging them on, bundling them in the cab to the
courthouse. When she thought back to last night, she
remembered watching Joe on stage, sweat dripping
from his forehead as he sang and rocked around the
stage. Him grabbing her hand and pulling her to the
dance floor when they'd gone on to a club after the
gig, when he hadn't wanted to talk business.

She remembered the touch of his mouth on hers, as
they were pronounced husband and wife.

But of course there had been witnesses, people who
knew as well as she did that this was all a sham.

'What if they say something? They could go to
the press.'

'They won't. Anyway, to everyone else it was just
a laugh. And if anyone did say something, it'd be up
to us to look so convincingly in love that no one could
possibly believe them.'

'Ah, easy as that, huh.'

As they sat in the diner she realised how little
thought they'd actually given this. She didn't even
know when she would see him again. Her flight was
booked back to London that night. She'd only been
in Vegas to take this meeting. Her boss had sent her
on a flying visit, instructed to try anything to get him
to sign. She'd given her word that she wouldn't leave
without the deal done. Would he see through them
when they got back? Would he realise how far she
had gone to keep to her promise?

'I'm flying home tonight,' she said.

He raised an eyebrow. 'You were pretty sure you'd

get me to sign, then. Didn't think you'd have to stick around to convince me?'

'I thought you'd be on the move, actually. I was told that you were only in Vegas for one night.' She knew that the band were renowned for their work ethic and their packed tour schedule, moving from city to city and gig to gig night after night. This had been her only chance for a meeting, her boss had told her as he'd instructed her to book a flight.

If he was always on the move like that, perhaps this would be easier than she thought. It could be weeks, months, before they actually had to live together. And by then, maybe… Maybe what. Maybe things would be different? There was no point pretending to be married at all if she thought that they would have changed their minds in a few weeks. They had to stick it out longer than that. If they were going to do this, they had to do it properly.

'I am, as it happens. I'm flying back to London tonight too.'

Why had he said that? They were meant to be in the States for two more weeks. Their manager had booked them into a retreat so that he could finish writing the new album. It should have been just a case of putting the finishing touches to a few songs, but he had an uneasy feeling about it this morning. He needed to go back and look at it again. There were a few decent tracks there, he was sure. But a niggling voice in his head was telling him that he still hadn't got the big hitters. The singles that would propel the album up the streaming charts and across the radio waves.

There was studio space booked for them in London in two weeks' time and it had to be fixed before then.

Their manager was going to kill him when he told him he wouldn't be showing up.

He could write in London; he had written the last album in London. It had nothing to do with Charlie. Nothing to do with her feelings, anyway. As she kept saying, this was just business. But it would look better for them to arrive home together.

Nothing to do with their feelings. Right. He would make her believe that today. Because her memory might be fuzzy but he could remember everything. Including the moment that they'd been on the dance floor, him still buzzing from the adrenaline of being on stage, her from the dancing and the music and the day and a half without sleep.

They'd moved together as the music had coursed through him, the bass vibrating his skin. She'd been trying to talk business, shouting in his ear. Contracts and terms, and commitment. But he hadn't been able to see past her. To feel anything more than the skin of her shoulder under his hand as he'd leaned in to speak in her ear. The soft slide of her hair as he'd brushed it off her face. 'Let's do this,' she'd said. 'We'd be a great team. I know that we can create something amazing together.'

She'd reached up then, making sure she had his attention—as if it would ever be anywhere but on her again. And then Ricky had said those idiotic words, the ones that no judge could take back this morning.

She'd laughed, at first, when he had proposed, assuming that he was joking. It had had nothing to do with the way she'd felt when his arm was around her. The way that that had made him feel. As if he wanted to protect her and challenge her and be challenged by her all at once.

He could never let her know how he had felt last night.

It was much better, much safer that they kept this as business. He knew what happened when you went into a relationship without any calculation. When you jumped in with your heart on the line and no defences. He wouldn't be doing it again.

And then there were the differences between them. Sure, it hadn't seemed to matter in that moment that he'd asked her to marry him, or when they were dancing and laughing and joking together, but a gig and a nightclub and beer were great levellers. When you were having to scream above the music then your accent didn't matter. But in the diner this morning there was no hiding her carefully Londonised RP that one could only acquire with decades of very expensive schooling, and learning to speak in the echoey ballrooms of city palaces and country piles.

He'd learnt that when he'd joined one of those expensive schools at the age of eleven, courtesy of his music scholarship free ride. His Bolton accent had been smoothed slightly by years away from home, first at school, and then on the road, but it would always be there. And he knew that, like the difference in their backgrounds, it would eventually come between them.

His experiences at school had made it clear that he didn't belong there.

And when he'd returned home to his parents, and

their comfy semi-detached in the suburbs, he had re-alised that he didn't belong there any more either. He was caught between two worlds, not able to settle in either. So the last thing that he needed was to be paraded in front of the royal family, no doubt com-ing into contact with the Ruperts and Sebastians and Hugos from his school days.

And what about his family? Was Charlie going to come round for a Sunday roast? Make small talk with his mum with Radio 2 playing in the background? He couldn't picture it.

But he would have to, he realised. Because it didn't matter what they were doing in private. It didn't mat-ter that he had told himself that he absolutely had to get these feelings under control, their worlds were about to collide.

It wasn't permanent. That was what he had to re-mind himself. It wasn't for ever. They were going to end this once a decent amount of time had passed, and in the meantime they would just have to fit into each other's lives as best they could.

Just think of the publicity. A whirlwind romance was a good story. No doubt a better one than a drunken mistake. But since when had he allowed the papers to rule on what was and wasn't a good idea for him? No, there was more to it than that. Something about waking up beside her in bed that he wasn't ready to let go of yet.

'I have an album launch party to go to first, though,' he said at last. 'What do you say to making our first appearance as husband and wife?'

CHAPTER THREE

CHARLIE ADJUSTED THE strap on her spike heels and straightened the seam of her leather leggings. As soon as the car door opened, she knew there would be a tsunami of flashes from the assembled press hordes. She was considered fair game at the best of times, and if news of the wedding had got out by now, the scrum would be worse than usual.

These shots needed to be perfect. She wasn't having her big moment hijacked by a red circle of shame.

It was funny, she thought, that neither she nor Joe had called his manager, or her boss yet, and told them about what had happened. Not the best start to a publicity campaign, which was, after all, what they had agreed this marriage was. It was more natural, this way, she thought. If there was a big announcement, it would look too fake. Much better for them to let the story grow organically.

As the limo pulled up outside the club she realised that no announcement was necessary anyway. Word had obviously got around. The hotel had arranged for them to be picked up from a discreet back door, an old habit, so she hadn't been sure whether there had been photographers waiting for her there. If there had, they'd taken a shortcut to beat them here. There were definitely more press here than a simple album launch warranted. The story was out, then.

Without thinking, she slipped her hand into Joe's, sliding her fingers between his. The sight of so many photographers still made her nervous. It didn't matter how many times she had faced them. It reminded her of those times in her childhood when she'd been pulled from the protective privacy of her family home and paraded in front of the world's press, all looking for that perfect picture of the perfect Princess. As a child she had smiled until her cheeks had ached, dressed in her prettiest pink dress, turning this way and that as her name was shouted. It had been a small price to pay, her parents had explained, to make sure that the rest of their lives were private. But as she'd got older she'd resented those days more and more, and her childish rictus grin had turned into a sullen teen grimace.

And then, when she was nineteen, and had realised that she would never be the Princess that her family and her country wanted her to be, she'd stopped smiling altogether. She remembered sitting in the doctor's office as he explained what he'd found: inflammation, scar tissue, her ovaries affected. Possible problems conceiving.

She might never have a baby, no chubby little princes or princesses to parade in front of an adoring public, and no hope of making the sort of dynastic match that would make her parents happy.

Her most important duty as a royal female was to continue her family's line. It had been drummed into her from school history lessons to formal state occasions from as far back as she could remember. Queens who had done their duty and provided little princes and princesses to continue the family line.

And things hadn't changed as much as we would all like to think, she knew. The country had liked her mother when she was a shining twenty-something. But it was when she'd given the country three beautiful royal children that they'd really fallen in love with her, when she had won their loyalty. And that was something that Charlie might never be able to do. She might never feel the delicious weight of her child in her arms. Never breathe in the smell of a new baby knowing that it was all hers.

What if she never made her parents grandparents, and saw the pride and love in their eyes that she knew they were reserving for that occasion?

And as soon as she'd realised that, she had realised that she could never make them truly proud of her, somehow the weight of responsibility had fallen from her shoulders and she'd decided that she was never going back. If she wanted to roll out of a nightclub drunk—okay. If she wanted to disappear for three days, without letting anyone know where she was going—fine. If she wanted to skip a family event to go and listen to a new band—who cared?

Her mother insisted on a security detail, and Charlie had given up arguing that one. Her only demand was that they were invisible—she never looked for the smartly dressed man she knew must be on the row behind her on the plane, and so she never saw him. And the officers didn't report back to her mother. If she thought for a second that they would, she would have pulled the plug on the whole arrangement. That was why they'd not intervened last night: they knew she had a zero-tolerance approach to them interfering with anything that didn't affect her physical safety.

She was never going to be the perfect Princess, so why build her family's hopes up? She could let them down now, get it out of the way, in her own way, and not have to worry with blindsiding them with disappointment later.

Except it hurt to disappoint them, and it didn't seem to matter how many times that she did it. Every time, the look on their faces was as bad as the time before.

What would they say this time, she wondered, when they realised that she had married someone she had just met—so obviously to scupper the sensible match that they were trying to make for her? And she had married a rock star at that, someone who couldn't be further from the nice reliable boys that they enjoyed steering her towards at private family functions. What was the point of going along with that? she'd always thought. Entertaining the Lord Sebastians and Duc Philippes and Count Henris who were probably distant cousins, and who all—to a man—would run a mile as soon as they found out that they might not be needing that place at Eton or Charterhouse, or wherever they'd put their future son's name down for school before they had even bagged the ultimate trophy wife.

Joe leaned past her to look out of the window, and then gave her a pointed look. 'I guess our happy news is out.'

'Looks that way,' she said, with a hesitant smile. 'Ready to face the hordes?'

'As I'll ever be.' He looked confident, though, and relaxed. As if he'd been born to a life in front of the cameras, whereas she, who had attended her first photo call at a little under a day old, still came out in a sweat at the sight of a paparazzo.

But she stuck on what she'd come to think of as her Princess Scowl, in the style of a London super-model, and pressed her knees and ankles together. It was second nature, after so many hours of etiquette lessons. Even in skin-tight leather, where there was no chance of an accidental underwear flash. She ran a hand through her hair, messing up the backcombed waves and dragging it over to one side in her trade-mark style. A glance in the rear-view mirror told her that her red lip stain was still good to go, managing to look just bitten and just kissed. She took a deep breath and reached for the door handle.

Joe stopped her with the touch of his fingertips on her knee. 'Wait.'

It was as if the leather melted away and those fin-gertips were burning straight into her skin. Wait? For ever, if she had to.

But before she could say, or do, anything, they were gone, as was Joe. Out of the door and into the bear pit. Then her door was wrenched open and his hand was there, waiting to pull her out into the bright des-ert sunshine. She gripped his hand as he helped her from the car, and the flashbulbs were going off before she was even on her feet.

Shouts reached her from every direction.

'When was the wedding?'

'Was Elvis there?'

'Were you drunk?'

And then there it was, the question that she'd never

anticipated but that she realised now had been inevitable from the first.

'Are you pregnant?'

She stumbled, and it was only Joe's arm clamping round her waist and pulling her tight that stopped her falling on her face in front of the world's press. And then she was falling anyway, because Joe's lips were on hers, and her heart was racing and her legs were jelly and her lips…her lips were on fire. One of his hands had bunched in her hair, and she realised that this, this look, this feeling, was what she'd been cultivating in front of the mirror for more years than she cared to think about. Just been kissed, just been ravished. Just had Joe's tongue in her mouth and hands on her body. Just had images of hot and sweaty and naked racing through her mind. He broke away and gave her a conspiratorial smile. She bit her lip, her mouth still just an inch from his, wondering how she was meant to resist going back for more.

And then the shouts broke back into her consciousness. 'Go on—one more, Charlie!'

And the spell was broken. She wasn't going to give them what they wanted. She turned to them, scowl back in place, though there was a glow now in the middle of her chest, something that they couldn't see, something that they couldn't try and own, to sell for profit.

She grabbed Joe's hand and pulled him towards the door of the venue, ignoring the shouts from the photographers.

She dragged him through the door and into a quiet corner.

'So I guess we survived our first photo call.'

She had hoped the relative seclusion of this dark corner would give her a chance to settle her nerves, for her heartbeat to slow and her hands to stop shaking. But as Joe took another step closer to her and blocked everything else from her vision, she felt anything but relaxed.

'Are you okay? You look kind of flushed,' he asked.

'I'm fine. I just hate…never mind.' Her voice dropped away as her gaze fixed on his lips and she couldn't break it away. This wasn't the time to think about what she hated, not when she was so fixed on what she loved, what she couldn't get enough of. Like the feeling of his lips on hers.

'Joe, I thought I saw you come in. And the new missus!'

Ricky, the drummer from Joe's band, Charlie recognised with a jolt.

More flashbacks of the night before: the band laughing with them in the taxi cab to the courthouse, joking about how they were going to have to sign with her now she'd done this. She had to convince them that they'd been mistaken last night. That she'd married Joe for love at first sight, before they started talking to journalists. If it wasn't already too late.

She reached for Joe's hand and gripped it tightly in hers, hoping that it communicated everything that she needed it to.

'Hi, Ricky,' she said, plastering on a smile that she hoped broadcast newly wedded bliss and contentment.

'So your first day as husband and wife, eh. How's it working out for you?'

She tried to read into his smile what he was really saying. If only she could fake a blush, or a morning-after glow. But in the absence of that, she'd have to go on the offensive.

'Pretty bloody amazingly, actually,' she said, leaning into Joe and hoping that he'd run with this, with her.

'Really?'

Ricky gave Joe a pointed look, and it told Charlie everything that she needed to know. He had thought last night that this was all a publicity stunt, and nothing that he had seen yet had changed his mind.

'Well, I'm just glad that you both decided to take one for the team.' He grinned. 'It was a brilliant idea. I wish I'd thought of it first.'

She opened her mouth to speak, but Joe got there first.

'I'm not sure what you mean, Ricky. We're not doing this for the team. I admit it was a bit hasty, but we really meant it last night. We wanted to get married.'

'Because you're both so madly in love?'

She felt Joe's hand twitch in hers and tried not to read too much into it.

'Because it was the only thing we *could* do,' he said. 'I don't care what we call it. Love at first sight. Or lust. Whatever. I just knew that once I had Charlie in my arms there was no way I was going to let her go. And if that meant marriage, then that's what I wanted.'

Bloody hell, maybe he should have been an actor rather than a singer. He certainly gave that little speech more than a little authenticity. She leaned into him again, and this time he dropped her hand and wrapped his arm around her shoulders. She looked up at him, and there was something about the expression in his face that forced her up onto her tiptoes to kiss him gently on the lips.

'Wow, okay,' Ricky said as she broke away. 'I guess I missed something last night. So, someone wants to chat with us about the new album, if you've got a minute.'

'Okay,' Joe replied, 'but you do remember what we decided last night. We're going to say yes to Charlie's label. I'm not going back on my word.'

'A bit early in the marriage for those sorts of ructions, is it?' Ricky looked at them carefully, and Charlie knew that they hadn't dispelled all of his doubts, regardless of how good an actor Joe was. 'Either way, we still need to speak to them. Until this deal is signed, we schmooze everyone, as far as I'm concerned. I know the others feel the same.'

She *had* to call her boss. She couldn't think why she hadn't done it before now. She'd do it on the way to the plane. She glanced at her watch. They couldn't stay long if they were going to make the flight. For a second she thought wistfully of her family's private plane, and how much easier life had been when she'd been happy to go along with that lifestyle, to take what she didn't feel she had earned. But it had got to the point where she simply couldn't do it any more. If she was never going to be able to pay her parents back with the one thing that everyone wanted from her, she couldn't use their money or their privilege any more.

She had some money left to her by her grandparents—despite her protestations, the lawyers had told her that it belonged to her and there was nothing that she could do about it—and her salary from the record label.

'I'm sorry, do you mind if I talk to them?' Joe asked, turning to her.

'Of course not.' She forced a smile, trying to live in the moment and forget all of the very good reasons she should be freaking out right now. 'Go on.'

But Joe turned to Ricky. 'You go ahead,' he said. 'I'll be there in a second.'

'You all right?' he asked, when they were alone. 'Still happy with everything? Because if you're going to change your mind, now's the time…'

She drew away from him and folded her arms. 'Why would I have changed my mind?'

She didn't understand what had happened to cause this change in mood. His shoulders were tense, she could see that.

Was it because he'd just reminded Ricky of their deal to sign with her the night before? The thought made her feel slightly sick, reminded her that whatever they might say to his band, whatever story they might spin for the papers, when it came down to it, this really *was* just a publicity stunt, or a business arrangement or…whatever. Whatever it was, she knew what it wasn't. It hadn't been love at first sight. It wasn't a grand romance. It wasn't a fairy tale, and there was going to be no happy ending for her. Well, fine, it wasn't like she deserved one anyway.

But now that they were married, they had to make it work. They had to appear to be intoxicated with one another. Luckily, intoxicated was one of her fortes. She forced herself to unfold her arms and smile. 'Of course I'm all right.'

Taking a deep breath, she stepped towards him, and with a questioning look in her eye snaked her arms around those tense shoulders. She placed another chaste peck on his lips, and smiled as she drew away. 'See? Picture perfect. Everything's as we agreed. Let's go say hi to everyone.'

Under the pressure of her arms, she felt his shoulders relax and his face melted into a smile. 'Well, we could give them something to talk about first.'

His arms wrapped around her waist, and she was reminded of the rush of adrenaline and hormones that she had felt outside when he had kissed her in front of the cameras. Her breath caught as her body softened into his hold. This time when his lips met hers, there was nothing chaste about it. Her arms tightened around him as he lifted her just ever so slightly, rubbing her hips against his as she slid up his body. His arms wrapped her completely, so that her ribs were bracketed with muscular forearms, and his hands met the indents of her waist. She was surrounded by him. Overwhelmed by the dominance of his body over hers.

His mouth dominated her too, demanding everything that she could give, and it was only with the touch of his tongue that she remembered where they were. She pushed both hands on his chest, forcing him to give her space, to unwind his arms from around her waist.

She smiled as she looked at him, both of them still dazed from the effect of the kiss. 'Do you think they bought it?' she asked, remembering that just a few moments ago they had been discussing the fact that this relationship was just a business deal—that the purpose of the kiss had been to keep up appearances. But Joe's face fell, and she knew that she had said the wrong thing.

'I think they bought it fine,' he said. 'It was a winning performance.'

Through the bite of his teeth, she knew that it wasn't a compliment.

She shook her head, then reached up and pecked him one last time on the cheek. 'Whatever it was, it blew my mind.' She met his eyes, and she knew that he saw that she was genuine. Whatever else might be going on, there was no denying the chemistry between them. It would be stupid to even try.

But beyond that, beyond the crazy hormones that made her body ache to be near his, was there something else too? A reason that the disappointment in his eyes made some part of her body hurt? She slipped her fingers between his and they walked over to where Ricky was holding court with a woman that she recognised from another record label, her competition, and a music journalist.

'So here's the happy couple,' the hack said with a smile, raising her glass to toast them. Charlie spotted a waiter passing with a tray of champagne and grabbed a flute for herself and one for Joe. She saw off half the glass with her first sip, until she felt she could stare down the journalist with impunity.

She watched Joe as they chatted, her hand trapped within his, and tried not to think about whether the warm glow of possessiveness she felt was because she'd bagged him as an artist, or a husband.

As they walked through Arrivals at Heathrow Airport, Joe felt suddenly hesitant at the thought of taking Charlie back to his apartment, definitely not something he was used to. It wasn't as if he were a stranger to taking girls home. Though in fairness home was more usually a hotel room or their place. But now that he and Charlie were back on British soil, he realised how little they'd talked about how this was going to work.

'So we said we'd stay at my place,' he reminded her as they headed towards the end of another endlessly long corridor.

'We did,' she agreed, and he looked at her closely, trying to see if there was more he could glean from these two words. But he had forgotten that his new wife was a pro at hiding her feelings—she'd had a lifetime of practice. Charlie offered nothing else, so he pushed, wanting the matter settled before they had to face the press, who were no doubt waiting for them again at the exit of the airport. Airport security did what they could to push them back, but couldn't keep them away completely. Not that he should want that, he reminded himself. They wanted the publicity. It was good for the band. It was the whole reason they were still married.

But even good publicity wasn't as important as finishing a new album would be—that thought hadn't been far from his mind the last few days. He couldn't understand how he had thought that it was nearly finished. He'd played the demo tracks over and over on the plane, and somehow the songs that he'd fine-tuned and polished so carefully no longer worked when he listened to them. They didn't make him *feel*. They had a veneer of artifice that seemed to get worse, rather than better, the more that he heard them.

His first album had come from the heart. He shuddered inwardly at the cliché. It was years' worth of pent-up emotion and truths not said, filtered through his guitar and piano. It was honest. It was him. This latest attempt... It was okay. A half-dozen of the tracks he would happily listen to in the background of a bar. But it was clean and safe and careful, and lacking the winners. The grandstanding, show-stopping singles that took an album from good to legendary.

He was still writing. Still trying. But he was out of material and out of inspiration. His adolescent experiences, his adult life of running from them had fed his imagination and his muse for one bestselling album. But he couldn't mine the same stuff for a second. It needed something new. So what was he meant to write about—how ten years on the road made relationships impossible? How his parents kept up with his news by reading whatever the tabloids had made up that week? That his only good friends had spent most of that time trapped with him in some mode of transport or another for the last decade? It was hardly rousing stuff.

'Do you want to go back there now, then?' he asked Charlie.

How was this so difficult? Was she making it that way on purpose?

She looked down at her carry-on bag. 'This is all I have with me.'

'We can send someone for your stuff.'

'No.' She didn't want anyone riffling through her things. Occasionally she missed the discreet staff from her childhood home in the private apartments of the palace, who had disappeared the dirty clothes from her bedroom floor before it had had a chance to become a proper teenage dive, but she loved the freedom of her home being truly private. That the leather jacket that she dropped by the door when she got home would still be right there when she was heading out the next morning.

She stopped walking and looked up at him. 'Okay, so we go back to yours tonight. Tomorrow we go to my place and pack some stuff. Does that work for you? Or I could go back to my place tonight. Sleep there, if we don't want to rush into—'

'You sleep with me.'

He couldn't explain the shot of old-fashioned possessiveness that he had felt when she suggested that they sleep apart. Except… The bed share of the previous night. That was a one-off, wasn't it? He supposed they'd find out later, when she realised that his apartment's second bedroom had been converted to a recording studio. Leaving them with one king-sized bed and one very stylish but supremely uncomfortable couch to fight over. He was many things, but chivalrous about sleeping arrangements wasn't one of them. He couldn't remember the last time that he had slept eight hours in a bed that wasn't hurtling along a motorway or through the clouds. So he could promise her a chivalrous pillow barrier if she absolutely insisted, but there was no way he was forgoing his bed. Not even for her.

'For appearances' sake,' he added to his earlier comment. 'What would it look like if we spent our first night back apart?'

CHAPTER FOUR

'WHEN ARE WE going to tell our families?' Joe asked as the driver slid the car away from the kerb, and the throng of photographers who had been waiting for them grew distant in the rear window.

He was probably just hoping to fill the awkward silence, Charlie thought, rather than trying to bait her. But the niggle of guilt that had been eating away at her turned into a full-on stab. She really should have called her parents before she had left the States, but she had just kept thinking about how disappointed they were going to be in her—again—and she couldn't bring herself to do it.

But now they had another load of morning editions of the tabloids to worry about, full of their red-carpet kisses from the night before. Or was it two nights? Losing a day to the time difference when they were in the air hadn't helped her jet lag, or her sense of dislocation from the world. Whenever it was that those kisses had taken place, somehow, she didn't think that they were going to help matters.

'When we get home,' she said, cracking open a bottle of mineral water and leaning back against the leather headrest. In theory she had just had a eleven-hour flight with nothing to do but catch up on missed sleep. And it wasn't even as if she and Joe had spent the time chatting and getting to know one another. He had pulled out noise-cancelling headphones as soon as he was on board and she'd barely heard a word from him after that.

She'd shut her eyes too, pulled on a sleep mask and tried to drift off. But sleep had been impossible. First her mind had run round in circles with recriminations and criticisms; then slowly, something else had crept in. The scent of Joe's aftershave, the drumming of his fingers on the armrest as he got into whatever he was listening to. Her body remembered how she had felt that morning waking up next to him, after her dream filled with hot, sticky caresses. Before her memory returned and she remembered the idiotic thing that they had done. When he was just a hot guy in her head and not the man she had married in a fit of self-sabotage. Lust, pure and simple.

Things were anything but simple now. Attraction could be simple. A marriage of convenience could be simple too, she supposed. She was the product of generations of them. But she and Joe had gone and mixed the two, and now they were paying the price. As Joe shifted on the seat beside her she opened her eyes and watched him for a few moments.

Their late night followed by a long, sleepless flight had left him with a shadow on his jaw that was more midnight than five o'clock. She could almost feel the scratch of it against her cheek if she shut her eyes again and concentrated. She snapped herself out of it. Too dangerous. *Far* too dangerous to be having those sorts of feelings about this man. They had made this arrangement complicated enough as it was. Attraction made it more complicated still. Acting on that attraction anywhere but in the safety of the public gaze was complete madness. No, they were just going to have to get really, really good at self-restraint. She was so looking forward to shutting her bedroom door on Joe and the rest of the world and finally being able to relax and sleep off the jet lag.

Their driver hauled their bags up the stairs to his first-floor warehouse conversion, and Charlie breathed a sigh of relief when they shut the door on him. Home and private at last, all she wanted to do was sleep.

'Do you mind if I just crash?' she asked Joe. 'Which is my room?'

He looked suddenly uncomfortable. 'About that, there's actually only one bedroom.'

Determined not to lose her cool in front of him, she forced the words to come out calmly. 'What do you mean there's only one?'

She crossed the huge open living space and stood on the threshold of Joe's bedroom, her mouth gaping at what he had just told her. He was the one who had suggested they live at his apartment. He couldn't have mentioned he didn't have a guest room?

'You can't think that I'm going to sleep with you.'

'As if, Princess. You're not that irresistible, you know.' Way to kill an ego. Not that she cared right now. All she wanted was to sleep. No, she corrected herself. She needed privacy to call her parents and let them know that she'd messed up—again. And then she needed to sleep. Probably for about three days straight.

'Look, Charlie. I'm tired, I'm grouchy. I have to go call my mum and explain why I decided to get married without her there, and then I'm sleeping. The mattress is big enough for us both to starfish without getting tangled. So you do what you like, but I'm going to bed.

He was tired? *He* was grouchy?

She stood for a moment in the doorway, and could almost feel the delicious relief of slamming it shut with her on the inside. Instead, she pulled herself up to her full five feet ten inches, turned on the spot and stalked off with a grace that her deportment coach had spent months all but beating into her.

Charlie plopped down onto the couch with significantly less grace—no way was she contorting on there to sleep—and pulled out her mobile. She dialled her mum's private number, and heard her voice after a single ring. She could picture so clearly the way the Queen would be working at her desk with her phone beside her blotter, just waiting for her to call.

'Caroline.'

So much said in just one word. She'd been worried about disapproval, disappointment. But the heartfelt, unreserved concern in her mother's voice was the killer.

'Hi, Mum.'

'Charlie, are you okay?'

She dropped her forehead into her hands and wished for the first time that she had gone to do this in person. Surely it was the least her mother deserved. But—like so many of her other mistakes—it was done now, and couldn't be undone.

'I'm fine, Mum. I'm sorry, I know I should have called earlier…' Her voice tailed off and she held her breath, waiting for forgiveness.

'I'm just glad to hear from you. Are you going to tell me what happened?'

She wanted to tell the truth. To confess and tell her that she had messed up again. Her mum would forgive her...eventually. But that wouldn't stop her being disappointed. Nothing could do that. So she steeled herself to lie, to trying to cover up just how stupid she had been this time.

'I met a guy, Mum, and I don't know what happened, but we just clicked. It was love at first sight, and we wanted to get married right away.'

The long pause told her everything she needed to know about how much her mum believed that story.

'If you've made a— I mean if you've changed your mind, Charlie, we can take care of this, you know.'

It was the air of resignation that did it—the knowledge that her mother had been anticipating yet another catastrophe that strengthened her resolve.

'It wasn't a mistake, Mum. It's what I wanted. What we both wanted.' Another long pause, followed by the inevitable.

'So when do we get to meet this young man and his family?'

Her heart kicked into a higher gear as she worried what her mother was expecting—how formal and official was this going to get?

'I was thinking family dinner this weekend. Fly in and stay Friday night—how long you stay is up to you. I've already told your brother and sister. My secretary will ring with the details.'

Charlie couldn't speak. So this was real. She was going to bring Joe to meet her family, pretend that they were crazy in love. She nodded, then realised what she was doing. 'Okay, Mum, we'll be there.' Because when your mum was the Queen it was hard to say no, even more so when you had just done something you knew must have bruised her heart, if not broken it completely.

'I can't wait, darling.' The truth she could hear in her mum's voice broke her own heart in return.

She hung up and for a second let the tears that had been threatening fall onto her cheeks. Just three. Then she drew a deep breath, wiped her eyes and set her shoulders. She had, once again, got herself into an unholy mess and—once again—she would dig herself out of it. There was one other call that she knew she had to make—to her boss, Rich. But she had just disappointed one person whose approval she actually cared about. She didn't have it in her to do the double. She'd need at least a couple of hours' sleep before she could think about that.

She scrubbed under her eyes with a finger, determined to show no signs of weakness to her new husband. This was a professional arrangement and she had no business forgetting that.

As she opened the bedroom door she squared her shoulders. For just a few more hours it was just her and Joe, before the lawyers and managers and accountants wanted to start formalising everything at work. Damned right she was going to enjoy the calm before the storm.

The door opened and she looked over to the bed. *Holy cra—*

She was never going to be able to sleep again. At least not while she was pretending to be married to this man. He hadn't been lying when he'd said that there was room for the two of them to sleep side by side. It was an enormous bed. But the man she had decided to marry had chosen to starfish across it diagonally. There was barely room for a sardine either side of him, never mind anyone else.

And space wasn't the only issue. She'd assumed no naked sleeping, but maybe this was worse. The white T-shirt he must have pulled on before climbing between the sheets hugged tight around his biceps, revealing tattoos that swirled and snaked beneath the fabric, tempting her to follow their lines up his arms. The hem of the shirt had ridden up, showcasing a strip of flawlessly tanned skin across his toned back. And, just to torture her, the sheets had been kicked down to below his tight black boxers—the stretch of the fabric leaving nothing to the imagination. For half a second she thought about sleeping on that back-breaking couch. Or even calling a cab back to her own flat. But the lure of a feather mattress topper was more than she could resist. She kicked off her jeans, noting that her black boy shorts underwear was more than a little similar to her husband's. Luckily *her* white shirt covered her butt.

She crawled onto the mattress beside Joe, trying to keep her movements contained and controlled. Waking him would open the door to a host of possibilities that she didn't want to—couldn't—contemplate right now. Lying on her side on the edge of the bed, she tried to ignore the gentle rhythm of Joe's breathing beside her. She balanced on her hip, the edge of the bed just a couple of inches in front of her. So much for a deep, relaxing sleep. There was no way that was going to happen with her frightened of hitting the floor on one side or Joe on the other. No, she had to start as she meant to go on, and there was no way she was enduring marriage to a man who thought she would perch on the edge of the bed.

She snuck out an experimental toe and aimed at the vicinity of Joe's legs. When her skin met taut, toned muscle, she wasn't prepared for the flash of warmth that came with it. For the memory of the night that flashed back with it. Of her and Joe heading for the bed in their suite, high from champagne, the roulette wheel and the new and exciting gleam on the third fingers of their left hands.

She'd jumped back onto the mattress, the bemused bellboy still standing watching them from the doorway. As Joe had approached her, the look in his eyes like a panther stalking its prey, the bellboy had withdrawn. Her eyes had locked on Joe's, then, and her breath had caught at the intensity in his gaze. And then he had tripped on the rug and fallen towards the bed headfirst, breaking the spell. She'd collapsed back in a fit of giggles, and as her eyes had closed she had been overtaken by a yawn.

She'd fallen asleep so easily the night before. Maybe she could kick him out completely. That might be the only way she was going to get to relax enough to fall asleep. She remembered the look on his face, though, when he'd told her he wasn't giving up his bed for her. She didn't think he'd take crashing to the floor well. And, really, they had enough troubles at the moment without him being any more annoyed with her. She braced herself for the heat that she knew now would come and pushed at his leg again. Success. He shifted behind her and she shuffled back a few inches on the bed. She could hear Joe still moving, but she lay stiff and still, determined not to give up her hard-won territory.

With a great roll Joe turned over, and their safe, back-to-back stand-off was broken. His breath tickled at the back of her neck, setting off a chain reaction of goosebumps from her nape to the bottom of her spine. Maybe she had been better off on the edge of the bed, because her body was starting to hum with anticipation. Her brain—unhelpful as ever—was reminding her of how good it felt to kiss him. How her body had thrummed and softened in his arms. She reached down for the duvet and tucked it tightly around her, though she didn't really need its warmth. But with her body trapped tight beneath it she felt a little more secure. As a final defence, she shoved in her earphones and found something soothing to block out the subtle sounds of a shared bed, and shut her eyes tight.

Joe stood in the bedroom doorway, surveying the scene in front of him. A pair of black skinny jeans had been abandoned by the bed, and silver jewellery was scattered on the bedside table. Dark brown hair was strewn across the pillow and one long, lean calf had snaked out from beneath the duvet. Along with the jeans on the floor, it answered a question that he'd been tempted but too much of a gentleman to find out for himself.

His wife. He had to shake his head in wonderment of how that had happened. A simple kiss from her did things to his body that he had never experienced before. He'd woken with his arms aching to pull her close and give her a proper good morning. And she was the one woman he absolutely couldn't, shouldn't fall for. They had gone into this marriage with ground rules for a good reason. They couldn't risk their careers by giving in to some stupid chemical attraction, or, worse still, by getting emotionally involved.

He'd made the mistake before of giving his heart to someone who was only out to get what she wanted. He'd learnt his lesson, and he wouldn't be making the same mistake again. And of all the women he could have married, it had to be her, didn't it? One who would throw him back into that world of privilege and wealth.

He'd spent just about every day since he was eleven years old feeling like the outsider. And now he had gone and hitched himself to the ultimate in exclusive circles. Once he and Charlie were married, there was no way of getting away from them. But he had learned how to deal with it a long time ago. Keep his distance, keep himself apart, to prevent the sting of rejection when he tried to fit in. The same rule had to apply to Charlie. It didn't matter what she had told her parents, how real they were going to make this thing look— he couldn't let himself forget that it was all for show.

He placed a cup of coffee down among her earrings and bracelets, and from this vantage point he could see the chaos emerging from her suitcase, where more shirts were spilling from the sides.

Charlie jerked suddenly upright, knocking his arm and sending the coffee hurtling to the floor.

'Crap!'

He jumped back as the scalding liquid headed for his shins. Charlie was scrambling out of bed, and grabbed her jeans from the floor to start mopping up the coffee from the floorboards. 'What the hell?' she asked, crouching over the abandoned coffee.

'I thought I'd bring you a cup of coffee in bed, you ungrateful brat.' She sat back at the insult and crossed her arms across her chest. 'I suppose I ought to expect the spoilt little princess routine,' he continued, and they both flinched at the harsh tone in his voice. 'Sorry. Look, you wait there. I'll grab a towel.'

He retreated to the kitchen and took a deep breath, both hands braced palms-down on the worktop; then grabbed some kitchen roll and headed back to the bedroom. Charlie was crouched like a toddler, feet flat on the floor, attacking the coffee with a hand towel from the bathroom. She took a slurp from the cup as she worked, swishing the towel around ineffectually, and chasing streams of coffee along the waxed floorboards and under the bed.

'Here,' he said, taking the sopping towel from her and holding out a hand to pull her up. 'I'll finish up. You drink your coffee.'

'Thanks,' she said, relinquishing the towel with a look of relief. 'And for the coffee. Sorry, I was just a bit disorientated.'

'Forgot you picked yourself up a husband in Vegas?'

'Something like that.' She grabbed her watch from the bedside table and shook off the coffee, leaving flecks of brown on the snowy white duvet cover.

'Ugh. I've got to be at work in an hour.'

She walked over to the bathroom, and he directed his gaze pointedly away from the endlessly long legs emerging from beneath that butt-skimming shirt. He had no desire to make this arrangement any more dif-

ficult than it undoubtedly was. Keeping it strictly business was the only way that it was going to work. She
eyed her suitcase uncertainly. 'I've got more jeans, but
I'm all out of clean tops. Can I raid your wardrobe?'

'Go for it. I'm jumping in the shower. We'll need
to leave at quarter to if we're going to walk.'

She stopped riffling through the rails in his dressing room for a second.

'We?'

'I think I'd better come talk to Rich. There's a lot
to go through before we can sign anything.'

Of course she hadn't forgotten that Rich had sent
her out to Vegas with a job to do. So why wasn't she
exactly thrilled about the prospect of going in and
seeing him this morning? Because this hadn't been
what he'd meant, she knew. It hadn't been what she'd
wanted either. If this was a casting-couch situation
she wasn't sure which of them had been lying back
and thinking of the job, but she knew that she was
good at what she did. She knew that she could have
bagged this signing without bringing her personal
life or family into the picture. But who was going to
believe that now?

Her face fell, and somehow he knew exactly what
she was thinking.

'You think he's going to be pissed at you?'

'Why would he be? He sent me out there to close
this deal. Job done, mission complete. He's going to
be thrilled.'

'Really? So why don't you look happy about it?'

'It's nothing.'

'It's clearly something.'

He sat on the edge of the bed as she turned back to

the wardrobe and started looking through his shirts again. Sliding them across the rail without paying much attention.

'I'm just not sure how he's going to react to…this.' She waved a hand between them so he understood exactly what 'this' was. His hackles rose.

'You told me you weren't involved with anyone. Are you telling me you and he are…a thing? Because that would be a major problem. I can't believe you'd—'

'It's nothing like that.' She grabbed hold of a shirt and pulled it from the hanger. 'God, why does everyone assume that any professional relationship I have is based on sex?' He lifted one eyebrow as he took in her half-dressed form and the unmade bed.

'Oh, get lost, Joe. This is nothing to do with sex. This was *your* idea. I'd have got you to sign anyway.'

'Really? Why did you say yes, then?' She had been starting off to the bathroom, but she stopped halfway across the room, his shirt screwed up and crumpled in her hand.

'Oh, why does a party girl do anything, Joe?' Her smile was all public, showing nothing of the real woman he had spent the last couple of days with. 'I'm an idiot. I was drunk. It was a laugh.' It was what everyone would assume, there was no doubt about that—but what was most shocking to him was that she didn't believe that any of those statements were true. So if it hadn't been just for a laugh, and it wasn't about her job either, then why had she done it?

He waited for the water to shut off and for Charlie to emerge from the bathroom before he grabbed his wash bag from his suitcase. She kept her back to him as she emerged and headed straight into the dressing room. Respecting her obvious need for privacy, and reluctant to continue their argument, he went straight into the bathroom and locked the door.

So what was the deal with her boss if she wasn't sleeping with him? Why was she so bothered about what he would think about their marriage? Their reasons for staying together were still good. The papers had been full of stories about the two of them, and there had been talk about the anticipation of their new album. It was exactly the sort of coverage that you couldn't buy. Her boss would be able to see that. He should be pleased that she'd got the job done and with a publicity angle to boot.

He stepped under the spray of the shower and let the water massage his shoulders. Maybe he should let her go and deal with her boss on her own. But he was keen to get this contract signed. He had meant what he had said. He'd been impressed with what the label had pitched to him—he would have signed even without Charlie turning up in Las Vegas.

He followed in her footsteps to the dressing room and wasn't sure whether to be disappointed or relieved that the towel had been discarded on the floor and she was fully dressed. One of his shirts was cinched in at the waist with a wide belt of studded black leather. A pair of black leather leggings ended in spike-heeled boots and she was currently grimacing into the mirror as she applied a feline ring of heavy black eyeliner.

'Walk of shame chic,' she said as she met his eye in the mirror. 'What do you think?'

'I think that now you're a married woman we can't call it the walk of shame. This is home. If you want it to be.' He leaned back against the wall as she paused with a tube of something shiny and gold in her hand. His eyes met hers in the mirror, and he gave a small smile. Relaxing in that moment, he enjoyed their connection—the first since they had woken up that morning. And he remembered again that feeling when he had first met her. When he had glanced across the stage and seen her in the wings, watching him. How they had danced and felt so in tune, so together, that the idea of marriage had seemed inevitable, rather than idiotic.

He laughed as she broke their eye contact to apply a coat of mascara, complete with wide open mouth.

'Come on,' he said, heading to the kitchen. 'I'll make another coffee.'

She glanced at her watch, returning his smile.

'We might have to drink on the go.'

He couldn't deny that he was startled. Princess Caroline all worried about being late for work the morning after bagging the biggest signing of her career. She was just full of surprises.

In the kitchen he set the coffee machine going and grabbed his only travel mug from a cabinet. 'Okay, but we're sharing, then,' he shouted back to her as he added frothy steamed milk.

By the door, he grabbed wallet and keys from the tray on the console where he'd dropped them the night before. Waiting for Charlie, he had an unimpeded view of her kicking her coffee-stained jeans towards her suitcase, and swiping some of the jewellery from the bedside table, but knocking the rest of it under the bed. Spot the girl who'd grown up with staff, he thought again to himself. They were going to have to talk about this at some point, he realised. He wasn't going to pick up after her like some sort of valet.

Was that how she saw him, he wondered—on a par with the staff? Barely visible in a room? She swept past him and out of the door; then drew up short in the corridor, clearly surprised that he wasn't just following in her wake.

'Are you coming?' she asked over her shoulder.

Slowly, Joe turned his key in the lock and then walked towards her. He took a long sip of coffee from the travel mug and then met her eye.

'You're not a princess here, sweetheart,' he told her gently. 'Home means you do your own fetching and carrying.'

Her brows drew together and he knew he'd pissed her off. 'I'll start by carrying this, then, shall I?' She took the coffee from him and walked into the lift, letting the door close in his face behind her.

Charlie swiped them into the office with her key card and waved at the receptionist on her way past. Avalon Records was based in a rundown old Regency villa on a once fashionable square. The grandeur of the high ceilings and sweeping staircases was in stark contrast to the workaday contents. Laminate wood desks had been packed into every corner of the building, and tattered swivel chairs fought for space with stacks of paper and laser printers.

She headed to her desk with eyes forward, intent on not letting anyone—especially Joe—see how nervous she was. Not that she needed to worry about that. She had been so keen to get into the office early that the place was practically deserted. She reached her desk and stashed her bag in a drawer, making herself busy for just a few more moments, turning on the computer and getting everything straight in her head so that the minute Rich arrived she could sell the hell out of this situation.

This was a good day, and there was no way she was leaving Rich's office until he agreed with her. Not only had she closed the deal that Rich had sent her out there to do, she had tied Joe and The Red Kites to their future in the closest way possible. Rich should—and he would—be eternally grateful. This was a massive coup for their indie label, tempting the hottest band of the year away from the big multinationals. She grabbed a couple of files and a notebook from under a pile of papers and then turned back to Joe.

He was staring at her desk with a mixture of shock and despair.

'What?' she asked, alarmed by his expression.

'Oh, my God. You're a slob.' He laughed as he spoke, his eyes wide. She leaned back against her desk and crossed her arms across her chest.

'I am so not.'

'You totally are. I thought maybe back at my place it was because we were both still living out of our cases. I need to clear you some space in the war...' His voice drifted and a shadow crossed his expression before he shook it off and got back to the point. 'But this proves it. I mean...how do you find anything?'

She waved the files in her hand at him.

'Because they're exactly where I left them.'

He shook his head again. 'But wouldn't they also be exactly where you left them if they were...say... filed neatly in a drawer?'

She raised her brows. 'You wouldn't by any chance be interfering, would you, Joe? Because this is my desk, and my office, and my job, and you don't get to boss me around here.'

He snorted out a breath. 'Oh, right, because at home you're so biddable and accommodating.' He laughed again, taking a step closer until she was trapped between him and the desk. She could smell his shower gel, the same one that she'd borrowed that morning, knowing even as she'd done it that she was going to be haunted by this reminder of him all day. She looked up at him, enjoying the novelty of a man who was still a smidge taller than her, even when she was in heels.

'I'm not interfering. I'm just getting to know you. We can talk about this more at home.' He took another half-step closer and she hitched a butt cheek onto her desk, looking for just a little more space, a little more safety. Breathing space for sensible, professional decision-making.

Then Joe lifted his hand and even without knowing where it was heading—hair, cheek, lips—she knew it would be more than her self-control could stand. She grabbed his hand mid-air, but that didn't help. It just pulled him closer as their linked hands landed on the desk by her hip. The front of his thighs pressed against hers, long and lean and matched so perfectly to her body he could have been made for her. She could feel the gentle pressure of his breath on her lips, and her eyes locked on his mouth as she remembered the times that they had pressed against hers. Her brain was desperately trying to catch up with the demands of her body. Remember the agreements they had made. They were meant to be madly in love in public. They were business associates when they were home. But what were they to each other here? In this public place, but with no one there to see them.

She dragged her gaze away for a moment, over Joe's shoulder to the still-deserted office. She had wanted to be in early. To show Rich that she was still as committed—as professional—as ever. But it had left her and Joe dangerously secluded.

His fingers untangled from hers, and she was hit with syncopated waves of regret then relief. But neither lasted long as his hand completed its original journey and landed this time on her cheek. His palm cupped her face as he tilted her head just a fraction. The sight of his tongue sneaking out to moisten his lips set off a chain reaction from the tight, hard knot low in her pelvis to the winding of her arms around his shoulders to the low sigh that escaped her throat as she closed her eyes and leaned in, waiting for the touch of his mouth.

A door slammed behind her and she jumped back, whacking her thighs against her desk in the process. She pushed at Joe's chest, knowing even before she turned to look at Rich's office what she was going to find.

Her boss was standing in front of the closed door to his office, leaning back against it with his arms crossed. Proof that the slam had been entirely for effect. Bloody drama queen, Charlie cursed him under her breath.

'The lovebirds return,' Rich said, leaning forwards and extending his arm to shake Joe's hand. 'It's good to see you again, Joe. We weren't expecting you. Are you just seeing the wife to work, or…?'

'Actually, Rich, we have good news.' Charlie

watched her boss's face closely, trying to judge his reaction. 'Joe and the rest of the guys are all in agreement. They want to sign with us. Joe wanted to come and give the good news in person this morning.'

Rich's professional smile didn't give anything away, but she knew him well enough to see the slight hint of tightness around his eyes that told her that this wasn't unmitigated pleasure.

'That is great news,' he said, clapping Joe on the back. 'I guess this is a pretty good week for us all, then. Congratulations to you both. Married? Love at first sight, the papers are saying. I have to admit, I was surprised not to hear it from the horse's mouth.' He gave Charlie a pointed look and she pulled herself up to her full height, determined not to act like a chastised teenager. She had every right to do just what she wanted. She didn't need Rich's permission, or his approval, to marry whomever she chose.

'You know how it is, Rich. The papers knew what was happening almost before we did. We didn't have a chance to tell people ourselves.'

'Funny how that happens, isn't it?' Rich said with a quirk of his eyebrow. So he definitely wasn't going to buy 'love at first sight' then. Time for Plan B.

Joe looked from her to Rich, and must have picked up on the atmosphere between them.

'Look, we just wanted to give you *this* news in person,' Joe said. 'I know that there's loads to work out with the lawyers and stuff so just let me know when you want to start.' He leaned forward to shake Rich's hand again before turning back to Charlie. She waited to hear Rich go back into his office, but the click of the door handle didn't come. Was this a test? Was he trying to see if this was all for show?

She didn't have time to worry about it as Joe's lips descended on hers. His hands framed her face, his fingertips just teasing at her hairline. His lips were warm and soft as they pressed against her mouth, full of promise and desire. But then his hands dropped to her shoulders as he broke away, and when she opened her eyes she was met by a twinkling expression in his. 'See you at home, love.'

He swept out of the office with a final wave at Rich, and she fought the urge to lean back against her desk to catch her breath.

Instead her hands found the files that she'd grabbed before Rich had arrived, and she stalked into his office with her head held high.

'Are you ready to get started? We've got a lot to cover.'

Rich stood in the doorway, not joining her at the table as she pulled out a chair and sat. Then shook his head as he took in her determined glare. 'I'll be with you in a second.'

Five minutes later he returned with two cups of coffee and a look of determination that matched her own.

She was reading through a boilerplate contract, making notes in the margin with a red pen, and Rich waited for her to finish scribbling before he sat.

'Here, have a caffeinated peace offering. Have you slept at all since you left for the airport? I'm betting your body has no idea what time zone it's in right now.'

'Thanks.' She took the coffee and realised that he was right. She should be exhausted, but she wasn't.

Something to do with having a brand-new husband she wasn't sure if she was meant to be keeping her hands off or not, she supposed.

'So are you going to tell me what happened?'

'I thought you said you already knew.'

'I told you I'd read the papers. I want the real story. From you, preferably. I think I deserve that. This affects us all. This is work. When I sent you out there to seal the deal, I didn't mean do *any*thing. I thought maybe… I don't know. The Princess thing: sometimes it works. I never expected you to… Just… What happened, Charlie?'

She looked him in the eye, still trying to work out her angle. How much she should share. How much she should hide. But Rich was right. This went beyond her personal life. She and Joe had made a calculated business decision—he couldn't expect her to keep it from the head of the business.

'We got carried away. Vegas, you know.' She gestured vaguely with her hands. 'We'd had too much to drink. We thought it would be funny. And that, you know, the publicity wouldn't be a bad thing for the band.'

'So it wasn't…' He hesitated, and Charlie just knew he was trying to find the right words. The ones that would annoy her the least. She prayed he wasn't about to ask the question she knew deep down was coming. 'It wasn't a quid pro quo deal. Nothing to do with the contract.'

She bristled, even though she'd been expecting it.

'What are you implying, Rich? Because if you think that I would do that—that I would need to… There's nothing I can say to that.'

Rich held out his hands for peace.

'I'm just trying to understand here, Charlie. I wasn't implying anything. So you thought it was a laugh, to celebrate the deal, and the publicity wouldn't exactly harm the band. But...now? What's going on now? You're living together?'

'We thought it would look better if it was love at first sight rather than a Vegas mistake. We're both committed to keeping up the pretence until the publicity won't be as harmful.'

'And it's all for show?' Rich asked. She nodded. 'So that little moment I walked in on earlier?'

'All part of the act.'

Rich sighed, non-committal. 'Okay, all of that aside, this is an amazing opportunity for us. Great job on getting the signing. I knew that I could trust you to take care of it.'

Charlie straightened the papers in front of her, enjoying the warm glow of Rich's praise for her work. She'd survived the first meeting: it could only get better from here.

'So how did it go with your boss after I left?' Joe asked when she arrived home that evening. 'It looked like things were about to get heated between you.'

She crossed to the fridge and surveyed the contents as she thought about it.

'It was a bit hairy at first,' she admitted as she grabbed a couple of beers and waved one in Joe's direction. He took them both from her and reached behind him into a drawer to find a bottle opener.

'Does he always get so involved in his staff's personal lives?'

'Only when they go around marrying potential clients.'

He raised his eyebrows in a 'fair enough' expression, pulling out the bar stool next to him at the kitchen island.

'Why do you care so much what he thinks anyway? If you're so adamant that there's nothing going on between you.'

'Jealous again, darling?' She threw him some serious shade while taking a sip of her beer and resting her hip on the stool. The hardness of his gaze drew her up short. 'Don't be an idiot, Joe. I'm not impressed or in the least turned on by the jealousy thing. Drop it.'

'Okay,' he conceded. 'So there's nothing romantic going on between you. Tell me what that weird vibe was, then. Why were you afraid of disappointing him?'

'He's my boss. I'd quite like to not get fired. Are you so much of a celeb these days that you don't remember what it's like to hold down a job?'

'Said the Princess.'

'You wanted to know why I don't want to disappoint Rich? Because he's the only one who doesn't call me Princess. Even when others aren't doing it to my face, they still treat me differently, and it drives me crazy. Rich is the only person who doesn't make exceptions or allowances. He's the one person who treats me like a normal goddamn human being and expects me to act like one. If I stepped out of line he'd fire me in a heartbeat.'

'And you'd walk straight into another job.'

She resisted the urge to throw her beer at him. 'Maybe I would. But not one that I deserve. Not one that I could do as well as the one I have now. Rich has made me work my arse off for every achievement. Every signing. Every bloody paycheque has been in exchange for my blood, sweat and tears. He's the only one who could see that I can do it. I work hard, I earn my keep. When I let him down, I'm proving them right. All the people who just expect the world to fall into my lap.'

Which was why there was no way that she was walking away from the life that she'd built for herself, just because she'd promised her parents she'd come home at some fixed point in time.

'I'm sorry, I didn't mean to.'

'It's a sore point, okay. Because I have let him down. This whole thing is stupid. It's beneath me. I messed up, and I don't like having it pointed out to me by the people whose opinion I value.'

He gave her a long, assessing look. 'We never talked about how it went with your parents, did we?'

She knocked back another long glug of beer.

'They want to meet you.'

'Mine too.'

She caught his eye, and managed a tentative smile. 'How do you reckon that's going to go?'

'My mum asked if she needed to wear a hat.'

Frothy beer hit her nose as she snorted with laughter.

'What did you tell her?'

'That I had no idea. I have no idea how this works.' The laughter died in his eyes and he looked suddenly solemn.

'Are you freaked out by it? The royalty thing? Because I thought you went to Northbridge School. My cousins are there. And you didn't seem all that impressed when I arrived in Vegas.'

He hesitated; the last thing that he wanted was to talk about his school days. He'd been awkward enough there, the scholarship kid from up north. And that was before the school's very own Princess—she didn't need the royal blood to call herself that—had used and humiliated him. 'Yeah, I knew your cousins at school,' Joe said, 'but we weren't friends. I didn't exactly click with my classmates.'

'School can be a cruel place.'

'I guess.' He took another swig of his beer and thought back. It had been a long time since he'd really thought about that part of his life. After he'd been ignominiously dumped in front of half his school year, he'd taken the lesson, moved on, and tried to forget about the humiliation. 'There wasn't any bullying or anything like that. The masters would never have stood for it. It's just, I didn't fit in, you know.' There was no need to tell her the whole ugly story. It had been embarrassing enough the first time around.

'And you're worried it's going to be like that with my family?' Charlie leaned forward and rested her elbow on the bar and her chin on her hand as she asked the question. 'They're really nice, you know,' she said earnestly. 'Well, my brother's an idiot, but every family has one of those.'

'I'm sure they are nice, Charlie. But they're different. We're different. And that's not something that we can change.' The last time that he'd been around people who moved in royal circles, the fact that he was different had become a currency in a market that he hadn't understood. Luckily, he was older and wiser now. He knew to look out for what people wanted from him, and to make sure he was getting a good deal out of it too. He also knew that no one was ever going to see their match as a marriage of equals.

'It's a good job that this is just all for show, then,' she added. 'So my family won't be making you uncomfortable for long.'

A look of pain flashed across her face, and he wondered what had caused it. It was too deep, too old to have been caused by this argument.

'It doesn't matter,' she said after a long pause, turning away from him almost imperceptibly. 'I'm never going to marry, so you don't have to worry about some future husband being trapped in that world.'

'I hate to break it to you, but it's a bit late for never.' He leaned in closer, nudging the footrest of her stool, trying to bridge the gulf that had suddenly appeared between them.

'Well, except this isn't real, is it?' she said.

He nodded, trying to hide his wince at the unexpected pain her statement had caused. Time for a change of subject, he thought. 'So why are you never getting married? Well, getting married again.'

'It's just not for me.' She shuffled to the back of her stool, reinstating the distance that he had tried to breach.

'Wow. That's enlightening.' She was hiding something from him, he knew it. Something big. And while she could keep her secrets if she wanted—it worried him. Because how was he meant to know how to handle this situation if he didn't have all the information? With all the women that had come before her, he knew exactly what they wanted, and they knew what he wanted in return.

With Charlie, despite their best efforts to keep this businesslike, he knew that everything she said carried shades of meaning that he didn't understand. It made him nervous, knowing that he was making calculations without all of the information he needed.

'Look, what does it matter, Joe? I wouldn't make a good wife, it wouldn't be fair for me to get married—not to someone who actually wanted to be my husband. But you'll have a chance to see them all for yourself. When I spoke to my mother yesterday she invited us over for dinner with the family on Friday. We'll need to stay. It's too far to fly there and back in an evening.'

'Yeah, great,' he said, though he knew that his lack of enthusiasm was more than clear.

'Anyway, I don't want to talk about this any more. How about we go out? I'm not sure what's going on with the jet lag, but I'm not sleeping any time soon. We could go get a drink—I know a place not far from here.'

'Like a date?' he asked, uncertainly. Had she suddenly decided that that was what she wanted?

'Like a chance for the press to see us as loved-up and glowing newly-weds.'

He nodded, trying to work out whether he was relieved or disappointed that it was all part of the act. 'Wouldn't newly-weds be more interested in staying home and getting to know one another?'

She spoke under her breath so quietly he could barely hear her reply: 'All the more reason to go out.'

CHAPTER FIVE

SHE PULLED THE front door closed behind them while she smudged on a bright red lip crayon. The bar was a ten-minute walk away. She'd been to their open mic night a few times, looking out for artists that she'd seen online but wanted to check out playing live before she decided if she was interested. As they turned the corner by the bar, though, she realised that this wasn't going to be one of those nights where she struck professional gold. And when they walked in and saw the screens showing lyrics, her worst fears were confirmed. It was no-holds-barred, no-talent-required, hen-parties-welcome karaoke. A trio of drunk students were belting out a rock classic, spilling pints of beer with their enthusiasm. Well, at least their taste in music couldn't be faulted, Charlie thought, boosting the roots of her hair with her fingers in honour of her spirit sister.

'Well, they're certainly going for it,' Joe said with a grin that slipped slightly as they hit a particularly painful note. 'This your usual kind of place?'

She looked around. The place itself was great: a shiny polished wood bar, real-ale pumps gleaming and—importantly—well stocked with decent beer.

Plus there was plenty of gin on the shelves, and good vodka on ice for later in the evening. But most importantly of all, the manager, Ruby, had her number and would call with any hot tips for new acts she might be interested in.

'Charlie!' Ruby greeted her with a smile. 'Don't usually see you here on a Tuesday. Don't tell me this is your honeymoon. That would be too tragic.'

Charlie forced a laugh at this reminder of her newly married status.

'I wish. No time for a honeymoon. But Joe—or we, now, I guess—live just round the corner and we fancied a quiet drink. I'd say you'd be seeing more of me, but...' She looked over at the singing students.

'Wanted to try something new. Don't worry, I won't be repeating the experiment.'

They all watched the tone-deaf trio with similar expressions of amusement.

'Sorry,' Charlie added, realising that she hadn't introduced Joe. 'Joe, this is Ruby, she runs this place. Ruby, this is Joe, my...er...'

'Her husband,' Joe filled in, sliding one arm around her waist and with the other leaning over the bar to shake Ruby's hand.

'I read about your news. Congrats! Vegas, huh. You guys have a wild time?'

'"Wild" is one word for it.'

'The best.'

Charlie, remembering her part, relaxed into Joe's arms. Ruby was watching them carefully, and Charlie wondered what she was thinking. Was she trying to judge whether they were for real? Were they going to face this scrutiny from everyone they met? She might not count Ruby as quite a friend, but Charlie would normally have at least considered her an ally. Well, they would just have to convince her, she decided. Because they were going to make this pretence of a marriage work. The alternative was to disappoint her family even more than she already had.

She just had to remember that it was all make-believe. She didn't get to be the glowing newly-wed in real life. Being a wife, like being a princess, came with certain responsibilities, certain expectations that she knew she couldn't fill. There was no point letting herself fall for a guy only to have him up and leave when he found out that she might not be a complete woman.

Charlie ordered a couple of beers and led Joe over to one of the booths in the back of the bar. It was comfy and private, upholstered in a deep red leather, and just the sort of spot that a loved-up couple would choose, she thought.

'They're really going for it, huh,' Joe said, indicating the girls on the karaoke, who had moved on from rock to an operatic power ballad. He took a swig of the ale, and Charlie watched as his throat moved. His head was thrown back, so he couldn't see her watching him. From inside the sleeve of his tight white T-shirt she could see half a tattoo, weaving and winding around his arm. She was concentrating so hard on trying to trace the pattern that she didn't notice at first that his eyes had dropped and she'd been totally busted.

'Looking at something you like?' It could have sounded cheesy. It *should* have sounded cheesy. But somehow the sincerity in his gaze saved it. 'You wanna see the rest of it?'

Okay, so that was definitely flirtatious. She looked around quickly to see if anyone was eavesdropping. Surely if they were already hitched she should know what his tats looked like.

Ruby was serving at the bar, the drunk girls were still singing enthusiastically, and most of the other customers had been scared off.

She slipped off her bench and darted round the table, sliding in beside Joe until her thigh was pressed against his.

'All yours,' he said, lifting his arm. Her fingertips brushed at the edge of the cotton T-shirt, which was warm and soft from contact with his skin. She traced the band that wound around his bicep, looking up and meeting his eye when he flinched away from her touch as she reached the sensitive skin near his underarm.

'Ticklish?'

'Maybe.' One side of his mouth quirked up in a half-smile, and she filed that information away, just in case she should ever need it.

She shouldn't ever need it, she reminded herself.

This was just an arrangement, and she had no business forgetting it. No business exploring his body, even something as seemingly innocent as an arm. Her body remembered being in bed with him. It remembered those kisses. The way that she had arched into him, desperate to be closer. She shot off the bench, diving for safety on the other side of the table.

'It's nice. I like it.' She tried to keep her voice level, to prevent it giving away how hard she was finding it to be indifferent to him.

'Well, there's plenty more. But maybe we should keep those under wraps for now.' She nodded. Not trusting herself to reply to that statement. She took a sip of beer, hoping the chilled amber liquid would cool her blazing face.

'So the open mic here's usually good?' Joe asked, and she jumped on the change of subject gratefully.

'It is,' she said. 'Very different from tonight. It's normally pretty professional. I've found a couple of great artists here.'

'You like to find them when they're still raw?'

'Of course. I mean a fully formed band with a track record is pretty great too.' She inclined her head towards him and he smiled. 'But there's something about finding raw talent and helping it to develop. It's… It's what gets me to work on a Monday morning when sometimes I'd rather drag the duvet over my head.'

'Must be tough to stay motivated when you don't really have to work.'

She dropped her bottle on the table a little harder than was strictly necessary. 'And why do you think I don't have to work?'

'Oh, I don't know, royal families are all taxpayer-funded, right?'

She placed both palms face down on the table, forcing herself to appear calm, not to slam them in a temper. 'The *working* royals are taxpayer-funded. Yes. And the key word there is "working". Do you know what the royal family is worth to my country's economy in terms of tourism alone? Not that it matters, because I opted out. I don't do official engagements and I don't take a penny.'

'Come on, though. You've never had to struggle.'

'Oh, because a wealthy family solves all problems. We all know that.'

She wished it were true. She had asked the doctor when she had first got her diagnosis whether there was anything that could be done, and the answer was a very equivocal 'maybe'.

Maybe if she threw enough money at the problem, there might be something they could do to give her a chance of conceiving. But it wouldn't take just money. It would take money and time and invasive procedures. Fertility drugs in the fridge and needles in her thighs. It could mean every chance of the world discovering she was a failure on the most basic level, and absolutely no guarantee that it would even work. No, it was simpler to accept now that marriage and a family weren't on the cards for her and move on.

'Where did you pick up this chip on your shoulder, anyway?' Charlie asked. 'I thought your education was every bit as expensive as mine.'

He looked her in the eye, and for a moment she could see vulnerability behind his rock-star cool.

'I had a full scholarship,' he said with a shrug.

'Impressive.' Charlie sat back against the padding of the bench. 'Northbridge don't just hand those out like sweeties. Was it for music?'

She was offended by his expression of surprise. What, did he expect her to recoil at the thought that he didn't pay his own school fees? God, he really did think that she was a snob. Well, it was high time she straightened that one out. Finishing her beer in one long gulp, she slid out of the booth and held out her hand to pull Joe up.

'Somehow,' she said, when he hesitated to follow

her, 'you seem to have got totally the wrong idea about what sort of princess I am. We're going to fix that. Now.'

His expression still showing his reluctance, he allowed her to pull him to standing, but leaned back against the table, arms folded over his chest.

'How exactly do you plan to do that?'

'We, darling husband, are going to sing.'

He eyed the karaoke screens with trepidation.

'Here?'

'Where else?' But he still didn't look convinced.

'Are you any good?'

'I'm no music scholar, but I hold my own. Now, are you going to choose something or am I?'

She grabbed the tablet with song choices from Ruby at the bar, who looked eternally grateful that someone would be breaking the students' residency.

'Are you going to help choose? Because I'm strongly considering something from the musical theatre oeuvre.'

That cracked his serious expression and he grinned, grabbing the back pocket of her jeans and pulling her back against the table with him, so they could look at the tablet side by side.

'As if you'd choose something that wasn't achingly cool.'

She swiped through the pages in demonstration.

'Hate to break it to you, but there's a distinct lack of "achingly cool". The only answer is to go as far as possible in the other direction. We go for maximum cheese.'

'I was so afraid you were going to say that.'

'Come on.' She swiped through another couple of

choices until she landed on a classic pop duet. 'It's got to be this one.' She hit the button that cued up the song and bought another round at the bar to tempt the drunk girls away from their microphones. With another couple of beers for her and Joe in hand, she stepped up onto the little stage.

She glanced around the bar—the girls had done a good job of emptying the place, but a few tables had stuck it out, like her and Joe, and now had all eyes on her. She could see the cogs whirring as they tried to place her face. Obviously not expecting to see a princess at the karaoke night. Even one with her reputation.

'It's a duet!' she shouted to him from the stage. 'Don't you dare leave me hanging!'

She held out her hand to him again and this time he grabbed it enthusiastically, pulled himself up to the stage beside her and planted a heavy kiss on her lips.

The surprise of it stole her reason for a moment, as her breath stopped and her world was reduced to the sensation of him on her. She lifted her hands to his arms, bracing herself against him, feeling unsteady on the little stage as one arm slid around her waist and his hand pressed firmly on the small of her back, pulling her in close.

Her fingers teased up his bicep; though her eyes were closed, her fingers traced the pattern of his tattoo from memory, nudging at the hem of his sleeve as they had earlier, keen to continue their exploration.

A wolf whistle from the crowd broke into their little reverie, and Charlie looked up, only to be greeted with the cameras of several phones pointing in her direction. Well, they'd be in the papers again. She shrugged mentally and reminded herself that that was the whole idea of this marriage.

That was why he'd kissed her.

It took a few moments for reality to break through. For her to remember that of course he'd only kissed her because they had an audience. This wasn't real— they just had to make it look that way. And just as her confidence wavered, and she wondered why that thought hurt so much, the music kicked in and Joe passed her a microphone.

'Come on then, love. Show me what you've got.'

She pulled her hair to one side, puckered up her finest pout and prepared to rock out.

They made it through the first verse without making eye contact, never mind anything more physical, but as they reached the chorus Joe reached around her waist and pulled her back, so her body was pressed against him from spike earrings to spike heels. She faltered on the lyrics, barely able to remember how to breathe, never mind sing.

She looked round at Joe to see if it had had the same effect on him, but when she saw his face she knew that he wasn't feeling what she was feeling. He was just feeling the music: every note of it. His throaty, husky voice giving the pop song a cool credibility it had never had before.

She pulled away to see him better, and though she picked up the words and joined in, it was only a token effort. Backing vocals to his masterful performance. This was why she'd agreed to marry him. The man Joe became on stage was impossible to refuse. She had kicked herself every minute since she'd woken up with a Vegas husband she no longer wanted, asking how she could have been so stupid.

But she hadn't been stupid, she realised now. It was just that they had been so magnetically drawn to one another because of his passion for music—any music—that it would have been pointless even trying to resist. Joe's eyes opened as the song slowed, and their gazes met, freezing them in the moment.

Does he feel it too? she wondered. Or had he just been so high on the adrenaline of performance that he would have agreed to marry anyone who had crossed his path?

She could see his adrenaline kicking up a notch now. His gestures growing more expansive, his grin wider, his eyes wilder.

She sang along, trying to keep pace with his enthusiasm, but whatever performance gene he'd been born with, she was clearly lacking.

The song finished with an air-guitar solo from Joe, and a roar of applause from the bar. She'd been so intent on watching him that she hadn't noticed the place fill up. From the many smartphones still clutched in hands, she guessed that they were about to go viral.

Joe grabbed her around the waist, and before she could stop him, before she could even think about whether she wanted to, his mouth was on hers, burning into her body, her mind, her soul, with his intensity. His hands were everywhere: on her butt, in her hair, gently traipsing up her upper arm. His lips were insistent against hers, demanding that she gave herself to him with equal passion. And his tongue caressed hers with such intimacy that it nearly broke her. Soft and hard, gentle and rough, he surprised her with every touch.

When, finally, he pulled away, they both gasped for air, and she was grateful his arms were still clamped around her waist, keeping her upright. And that she'd turned so that her back was to the bar, so no one would be able to see her flaming red cheeks or the confusion in her eyes.

'Uh-oh. Looks like we've got an audience,' Joe said, and Charlie registered that the surprise in his voice seemed genuine. Had he really not noticed that they were being watched? Because if not, that kiss needed an explanation. The knowledge that it was all for show had been the only thing keeping her from losing her mind. He couldn't go and change the rules now.

'Are you up for another?' Joe asked.

Another song? Another drink? Another kiss? None of the options seemed particularly safe after that performance.

'I think my singing days are done,' she said with a smile, jumping down from the stage and heading back to the relative safety of their booth.

'Where did they all come from?' Joe asked, drinking the beer he'd abandoned when he'd gone into performance mode.

'Happened quickly, huh.'

'So fast I didn't even notice.'

Then why did you kiss me? The question hung, loud and unspoken, in the air.

'So what's your family like?' Charlie asked, suddenly desperate for a change of subject. 'You're from up north, right?'

Joe nodded, and named a town near Manchester. Of course she already knew where he'd grown up from her research into the band, but small talk seemed the safest option open to them at the moment. 'They must have been proud of you. For the scholarship. For everything since.'

'Of course. They were chuffed when I got into the school. It was their idea, actually. My mum was a gifted pianist but never had the opportunity for a career in music. They wanted me to have the best.'

'Sounds like a lot of pressure.' If there was one thing she understood it was the heavy weight of family expectation. But Joe shrugged, non-committal.

'Their motives were good. Still are.'

'But you weren't happy?'

'It was an amazing opportunity.'

'That's not what I asked.'

He sighed and held up his palms. 'I don't like to sound ungrateful. I have no reason to complain. The school funded me. My parents made sacrifices.'

'You remember who you're talking to, right? I do understand that having the best of everything doesn't always make you happy. It doesn't make you a bad person to acknowledge that. It makes you human.'

He was quiet for a beat. 'So what's making you unhappy, Princess Caroline?'

'Oh, no. You are so not changing the subject like that. Come on. Mum and Dad. What are they like? How did they react to…' she searched for the words to describe what they were doing together '…to Vegas?'

He grimaced; she cringed. 'That bad?'

'They weren't best pleased that we did it without them there. They're hurt, but happy for me. I don't know, but I think that made me feel worse.' He was silent for a moment, fiddling with the label of his beer bottle. 'They want to meet you.'

And she was every bit as terrified of that as he was about meeting her family. She knew that she had a reputation that was about as far as you could get from ideal daughter-in-law. 'I could ask my mother to invite them this weekend? Face everyone at the same time?'

He choked on his beer, caught in a laugh.

'That's sweet, Charlie, but how about we start with introducing them to one royal and go from there. Not everyone is as super cool as me when it comes to meeting you and yours.'

'Oh, right,' she laughed. 'Because you were so ice-cool you practically dropped to one knee the night that we met.'

She wondered whether her tease had gone too far, but his mouth curved in a smile. 'What can I say? You give a whole new meaning to irresistible.'

She could feel herself blushing like a schoolgirl and incapable of stopping it. 'So we see my parents Friday night. Do you want to see yours this weekend too? If you wanted to go sooner I guess I could talk to Rich. Work remotely or something.'

He shook his head. 'Don't worry. I think this weekend will be plenty soon enough. We can fly into Manchester on Saturday. Be back home by Sunday night. No need to miss work.'

'Actually, I could do with stopping by a festival on Sunday, if you fancy it. There's a band I'd like to see perform, and try and catch them for a chat.'

He nodded, and then Charlie glanced at her watch, realising with surprise that over an hour had passed since they had left the stage. The bar had thinned out a little again, leaving the atmosphere verging dangerously on intimate.

'Speaking of work, I've a fair bit to catch up on. I need to be in the office early tomorrow. Mind if we call it a night?'

He swigged the last of his drink and stood, reaching for her hand as she slipped off the bench. 'I like that you're tall,' he said as they left the bar with a wave to Ruby. 'As tall as me in those shoes.'

'Random comment, but thanks,' she replied, trying to work out if there was a hidden message in there that she wasn't getting. 'Are you just thinking out loud? Is this going to be a list?'

'I'm just… I don't understand. You're right. I didn't play it cool, that night. I didn't play it cool on stage just now. I'm just trying to figure this out. Maybe it is the royal thing, but I didn't struggle not to kiss your cousins when I was at school with them.'

'So you think it's because I'm tall?' Really thinking: What are you saying? Are you saying you like me? That this is real for you?

'I'm thinking about everything. I just figure that if I can work out what it is…you know…that makes us crazy like that, we can avoid it. Stop it happening again. Keep things simple.'

Her ego deflated rapidly. So it didn't matter what he was feeling, because all he wanted was a way of not feeling it any more. After their madness on stage, they were back on earth with a crash, and she had the whiplash to prove it.

'Well, I'm sorry, darling, but I'm not losing the heels.'

'God, no. Don't,' he said with so much feeling it broke the tension between them. 'I love the heels.'

Which was meant to be a bad thing, she tried to remind herself, but the matching grins on their faces proved it would be a lie.

'Or maybe it's the hair,' he came up with as they walked back to his flat, their fingers still twined. 'There's so much of it. It's wild.'

She tried to laugh it off. 'So we've established you have a thing for tall women with messy hair. I guess I was just lucky I fit the bill.' She turned serious as they reached the front door of the warehouse and stepped into the privacy of the foyer. 'Are your parents going to hate me?'

'Why would they hate you?'

'Notorious party girl seduces lovely northern lad into hasty Vegas marriage. Am I not the girl that mothers have nightmares about?'

'Is that how you see what happened? You seduced me? Because I remember things differently…'

'It's not about what I remember. It's about what your mum will think.'

'My mum will think you're great.' But his tone told her that she wasn't the only one with reservations about the big introduction. 'You'll mainly be busy with dodging hints about grandchildren.'

Her stomach fell and she leaned back against the wall for support while the rushing in her ears stopped.

'She won't seriously be expecting that, will she?'

'She's been bugging me for years about settling down and giving her grandkids. Isn't that what all mums do?'

Apparently they did—that was why she made a point of seeing hers as little as possible.

She drew herself up to her full height again, not wanting Joe to see that there was anything wrong.

'Well, we'll just have to tell her that we don't have any plans.'

Joe was looking at her closely, and she wondered how much he had seen. Whether he had realised that she had just had a minor panic attack.

'It's fine; we'll fend her off together. Are you sure you're okay?'

So he had noticed. She pasted on a smile and pushed her shoulders back, determined to give him no reason to suspect what was on her mind. 'Of course. Just tired. That jet lag must be catching up with me after all.'

It wasn't until she reached his front door that she remembered the whole bed situation. How was she meant to sleep beside him after a kiss like that? After he'd all but told her that he was finding it as hard to resist her as she was to resist him.

She dived into the bathroom as soon as they got into the apartment, determined to be the first ready for bed, and to have her eyes closed and be pretending to sleep by the time that Joe came in. Or better still, actually *be* asleep, and not even know that he was there. She pulled a T-shirt over her head, still warm from the dryer, and gave herself a stern talking-to. She couldn't react like that every time someone mentioned babies or pregnancy. There were bound to be questions after the hasty way that they had got married, and she was going to have to learn to deal with them.

CHAPTER SIX

THERE WAS DEFINITELY something that she wasn't telling him. Something to do with the way that she'd reacted just now when he'd warned her that his mum would probably be hinting about grandchildren.

What, did she already have an illegitimate kid stashed away somewhere? No. It couldn't be that. There was no way that she'd be able to keep it out of the papers. What if she was already pregnant? That could be it. After all, she had accepted a completely idiotic proposal of marriage from a man that she barely knew. Was she looking for a baby daddy, as well as a husband?

And how would he feel if she was? That one was easy enough to answer: as if he was being used. Well, there was nothing new in that. He'd learnt at the age of eighteen, when it transpired that the girl he had been madly in love with at school was only with him for the thrill of sleeping with the poor northern scholarship kid, and bringing him home to upset her parents in front of all their friends, that women wanted him for *what* he was, not who.

And after years on the road, meeting women in every city, every country that he had visited, he knew that it was true. None of them wanted him. The real him. They wanted the singer, or the writer, or the rock star, or the rich guy.

Or—on one memorable occasion—they wanted the story to sell to the tabloids.

Not a single one of them knew who he really was. Not a single one of them had come home to meet his parents. And that was fine with him. Because he knew what he wanted now too. And more importantly he knew that relationships only worked if both of you knew what you wanted—and didn't let emotions in the way of getting it.

But it didn't mean anything, he told himself, Charlie coming home with him at the weekend. Like all the others, she was just using him. He provided a nice boost to her career, and a new way of causing friction with her family, though he couldn't pretend to know why she wanted that. And he was using her to get exposure for his band, and sales for his new album. If he ever finished it.

He tidied up the bedroom while he waited for her to finish in the bathroom, chucking dirty clothes in the laundry hamper and retrieving the rest of Charlie's jewellery from under the bed. They would have to pick up the rest of her stuff from her flat at some point. He'd clear her a space in the wardrobe. Of all the things that he'd thought about that night that they got married, how to manage living with a slob hadn't been one of them. He surveyed the carnage in his apartment, and shrugged. Lucky his housekeeper was going to be in tomorrow. He'd leave a note asking her to clear some space in the drawers and wardrobe.

The thought of it was oddly intimate. Strange,

when they were already having to share a bed. Sharing hanging space should have been the least of their worries. But there was something decidedly permanent, committed, about the thought of her clothes hanging alongside his.

It wasn't permanent.

They'd both known and agreed from the start that this wasn't real, and it wasn't going to last. They just had to ride out the next year or so. Let the press do their thing, and then decide how they were going to end things in a way that worked out for both of them. It was as simple as that.

Joe waited outside Charlie's office, wondering whether she'd be pleased or not if he went in. Somehow, over the past three days they'd barely seen each other. That night after the karaoke she'd been asleep by the time that he'd got out of the bathroom, lying on her side on the far side of the bed, so far away that they didn't even need a pillow barrier as a nod to decency. Then she'd been up before him the next morning, though she had said that she had a lot to catch up on. The pattern had stayed the same ever since. She was in the office before he'd had his breakfast every morning, and came home late, clutching bags and suitcases from her flat.

The only sign that they were living together at all was the increasing chaos in his apartment. His housekeeper did her best in the daytime, but once Charlie was home she was like a whirlwind, depositing clothes and hair grips and jewellery on every surface. Leaving crumbs and coffee rings all over the kitchen and the coffee table. He wasn't even mad: he was amused.

How had the prim and proper royal family produced such a slob?

It wasn't as if she were lazy. The woman never stopped. He knew that of her reputation at work. That she worked hard to find her artists, and then even harder to support them once they were signed. She was on the phone to lawyers, accountants, artists all day long, and then out at gigs in the evening, always looking for more talent, more opportunities.

Perhaps that was it, he thought. Why waste time picking up your dirty clothes when there was new music to be found?

The pavements started to fill with knackered-looking workers as the clock ticked towards six. As East London's hipster types exited office buildings and headed for the craft-beer-stocked pubs as if pulled by a magnet.

She'd told him she'd arranged for a car to collect her from work and swing by the apartment to pick him up, but as the hours after lunch had crawled by he'd realised that sitting and waiting for her was absolutely not his style.

He strode into the building, mind made up, and smiled at the receptionist.

'Hey, Vanessa. I'm Charlie's husband. Okay if I go straight through?' There. He made sure he sounded humble enough not to assume that she'd know who he was—though he would hope that the receptionist at his own label would recognise him—but confident enough to be assured that he wouldn't be stopped. He breezed past her, wondering why he felt so nervous. All right, he hadn't even visited Afland before, never mind the private apartments at the royal palace, but he had met a fair few royals, between his posh school and attending galas and stuff since his career took off. Deep down, he knew it wasn't who her family was that was making him nervous. It was the fact that he was meeting them at all.

He'd not been home to meet the family for a long time. Not since the disaster with Arabella.

That weekend when he was eighteen, he'd thought he had it made. His gorgeous girlfriend, one of the most popular girls in school, had invited him and a load of their friends to a weekend party at her parents' country house. For the first time since he had started at the school he had felt as if he had belonged. And more importantly had thought it meant that Arabella was as serious about him as he was about her. He'd been on the verge of telling her that he loved her. But as soon as he'd arrived, he'd realised that there was something wrong. She'd introduced him to her parents with a glint in her eye that he knew meant trouble, and had stropped off when they'd welcomed him with warm smiles and handshakes.

Turned out, he wasn't the ogre she'd been expecting them to see. And if he wasn't pissing off her parents, he was no use to her at all. So she'd broken it off, publicly and humiliatingly, in front of half the school and their parents.

Was Charlie doing the same thing? Perhaps marrying him was just one more way for her to stick her middle finger up at her family. Another way to distance herself from her royal blood. But instinctively he felt that wasn't true. Whenever they'd discussed her family, she'd made it clear that she didn't want to upset them. That had been the main thing on her mind that first morning in Vegas. But she hadn't been so concerned about it that she hadn't married him in the first place.

He showed himself through the office, over to where he remembered Charlie's desk was. She couldn't see him approach, her back to him, concentrating on her computer. Her hair was pulled into a knot on the top of her head, an up-do that could almost be described as sophisticated, and a delicate tattoo curled at the nape of her neck. He'd never noticed it before—and that knowledge sent a shudder of desire through him. How many inches of her body were a mystery to him? How many secrets could he uncover if they were to do the utterly stupid thing and give in to this mutual attraction?

They couldn't be that stupid. *He* wouldn't be so stupid. Opening up to a woman, especially a woman like Charlie, was like asking to get hurt.

By the time that he reached her desk, she still hadn't looked up. He couldn't resist that tattoo a moment longer. He could feel the eyes of her co-workers on him, and knew that they were watching, knew that they had read the gossip sites. It was all the excuse he needed, the reminder that he had a part to play.

He bent and pressed his lips to the black swirl of ink below her hairline.

The second that he met her skin a shot of pain seared through his nose and he jumped back, both hands pressed to his face.

'What the h—?'

'What the h—?'

They both cried out in unison.

'Joe?' Charlie said, one hand on the back of her

head as she spun round on her chair. 'What were you *thinking*?'

He gave her a loaded look. 'I was thinking that I wanted to kiss my wife. What I'm thinking now is that we might need a trip to A&E.' She looked up then, clocked the many pairs of eyes on them, and stood, remembering she needed to play her part too.

'Oh, my goodness, I'm sorry, darling.' She reached up and gently took hold of his hands, moving them away from his nose. 'Does it still hurt?'

She turned his head one way and then the other, examining him closely as she did so.

'Not so much now,' he admitted, finally making eye contact with her. It was the truth. With her hands gently cupping his face like that, he could barely feel his nose. Barely think about any part of his body that didn't have her soft skin against it.

'No blood anyway,' she added.

He smiled. 'Can't meet the in-laws with a bloody nose and a black eye,' he said. 'Not really the best first impression.'

'They'll love you whatever,' she said, returning his grin, but he suspected it was more for their audience than for him.

She was wearing a black dress, structured and tight, giving the illusion of curves that her tall, athletic figure usually hid. Was this what her parents wanted of her? he wondered. For her to tone herself down and wear something ladylike?

Her phone buzzed on the desk behind her, breaking the spell between them. 'That'll be the car,' she said, gathering up her stuff and shutting down her computer. As she grabbed her purse off the desk she sent a glass of water flying, soaking a stack of scrawled notes.

'Argh,' she groaned, reaching into a drawer for a roll of paper towels. 'Last thing we need.'

'It's fine,' he said, grabbing a handful of the towels. 'Here.' He mopped up the puddle heading towards the edge of the desk and spread out the soggy papers. 'They'll be dry before we're back on Monday. No harm done.'

She blotted at them some more with the paper, glancing at her phone, which was buzzing again on the desk.

'Is it time we were going?'

'Mmm,' she said, non-committal, silencing it. 'It's okay, we've got time.' She started straightening up another stack of papers, and throwing pens in a cup at the back of the desk.

'Wait a minute. Are you tidying?'

She shrugged. 'It's happened before, you know.'

'Maybe, but right now you're stalling, aren't you?'

She stopped what she was doing and looked him straight in the eye, leaning back against the desk with her arms crossing her chest. 'Says who?'

'Well, you just as good as admitted it, actually. What's going on? Ashamed to introduce me to your family?'

She started with surprise. 'Why would I be ashamed?'

'Because you're nervous. Why else would you be?'

'Maybe I'm desperate for them to fall in love with you.'

'Maybe.' He watched her with a wry smile. 'I guess we're going to find out. Are you ready?'

She sighed as she pulled on her jacket and swung her bag over her shoulders. 'Ready.'

As the car pulled through the gates at the back of the palace a few hours later, Joe took a deep breath. He might have been all blasé with Charlie, but now that he was here at the palace, with its two hundred and fifty bedrooms and uniformed guards and a million windows, perhaps he was feeling a little intimidated. Regardless of what he'd thought earlier, his brief brushes with royalty before he had met Charlie hadn't left him at all prepared for this.

Throughout the short flight to the island, he'd been making a determined effort not to feel nervous—forcing his pulse to be even and his palms dry.

And now, as they stepped out of the car and through the doors of the palace, perhaps if he closed his eyes, shut out the scale of the entrance gates, the uniformed staff in attendance, and the police officer stationed at the door, he could almost imagine that this was just any other dinner.

Eventually, following Charlie into the building and through a warren of corridors, he had to admit to himself that there was no escaping it. 'The private apartments are just up there,' Charlie told him as they rounded yet another corner.

He nodded, not sure what the appropriate response was when your wife was giving you the guided tour of the palace she had grown up in. In fact, he'd barely spoken a word, he realised, since the car had pulled through the gates.

The uniformed man who had met them at the door faded away as the policeman ahead of them opened the door. He nodded to them both as Charlie greeted him by name, and Joe followed her through the door. Unlike the corridors they'd followed so far, the interior of the private rooms was simple. Plush red carpets, gilt and chandeliers had fallen away, leaving smart, bright walls, soft wood flooring and recessed lighting.

'It's like another world in here,' Charlie said with a smile. 'My parents had it renovated when we were small. They were doing big repair work across the whole palace, so they took the opportunity to modernise a bit.'

'No chandeliers, then?'

'Not really my mother's style. They keep them in the state rooms for the visiting dignitaries and the tourists. But my parents have always preferred things simpler.'

He followed her down the corridor, and she paused in front of a closed door. 'Ready?' she asked.

He took her hand in his and squeezed. 'Let's do it.'

She opened the door into a light-flooded room.

Her parents were seated on a sofa to one side of a fireplace, what looked like gin and tonics on the coffee table in front of them.

'Oh, you caught us!' said Queen Adelaide, Charlie's mother. 'We started without you. I know, we're terrible.' She stood and kissed Charlie on the cheek.

Joe just had time to register the stiffness in Charlie's shoulders before her mother, Her Majesty Queen Adelaide of Afland, was stepping around her and holding out her hand.

He held his own out in return, but couldn't find his feet to step towards her. Was it because she was the head of state or the head of Charlie's family that was making him nervous?

'You must be Joe,' Queen Adelaide said, smiling and filling the silence that was threatening awkwardness. 'How do you do?'

Charlie's father stepped forward and shook his hand too, but he wasn't as skilled as his wife at hiding his feelings, he noted. And in his case, his feelings appeared to be decidedly frosty.

'Joe. How do you do?'

He wasn't the only frosty one, Joe realised, watching Charlie as they took a seat on the sofa opposite her parents. Her shoulders were as stiff as he had ever seen them, and her back was ramrod straight. She reached for one of the drinks that had appeared on the coffee table while they were getting the formalities out of the way.

They sipped their drinks as silence fell around them, definitely into awkward territory now. And still a distinct lack of congratulations. Perhaps they were waiting for the others to arrive.

Just as he was taking a deep breath, preparing to dive into small talk, he heard a door open, and the apartment filled with the noise of rambunctious children.

'Grandma! Grandpa!'

The kids barrelled into the room with squeals of excitement. The tense atmosphere was broken, and Queen Adelaide and Prince Gerald beamed with proud smiles and stood to scoop up their grandchildren. But Charlie stayed seated; though she smiled, the expression seemed forced.

Three adults followed the kids into the room. Joe recognised Charlie's sister and brother-in-law, and a second woman who he guessed must be the nanny.

She drifted out of the room after seeing the children settled with book and toys, and Joe shook hands with his new in-laws.

'So, Vegas!' Charlie's brother-in-law said as they all sat down. 'Wish we could have done that. Would have given anything to avoid the circus that we had to endure.'

'Endure?' Charlie's sister, Verity, slapped her husband's leg playfully. 'If that was a circus, I don't know how you'd describe our life now, chasing after these two.' But she smiled indulgently as she said it. Charlie leaned forward and helped herself to her sister's drink, uncharacteristically quiet.

'It was definitely low-key,' Joe said. 'Just us and a couple of friends.' He took hold of Charlie's hand, wondering whether she was planning on checking back in to this conversation again at any point. He withheld the details of the kitschy chapel they had chosen: it had seemed so funny at the time, but less so now that they were facing the consequences of their actions. He looked across at Charlie, and saw the tension in her expression that revealed how uncomfortable she was.

Isn't that what I'm meant to be feeling? he thought. You're back in the bosom of your family. This is meant to be your home, so why are you so uncomfortable?

He was so distracted by wondering what was preoccupying her that he forgot that he had been nervous about meeting the family. Her family were half of the reason he was so sure that this relationship wouldn't work so if it wasn't her family causing the problems, then where did that leave them?

Using one another—that was it. And he knew that

he had to keep his head if he was going to stay ahead of the game, make sure that she was never in a position to hurt him.

His thoughts were interrupted by the arrival of Charlie's brother, Miles, who bowled into the room wearing an air of privilege that outshone his exquisitely tailored suit. He greeted Charlie's brother-in-law with hearty slaps on the back—they'd been friends at school, Joe seemed to remember—and then doled out kisses on the cheek to his female relatives.

'So you're the guy who seduced my sister,' he said when he reached Joe.

He gave Miles a shrewd look. Was he trying to get a rise out of him? Well, he'd have to try harder than that.

'I'm Joe,' he said, standing to shake his hand. 'It's good to meet you.'

Charlie had risen beside him and he wrapped an arm around her waist. She seemed calmer with her brother than with her sister. Interesting, Joe thought. Because so far, her brother seemed like a bit of an ass. But families were strange, he knew. Maybe she'd always been closer to her brother. He tried to push it from his mind as they all sat down again. The nanny came back in, then, and the room was suddenly in chaos as toys were put away, negotiations for 'just five more minutes' were shut down and a pair of desultory kids doled out goodnight kisses.

When they got to Charlie, that stiffness came back to her shoulders, and she straightened her spine, sitting beside Joe on the sofa as if she were in a job interview. She sat deadly still as the children climbed up onto the couch, still offering kisses and messing around.

In contrast to all of the other adults in the room, who were joining in with the kids' silliness, Charlie pretty much just patted them on the head and dodged their kisses.

What was her issue with the kids?

There was no getting away from the fact that there *was* something going on. Joe looked over at Charlie's mum and sister to see if they had noticed—looking for any clues to what was going on—but their attention was completely on the children. Joe's earlier suspicion came back to him. Could she be pregnant? Did that even fit with what he was witnessing?

It did if she was in denial, he supposed. If she was pregnant and didn't want to be. Or didn't want to be found out.

Finally, the kids were bundled out of the room by the nanny, and a member of staff appeared with a silver tray bearing champagne flutes and an ice bucket.

'Ah, perfect timing,' Adelaide declared as the glasses were handed round and champagne poured.

The tone of her voice shifted ever so subtly, from relaxed and convivial to something more formal. Maybe more rehearsed. Charlie was close by Joe's side still, and this time it was she who took his hand, and ducked her head under his arm as she wrapped it around her shoulders and turned in towards him, until she was almost surrounded by his body. He tried to meet her eyes, but she evaded him. He couldn't be sure with her avoiding eye contact, but if he didn't know better he'd say that she wanted him to protect her. From her own family? Who seemed—to his surprise—a bunch of genuinely nice people who cared about one another. Her slightly annoying brother aside. It just didn't make any sense. Not unless she was keeping all of them—him included—in the dark about something.

'Joe and Charlie,' Adelaide began, 'I'm so pleased that we are all together this evening. While we can't say that we weren't surprised by your news...' her raised eyebrows spoke volumes about how restrained she felt she was being '...your father and I are delighted you have found someone you want to spend your life with. Now we didn't get to do this on your wedding day, so I'm going to propose the traditional toast. If you could all charge your glasses to the bride and groom. To Charlie and Joe.'

Queen Adelaide took a ladylike sip, while Charlie polished off half her glass and pulled Joe's arm tighter around her.

'Joe, we're absolutely delighted to meet the man who wants to take on, not only our wonderfully wild Caroline, but also her family, with everything that entails. We're always so happy to see our family grow, and, who knows, perhaps over the next few years it might be growing even further.'

From the corner of his eye he saw Charlie flinch, and he knew exactly how she had taken that comment of her mother's, whether it had been meant as a jibe about grandchildren or not. He sipped at his champagne, having smiled and nodded in the right places during Queen Adelaide's speech.

'Are you okay?' he whispered in Charlie's ear when the toasts were done and attention had drifted away from them.

She nodded stiffly, telling him louder than words that she absolutely wasn't.

'Want to try and make a break for it?'

She cracked half a smile. 'We'd better stay. I'd never hear the end of it.'

He wondered if that were true. Charlie's parents looked delighted to have her home. But were they really the types to nag and criticise if she left? They'd welcomed him with good grace in trying circumstances. Perhaps they deserved more credit than Charlie was giving them.

But there was no getting around the fact that she was still on edge, even after all the introductions were out of the way and they were all getting on fine. Which meant there was more to this than just her worrying whether they were going to buy their story.

What if he was right? What if she was pregnant, and was using him? Would he walk away from her? From their agreement? How would that look to the press…?

He suspected there was nothing worse as far as the tabloids were concerned than walking away from a pregnant royal wife.

He still had his arm around Charlie's waist, but he could feel a killer grip closing around him, making it hard to breathe. He'd thought that he'd gone into this with his eyes open. He'd thought he'd known what she wanted from him. Had he been duped again? Was he being used again, without him realising it?

'So, Joe, you were at school with Hugo and Seb, is that right? At Northbridge?' Charlie's brother had come to sit beside them, dragging his thoughts away from his wife.

'Yeah, they were a year or two ahead of me though. You know what it's like at school. A different year could be a different planet.'

'They remembered you, though.'

He heard Charlie move beside him, and, when he glanced across at her, she looked interested in the conversation for the first time since they'd arrived.

'What did they tell you?' she asked, a glint in her eye. 'You have to share. Don't you dare hold out on me, big brother.'

'Oh, you know, the usual. Ex-girlfriends and kiss-and-tells. God, you've let your standards slip, getting yourself hitched to this one.'

'Standards? Really? Who did he date at school?'

'You really want to know?' Miles laughed and rolled his eyes. 'Masochist. Fine, it was Arabella Barclay,' Miles said.

He watched Charlie's reaction from the corner of his eye. It was clear that she knew her, or knew of her.

'Wow. Miles is right, Joe. Blonde, skinny, horsey. If you've got a type, I'm definitely not it.'

Her brother laughed, and Joe resisted the urge to use his fists to shut his mouth.

'Thank God I came to my senses and left all that schoolboy rubbish behind,' he said. Trying not to think of that leggy, horsey girl. Or maybe he *should* be thinking about her. Really, looking back, he owed Arabella a big thank you. She'd done him a favour, teaching him about how relationships *really* worked, rather than the schoolboy idealism he'd had at eighteen.

'Trust me,' Joe said, dropping his arm from Charlie's shoulders to her waist, 'you were everything I didn't know I was looking for.' He closed his eyes and leaned in for a kiss, thinking that a peck on the lips would finish off their picture of newly wedded romance nicely. And banish bitter memories of Arabella into the bargain.

How could he have forgotten? Perhaps his brain erased it on purpose, in an attempt to protect him? The second his lips met Charlie's a rush of desire flooded his blood, and he clenched his fists, trying to control it. To control himself. Was this normal? This overwhelming passion from the most innocent of kisses? He pulled away as Charlie's lips pouted, knowing that another second would lead them to more trouble than he could reasonably be expected to deal with.

Her eyes were still closed, and for the first time since they'd arrived at the palace her features were relaxed. A hint of a smile curved one corner of her lips, and the urge to press just one more kiss there was almost overwhelming.

'Okay, you've proved your point.' Miles laughed. 'I will never mention Arabella again. Or the fact that she's still single and still smoking hot.'

Charlie opened her eyes to roll them at her brother.

'Do you think we can stop trying to set my husband up with his ex?'

Miles held up his hands. 'You're the newly-weds. Your marriage is your own business. I was just providing the facts,'

'Well, as helpful as that is, darling,' Charlie's mother interjected, 'I think we can leave gossip about school friends for another time.'

Joe glanced at Adelaide, and as she met his eye he realised that he had an unexpected ally. He smiled back, curious. Charlie had been so worried about how her parents were going to react that it had never occurred to him that they'd actually be pleased to meet him.

They sat down for dinner in one of the semi-state-rooms, and Joe looked around him in awe. Away from the modest private apartments, it struck him for the first time that this really was Charlie's life. She'd grown up here, in this home within a palace. Her life had been crystal and champagne, gilt and marble and staff and state apartments. Carriages and press calls, church at Christmas and official photographs on her birthdays. And she'd walked away from all of that.

She'd chosen a warehouse apartment in East London. A job that demanded she work hard. A 'floor-drobe' rather than a maid. A real life with normal responsibilities. It occurred to him that he'd never asked her why. He'd mocked the privileges that she'd been born with, but he'd never asked her about the choices that she'd made.

As the wine flowed and they settled in to what to Joe seemed like a banquet of never-ending courses, Charlie relaxed more. He watched her banter with her brother and sister, and marvelled at the change in her since they had first arrived. When her hand landed on his thigh, he knew that it was all for show. Part of appearing like the loved-up new couple they were meant to be. But that didn't stop the heat radiating from the palm of her hand, or the awareness of every movement of her body beside him.

It didn't stop his imagination, the tumble of images that fell through his mind, the endless possibilities, if this thing weren't so damned complicated.

He wanted her. Could he have her? Could they go to bed, and wake up the next morning and *not* turn the whole thing into a string of complications? Could they both just demand what they wanted, take it, and then agree when it needed to be over?

They shouldn't risk it. He looked down at her hand again and caught sight of the gold of her wedding ring. It would never be that simple between them. They were married. They worked together. There was unbelievable chemistry between them, but that didn't mean that a simple night in bed together could ever be on the cards. They'd acted impulsively once, when they'd decided to get married, and that meant that the stakes were too high for any further slips on the self-control front.

Work. That was what he should be concentrating on. Like the fact that he still hadn't managed to write anything new for the album. He'd told Charlie and her boss that it was practically finished when he'd agreed to sign the contract. It *had* been finished. It still was, he supposed, if he was prepared to release it knowing that it wasn't his best work. What he really needed was to lock himself in his studio for a month with no distractions. Unfortunately, the biggest distraction in his life right now was living with him. And then there was the fact that if he was holed up in his studio, then where was the inspiration supposed to come from? What he'd end up with was an album about staring at the same four walls. What he needed was a muse. A reason to write.

Taking Charlie to bed would give him all the material he needed. He was sure of that. But at too high a cost.

They left the drawing room that night and headed to bed with handshakes and kisses from Charlie's family. Charlie stiffly accepted the kisses from her mother, and she climbed the stairs stiff and formal with him.

Joe watched her carefully as she led them down corridor after corridor, low lit with bulbs that wouldn't damage the artworks. He was vaguely aware of passing masterpieces on his left and right, but his attention was all on Charlie.

'Did you have a good time?' he asked. 'I thought it went pretty well; I liked your family.'

She nodded, staring straight ahead instead of at him. 'They liked you. Even Miles.'

'That's how he acts when he likes someone?'

She huffed an affectionate laugh, and turned to face him. 'I know. He's an idiot. We keep hoping he'll grow out of it.'

'Do you think they bought our story?' he asked. Her eyes seemed to turn darker as she looked ahead again. The sparsely spaced lights strobed her expressions, yellow and dark, yellow, dark.

'I'm not sure,' she admitted. 'But I don't think they're going to call us out on it. My mum already—'

She stopped herself, but he needed to know. 'What?' he asked.

'When I first called and told her what we'd done, she told me that she'd take care of it. If we wanted this marriage to go away.'

'And you didn't take her up on it?'

'We'd already talked about why that would be a bad idea. We made an agreement and I'm sticking to it.'

Her face was still a mystery. She was hiding something else. He knew that she was. Something that meant she was happy with their lie of a marriage rather than the real thing. Maybe he'd shock it out of her with some brutal home truths.

'Charlie, I want you. I know we said that sleeping together would be a disaster. But what if it wasn't?'

She turned to him properly now, her eyes wide with surprise. 'And where the hell did that come from?'

'It needed saying. Or the question needed asking. Maybe it could work. Maybe we could give it a go. I mean, we're acting out this whole relationship, so why not make it that bit more believable?'

'Why not? Do you really need me to list the million reasons it's a horrendous idea? As if our lives weren't complicated enough—you want to add sex to the mix?'

'But that's what I'm saying. Maybe it doesn't have to complicate things. Maybe it would simplify them. We're living together. We're married. We're making everyone believe that we're a couple. I mean, how would sex make any of that more complicated?'

'Because you forgot the most important thing— we're pretending. Yes, we had a wedding, but this isn't a marriage. We're not a couple. We're doing this for a limited time only, and mixing sex in with that would just be crazy.'

'So you don't want to. Fine, I just thought I'd ask the question. Clear the air.'

'Whether I want to or not isn't the issue, Joe.'

'So you do.'

'Urgh.' She threw her head back in frustration. '*Totally* not the point. And to be honest I'm surprised you're asking, because we both know that there's some crazy chemistry between us. We've talked about it before. And at no point has either of us thought that doing something about it was in any way a good idea. I don't know why we can't just drop it.'

'Maybe I don't want to.'

They stopped outside a door and Charlie hesitated with her hand on the doorknob, a frosty silence growing between them. Joe decided to take a punt, knowing that he could be about to set a bomb under their little arrangement. But if she wasn't going to volunteer all the facts, he had to get them out of her somehow. A pregnancy wasn't the sort of thing you could ignore for ever.

'How are you planning on passing me off as your baby daddy, then, if we're not sleeping together?'

Charlie took in a gasp of a breath, and as he watched her straighten her spine he realised that he'd been right about one thing—this was going to be explosive. But a shiver ran through him as Charlie walked into the room and he wondered whether he had just made an enormous mistake.

CHAPTER SEVEN

CHARLIE KEPT WALKING, calm and controlled, past the four-poster bed, trying to cover the typhoon of emotions roiling through her. She stopped when she reached the bathroom, an island of cool white marble after the richness of the bedroom.

'What are you talking about, Joe?'

Her teeth were practically grinding against one another, and she didn't seem to be able to unclench her fists.

'You're pregnant, aren't you?' His voice faded towards the end of the sentence, as if he were already regretting asking. But she didn't care about that, because the grief and pain that she had been holding at bay all night, seeing her sister's happiness with her children, her easy contentment, broke through the dam and flooded her. Winded, as if she'd been punched in the gut, she turned. She retched into the sink, as a week of new pain caught up with her. This had been building since she'd seen the newspaper headline announcing her own imminent engagement. She'd held it at bay, distracted herself with her stupid Vegas wedding and then burying herself in her work. But with Joe's crazy, heartless words—his absolutely baseless accusation—the pain had gripped her and wouldn't let her go.

Joe caught up with her and leaned against the bathroom door frame as she retched, hoping that she wasn't going to get a second look at her dinner.

'Are you okay?'

She threw him the dirtiest look that she could muster before hanging her head over the sink.

'Is it morning sickness?'

It took every ounce of self-control she possessed not to howl like a dog and collapse in a heap on the floor. Instead she forced herself upright, regaining control over her body.

'I. Am. Not. Pregnant.'

She forced the words out as evenly as she could, determined not to give him the satisfaction of seeing how he was hurting her, driving the knife deeper and twisting it with everything that he said.

'Are you sure? Because—'

She broke.

'I'm infertile, Joe. Is that sure enough for you?'

Her spine sagged and her legs turned to jelly as she spoke the words that she'd buried for so many years. She didn't even put out her hands to break her fall. There was no point—what could hurt more than this?

But instead of hitting cold marble, she landed on soft cotton, hard muscle. Joe's arms surrounded her, and her vision was clouded by snowy white shirt. She pushed away, not wanting him here, wanting no witnesses to her despair. But his arms were clamped around her, his lips were on her temple and his voice was soft in her ear.

'God, Charlie, I'm so sorry. I never would have said that if… I didn't know. I'm sorry.'

More murmurs followed, but she'd stopped listening. The tears had arrived. The ones that she'd kept at bay since she was a teenager. That she'd forced down somewhere deep inside her.

They tipped off the mascaraed ends of her lashes, streaking her cheeks, painting tracks down Joe's shirt as he held her tight and refused to let go, even as she struggled against him. Eventually, she stopped fighting, and accepted the tight clamp of his arms around her and the weight of his head resting against hers. She listened to the pulse at the base of his throat, heard it racing in time with her own. And then, as her heaving sobs petered out to cries, and then sniffs, she heard it slow. A gentle, rhythmic thud that pulled her towards calm. They'd slumped back against the claw-footed bath, her legs dragged across Joe's when he'd pulled her close and she'd fought to get free. The shoulder of his shirt was damp, and no doubt ruined by her charcoaled tears.

'You know,' he said eventually, 'we'd be more comfortable in the other room.' Their conversation in the corridor, when he'd oh-so-casually asked if she wanted to sleep with him, felt like a lifetime ago. Surely he couldn't be suggesting…

But he was right. The floor was unforgiving against her butt, and as comfortable as the bath probably was once you were in it, it didn't make for a great back rest.

She stood, pulling her dress straight and attempting something close to dignity.

'Let's just forget this whole conversation. Please,'

she added, when he stood behind her and met her gaze in the mirror.

He crossed his arms.

'I'm not sure that I can.'

'Well, I'm sure that if I can manage not to think about it, you can too.' She didn't care that he'd just been gentle and caring with her. Spiky was all she had right now, so that was what he was going to get. She walked through to the bedroom, her arms crossed across her chest and her hands rubbing at her biceps. She was cold, suddenly. Something to do with sitting on a marble floor perhaps. She climbed under the crisply ironed sheets and heavy embroidered eiderdown, pulling it up around her shoulders in a search for warmth. She figured she didn't need to worry about Joe's suggestion about sleeping together. There was no way that he was going to be interested in her now, with her messed-up mascara and malfunctioning uterus. When she looked up he was still standing in the doorway of the bathroom, watching her. She pulled the sheets a little tighter and sank back against the padded headboard, wondering if he was going to drop the subject.

'So how's that going for you?' he asked eventually. 'Not thinking about it, I mean.'

She shut her eyes tight, trying to block him out. She didn't need him judging her on top of everything else. But he wasn't done yet. 'Because it looks to me like burying your feelings isn't exactly working.'

Throwing the sheets down, she sat up, and met Joe's interested gaze with an angry stare. 'Just because you catch the one time in goodness knows how many years that I let myself think about it and get upset—all of a sudden you're a bloody expert on my feelings.'

'You might not think about it, but that doesn't mean that it's not hurting you.' His voice was infuriatingly calm, just highlighting how hard she was finding it to keep something remotely close to cool. If she didn't get a handle on her feelings, she was heading for another breakdown, and that little scene in the bathroom did not bear repeating.

'God, Joe. Stop talking as if you know me. You know *nothing* about this.'

He came to sit beside her on the bed, and his fingertips found the back of her hand, playing, tracing the length of her fingers, turning them over to find the lines of her palm. 'I know that it's getting between you and your family,' he said at last. 'I know that it hurts you every time you see your niece and nephew. Every time your mother casually mentions grandchildren.'

She looked up from their joined hands to meet his eye. He'd seen all that? 'You think you're so insightful, but an hour ago you thought that I was pregnant,' she reminded him.

He boosted himself up on the bed, and with a huff she scooched over, making room between her and the edge of the bed. He picked up her hand again, and focussed intently on it as he spoke. 'So I misinterpreted the reason you were acting funny. That doesn't mean I didn't see it. That I don't understand.'

'You don't. How could you?' She tipped her head back against the headboard and closed her eyes, wishing that he would just drop this. It wasn't as if it really affected him. He had no vested interest in whether she could procreate. It wasn't fair that he was pushing this when she so obviously didn't want to talk about it.

But if she could admit it to herself, perhaps talking felt almost...good. She realised that there had been a heavy weight in her stomach, sitting there so long that she'd forgotten how hard it had been to carry at first. Over time, she had got so used to the pain that she had lost sight of how it had felt not to have it there.

'I know that you let it push you into doing stuff that you regret. What happened that night in Vegas. Was it something to do with this?'

'I was just letting off steam. Having fun.'

'I don't believe you. I've not known you long, Charlie, but I can see straight through you. If I'd known you better that night I'd never have gone through with it. If I'd been able to see how you were hurting.'

'Hurting? I was enjoying myself. I got carried away.'

'For God's sake. Can you still not be honest with me, even now? I'm trying to tell you that you don't have to bury this any more. That if you want, we can talk about it. But you're trying to tell me you don't even care and I know that that isn't true. This is why you said you never wanted to get married, isn't it?'

She rolled her eyes, and tried to fake a snort of laughter. 'As if I even have to worry about that. Who would marry me if they knew?'

'Is that really what you think?' Pulling back, he put some distance between them so he could look her in the eye.

'It doesn't matter, Joe. I came to terms with it a long time ago. But yes, it's what I think. What would be the point of getting married?'

'I don't know. Speaking hypothetically here…isn't it usually something to do with spending your life with someone that you love?'

She snorted. 'Who knew you were such a romantic? But in a real marriage, sooner or later, kids always come up. Everyone's expecting it. Everyone's waiting for it. When you come from my family, especially.'

'And you're going to let that dictate what you do— who you date. What the great unwashed masses expect of you?'

'It's not just them, though. You don't understand. You don't understand my family. It only exists to perpetuate itself. To provide the next generation.'

'And that's the sort of person you'd want to marry, is it? The sort of person who sees you as a vessel for the next generation? If someone's looking at you like that, Charlie, you need to run, as fast as you can, and find someone who deserves you.'

The fire in his voice and in his expression was disconcerting, so much so that she found that she didn't have a counter argument. Because how could she argue with that? Of course she wanted someone who saw her as more than just a royal baby maker, but that didn't mean that he existed.

Joe's arm came around her shoulders, and she turned in to him, accepting comfort from the one person who could truly offer it. The one person who knew what she was going through—even if he couldn't really understand.

Listening to the rhythmic in–out of his breathing, she gradually felt her muscles start to relax. First her shoulders dropped away from her ears as her own breaths deepened to match Joe's. Then her fingers unclenched from their fists, her back gave out as she let Joe's side take her weight, and then her legs, bent at the knee and pulled up to her chest, tipped into Joe's lap, and were secured by the presence of his hand tucked in behind her knee.

With everything that had been said and revealed in the course of a night, there was no danger of things turning sexy. Charlie could feel that her eyes were swollen, and her skin felt red and tight from tear tracks. She felt anything but desirable. Burying her face in Joe's shirt, she tried to decide what she *did* feel.

Secure.

Anchored.

Not that long ago, an emotional night like this one would have seen her out on the town, running from her problems, looking for a distraction. But tonight, with Joe's solid presence beside her, she was exhausted. And where had running got her over the years anyway? Right back here in the palace, with her problems exactly where she'd left them.

She took a deep breath in, and as she let it go she released the remaining tension in her arms and legs, concentrating on loosening her fingers and toes. Her eyelids started to droop, and she knew that there was no point fighting it. She was going under, and she didn't want to go alone.

CHAPTER EIGHT

CHARLIE SNORED.

As in she was a serious snorer.

As in it sounded as if he were sharing a bed with a blowing exhaust pipe.

It seemed there was no end to the ways that this woman kept on surprising him.

Not that the snoring was bothering him, particularly. After all, there was no way that he was ever going to be able to get back to sleep. Not with the way that she had turned her back to him and scooted in, tucked inside the circle of his arms, and pressing back against him. Every time that he moved away, she scooted again, fidgeting and squirming in a way that was just…too good. So he'd stopped fighting it and pulled her in close, where at least she kept still, and his self-control had half a chance of winning out over his libido.

When they had fallen asleep last night they had been sitting against the headboard, one of his arms draped loosely around her shoulders. She had been curled up and guarded. Forcing herself into the relaxed state that she couldn't find naturally. He'd felt protective. As if he wanted his arms to keep out all the hurts that seemed to be circling her, waiting to strike. And he'd wanted to get into her head, to show her that the way she saw herself wasn't the way the rest of the world saw her. He certainly didn't see her as damaged goods. As being less than a woman whose insides happened to work differently. But he knew she wouldn't believe him if he told her that.

And more to the point, he didn't want her to think that he had some vested interest in the matter. He'd crossed a line yesterday by suggesting that they sleep together, and, now that he knew how narrow a tightrope she was walking, he felt like kicking himself for adding more uncertainty and confusion into the mix. They weren't going to sleep together. She had been right—it would make an impossibly complicated situation even worse. He didn't want to lead her on. This was a limited-time deal, and it would end when they thought the timing was right for both of their careers. He wasn't getting involved emotionally—he had known all his adult life that relationships worked best when both parties knew exactly where the boundaries were, exactly what they wanted to get out of it. They would be crazy to go back on those agreements now.

He just had to remind himself that she didn't want that either. She wanted this marriage for what it could do for her career. For the ructions it would cause with her family. And, in light of recent revelations, perhaps she wanted it as a hide-out. An excuse not to meet some suitable guy who might have marriage and babies on his mind.

But that was last night. This morning, 'protective' had well and truly taken a back seat. There were more pressing things on his mind, like the way that her legs fitted so perfectly against his: from ankle to hip they were perfectly matched. Or the way that his arm fitted into the indent of her waist.

Or the fact that if she were to wake up this minute, she'd know exactly how turned on he was, just by sharing a bed fully clothed.

How had his life got so complicated? In bed with a woman he wanted desperately—whom he had already married—but whom he knew he absolutely couldn't have. He cursed quietly, trying to pull his arm out from under her. If he wasn't getting back to sleep, he could be doing something useful, like taking a cold shower and then trying to write.

They were due to fly back to the UK and be up at his parents' house by tea time—they'd made no plans for the rest of the day, and he wondered whether he might be able to find some time alone to work. Last night, Charlie had promised to show him the music room, and the urge to feel the keys of a beautiful grand piano beneath the pads of his fingers had been niggling him since he'd woken. But every time he'd tried to make his escape, Charlie had pressed back against him again and he'd thought…not yet. Just another few minutes.

When she settled, he went for it again, this time pulling his arm out firm and fast, determined not to be seduced into laziness another time. His arm was free at last, and Charlie rolled onto her front, a frown on her face as she turned her head on the pillow first one way and then the other. He felt bad, seeing her restless like that. She had had too little sleep since her overnight stop in Las Vegas, and he knew that for once the black rings under her eyes had nothing to do with eyeliner. He stood watching her for a moment, reminded of that first morning, another night where they had collapsed into bed fully clothed.

He pulled off his T-shirt as he headed for the bathroom, and turned on the shower. He let it run cool before he climbed underneath, concentrating on the sensation of the water hitting his head and shoulders, trying not to think of the beautiful woman lying in his bed.

He wished that they could get out of their second trip this weekend. He wasn't sure that there was a good time to introduce your parents to your fake wife, but he guessed that the morning after a huge row and a heartfelt confession was pretty low on the list. Would Charlie be funny with him this morning? He tried to guess how she would act—whether she'd want to talk more, or pretend that it had never happened and she had never said anything—but had to admit to himself that he didn't even know her well enough to predict that.

By the time that he got out of the shower, she was sitting on the edge of the bed, rubbing at her eyes. So much for some alone time. He secured his towel firmly around his waist before he called out to her.

'Morning.'

Really, was that the best he could come up with? he asked himself.

'Hey,' she said back, tying up her hair and stretching her arms up overhead. 'Have you been up long?'

'Just long enough to shower. I was going to take you up on the offer to play in the music room. Have you got stuff you need to do this morning?'

She frowned, and he realised how that had come

across. But was it really so unreasonable of him to tell her that he needed some space? She had no problem with staying at the office late when she didn't want to see him—this was practically the same thing.

'I was just going to chill. Maybe hang out with Miles for a bit. I've not had a chance to do that since we got back.'

He nodded, trying not to show how claustrophobic he was starting to feel. Was this a normal part of newly married life? he wondered. This discomfort with sharing your personal space?

He crossed to the bureau, where he'd discovered their clothes had been unpacked, and pulled on a T-shirt and a pair of jeans. He'd wondered when he first woke up that morning whether she'd be uncomfortable with him today, he'd not expected when he'd been lying next to her that he would be the one trying to put space between them.

But it wasn't about her, or even about him. It was about feeling inspired to write for the first time all week, and wanting to make the most of it before the motivation deserted him again.

'You don't mind, do you, if I go?'

He was already halfway out of the door as he asked the rhetorical question, hoping that he remembered how to find his way back to the room she'd pointed out to him the day before.

When he eventually saw the piano in front of him, he let out a long sigh of relief. Then sat on the stool and let his fingertips gently caress the keys, pressing first one, then another, and listening to the beautiful tone of the instrument. One to one with a beauty like this, he could forget that he had a wife somewhere in this maze of a palace. Forget all of the complications that she had brought into his life.

He ran up and down a few scales, warming up his hands and fingers, trusting muscle memory to conjure up the long-memorised patterns. He'd been no more than a baby the first time he'd played the piano, he knew. Remembering family photos with him perched on his mother's knee as they picked out a nursery rhyme together.

These scales and arpeggios had taken him through recitals and grade exams. From his perfectly average primary school to the most influential and exclusive private school in the country.

They never changed, and he never faltered when he played them. From the final note of a simple arpeggio, his fingers automatically tipped into a Beethoven piece. His mother's favourite. The one that he'd practised and practised until his hands were so sore they could barely move, and he could see the notes dancing before his eyes as he tried to get to sleep. It was the piece that he'd perfected for his scholarship interview. The one that had opened up a new world of possibilities in his career—and had eventually taught him the truth about human relationships. Okay, so he wasn't writing any new material. Not yet. He let the thought go; saw it carried away by the music. Because this was important too, these building blocks of his art and his craft.

He let his hands pick through a few more pieces, and he stretched his fingers, feeling the suppleness and strength in them now that they were warmed up. He placed his tablet on the music stand, flicked through folders, looking for where he'd jotted down ideas for new lyrics and melodies, stored away for future development.

There'd been nothing new added for a while. Lately, when he'd been working on songs for the album, he'd been much further down the line than this. It was ages since he'd been at square one with a song.

He listened to a few snippets of audio that he'd recorded. A few odd words and phrases that had struck him. None of it was working. He'd been right the first time around when he'd chosen other ideas over these. He shut off his tablet and returned his fingers to the keys. It was only since he'd met Charlie that he'd been so dissatisfied with the songs that he'd written before. Why should that be? He tried to reason it out logically. Because maybe if he could work out why he suddenly hated those songs, he could work out how to write something better. He let his fingers lead, picking out individual notes, and then chords, moving tentatively across the keyboard as he experimented with a few riffs.

A combination of chords caught his ear, and he played them back, listening, seeing where his fingers wanted to trip to next. Maybe that was something…it was something for now, at least. He grabbed a guitar from beside the piano and tried out the same chords. Then picked a melody around them. He turned on the recorder on his iPad. He wasn't in a position to risk losing anything that might be any good. He turned back to the piano and tried the melody again, tried transposing it down an octave, shifting it into another key. He crashed his fingers onto the keyboard harder. There was something there, he knew it. Some potential. He just couldn't crack it. He needed to get through to the nub of the idea to find out what made it good. How to work with it to make it great.

He'd just picked up his guitar again, determined to at least make a start on something good, when the door opened behind him. He spun round on the stool and threw an automatic glare at the door.

Charlie drew up short on the threshold.

'S-sorry,' she stammered, and he knew his annoyance at being disturbed must have shown on his face. 'I brought you a coffee.'

He noticed the tray in her hands and thought twice about his initial instinct to kick her straight out. Maybe he could do with the caffeine, something to get his brain in gear.

'Thanks,' he said grudgingly. 'You can come in— you don't have to stay in the doorway.'

He set the guitar down and turned back to the piano, hoping that she would get the hint, but, instead of hearing the door shut behind him, he was being not so gently nudged to the side of his stool while Charlie held two cups of coffee precariously over the keyboard.

'That sounded interesting,' she said. 'What was it?'

He fidgeted beside her, wishing she'd just go and leave him to it.

'It's nothing. Just playing around with a few ideas. Trying to generate some inspiration.'

She plonked herself down beside him and he held a breath as the hot dark liquid sloshed dangerously close to the piano. Somehow, miraculously, the coffee didn't spill. 'What for?' she asked. 'I thought the songs for the album were all done.'

He shrugged. He really didn't want to go into this now. 'They were.'

'Were?' She finally placed the drinks down on the top of the piano and turned towards him, trying to catch his eye. 'Are they not any more? What happened to them?'

He kept his eyes on the keyboard, his fingers tracing soundless patterns in black and ivory. 'Nothing happened to them. I'm just not sure that I want to include all of them. There's one or two I'm looking at rotating out.' He kept his voice casual, trying not to show the fear and concern behind this simple statement. It didn't work. Charlie's back was suddenly ramrod straight.

'And you're telling me this now? How long have you been thinking this?'

'Are you asking as my wife or as a representative of Avalon?'

'I thought they were the same thing.' The monosyllables were spoken with a false calm, giving them a staccato rhythm. But then she softened, leaned forward and sipped at her coffee, looking unusually thoughtful before she spoke.

'What can I do to help?'

His first instinct was to tell her to leave him in peace—that was the best thing she could do for him. But the timing of this creative crisis suggested that she was in some way to blame for his current dissatisfaction with his work. So maybe she could be the solution too. 'What about a co-writer? I can call a couple of people. Maybe someone to bounce ideas off.'

'I'm not sure,' he said eventually. 'I was happy with

everything before we went to Vegas. I didn't feel like I had to do anything more to it.'

'And now?'

'I don't know. I listened to the demo when we were on the plane. I reckon half the tracks need to go.'

She visibly paled. But to her credit she clearly tempered her response. Regardless of the fact that losing half the tracks would throw a complete spanner into the plan that she and Rich had been working on for recording and releasing the album.

'Can we listen together?' she asked. 'You can talk me through what you're worried about.'

He hesitated. No one outside the band had heard the new tracks. The record companies that had been so keen to fight over them had taken their history of big sellers, and not insisted on listening to the new material. Letting his songs loose on the world was hard enough when he was happy with his work. Letting someone listen to something he knew wasn't right… It was like revealing the ugliest part of his body for close inspection.

But this was what Charlie did. He knew her reputation. He knew the artists and albums that she had worked on. She got results, and her artists trusted her. Maybe he should as well. He'd spent the last week with his head buried in the sand, trying to ignore the problem. It was time to try something different.

He reached for the tablet, ready to cue up the demo, but Charlie stopped him with a hand on his arm.

'Why don't you play?' she asked, nodding at the piano keyboard in front of them. 'One-man show.'

He shrugged. It didn't make much difference to

him. The songs weren't good enough, and it wouldn't matter how she heard them.

He rattled through the first bars of a track he picked at random. Trying to show her with his clumsy hands on the keys how far from good the song was.

She didn't say a word as he played, but her knee jigged in time with the music, and as he reached the middle eight her head nodded too.

He reached the end and looked over at her—ready for the verdict. 'I don't hate it,' she said equivocally. 'Are there lyrics?'

'The chorus maybe. The verses are definitely going.'

She nodded thoughtfully.

'Well, let's hear it before we do anything drastic.'

He returned his hands to the keys and took a deep breath, straightening his back until his posture rivalled hers. He'd been taught to sing classically at school, and there was a lot to be said for getting the basics right.

It had been a long time since he'd sung to someone one-to-one, with just a piano for company. In fact, he couldn't remember ever sitting like this with someone. With so much intimacy.

A lump lodged itself in his throat. Was he really nervous? He'd sung to her the first night that he'd met her. Spotted her on the side of the stage halfway through the gig and made eye contact. Had that been it? The moment that everything had changed for them?

There had been thousands in the audience that night. He'd played at festivals where the audience stretched further than he could see. Just a couple of days ago he'd sung with her in front of a growing crowd of Londoners. It hadn't occurred to him that day to be nervous.

But the thought of singing with her sitting beside him at the piano was bringing him out in a sweat.

She waited, letting the silence grow. Waiting for him to fill it. He pressed a couple of keys experimentally then worked his way into the intro.

Her thigh was pressed against his leg; he felt the pressure of it as he worked the piano pedal. He closed his eyes, hoping that banishing her from at least one of his senses would get his focus back where it needed to be.

He took a deep breath and half sang the first words of the verse. His hands moved without hesitation and he felt his voice grow stronger as he moved from verse to chorus and back again. He winced as he sang the second verse, aware that the lyrics were trite and cliched.

He'd written about love. Or what he thought love might feel like as a thirty-something. The more he thought about the only time he'd thought he'd been in love, the more uncertain he was that that was what he had really felt for Arabella. Sure, it had been intense at the time. There were songs that he'd written then that still tugged at the heart strings. But something told him that love was meant to be…bigger than that. The connection he felt with Charlie right this second, for example. That was big. In fact, he couldn't quite decide if it was warm and enveloping big, or heavy and suffocating big. All he knew was that it was scary big. And a million miles from what he had felt for Arabella when he was eighteen.

And of course all that was seriously bad news—

because big scary feelings did not make for a happy marriage of convenience. He tackled the middle eight with energy, abandoning his original lyrics, and just singing what came into his head. Trying to lose himself in the notes and not overthink.

He sang the last chorus as if there were no one else listening, new lyrics streaming through him as if he were a vessel for something greater than him.

He let his hands rest on the keyboard when he finished, and kept his eyes locked on them as well. He couldn't let her see. It was too dangerous. Too risky to the arrangement that they had both agreed to. He waited until he could be sure his expression was neutral before he picked up his mug from the table beside the piano and took a sip.

'So?' he asked, not sure that he wanted to know what she thought of it.

'Please, please tell me that's not on the cull list.'

He took a second to really look at her. Her eyes were wide, almost surprised. Her bottom lip was redder and fuller than the top, as if she had been biting on it and had only just let it go. He imagined that if he looked hard enough he would be able to see the shadowed indentation of her top teeth still there. That if he leaned down and brushed his own lips against it it would be hot and welcoming.

'I'm not sure about the first half,' she went on at last, 'but the lyrics in the second? The bridge? That last chorus. That's winning stuff, Joe. That's straight to number one and stay there. That's break the internet stuff. I can't believe you were going to toss that.'

'The first half though.'

'The first half we can fix. Anyone who can write the second half can fix the first, I promise you that.'

He stayed quiet for a long moment. He could ask himself what had just happened, but the truth was that he already knew. She had happened. She was what was different about his writing. He finally had the inspiration that he needed.

He had no doubt that he still had a lot of work to do, but maybe working with Charlie would be a good thing. It had certainly helped with these lyrics; they'd worked their way into his brain as he was singing, reaching his lips as if he were channelling them, not writing them.

He launched into the opening chords of another song. One he was more sure of. He tweaked the words as he sang, reaching for more unusual choices, to pin-point emotions he'd only been able to sketch before.

He glanced across at Charlie and she was smiling. A weight of pressure lifted slightly; a measure of dread fell away. They could fix this. Together.

More than anything, this was what really brought it home to him what they'd done. They had tied themselves together in every possible way. His career and his personal life were indivisible now.

For so long 'personal life' had been synonymous with 'sex life'. When Charlie had stipulated *no cheating* he'd known that it was a no brainer. Of course he wouldn't sleep with anyone else. But had he really thought it through? He'd voluntarily signed up for months of celibacy. Maybe years. Perhaps he had assumed unconsciously that 'no cheating' and celibacy weren't necessarily the same thing.

Everything seemed to keep coming back to that

question—even though they had agreed right from the start that that wasn't going to happen. And now he had acknowledged that his feelings for her were so much more serious than he had originally thought. Had he really thought the word 'love' earlier?

He finished the song on autopilot and knew from Charlie's expression that she could feel the difference. Her smile was more polite and that sparkle had gone from her eyes.

'Lots of potential in that one,' she said diplomatically. 'Definitely one we can work on.' She glanced at her watch and had a final sip of her coffee.

'I should let you work. Are you sure I've packed the right stuff for your parents' house? Because I can go out and pick something up if I need to.'

'Well, you probably can leave your tiara here,' he said with a smile, so she knew it wasn't a dig. 'Just something for dinner tonight. Doesn't need to be as fancy as at your place.'

Had he really just referred to the palace they were sitting in as 'your place'? Perhaps he was getting more used to this royal thing than he had thought. Getting used to her.

It was getting harder and harder to remember they were only in this to forward both of their careers. The lines between business and personal were blurring to the point that he couldn't see them any more. And that was dangerous, because the further they moved away from that simple transactional relationship, the more at risk his heart and his feelings would be.

'And make sure you've got something you don't

mind getting dirty if we're going to that festival. I'm not going to spend the whole time in VIP.'

She rolled her eyes.

'You so don't need to worry about that.'

CHAPTER NINE

CHARLIE CRAWLED UNDER the duvet and across the tiny double bed until she was almost pressed against the wall. Really, the sleeping arrangements in this marriage kept going from bad to worse.

'Do you think they liked me?' she whispered as Joe unbuttoned his shirt and pulled it back over his shoulders, revealing those tattoos she was still getting to know. He pulled a T-shirt from his bag, and then they were covered again. She almost spoke up and asked him not to, but stopped herself. Cosy sleeping arrangements or not, she had no rights over his body. No authority to ask for a few more minutes to look at his skin.

'They loved you,' he replied, sitting on the side of the bed and pulling off his jeans. 'Of course they did. What did you expect?'

'You know what I expected,' she said, tucking her hand under her pillow and turning on her side to face him. He slid between the sheets and lay beside her, mirroring her posture until they were almost nose to nose in the bed.

'And I told you that you didn't have to worry,' he said, though she didn't quite remember it that way.

Why should she care anyway? In a few months these would be her ex in-laws. She wouldn't ever see them again.

He wondered whether his parents had suspected that there was something off about their relationship. But they had been so distracted by Charlie, and protocol and the whole Princess thing that they hadn't seemed to notice anything.

He could feel the warmth of her under the cool sheets, and for a second was flooded by the memory of waking up with her that morning, with her legs fitting so closely to his. Did she even know what she had done?

'Did you know you're an aggressive spooner?' The question just slipped out of him. She looked shocked for a second, but then had to stifle a laugh.

'What's that meant to mean?'

'It means you were grinding into me like a horny teenager this morning. I didn't know where to put my hands.'

Her mouth fell open. 'I did not.'

He couldn't resist smiling. 'You so did. Forced me out of bed.'

Not strictly the truth, of course. He'd lain there so much longer than was a good idea, just soaking up the feel of her.

'A gentleman would have moved away,' she said.

'A lady wouldn't have reversed straight back in again every time I did.'

She kicked out at his leg. 'You're totally making this up.'

'Why would I do that?' he asked.

'I don't know. Maybe you want me to do it again.'

'Would you?' The very air around them seemed to be heavy with anticipation as he waited for her to answer.

'I asked first,' she said at last, deliberately not answering his question.

Was she serious? Were they really talking about this as if it might happen? She looked as if she wanted it. Her eyes were wide, her lips moist and slightly parted. One hand was tucked under her cheek and the other below her pillow. He didn't dare look any further down. He'd seen her pull on a pyjama top and shorts earlier, and he knew that gravity would be making the view south of her throat way too distracting. Too tempting.

'Maybe,' he replied at last.

Such a simple word. Tonight, such a dangerous one.

She turned her back to him but didn't make any effort to come closer. Was she testing him? Seeing if she came halfway whether he would come forward the other half.

With her back to him it was safe at last to look down. From where she'd tied her hair in a messy knot, the ink at the nape of her neck, down the length of her long, elegant spine. The tapering of her waist disappeared into the shadows under the sheets.

If he reached for her, would that be the point of no return?

Would the touch of his hand on her waist be the same as telling her that he wanted a relationship? That he loved her?

Were those statements true?

He wanted her. He knew that. That was the easy question. But how many times did he have to tell himself that having sex with the woman pretending to be his wife was a bad idea? That it could never be just sex, because it was already so much more than that.

What would she want from him in return? More than sex meant thinking with his heart, rather than his head, and that had got him badly hurt—and embarrassed—before.

He had tried his hardest to learn his lesson after Arabella, but even that humiliation hadn't been enough for him to spot the woman who was only with him so she could sell his secrets to the highest bidder.

Could Charlie really want him for who he was, rather than what he could do for her?

He couldn't remember ever being more turned on, more tempted than he was right now, but he had to be smarter than that.

Taking what he wanted came with a price tag. But tonight he couldn't be certain what the price was, or whether he would be willing to pay. And so as much as it killed him to do it, he turned over, pulled the duvet high on his chest and squeezed his eyes shut.

He heard a rustle behind him and tried not to imagine Charlie lifting her head from the pillow and looking over at him, wondering what had happened. He didn't want to see her confusion as he cut dead their flirtation. Her head hit the pillow hard, and the duvet pulled across to her side of the bed.

'Night, then,' she said, nicking territory and duvet as she spread out her limbs.

He was so tempted to retaliate. Almost as tempted as he had been to kiss her. To be pulled back into their banter. But he kept silent and still, feigning sleep.

* * *

Had she imagined it, last night? she wondered, trying to decide if she should be blaming Joe or her over-active imagination for what had happened. Why, oh, why had she had to be so insistent that they didn't have sex? Because that was where this relationship had been heading, before they were so stupid as to get married.

If they'd done the sensible thing and had a one-night stand that first night, like any self-respecting party girl meeting a rock star, they could be thousands of miles apart and a week into forgetting it all by now. Instead she had been shacked up at her new in-laws', trapped in the world's smallest double bed and ready to explode from frustration.

Surely her imagination wasn't good enough to have imagined that flirtation last night. Joe was the one who had brought up the subject of spooning, and when she'd decided she was so goddamned turned on that she didn't care any more whether it was a good idea or not, and all but wiggled her arse at him, he'd literally turned his back on her—the body-language equivalent of 'thanks, but no thanks'. Only less polite.

So when she'd woken first this morning, there was no way she was going to hang around for him to wake up and rehash the whole thing. One rejection was plenty, thanks. She'd known as soon as she told him about her infertility that she was taking herself well and truly off the market as far as he was concerned. It had been stupid to expect any other reaction to her advances than the one that she had got.

So she'd got up and found Joe's mum already in the kitchen, and before she quite knew what was happening there was a cup of strong tea in front of her and the smell of bacon coming from the stove.

'Did you sleep well, then, love? Oh, I shouldn't ask that really, should I? Not to a newly-wed. And that bed in there's so small. Not even a proper double. Hardly room to—'

'Shall I put the kettle on?'

Charlie breathed a deep sigh of relief—not the emotion she'd expected to feel when setting eyes on Joe that morning. He leaned in the kitchen doorway, colour high on his cheeks as he crossed his arms and gave his mum a look.

'No need, love.' His mum bustled round, pouring another cup from the pot and setting it on the table for Joe.

'I was just saying to Charlie—you are sure it's okay for me to call you Charlie?' She didn't stop for an answer. 'I was just saying that the bed in your room. It's hardly big enough for you on your own, never mind for the two of you great tall things. We'll have to do something about that. Maybe you should have our room.'

Joe kissed his mum on the cheek and extracted the tongs from her clasped fist.

'You're babbling, Mum. Sit down and drink your tea.'

His mum sat and he shot a glance over her head to Charlie, who smiled conspiratorially in return.

'You sure you don't want to come with us today, Mum?' Joe asked as he served up the bacon sarnies.

'Me in all that mud? You must be mad, love.'

'Mud? It's twenty-five degrees outside. Not every festival is Glastonbury in the rain, you know.'

'I've seen these things on the telly, love. Maybe if you were playing, but I'll give it a miss. You two love birds don't want me and your father there playing gooseberry anyway.'

Joe rolled his eyes as he picked up a sandwich, 'Mum, there'll be thousands of people there. It's not like we're expecting to be alone.'

'Don't be obtuse, Joe. You know full well it's not the same.'

'I feel awful shooting off like this,' Charlie said. They'd sat down to dinner barely an hour after they had arrived last night, and she'd been so beat after four courses and dessert wine that they'd retreated to bed long before midnight.

'Don't be daft, love. You young people are so busy, and Joe's already told me how hard you work.' Interesting…when had he told her that? 'It's been lovely that you made it up here with everything that you've both got going on. Don't go and spoil it by overstaying your welcome.'

Charlie smiled, surprised by how at home she felt with Joe's parents already. As if she really were becoming part of the family. Probably best that they were leaving this afternoon, then. Before this became another reminder of how hard it was becoming to keep reality and pretence straight in her head.

They climbed into Joe's car, chased by kisses and offers of baked goods for the journey. The festival was out in the countryside, about half an hour from his parents' house. Thank God it was no further, Charlie thought, twenty minutes of isolated confinement later. There was a limit to the tension that her body could take, and she was rapidly approaching it.

They were going to have to talk about what had happened last night. She'd hoped that maybe they could just ignore it—forget it had happened. And then his mum had been so funny with her babbling that she'd thought that they'd taken a shortcut and moved past it. But after breakfast they had been back in Joe's tiny bedroom, trying to pack their bags without touching. Moving around each other as if they were magnets with poles pointing towards one another. And she knew it would take next to nothing for those poles to flip and they would be back where they had been last night, drawn together, with only their self-control and better judgement fighting against the inevitability of the laws of nature.

She rested her chin on her hand; her elbow propped on the door as she gazed out of the window. They had barely spoken a word since they'd climbed into the car.

'Have you played here?' Charlie asked, needing the tension broken—before it broke them. The question counted as work. Talking about the band and work was safe. It was the only safe zone they had.

'Two years ago,' Joe replied, his eyes still locked on the road. They hadn't left it for a second since they'd left his parents' driveway. 'Were you here?' he asked.

'Yeah, with one of my artists. I didn't see you.'

'I wonder how many times that's happened,' he said, and for the first time he glanced over at her.

She furrowed her brow. 'That what's happened?'

'That our paths have crossed and we've not seen each other.' His eyes were back on the road now, but he looked different somehow, as if he was having to work harder to keep them there.

She tried to keep her voice casual, not wanting to

acknowledge the way the tension had just ratcheted up another notch. 'I don't know. Must be loads if you think about it.'

'I can't believe it,' he said.

She looked over at him again, to find him watching her. They'd pulled up at a junction, but his attention was all on her, rather than looking for a gap in the traffic crossing their path.

'Why?'

'Because...*this*. Because of the atmosphere in this car for the last twenty minutes. Because of how it felt in Vegas, knowing that you were watching me. I just can't imagine being in a room with you and not feeling that you were there.'

How *what* had felt in Vegas? She thought back to that moment when she was watching him from the side of the stage and their eyes had met. He had felt that too?

He reached for her hand. She considered for a split second whether she should pull away. It was what he'd done last night. She'd reached out to him, and he'd known it was too dangerous. A bad idea.

Could she be as strong as he had been?

His hand cupped her cheek, and she knew she could. She could be strong and resist, as he had. But maybe she could be a different kind of strong. Maybe looking at all the reasons this was a bad idea, all the reasons it was a terrifying choice, and *still* choosing it, maybe that was strong too.

She leaned forward across the centre console, sliding her hands into his hair and bringing their mouths together.

Her body sighed in relief and desire as his tongue

met hers, simultaneously relaxed and energised by this feeling of…perfection. This was it. This sense of fitting together.

A horn blared behind them and she sprang back, reeling from her realisation.

He grimaced as he slid the car into gear and pulled away, with just a slight lurch as the clutch found its biting point. This was what she'd been waiting for; and it was what she'd been dreading. She'd been running from it her whole adult life. She didn't want to be completed. She didn't want to belong with someone. Her one-off dates and casual boyfriends—she never had to tell them she was infertile. Never had to spell out the future that they would never have. Never had to explain that if she shacked up with someone long-term and the babies didn't come that they'd be hounded by the press and his virility would be called into question. Their bins would be searched and their doctors harassed. Her body had been public property since before she was born. Anyone who wanted to spend their life with her would be volunteering for the same deal—who in their right mind would do that?

Ten more minutes. She had to survive just ten more minutes in this space with a man she was finding it impossible to remember to resist. They showed their passes at the gate and, in silence, Joe directed the car through the gates and down a rucked track towards the VIP parking, waved along by marshals. When they arrived, Joe pulled on the handbrake and opened the door, while she gathered her things from the footwell. Her door opened, and Joe was there, holding out his hand like a cartoon prince.

'Very gallant,' she said lightly, knowing that her

confusion was causing a line to appear between her eyebrows.

He handed her down from the car, and as her feet reached the ground he pressed her back against the rear door, one of his knees nudging between hers. His hand caught at the ends of her hair and he pulled gently, bringing a gasp of pleasure and anticipation to her lips. She tilted her head to one side as she met his eyes, and saw passion and desire. Another inch closer and she was trapped. Car behind, hard body in front, and still that hand in her hair, pulling to one side now, exposing the pulse of her throat. She licked her lips in anticipation and closed her eyes as Joe moved closer. First cool lips descended and then a flicker of warm tongue in a spot that made her shudder. The butterfly caresses of his mouth traced up the side of her neck, then suddenly down to her shoulder, where her shirt had slipped, exposing her collarbone. The sharp clamp of his teeth on her sensitive skin made her gasp in shock. But the noise was lost as his lips were suddenly on her mouth, and his tongue was tangling with hers.

She wound her fingers in his hair, levering herself a little higher, desperate to bring their bodies in line. Cursing her decision to wear flat biker boots instead of her usual heels. Who cared about practicalities when there was a man like this to kiss?

Joe pressed into her with an urgency she'd not felt from him before. An urgency that made her wonder how spacious the back of his car was, and how much faith they wanted to put in the tinted windows.

It was as his lips left hers, to dip again to her neck, that she heard it.

Click.

Her eyes snapped open and she pushed at Joe's chest. She didn't have to look far over his shoulder to see the photographer. She took a second, breathing heavily and trying to remember that she was meant to be pleased about the press involvement in her life for once, before she spoke.

'You knew he was there?' she asked quietly, her lips touching Joe's ear. Her calves burned as she stretched up on tiptoes, but she wasn't ready to back down, back away, just yet.

'Spotted him as I got out of the car,' Joe whispered back.

Which explained the little display he'd just put on, then. Thank God she hadn't suggested taking the party back into the car.

'You okay?' he asked, and she forced a smile, pushing slightly on his chest and trying to regain her equilibrium. Desperate for a balance between trying to convince the photographer that that kiss had rocked her world, and not letting Joe see the truth of it.

'I'm fine.'

Their encounter with photographers at the airport seemed a long time ago and a long way away. She'd barely noticed over the past week that they hadn't been harassed by the paparazzi as much as she'd thought they might be—perhaps her mother had had a discreet hand in that. But there was no way that even her mother could keep them away here. The reality of the situation struck her—something she'd not counted on when she and Joe had been making plans for seeing family and work: they were going to be on display, all day. They couldn't afford to slip up. She closed her eyes and kissed Joe lightly on the mouth, telling herself it was just her way of warming up for the performance she knew that they had to nail.

'Want to go listen to some music?' she asked.

'No,' he said with a smile. 'I want to stay here and kiss you.'

She couldn't help grinning in return, not even trying to work out if it was for real or for show. Leaning back against this car in the sunshine, kissing a super-hot guy—that sounded pretty good to her too. But the moment was gone, and she couldn't lose the photographer from the corner of her eye.

'You're so going to get me fired,' she said. 'I'm meant to be working.'

'Well, then, jump to it, slacker. I'm not going to be one of those husbands who expects you to stay home and play house. Get out there and earn your keep.' He took a step back from her, and she slid her hands behind her butt. She knew real life was waiting for them, but what was just a few more minutes?

'I'd make a lousy housewife.'

'Oh, I don't know,' he said with a laugh. 'Some people like the hovel look. I hear it's big this year.'

She poked him in the ribs and laughed back.

'I'm not that bad.'

'You're worse.' He turned and stood beside her, draping a casual arm around her shoulder and pressing a kiss to her temple.

It would be too easy to take this little scene at face value, she knew. A week ago she'd be giving herself a stern talking-to. That all this was for the benefit of the photographers and the eager public. But today... today the line was more blurred. Her first thought had been that Joe was just putting on a show, but they had been moving so much closer for the last few days that she knew that some part of it was real. Their performance, it didn't feel like some random invention—it was more… Maybe it was what their relationship might have been if their lives were simpler. If she weren't a princess with a wonky reproductive system. If he formed actual emotional relationships rather than using women to get what he needed. Would it work? she couldn't help but wonder. If they had been two ordinary people, with ordinary lives, would they have been happy together?

'Come on, then,' she said at last, pushing herself away from the car, trying to shake the thought from her mind. It didn't matter if it would work that way, because they weren't those people, and never could be. Joe moved with her, his arm still around her shoulders as they made their way into the festival.

As Joe had promised, they were in the VIP zone for no more than half an hour before she was dragging him through a dusty field of festivalgoers, littered with abandoned plastic cups. She refused to watch the band from the side of the stage—she wanted the full experience, to see what she would be working with if she ever got this band to agree to sign with her.

The Sunday afternoon vibe was chilled and relaxed, with families dancing to the music, kids on shoulders, or eating on picnic rugs on the ground. Groups of people sat on the floor, passing round cigarettes and bottles of drink.

The sun was hot on her back, and she was pleased she'd pulled on one of Joe's long-sleeved shirts with her denim shorts, protecting her shoulders from burning.

For a while they just wandered, soaking up the atmosphere of a group of people united by a passion for music. Joe's fingers were loosely wound between hers, keeping her anchored to him. To their story. The impression of that kiss was still on her lips, and had been refreshed every now and again with a brief re-enactment. They couldn't just keep an eye out for cameras and people watching. For the first time since they had arrived back in the UK, they were truly having to live out their fake marriage in full view of the public.

And the weirdest part…it wasn't weird at all. In fact, it felt completely natural to be walking round with her hand in his. The way he threw an arm over her shoulders if they stopped to talk to someone. For once, she decided she actually liked being in flat shoes. Liked that his extra height meant that she was tucked into his body when he pulled her to him. It felt good—warm, safe, protected. Everything she'd been telling herself she didn't want to be.

'Want to find something to eat?' Joe asked when the band they had been watching finished.

'Dirty burger?' she asked, with a quirk of her brow.

'Whatever turns you on.'

You know what turns me on. The response was right there on the tip of her tongue, but she held it back, not trusting where it might lead them.

'Come on,' she said, pulling him towards a van selling virtuous-looking flatbreads and falafel. 'These look amazing. I'm having a healthy lunch, then I'm going in search of cider.'

With lunches in hand, they picked their way across to another stage, where Casual Glory, the band Charlie wanted to see, were just warming up at the start of their set.

'I saw these guys in a pub last year,' she told Joe. 'I wanted to sign them then and there. But then all the suits got involved and… I don't know, maybe they got spooked but somehow it didn't come off. I don't want to let them out of my grasp again.'

'They're still not signed?' Joe asked.

She dropped to the floor and sat cross-legged, watching the band while she ate.

'Free spirits. Didn't like the corporate stuff. And I'm not sure what I do about that, to be honest, because the music business doesn't really get much more laid-back than with Avalon.'

'You think you can get them to change their minds?'

Charlie nodded. 'I'm going to. I'm just not sure how yet.'

'You're not going to marry him, right?'

She laughed under her breath.

'One husband's already too many, thanks.'

He wound an arm around her neck, pulling her close and planting a kiss on her shoulder.

'You're right: they're good,' Joe said after they finished another song. 'Loads of potential. You should bag them.'

'Yeah, well, try telling them that,' she joked.

'I will, if you want. Are we going to say hi when they're done?'

'That's the plan.'

She leaned against his shoulder, soaking up the sun warming the white cotton of her shirt. Her head fell to rest against Joe's and she shut her eyes so she could appreciate the music more.

'Tired?' Joe asked in her ear, and she 'mmm'ed in response. She couldn't remember the last time she'd had a properly restful night's sleep. Turned out being married was more likely to give you black bags than a newly-wed glow.

'Come here, then.'

Joe pushed her away for a moment, then slung his leg around until she was sitting between his thighs, her back pulled in against his front. She relaxed into him, shutting out all thoughts of whether this was a good idea or not. Just letting the music wash through her. Soak into her skin and her brain.

'Comfortable?' Joe whispered in her ear.

'Too comfortable.'

She felt more than heard him chuckle behind her as his arms tightened. A press of lips behind her ear. A kiss on the side of her neck. A tingle and a clench low in her abdomen: a silent request for more and a warning of danger ahead.

Instead of heeding it, she let her head fall to one side, just as she had done by his car. They were in public, she reasoned with herself. There was only so far this could go. It was all a part of their performance.

'How about now?' he asked, pulling her hair over to her other shoulder. 'Feeling sleepy still?'

God, he was driving her insane.

'Like I could drop off at any moment.'

He growled behind her and she smiled, revelling in the way she was learning to push the boundaries of his self-control. His hand in her hair was tough and uncompromising now, and she let out a gasp as he pulled her back slowly, steadily, never so hard that it hurt. Making her choose to come with him rather than forcing. She opened her mouth to him without question. The hand still round her waist flattened on her belly, pressing her closer still.

She let out a low sigh of desire and her arm lifted to wind round his neck, opening her body. Was Joe controlling her without her realising? She didn't remember meaning to do it. Then his hand dropped from her hair and cupped her jaw: the kiss gentler now, sweeter.

She opened her eyes and smiled back at him, and she knew her eyes must look glazed, dopey. 'All right, I'm not likely to sleep in the next year. Is that what you wanted?'

'I'll take it,' he said with a smug smile. She leaned back into him again, languor and desire fighting to control her limbs.

CHAPTER TEN

'I WISH WE didn't have to go back tonight,' Joe said, stretching out his legs and leaning back on his elbows. Maybe it was the sun making him lazy, making him feel that he never wanted to leave this place. Charlie moved so she was lying to one side of him, her head propped on her hand.

'I thought you'd be dying to get back in your studio,' she said. 'You seemed all…inspired and stuff yesterday.'

'I am. I do want to write.' He'd had ideas swirling round his brain for two days; when they'd been at his parents' house he'd been desperate for a bit of space and time to try and get them down on paper, or recorded on his phone. But since they had arrived at the festival, since that kiss, everything felt different. 'I can't remember the last time that I was relaxed like this. The last time I felt still. I like it.'

'You can be still in London,' Charlie said.

He shrugged—or as best he could with his body weight resting on his elbows. 'I don't know if I can. Or maybe it's that I know that I won't.'

She sat up and gave him a serious look. 'Not every day can be Sunday afternoon at a festival. Real life is still out there, you know.' Of course he knew, but somehow he was managing not to care.

'I do know. But it feels that it can't get us here.'

'What are you worried about "getting us"?' she asked.

Why did they have to think about that now? Why couldn't they just enjoy this? He wished he knew. He'd just told her he felt still—what he'd wanted to say was that he felt happy. Content. He'd wanted to say that he'd stopped trying to work out if what she was saying was loaded. A way to get something more than they'd agreed from their arrangement.

Here at the festival, life was simpler. He could kiss and touch her. Laugh with her. Treat her as the woman he was in love with. No holding back.

Was that really it? Was that what was making him feel so…serene? Because he didn't have to pretend not to love her?

His phone chirped and he fished it out of his pocket, grateful for the distraction from his own thoughts.

'Amazing, they're here. Some friends of mine have stopped by,' he told Charlie. 'Want to say hi after you've done your work stuff?'

'Sure, why not? Who are they?'

'Owen's band supported us at a couple of gigs a few years ago. We hung out a bit. His wife's lovely too. You'll like them.'

He stood and pulled her up as Casual Glory finished their final number. His arm fell round her shoulders in that way that felt so completely natural. Perhaps it was just their height, he thought. He'd told her that he'd liked that she was so tall, but her flat biker boots today meant that he was a few inches

taller than her. Or maybe it was something else—
something to do with escaping their real lives and real
pressures. They were meant to be putting on a show
to the public today—but in reality it had given them
permission to stop pretending for the first time since
they had woken up married.

They passed through security to the VIP area,
and Charlie headed straight for the lead singer of
Casual Glory and gave him a hug. Joe hung back a
little, watching her work, impressed. She didn't just
schmooze—though she did compliment them on
their awesome set. She also challenged them, asked
them about their goals and their hopes for the future.
Showed them subtly that she would be their ally if
they wanted to make that a reality. And she made sure
that each member of the band left with her business
card in their pocket and some serious thinking to do.

Charlie cut the conversation short before they out-
stayed their welcome, and they headed over towards
the bar. He surveyed the room once he had a jar of
craft cider in hand—it was full of people resting their
feet, snatching glasses of free champagne, and trying
to get a sneaky snap of the VVIP whose hen do was
in full drunken flow in the corner.

He tapped the side of his glass, wondering whether
he had missed his friend, and whether they should
commandeer one of the golf buggies to go in search
of him when he recognised Owen's shaggy, shoulder-
length hair and waved at him from across the crowd,
squeezing Charlie's hand at the same time. He wondered for a split second whether he had done the right
thing in looking Owen up, but it was too late to back

out now. Owen turned and saw him, waving from across the tent.

'Hey,' Joe called out, making a move towards his friend.

Charlie followed the direction of Joe's wave and saw Owen—she recognised him from a gig she'd been to last year. And then a blonde woman—polished and beautiful—stepped from behind him, a chubby baby settled on her hip. Charlie's stomach lurched and she felt bile rise in her throat. Joe should have warned her.

He was the one who had called her out on how uncomfortable she had been acting around her sister and her kids. He had to know just how hard this would be for her. Especially with the way that talking about everything had been tearing open old wounds recently.

She realised that she'd come to a halt, and only Joe's hold on her hand pulled her forwards.

'Owen, hey, man. Alice, you look gorgeous.' Joe shook his friend's hand and kissed Alice's cheek. 'Guys, this is Charlie.' He'd pulled her to him and wrapped his arm around her waist. He was putting her through this and he didn't even care—didn't even think to try and understand how much this was hurting her.

Alice leaned in and kissed her cheek and Owen shook her hand.

'Congratulations, you two!' Alice said with a friendly smile. 'I can't believe someone's tied this guy down. You deserve a medal, Charlie. I can't wait to hear all the details.'

Charlie tried to return her smile, but felt her facial muscles stiffen into a grimace.

'And who's this?' Joe asked, chucking the baby's cheek and being rewarded by a belly laugh. 'Looks like we should be the ones saying congrats.' Charlie sensed something slightly forced in his cheerful tone. What was he up to?

'This is Lucy,' Alice said, and shifted the baby to hold her out to Joe. 'Want to hold her?'

'Are you sure?' He took the baby awkwardly and held her up to his face, pulling funny faces. Joe with a baby. Charlie watched him closely, trying to work out what he was feeling. His smile was open and straight-forward, and she envied him for it. She wished she could enjoy the sweet, heavy weight of a baby in her arms without being haunted by the inevitable regret and sadness.

'That must have moved quickly, then,' Joe was saying. She struggled to follow the conversation—feeling as if she had missed some vital part. 'The last time I saw you, you were still mired in bureaucracy trying to bring this one home.'

'Our social worker was awesome,' Alice replied. She turned to Lucy with another megawatt smile. 'We've adopted Lucy,' she said.

And the bottom fell out of Charlie's stomach. She stumbled, and the only thing to grab hold of to stop her falling was Joe. Again, goddamn him.

Had he planned this? Manipulated her into meeting this gorgeous family, with their beautiful baby?

Of course he had—that was what she'd heard in his voice. He'd been planning this behind her back. So after everything he had said about her being enough for any man just as she was, and it didn't matter if she could have children or not, here was the proof that he felt otherwise. She'd always known that it was always going to be true in the end.

It was as if he'd not listened to a word she'd said since they'd met. As if he didn't know her.

'L-lovely to meet you,' Charlie managed to stammer, and then she turned and started walking. She didn't even care where she was going. She just had to get out of there. Away from Alice and her gorgeous baby. Away from Joe and his lies and manipulations.

She reached sunshine and fresh air but kept walking, wanting as much distance as she could get between her and Joe. She couldn't remember where the car was so she just walked out. Out as far as she could. Tears threatened at the edges of her eyeliner, but she knew that she must not let them fall. Even now, they had to make this deception work, or what had been the point of any of it? She spotted the VIP car park and headed towards Joe's car. She just wanted to not be here.

The keys. Damn it. Well, maybe there would be someone else leaving and she could hitch a ride—

'Charlie!'

She recognised Joe's voice, her body responded to it—to him—immediately, but she fought it and kept walking. He couldn't possibly have anything to say to her that she would want to hear.

'Charlie, stop. Please!'

Ahead of her, someone was staring at them. She wanted so much not to care. To be a nobody—unrecognisable in a crowd. Someone no one knew or cared about. But she stopped, because she wasn't that person. She could never be that person.

Joe caught up with her, rested his forearms on her

shoulders. God, if he asked her what was wrong, that was it. She was running and crying and she didn't care who saw.

'I'm sorry,' he said. 'I should have warned you that they have a baby.'

She shrugged his arms off her shoulders. He was trying, but he still didn't get it. 'I'm not angry about the baby, Joe. Babies don't make me mad. I'm angry because you tried to manipulate me.'

'Manipulate you? How?'

He'd raised his voice, but then looked around. Remembered where they were.

'Maybe we should talk about this in the car.'

She narrowed her eyes. Right—they needed to protect their secret. He climbed into the car and she sat on the passenger seat, looking straight out ahead, not able to face looking at him properly.

'I should have warned you about the baby,' he said again. 'But I thought I was doing something good. I thought seeing how happy they are to have her would help. That they're a family, even if not by conventional means.'

'So what are you telling me—you want to adopt a kid? Is that your next big idea? Your next publicity campaign? It doesn't matter that I'm damaged goods, because you can always stick a plaster on that?'

'Don't be ridiculous, Charlie. This isn't about me and you know it.'

'Oh, of course, because all this is just for show. It's all about your career.'

'Yours too,' he bit back. 'You make me out to be mercenary, but don't pretend that you're not using me every bit as much as I'm using you.'

He was using her.

Of course he was, she had known that from the start. But to hear him say it like that—no sugar coating—it winded her. And he thought that she was just as bad as him. That she had made a cold, calculated decision to use him. Well, she couldn't let him go on believing that. She wasn't that much of a bitch.

'My career? You know that that wasn't why I married you. Unlike you, I'm not that mercenary. I saw a headline in the news, that night. My parents trying to marry me off to one of those suitable husbands who'd be waiting for his heir and spare. I married you because my family were trying to force me into being the happy wife that I knew I never could be. When I have reminders of my infertility thrust in my face, Joe, I have been known to go a little crazy and act out. I could see the life I had built for myself slipping away and I was so heartbroken I couldn't think straight. That doesn't make us the same.'

CHAPTER ELEVEN

'You were still using me,' Joe said. Charlie rolled her eyes at him, but he was still reeling.

'Oh, because you're such a goddamn expert, are you?' she said. 'Is it all women that you know so well, or is it just me? Because I've been on your telly and in your newspapers my whole life you think you know what I'm feeling.'

'I never said I think I know you—but I think I know something about women. About relationships. I do have some experience of this.'

'Oh, so we're finally going to get to the bottom of this. Good. It was Arabella, I assume, who broke your heart.'

'Nobody said my heart was broken.'

'You scream it without saying a word, Joe. You with your trust issues and fear of commitment. You've already seen every article of my dirty laundry. Are you going to tell me what went on to make you such a cynical son of a b—? Or are we going to carry on trying to work out what's going on with us while having to avoid stepping on the elephant in the room?'

He slapped the steering wheel. Why was she so determined to make this about him—to make him the bad guy? He had been trying to help, and now she wanted to drag up his past as if that had anything to do with what they were arguing about. 'There is no elephant. Arabella and me—it wasn't a big deal. I wasn't heartbroken. If anything I'm grateful to her. She taught me a lot.'

'Like what?'

'Like how relationships actually work—and I don't mean the hearts and flowers rubbish. I'm talking about real adult relationships where both partners are upfront and honest about what they expect.'

'And let me guess, what Arabella expected wasn't just to enjoy your company. What else did she want?'

He tried to wave her off, but he knew that she wasn't going to let this drop. The fastest way out of this argument was just going to be to tell her the truth. Then she'd see that Arabella had nothing to do with any of this.

'She wanted to piss off her parents. She thought that taking me home to meet them would do that.'

Charlie raised her brows. 'And when did you find this out?'

'When we turned up at her house for the weekend. They were perfectly nice to me and Arabella was furious. I think that she thought that one whiff of my accent and they'd be threatening to disinherit her. She'd read too much D H Lawrence.'

'And before that… Were you in love with her?'

He shrugged, because what did it matter how he had felt when he was a naïve eighteen-year-old?

'Before that, I thought things were as simple as being in love with someone. I know better now.'

'That's a pretty cynical way to go through life.'

'Is it? Are you telling me that if you meet a guy you love you'll just marry him—no thinking about real life, your family, your career? Children?'

'I married you, didn't I?'

He didn't know what he could say to that. She had just told him that she hadn't been thinking straight. Surely she couldn't be saying that she loved him. But she didn't deny it either. He shook his head—he had to try and make Charlie understand how Arabella had helped him. That he was happy with his life as it was. Or he had been, until he had met her.

'All I know is that since Arabella, I've not been hurt,' he said. 'Someone tried. Pretended that she wanted me, when all she wanted was something she could sell to the papers. If I'd not learnt my lesson after Arabella, maybe that would have affected my heart too. But I'm a quick study.'

Charlie reached for his hand and absent-mindedly traced the lines of the bones beneath the skin. He tried not to notice, tried not to feel that caress in the pit of his stomach. She was still looking out of the window, and he was cowardly grateful that she wasn't making him do this eye to eye.

'And is that what you want from life?' she asked. 'From the women in your life—just to not get hurt? Or, one day, are you going to want more than that? Are you going to want to risk going all-in? Risk your heart, and see what you get back.'

He let his head fall back against the head rest, and let out a long, slow breath. 'I don't know, Charlie. What could be worth that?'

She turned to face him, and he knew that she was not going to put up with his evasion any more. That all pretence that they were not talking about them now was flying out of the window.

'Are you serious?' she said, her eyes blazing. 'Don't you think that this could be worth it? That *I* could be?'

Her expression was wide open—she was holding nothing back, now. No more secrets. Nowhere left to hide.

'This was meant to be all for show,' he said.

'And yet here we are. We both know we didn't go in to this for the right reasons, Joe. But the more time we spend together, the more I feel this…this pull between us that I've never felt before. And I don't know what to call it. I'm scared to call it love, but nothing else seems to fit.'

'But what do you *want*, Charlie?'

'For God's sake. Why do I have to want anything, Joe, other than you? Why can't you believe that that's enough? I want what we had last night, whispering and laughing in bed together. I want yesterday, at the piano, feeling like I can see into your soul when you play and sing just for me. I want this afternoon, sitting in the sun with my eyes closed and your arms around me, not able to imagine feeling more complete. But what about you? Do you want a string of girls who will give you what you ask for and nothing more, or do you want a relationship? A connection. Something *real*.'

He opened his mouth to speak, but she held up a hand to stop him. He wanted to tell her that of course he wanted all that, but how was he meant to know if that was what she really wanted too? That laying his heart out there in the open felt like asking to have someone come and smash it until there was nothing left.

'I don't want your knee-jerk reaction,' she told him. 'Whatever the answer is going to be, I need to know that you've thought about it. That you mean it.'

They sat in silence for a long minute.

'I think we both need some time,' he said eventually. 'And some space. I don't think you should come back to London,' Joe said. 'Not yet.'

Her face dropped instantly, and he knew that he had hurt her. He reached out to her and softened his expression. 'Go back to your mum. Tell her what you've told me, and make your peace with her. Make your peace with what your parents want for you, and decide, with all your cards on the table, whether it's what you want too. If it is, we'll find a way to get it for you. I'll disappear from your life if that's what you need from me.

'But if you don't…even if, with no secrets, you still want to be married to me? Come home to me, Charlie.'

CHAPTER TWELVE

CHARLIE SAT IN silence as the car sped along the roads that were so familiar to her from her childhood. She had spoken to her mother as soon as she had set off for the airport, and sensed that she wasn't entirely surprised that she was on her way back already.

She still hadn't decided what she wanted to say to her. How she would explain that she loved her parents, all her family, but that she didn't want the life that they had decided on for her.

Now the heat of the argument had faded, she could see that Joe hadn't been cruel to introduce her to his friends. The opposite, in fact. He'd shown her what she should have seen all along. Her ability to bear children or not had never been the problem—if she couldn't have kids naturally that was something that might be sad, and difficult for her and a husband to overcome. But it didn't mean that she could never have a family on her own, and it definitely wasn't a reason not to marry at all.

No, her reason for not marrying the men that her parents had introduced to her was much simpler—she didn't want them.

She didn't want the men, or the families, or the life that they represented.

She didn't want to give up her home in London, or her job, or the pride that she had built in herself and her abilities since she had left home.

She didn't want to go back to Afland just because of a promise she had made when she was eighteen and wanting to leave. Didn't want the life that she had made for herself to be over just because the date on the calendar ticked over and she was twenty-eight years old instead of twenty-seven.

Charlie bit at a nail as the car pulled through the gates of the palace and her hand barely moved from her mouth until she was in her mother's study, sitting on the other side of her expansive desk, feeling more like a job candidate than a daughter. And then she remembered that she was the one who had stalked in here and sat, leaving her mother standing on the other side of the desk, arms raised in greeting.

'So, was there something in particular you needed to talk about, sweetheart?' Adelaide asked, drawing her chair around the desk to sit beside her daughter.

Charlie felt her spine stiffen as she thought about all the things that she'd not said to her mother over the past ten years, not knowing where to start.

'I don't want to come back, Mother. After my birthday. I know I promised I would—'

'That was a long time ago,' her mother interrupted gently. 'I'd hoped that you would want to come back to live here, that your father and I might see a little more of you. But I'm not going to force you. I don't think I could if I wanted to. Now, are you going to tell me what this is really about? Is it Joe? Because we never really had a chance to talk properly before. I thought when you called after the wedding, maybe you had done something that you regretted, but then when you were here…honestly, darling, the atmosphere between you.'

Charlie couldn't help but smile when she thought of him.

'So I'm right,' her mother continued. 'You two are crazy about each other.'

'It's complicated,' Charlie said with a sigh.

'Well, I think it often is.' Her mother gave her an encouraging smile. 'Maybe if you tell me everything, it would help.'

'I wish it would, Mum. But the thing is…' She couldn't believe that she was about to volunteer the information that she'd held secret for so long, that she'd had nightmares about her mother finding out. What if she did react as she had in her dreams? Pushing her out of the family, banishing her from the island of Afland for ever? But wasn't that what Charlie had done to herself? She'd all but cut herself off from her family—her mother couldn't do any worse than that. She took a deep breath, squeezed her fingernails into her palms and spoke.

'The thing is, I might not be able to have children.' The words tumbled from her mouth in a hurry, and she kept her gaze locked on the surface of the desk, unable to meet her mother's eye.

Adelaide reached for her hand, and held it softly in her lap. 'I'm so sorry, darling. That must be terribly hard for you. And is having children important to Joe?'

'No.' She shook her head, and finally lifted her

gaze to meet her mum's eyes. The gentle kindness and love on her face made a sob rise in her throat, but she forced it down, wanting to finish what she'd started. Wanting, more than anything, her mum's advice. 'He says… It doesn't matter, does it? It's not about Joe. It's about me, it's about the fact that I'm never going to be who you want me to be.'

'I just want you to be *you*, darling. And more than that, I just want you to be happy.'

But that was crap, because she'd seen for herself what her mum wanted for her. A suitable husband, marriage, babies. 'Then what was all that with Philippe?' she asked, an edge to her voice. 'Why was he talking about engagements and moving to Afland with your blessing? Why did I have to read about it in the paper?'

'Honestly, Charlie, after all this time how can you believe anything that you read? Philippe came for dinner with his parents and he asked if you were still single. You know that he'd always had a soft spot for you. Then his father asked if you were planning on moving back to Afland. I don't know where he got the rest of it from. If I know his father as well as I think I do, the story probably came directly from him. I'm sorry that the press team weren't able to keep his mouth under control. I'm not going to lie and say that I haven't thought that you might be happier if you moved home and made a good match. It's kept your father and I happy for thirty-odd years, and your sister fairly blissful for the last seven. But we were never going to force you. Did you really think that we would?'

Yes, she had. She'd thought that there was only

one way that she could make her parents happy and proud of her, but she could see from her mum's face that she'd got it wrong.

'No, I don't think you'd force me, Mum.' She stayed silent for a moment. 'I'm sorry that I've not been home much.' Her mum wrapped an arm around her shoulders. 'But seeing Verity, and the children...'

'That must have been hard.'

'I just knew that that might never happen for me, and if it doesn't then where do I fit in this family?'

Adelaide squeezed her shoulders and reached for a tissue from the silver dispenser on her desk. 'You're my little girl, Charlie. That's where you fit. Where you'll always fit. But maybe things aren't as bad as they seem. Have you seen a doctor about it?'

'Not since I first found out. I didn't want to talk about it, didn't want the press getting hold of anything.'

'Well,' Adelaide said. 'How about I set up an appointment with my personal doctor, and you can have some tests? At least then you might know where you stand. If you knew the secrets that man had kept for me...well, let's just say I know that he can be discreet.'

'And if I definitely can't have children?' Charlie asked, a shake in her voice.

'Then it won't change the way I feel about you even a tiny bit, Charlie. Surely you know that. I just want you to be happy. Is Joe making you happy?'

'He's trying. I'm trying.'

'That's good. Keep trying, both of you.'

Charlie looked up and smiled at her mum, and could see from her expression that they weren't finished yet.

'What, Mum? I know there's something else you want to say.'

'I just… I'd like to see you at home more, darling. I know that you want to stay in London. I know how important your career is. But it doesn't have to be all or nothing. You could come back to visit more. We'd love to see you. And maybe you could do a few official engagements. I can't tell you how much I've missed you.'

Charlie plugged in her headphones as she climbed into the car and cued up the tracks that Joe had sent her. They had only been apart for a night—nothing in the grand scheme of things—but the already so familiar resonance and tone of his voice managed to relax her muscles in a way she didn't know was possible. She closed her eyes as the car crept along the London streets from the airport, drumming her fingers in time to the music in her ears, remembering the morning they'd been in the music room, sitting at the piano where she'd taken lessons as a girl, next to a man who made her skin sing.

Was it pathetic that she'd broken into a smile as soon as she'd seen his name on her phone?

She tapped at the screen to bring the message up again.

Call me when you get in.

Did he mean it? Or was it just a pleasantry? Like, *Call me when you get in, but obviously not if it's late, or inconvenient. Maybe just leave it till morning.*

Ugh. She was irritating herself, sounding like one

of those pink glitter princesses she'd tried all her life not to be.

She shot off a text, the traditional middle ground between calling and not calling, telling him she'd landed and was heading back to her place. It was too much to just turn up on his doorstep, especially when she wasn't even sure that he wanted her there.

The car twisted through the darkened streets of the city, over brightly lit dual carriageways, past the twisted metal of the helter-skelter sculpture in Stratford, and on towards her flat.

Her stomach sank at the thought of another night sleeping without Joe. She told herself that a month ago she'd been perfectly happy barely aware that he existed. But that had all changed the minute that she had set eyes on him, and they couldn't change that now. Somehow, she knew that without him her flat would feel empty, even though he'd never set foot there before.

As the car approached the stuccoed, pillared front of her apartment building, she spotted a dark shadow on the front steps and her stomach lurched. She glanced back through the windshield, checking that the police officers she knew should be on her tail were there, and breathed a sigh of relief when she saw one of the officers speaking into a radio.

Just as the driver asked her over the intercom whether she wanted him to drive on, the headlights illuminated the steps, throwing light onto Joe's face, and shadows into the space behind him. She let out the breath she had been holding, and told the driver that it was fine, he could stop. She took a moment before she opened the door to gather herself, prepare for what might come with Joe.

Had he come to tell her that he wanted her? That he wanted to make this a real marriage, or that he wanted out?

'Hi,' she said as she stepped out of the car and up the steps.

'Hey,' Joe replied, giving nothing away.

She grabbed her bag from the driver and stepped past Joe, unlocking the door and pushing it open.

She reached down to grab the mail and then dumped it on the hallway table, glancing round and trying to remember what state she'd left the place in. She didn't normally care about the condition of the flat, as long as it was warm and watertight. She had spent her whole childhood and adolescence looking forward to the freedom of space that was entirely her own. But there was something selfish and lonely about that, about the fact that she didn't have to consider a single person's feelings except her own. Maybe that was why she felt irrationally pleased that the worst of the mess had been bundled into bags and carted over to Joe's place. Her flat was usually her sanctuary but today it felt cold and unloved, and for a second she thought about the warm exposed brick and softly waxed wood of Joe's warehouse and felt a pull of something like homesickness.

She shook herself as she crossed to the windows and pulled back the curtains and blinds and opened a window. It was just feeling a bit neglected in here, because she hadn't been home for a few days, she reasoned. It was nothing a bit of fresh air and the warm light of a few lamps wouldn't fix.

'Want a drink?' she called out to Joe—anything

to stall actual, meaningful conversation. She grabbed them both a beer from the fridge and handed one to him.

'Nice place,' Joe said. Small talk. Good—she could handle small talk. She had plenty of formal training. Or maybe it had been bred into her. Either way, she grabbed his opening gambit and held onto it like a raft.

She chatted about the flat. How she'd chosen it for the big south-facing windows. The French doors out into the shared garden. The view of the park and lack of traffic noise from the front. She sounded like a desperate estate agent trying to close a sale.

Opening the French doors, she took her beer out to the patio, dropping onto one of the chairs and propping her knees against the edge of the little bistro table. The fairy lights her upstairs neighbour had threaded through the boughs of the trees twinkled at them, creating a scene she could have found in a fairy tale.

Shivering, she wished she'd grabbed her jacket, but she was too bone-tired to move.

'You're right, it's quiet out here,' Joe said, following her. 'Peaceful, and pretty. I can see why you like it so much.'

She looked up and met his eye, trying to judge if he was being sarcastic. But he looked genuine. He sat in the seat beside her, his thighs spread wide as he leaned back and let out a sigh.

'Long trip back,' he commented. 'For both of us.'

She 'hmm-ed' in agreement.

'Lots of time to think,' he added.

She looked up at him, wondering if this was it. When all their tiptoeing finally stopped and they decided if they wanted to run from the relationship they'd both been fighting from the first.

'Come to any conclusions?' she asked.

She wasn't sure she even wanted to know, because, whatever the answer, she knew that they still had a lot of work to do. He could declare his undying love for her this minute and that wouldn't remove a single one of the obstacles in their way. Still, even the thought of it made the hairs on her arms stand up.

'You're cold,' Joe said, stripping off his jacket and handing it to her. She draped it round her shoulders, refusing to acknowledge how delicious it felt to be wrapped in the warm, supple leather that smelt of him.

'I care about you, Charlie. I think you know that I do. But it's not as simple as that, is it?'

'I don't think that it ever is.'

'Honestly, after Arabella, and then the kiss and tell, when I'd picked myself up and convinced myself it hadn't been that bad, I thought I'd cracked it. That I'd finally figured out how these things work. And I've had no reason to doubt that I was right. What I was doing—it was working for me. Honestly, I've had no complaints.'

'So that's what—'

'Please, let me finish,' he said with a gentle smile. 'It was great, until I saw you watching me from the side of the stage in Las Vegas, and I felt something so overwhelming I still don't have the words to describe it. And I told myself that getting married was a great joke, or a killer career move or… I don't know. I told myself it was about anything except falling in love with you before I'd even said hello.'

Her heart pounded. She was desperate to say something, to ask if that was what he felt now—love. But he'd asked her for space to talk, and he deserved that.

'But I was kidding myself. I love you, Charlie. I think you knew that before I did.'

She let out the breath she had been holding, her thoughts whizzing by so fast it was impossible to concentrate on just one of them.

He sat watching her for a moment, and then grinned. 'That's it. I'm done,' he said. 'Twenty-four hours' thinking and that's all I've worked out. Say anything you like.

'Did you speak to your mum?' he asked eventually, his face falling when she couldn't think of what to say in response.

She nodded, still searching for the words. 'It was good,' she said eventually. 'I think… I think I got a lot of things wrong.'

'About me?'

She smiled, tempted to call him out on his self-centredness that only a rock star could get away with.

'About family, about children, about myself.' She looked up and met his eye. 'Yes, probably a few things wrong about you too.' She sighed, knowing that she was going to have to dig deeper than that. For so long, she'd kept as much as she could get away with to herself, but Joe deserved more than that from her.

'I'm not going back, to Afland. Well, not properly. I told my mum I'd take on some official duties, but my life will be here, Joe. I'm staying in London. And I hope to God that it's with you, because I've missed you like… I don't know. Like I suddenly lost my hearing and there was no music in the world.'

Now it was her turn to squirm, looking into her

man's eyes as she waited for him to reply. 'Is that what you want, Joe?'

'I want you, Charlie. Any way I can have you. Is that enough?'

She leaned forwards and pressed a hard kiss against his lips, gasping with pleasure as his hands wound around her waist under the warm leather of his jacket. 'It's enough,' she managed to whisper between kisses. 'We can make it enough—if we both want it.' His arms pulled tighter around her waist and she moved away from him for just a split second, and then she was sitting on top of him, her legs straddled around him and the chair. He leaned back, meeting her eyes as she settled on top of him. 'We're doing this?' he asked.

She answered him with a kiss.

EPILOGUE

'YOU KNOW, YOU HAVEN'T said it,' Joe said sleepily, brushing a strand of her hair back from her shoulder. He pulled the duvet up around them and Charlie in close, settling her in the crook of his arm as he laid his head on the pillow.

'Said what?'

Her eyes were shut, her body loose and languid, and her voice so sleepy she barely formed words.

'You know what.'

She opened her eyes and looked up at him, a teasing smile on her lips. 'I can't say it now that you've asked.'

Joe pressed a kiss into her hair. 'I don't need you to. But, you know, tomorrow, if you happened to feel the urge…'

'I predict lots of urges, tomorrow.' She smiled wickedly. 'It's a long, long list. But if that's the one that you want to put at the top…'

If he'd had any energy left, he would have rolled on top of her and taken care of a few of those urges right now. But instead he pinched her waist. 'Give me an hour's sleep and I'll put myself entirely in your hands.'

'Good. Exactly where I want you. Later,' she said,

with another kiss against his chest. 'I think there's something we need to talk about first.'

He sighed sleepily. 'I thought we were done talking.'

She shuffled away from him on the bed, pulling up the sheets to try and find some modesty.

'It's important, Joe,' she said, and he opened his eyes properly at the serious tone of her voice. 'There's a lot we didn't talk about. Children for one. It's not a fun conversation, but we have to have it. I'm going to see my mum's doctor, but there are no guarantees. What if it never happens for us?'

He rubbed his face and sat up. 'If it comes to that, Charlie, we'll deal with it. Together. There are other ways to have a family.'

'Is it what you want?' she asked, a wobble in her voice. 'Because I don't know if adoption is something that I could take on. With my family, the succession, it's complicated.'

He kissed her on the forehead, smoothing a hand down her spine. 'I know that. But no, it doesn't matter to me. You're what matters to me.'

'But I might never have a family, Joe. And there's no point taking this any further if that's not something that you can live with. If you're always going to want more.'

He stopped her with a kiss on the lips. 'The only thing I want in my future is you,' he said, between kisses. 'We're going to travel the world. We're going to make beautiful music. We're going to party until we can't take any more. If children come along, the more the merrier. But nothing, *nothing* is going to make me a happier man than knowing that you will come home with me every night, and wake up with me every morning.'

'I love you,' she whispered, and he smiled as he squeezed her tight and pressed a kiss against her hair. She ran her hands over his chest, and he stretched, bringing their bodies into contact from where she had propped herself on his chest right down to their toes.

'And I love you too. Now, are we making a start on that list of yours?'

* * * * *

ISLAND FLING
TO FOREVER

SOPHIE PEMBROKE

To Jessica,
For making this book twice as fun to write.

CHAPTER ONE

ROSA GRAY TIED her dinghy up on the jetty and looked out across the water behind her, back towards the mainland. It would be so easy to just hop back in the boat and set sail again for mainland Spain. And, actually, it was entirely possible that no one would even miss her. Especially her sister, Anna.

Except that her mother had sounded panicked when she called. Sancia Garcia never panicked. Not when she decided to leave her husband when Rosa was sixteen, not when Rosa's grandfather died three years ago and left Sancia in sole charge of the luxury island resort of La Isla Marina. Not even when Rosa was eight and had tried a flying dive off the highest point of the island coastline, and almost brained herself on the rocks below.

No, Rosa's mama was the epitome of laid-back grace. Of letting things work themselves out in time, and trusting the universe to provide.

Until, it seemed, she was faced with the wedding of a New York socialite, and the realisation that the luxury island resort was no longer quite so luxurious.

Rosa stared up the wide, open path that led to the main villa at the centre of the island. Dotted on either side were a few of the low, white bungalows that made up the island's accommodation, all shining bright in the fading afternoon sun.

It still looked pretty good to her. But then, maybe she had a slightly skewed view of luxury, after a month spent deep in a South American jungle for a job. Or, more likely, St Anna had already fixed whatever she believed was wrong with La Isla Marina.

Anna always believed she could fix anything, if she just made enough lists, worked hard enough, or nagged often enough. But she hadn't been able to fix their family, had she? Rosa was almost hoping she'd given up trying by now. If she'd learned anything from her mother it was that, at a certain point, the only thing to do was to cut and run. No point flogging a dead horse and all that.

Or, in Rosa's case, no point dreaming that her family would ever be the sort of Christmas-advert perfect family where everyone was equally respected and listened to. So why hang around and wait for the impossible?

Which didn't explain why she was on the damn island in the first place. The only thing Rosa could put that down to was that thin thread, the one that started deep down inside her, connecting her to her mother, her sister, even her father. The one she'd never been able to sever, no matter how far or how fast she ran.

Maybe Anna felt the same. Why else would Rosa's big sister be here fixing everything for the mother who'd run off and left her in charge when she was only eighteen? Unless it was just to prove she could.

Either way, Rosa was about to find out.

Shouldering her rucksack, Rosa set off for the central villa at a steady pace. No point putting it off now she was here: it was time for the grand family reunion.

La Isla Marina was less than a mile across, so it didn't take her very long to reach the villa that housed the family and staff accommodation, as well as the administrative offices for the island. On the way, Rosa searched for changes that had taken place since she was last there, for her grandfather's funeral, three years ago. Surely there must be some? But she was hard pressed to find them.

Pausing on the path, Rosa drank in the view of the central villa, surrounded by lush greenery and bright flowers. The large white building, with its graceful arches and turrets, and tiled courtyards within, looked more like a Moorish palace than a Spanish villa, but to Rosa it had always felt like home in a way that nowhere else in the world did. Its twin turrets, housing two bedrooms—one for her and one for Anna—had seemed like the most magical places ever, when she was small. In some ways they still did.

How strange to be back again, without her grandparents there to welcome her home. Three years since her *abuelo* had died, and another year before that without her grandmother, and Rosa knew that she'd never grow used to it. It was almost as if the soul had left the island when theirs had.

Another reason she hadn't made it back for so long.

Her fingers itched for her camera, packed safely in her bag, to capture this perfect moment—the villa almost glowing in the sunshine, the azure sky behind it—before any people intruded on the picture and the calm was broken.

She wondered what sort of a welcome *would* be waiting for her. Sancia would be pleased to see her, as always. Rosa was her baby girl, and for ever would be. She might not be the academic success her sister was, or be the useful, sensible sort of daughter that parents wanted, but Rosa knew her mother would always adore her all the same. And, unlike her father, respect her life choices, which meant a lot.

Of course, it was probably easier for Sancia to let Rosa be Rosa from afar, wasn't it? When she only saw her for holidays and high days, even before she left to explore the world, as soon as she turned eighteen? That was what Anna would say, anyway. Anna who had taken over to deal with Rosa's 'difficult teenage years', as their father referred to them.

She needed to stop channelling Anna's thoughts, or she was going to drive herself mad. Except Sancia wasn't the only family member waiting on the island. She might have called Rosa for help, but Rosa knew she wasn't Sancia's first call. That had gone to Anna, the useful, sensible daughter. As always.

And St Anna wouldn't have made their mother wait two weeks, as Rosa had. Whatever their differences— and there were plenty—Anna would have dropped everything to help Sancia. In her defence, Rosa had been stuck in the middle of a South American rainforest at the time, and contractually bound to stay there until she had the full story and photos she needed for the magazine hiring her. But that didn't mean that Anna wouldn't have something to say about that delay. Or, knowing her sister, many somethings.

And nothing at all to say about Rosa's career successes. Anna probably didn't even know that Rosa was booked up months in advance, when she wanted to be, by publications looking for her particular style of photo journalism. Rosa was making quite a name for herself in her industry, not that it would mean anything to Anna and their father. Anything that happened outside the dreaming spires of Oxford's academic elite simply didn't matter to either of them.

Oh, well. La Isla Marina might not be huge, in island terms, but it had plenty of hidden corners and secret places—and Rosa had discovered all of them over the years. From secret coves for skinny-dipping to secluded bars and 'relaxation zones' dotted between the bungalows, Rosa could always disappear when she needed to. And if the worst came to the worst, she could pick up one of the island's boats and head across to the mainland and Cala del Mar for some truly excellent tapas and views.

And she didn't have to stay long. She never did. Her *modus operandi* was get in, get what she needed, and move on again. Always had been. It served her well in her work, and she had a feeling it would serve her just as well on La Isla Marina this week. She loved her mother dearly, but it was generally better for everyone if they didn't spend more than a couple of weeks in each other's company. They were just too alike—in the same way that she and Anna were just too different—to get along all the time.

It was all about identifying objectives. On assignments, she knew which shots she needed to tell the story that was playing out before her. Here, it was about reassuring her mother, making sure that everything was stable on the island again, then moving on guilt free.

Chances were, Anna would already have done all the hard work for her, and Rosa could be on her way again inside the week. There was a situation in Russia that she'd been keen to get closer to...

A pang of guilt twanged through her as she thought about her sister. How bad had things on the island really had to get for Sancia to call *her*? And how mad would Anna be that Rosa had left her to deal with it?

The thing was, it wouldn't have mattered if Rosa had taken the first flight out. Anna, based over in Oxford, would still have beaten her there by sheer virtue of time zones and air miles. Which meant that Anna would have already taken charge, and taken over the island.

Anna had always made it very clear that she expected to do everything herself, her way, and to feel martyred about it afterwards. So really, what point had there been in rushing?

Besides, it wasn't as if Sancia had dragged Anna away from anything important. Probably. Last time they'd spoken, Anna had been busy living up to their father's academic ideals, and giving up any semblance of fun or a social life to mother him excessively in Sancia's absence— despite the fact Professor Ernest Gray was an intelligent, grown man who could clearly take care of himself.

Rosa couldn't really imagine that that situation might have changed in the last three years.

Three years. Had it really been three years since she last spoke to Anna? Three years since their grandfather died? Three years since she'd yelled back a whole host of home truths at her sister, then left the country? Three years since she'd been back in England, or to La Isla Marina? Three years since…well. She wasn't thinking about that. About him.

She'd made a point of not thinking about Jude Alexander for a grand total of thirty-six months. She wasn't breaking that streak now.

It was just that it was all tied up together in her head. That awful argument with Anna, everything that happened with Jude, why she had to get out of the country… and now, knowing she was about to see Anna again had brought it all back.

Well, tough. She was going to rock up to the villa, deal with her sister, hug her mother, accept the inevitable offer of a glass of wine, check that everything was fine now, and make plans for leaving again.

Easy.

Hopefully.

With a sigh, Rosa shifted her bag higher on her shoulder and carried on walking. She'd already lingered on the side of the path longer than necessary. The last thing she wanted was one of the guests reporting some suspicious character with a bag loitering in the greenery.

She frowned. Actually, she hadn't seen any guests. At all.

It was late May; the island should be teeming with holidaymakers, enjoying all the luxuries the resort had to offer. So where was everyone?

Unless things were worse than she thought…

Rosa quickened her step and, in a brief few minutes, found herself standing in the cool, tiled reception area of the central villa. White arches soared overhead, leading to small, secluded balconies with wrought-iron bars and plenty of brightly coloured cushions on their chairs. Just beyond the main area, through wide open doors, was the central courtyard, with reflecting pool and more lush potted greenery, and plenty of places to sit and take in the view. In high season, it was used as the main restaurant area for breakfasts, and even now it should be buzzing with early evening cocktail seekers.

It was empty. As was the reception desk.

Refusing to ring a bell in her own home, Rosa dropped her bags by the desk, bypassed the winding staircase to the upper levels, and the hidden doorway that led to the private, family quarters. Instead, she moved through the courtyard, and out the other side of the villa onto the sheltered patio that overlooked the beaches and the wide expanse of turquoise sea on the more exposed side of the island.

There, at last, she found signs of life, and her family. If not exactly the ones she'd been expecting.

She froze, her chest tightening, as if she were preparing to run—or hide. Surely her eyes were playing tricks on her?

'Dad?' Rosa pulled her sunglasses off to be absolutely sure of what she was seeing. Nope, she hadn't imagined it. There, looking incongruous in a white shirt and stone-coloured jacket over chinos, and a panama-style hat, sat Professor Ernest Gray himself, a thousand miles and more away from where Rosa had expected him to be, locked up in the ivory towers at Oxford.

Of course, he was playing Scrabble with a dark-haired guy who had his back to her, so he was still finding some way to demonstrate his mental prowess. As usual. Rosa pitied his opponent.

Except now she'd drawn his attention, she'd given him a new target. It could only be a matter of time now before he turned his sharp mind and sharper words onto her—her choice of career, her lack of education, her inability to stay in one place, her unreliability... How could he possibly get through all her faults in one short visit?

'Rosa.' Her father inclined his head towards her, without smiling. 'Your mother told us you'd be joining us. Eventually.'

And that was about all the family love and welcome she could expect from him, Rosa supposed. What was he even doing here? As far as she knew, he'd had as little contact with Sancia as possible, after she left, and they'd been separated ten years or more now. In all that time he'd *certainly* never visited the island that she'd escaped to. Why would he? Following Sancia to La Isla Marina would have been tantamount to admitting that he'd made a mistake, given her reasons to leave him. And if Rosa understood one thing about her father it was that Professor Ernest Gray would *never* admit that he was wrong.

So what could have brought him here now? Were things worse than she thought? Maybe it wasn't the island that had Sancia panicked. Maybe it was something else. She should have got here sooner…

Her heart raced as all the worst-case scenarios flooded her mind. Rosa grabbed for the memory of meditation practice in India, two years ago, and focussed on her breath until she had it under control again.

No point getting worked up until she had some answers. Which meant asking questions. 'Where is Mama? And Anna? And the guests, come to that? I was expecting—'

She didn't get any further, because as she started talking her father's Scrabble companion turned around and Rosa got a good look at his face, pale and shadowed in the cool of the patio shade but still absurdly perfect, with cheekbones that emphasised the beautiful shape of his face, and the incredible blue of his eyes.

It was too late to run. Too late to hide. And Rosa didn't even know *how* to fight this sudden intrusion. Her whole body seemed fixed to the spot as a hundred perfect memories ran through her mind, racing over each other, all featuring the man in front of her.

Whatever she'd been expecting from her return to La Isla Marina faded away. Because there in front of her, on her Mama's back patio, sat the last person she'd ever expected to see again—and a perfect reason to join Sancia and start panicking.

Jude Alexander.

La Isla Marina, Jude had decided within a few hours of his arrival, was the perfect hideaway from the real world. It had sun, sand, sangria and—most importantly for him—solitude. In fact, he wasn't all that bothered about any of the first three items on the list, as long as he was left alone while he was there.

Fame, it turned out, was overrated. Especially the sort of fame that meant he couldn't go anywhere without being recognised, or do anything without the world having an opinion about his actions. It might have taken him a while to see the downsides of celebrity, but now that he had...well, Jude was experiencing them in spades.

So it was sort of ideal that his main companion on the island was an ageing Oxford professor who hadn't got the slightest idea who Jude was. Professor Gray was perfectly content to play Scrabble for hours, or talk about events of the last century, or the one before—without ever asking a question about Jude's own life. The man's self-absorption—or perhaps his preoccupation with the historical world—made Jude's quest to escape the person he'd become all the easier. The professor hadn't even explained why he was there himself, let alone asked Jude what had brought him to the remote Spanish island.

If Professor Gray didn't know or care who Jude was, his ex-wife, Sancia, and daughter Anna were too busy to even notice. Apparently there was some sort of event happening at the island later in the month—Sancia hadn't gone into details—and it was all hands on deck to prepare for it. All hands except his and Professor Gray's. Jude got the feeling he'd been cast in the role of companion, or perhaps nurse, to the professor since they'd arrived together. Whatever the reason, it was all working out fine for him.

Until a voice he'd never dreamed or hoped he'd hear again spoke.

'Dad?' He hadn't realised what he was hearing, at first. That one word wasn't enough to make the memories hit—which surprised him, given how many other things seemed to trigger them.

'Rosa.' That name, spoken in Professor Gray's cultured tones. That was his first clue. 'Your mother told us you'd be joining us. Eventually.'

But still, Rosa had to be a reasonably common Spanish name, right? There was no reason to imagine it was *his* Rosa. Or, rather, the Rosa who'd made it very clear that she'd rather leave the country than belong to him.

The Rosa he'd known, three years before, was probably still thousands of miles away on the other side of the world, chasing whatever dreams he couldn't be a part of. Dreams she'd never even told him about, even as he'd spilled every one of his to her.

That Rosa couldn't be here. That was insane. Maybe the latest events in New York had actually driven him mad after all. It would explain the midnight flight to Spain, anyway.

'Where is Mama? And Anna? And the guests, come to that?' But as she spoke Jude realised there was no point denying what he was hearing, not any more. Only one person, one voice, had ever made his heart shudder like that.

There was no point hiding. La Isla Marina was his best shot at a hiding place, and she was already here.

Time to face his demons.

Jude turned around.

'I was expecting—' Rosa cut herself off, staring. 'Oh.'

She looked just the same—same wild dark hair, same wide, chocolate eyes with endless lashes. Same sweet, soft mouth. Same curves under her jeans and T-shirt, same smooth skin showing on her bare arms. Same neat, small feet shoved into flip-flops.

Same woman he'd fallen in love with, last time they met.

'Hello, Rosa.' Jude tried for a smile—that same smile

that graced album covers and posters and photo shoots. The one that never felt quite real, any more. Not since Rosa left. And definitely not since Gareth.

There was no answering smile on Rosa's face though, only shock. Who could blame her? It wasn't as if he'd planned this, either.

He might have done, three years ago, if he'd known about this place—or rather, known that this was her home. Because now, too late, all the pieces were falling into place. She'd left him to go back to her mother's family home, for her grandfather's funeral—and never come back again. La Isla Marina must have been where she'd run to.

If he'd known that then, would he have followed?

Or would he have accepted that she'd not told him where she was going for a reason?

Oh, who was he kidding? Even if he'd known where she was, he'd have sat there waiting for her to come back because he'd had *faith* in her. Something that had turned out to be seriously misplaced. And the day he'd realised that was the terrible day that everything had happened with Gareth, and he wasn't going anywhere for a while. Except down, in a despair spiral he almost hadn't made it out of. And then, suddenly, up the charts, for all the wrong reasons.

After Gareth, how could he have let himself see her again, anyway? He'd broken every promise he'd ever made for this woman, and she'd walked out anyway, leaving his world destroyed and empty.

Of course he hadn't chased her across the globe. Even if he'd wanted to, and hated himself for that.

So many conflicting emotions tied up in the curvy, petite woman standing in front of him, all tangled and tight around his heart. Would he ever escape those bonds?

Rosa was still staring at him, stunned, and Jude hunted around for something to say. For some of the many, many words he'd wished he could say to her over the last few years. The accusations, the questions, the declarations, anything. But nothing came out.

'You two know each other?' Professor Gray was looking between them, confused.

Something about his voice seemed to snap Rosa out of her shock, as she gave them both a lopsided smile that never quite reached her eyes. 'Oh, Dad, everyone knows Jude Alexander. He has possibly the most recognisable face in the world, right now.'

Professor Gray turned his curious gaze onto Jude, as if searching for fame in his features.

'Your daughter photographed me for a publication a few years ago,' he explained, blandly. No hint of the true story between that four-week study when Rosa travelled with them on tour, capturing every moment of their rise to fame. Of Gareth's last tour. 'I'm in a band, you see.'

'*A* band?' Rosa scoffed. 'Jude is the frontman of The Swifts, Dad. Hottest band of the decade, some are saying.' She raised an eyebrow at him, and Jude tried not to squirm under it. Not just because of the inevitable uncomfortableness that always came when someone referred to *him* as the frontman, instead of Gareth. But because he had *so* been enjoying not being *that* Jude Alexander for a while.

'You know I don't follow popular culture, Rosa.' Professor Gray dismissed his daughter's words with a wave of his hand. 'But Jude here is an almost competent Scrabble player, at least.'

Jude watched as Rosa's gaze flicked over to him at her father's words, meeting his for just a second. Just long enough for him to feel the same connection he'd experienced the night they'd met. It hit him deep, inside those tangled threads around his heart, a piercing guilt tied up with want and need and lust.

Still. Nice to know he hadn't imagined it, that connection. Even if it clearly never had the same effect on Rosa as it had on him.

'I'm so glad you've found a playmate, Father,' Rosa said, her tone scathing. 'But Jude's Scrabble abilities don't answer any of my questions. Where are Mama and Anna? And what on earth are you doing here?' She glanced at Jude again as she asked the last question, leaving him uncertain as to whose presence she was most baffled by.

Jude didn't blame her.

Now the initial shock of her arrival had passed, he found himself watching her more closely, looking beyond the familiarity of the woman he'd known so intimately— if, apparently, incompletely—three years ago. There *were* changes, ones he hadn't initially spotted. She was leaner now, he realised, harder even. Her mass of long, dark curls had been tamed back into a braid that hung over her left shoulder, and her dark eyes were far more wary than he remembered. Even in her relaxed jeans and fitted T-shirt, her sunglasses dangling loosely from her fingers, she looked poised to run at any moment. As if this beautiful island resort was more of a trap than her home.

What had made her look that way? And why, after all this time, did he even care?

'Your mother is talking with the cook about dinner, I believe,' Professor Gray said. 'And as for your sister, I have no idea.'

'She went to Barcelona with Leo,' Jude put in, since apparently he was paying more attention to the professor's family than he was.

'Leo?' Rosa's nose crinkled up as she said the name. 'Who on earth is…? Never mind. Dad, why are you here?'

Professor Gray observed his daughter mildly. 'Why, is it such a crime for a man to wish to spend time with his family?'

From the look Rosa gave him in return, Jude rather thought her answer might be yes.

'Professor Gray?' Maria, the only non-family member of staff that Jude had actually met on the island, appeared in the villa doorway. 'There is a phone call for you at Reception? From Oxford?'

'Still no mobile phone, huh, Dad?' Rosa asked.

'I have one,' Professor Gray answered, loftily, as he got to his feet. 'I merely do not see the requirement for it to always be on my person. Or switched on.'

'Of course you don't.'

As Professor Gray made his way into the villa, Jude found himself staring at Rosa again. What was it about this woman that captivated him so, that he couldn't look away, even now, after everything that had happened because he'd fallen for her? He wished he knew. Maybe then he could break free of it. As it was…

'So.' Rosa moved to take her father's chair opposite him, and Jude knew exactly what was coming next.

She was going to ask him a question, and he was going to have to decide how much of the truth he wanted to tell her. Given that last time he'd told her everything—opened up every part of himself and shared it with her—and she'd left anyway, he had a feeling that this time discretion might really be the better part of valour.

Or, as Gareth would have said, if he were still alive to say it, *Screw me once, shame on you. Screw me twice…*

Jude wasn't going to let that happen. In any sense of the word.

Rosa sat down, and caught his eye across the table.
'What are you doing here, Jude?'
Jude opened his mouth, and prepared to lie.

CHAPTER TWO

HE WAS GOING to lie to her.

Three years, and Rosa could still see the tell in the way Jude glanced to the side before speaking.

She supposed she couldn't blame him. She hadn't exactly done much to earn the truth from him.

But on the other hand, this was her home, her place—and she'd never told him about it. Had he been stalking her, searching for her, these last three years? Had he come here to find her? And if so, why on earth now, not three years ago?

No, that was ridiculous. She hadn't known she was coming herself until two weeks ago, and she had a hard time believing that Sancia and Anna had teamed up to come up with some outrageous story to get her there, just to help Jude out.

Unlikely as it seemed, this had to be some kind of crazy coincidence.

Rosa wasn't entirely sure if that made it better or worse.

'Believe it or not, I came here to work on some new music,' Jude said. Just the words conjured up memories of watching him composing, trying out new melodies on his guitar at the back of the tour bus, folded up to sit on the narrow bunk she lay in. Some of the most precious moments they'd spent together in that too-short month were times like that, when no one else was there or awake, when it was just them and the music.

But she couldn't think about that now. Memories weren't going to help her figure out what the hell was going on here.

'So you had no idea that this was my mother's family home?' Rosa asked, her eyes narrowing. It didn't hurt to double check these things, right?

'None at all.' That, at least, seemed to be the truth. So where was the lie? He was a musician, of course he'd come here to work on music. Except where was the rest of the band, in that case? Or what was left of it.

The memory hit her harder than she'd expected. An article online she'd caught by chance, that had left her crying in a foreign airport for a man she'd known and grown fond of. For another star gone too soon. And for Jude, left behind—the only time she'd let herself cry for him at all.

The band she'd known, when she'd toured with Jude that summer, wasn't the same band he was with now. Not without Gareth.

No wonder he hadn't come after her. He'd been dealing with his own tragedy, while she'd left to attend her *abuelo*'s funeral and had her whole world changed.

But that didn't change the truth of him being here, now. 'So you expect me to believe that this is just a bizarre and unfortunate coincidence?'

'If you like.' Jude gave a small, one-sided shrug, but the smile on his lips told her that wasn't entirely how he'd put it. 'To be honest, it doesn't much matter to me what you believe, any more.'

It had once, though. For one brief, shining month in time, what Rosa had believed had mattered to Jude Alexander. And what he'd believed about her had mattered to her, too.

Which had only made it harder to let him down when she'd walked away.

Of course, that was how she knew it was the right decision, too. But that didn't mean there hadn't been moments since, days when she'd been lost and alone and confused, when she'd wondered how different things would be if she'd gone back to him when she'd left La Isla Marina, instead of hightailing it for the Middle East, then Australia, then the Americas.

A whole life she'd thrown away and never lived. Of course she thought about it. She just didn't let herself imagine it too often, or in too much detail. She didn't want the regrets—not when she'd done the right thing, and found the life she'd always promised herself because of it.

She wondered if Jude would understand that, if she told him. Or maybe he'd been relieved when she hadn't come back. After all, he'd chased and caught his own dreams, too. But they'd come at a high price.

Rosa picked up a few of her father's Scrabble tiles, and began rearranging them on the rack, spelling out Spanish words he'd never use, for her own amusement, trying to find the words she needed to say.

In the end, she settled for blunt. It was her style, after all.

'I heard about Gareth. I'm sorry. You know how fond I was of him.' It had been hard not to adore Gareth. His optimism, his openness, the joy he'd found in the world… It was hard to imagine the band without him.

Hard to imagine Jude without his best friend.

Jude looked away. 'Yeah.' The curt word told Rosa her sympathies weren't enough. Of course they weren't.

Nothing could make up for Gareth's death. Certainly not anything *she* had to offer.

It wasn't her place to ask what happened, to tell Jude he could talk to her, if he needed to. Wasn't her place to comfort him for a three-year-old tragedy that obviously still cut him deep.

She'd given up that place when she left.

Time to move on. She was never good at the touchy-feely stuff, anyway.

'So, where are the others?' Always a good way of figuring out whether a person was lying to her—ask a question she already knew the answer to. 'Jimmy and Lee and Tanya?' The rest of The Swifts. After all, Jude hadn't got this famous all on his own, whatever the gossip magazines seemed to think.

And right now, the gossip sites didn't seem to know *what* to think. Rosa didn't make a point of following Jude's every career move, or anything—in fact, she made a point of not listening to his music any more than she had to, which was made more difficult by the fact it seemed to be playing *everywhere* at the moment. Even in the rainforest, someone had brought speakers and been playing The Swifts when they'd set up camp the other week.

But even she hadn't been able to avoid the news that Jude Alexander had dropped off the face of the earth. The rest of the band had been photographed out and about in New York City, but there had been no sign of their lead singer.

Not that Rosa had been concerned about that. Much.

'New York, I think.' Jude looked away again, down at his own tiles. He wasn't lying, so maybe just hiding something? Rosa couldn't tell, any more. 'I'm working on some…different stuff.'

'Solo stuff?' Because *that* she hadn't read anywhere online. 'You're planning on leaving The Swifts?'

'No,' Jude said, too quickly. 'I'm not. I couldn't. I just... I needed some time away, is all.'

'And you picked La Isla Marina?' Because, really, that was too much of a coincidence to not bear some investigation.

'I heard someone talk about this place once. I can't remember who, exactly. One of Sylvie's friends, maybe.'

Sylvie. That would be Sylvie Rockwell-Smythe, Rosa's ever-helpful brain for useless knowledge filled in. Jude's beautiful, red-headed, heiress and model girlfriend. Exactly the sort of woman a celebrity like Jude should be dating.

Except, if he was here in paradise, and she was still in New York... 'How is Sylvie?'

'We split up,' Jude said, shortly.

'Ah. Sorry.' There was that old talent for putting her foot in it, rearing up again. One day she'd learn not to just say the first thing that popped into her head. Maybe.

Jude shrugged. 'I wouldn't be.'

'Like that, huh?'

'Pretty much.'

Rosa sat back and surveyed him, taking in the changes the last three years had wrought on a face she'd known so well, once. He looked thinner. No, not thinner, exactly. Leaner. As if some stylist had decided to play up his pale and interesting aspect. But they couldn't style away Jude's broad shoulders, or the muscles in those arms.

But he looked tired. Worn down, maybe.

'So. How's fame going?'

'Overrated.' Jude met her eyes. 'Haven't you heard the latest? The entire of the continental US is talking about it.'

'I've been kind of out of touch,' Rosa admitted. 'I was working on a story down in South America...wait.' Hadn't she read something about a book, somewhere? A kiss-and-tell sort of a book, all about Jude? Maybe Sylvie had something to do with that... 'Is this about the book?'

'*Jude: The Naked Truth.*' Jude shook his head in disgust as he quoted the title. 'That's the one.'

Whoever had written it should have come and found Rosa. She could have told them plenty of secrets about Jude Alexander.

She wouldn't have, of course. That was just one of the many differences between her and Sylvie. That and the fact that the other woman was a supermodel. And at five feet three and with too many curves, Rosa would definitely never be that.

'I haven't read it.'

Jude didn't respond, and Rosa resigned herself to looking him up on the internet once she'd got her laptop hooked up to the island Wi-Fi. It wouldn't be the first time, anyway. And Jude didn't have many secrets from the media these days, it seemed to Rosa. She could probably download the eBook and know everything she wanted to about him in a couple of hours of reading.

Except she didn't want to. Those books never told the whole truth, anyway. And she knew more about him than any pages could contain.

Or she had. Once.

Before.

She turned back to her father's Scrabble tiles, and ignored the letters 's' 'e' and 'x' to find something else to think about.

'So. Been a while,' Jude said, and Rosa looked up from her Scrabble tiles to take in the sight of him in the sunshine again.

He was too pale, she decided. He couldn't have been on the island long or he'd have lost that grey pallor that came from too long spent inside with only his guitar for company.

But he was still every bit as gorgeous as she remembered. As she'd tried to forget.

Her fingers flexed, reaching for the camera that wasn't hanging around her neck for once. She wanted to capture him here, now, in the moment. A comparison piece to the famous, laughing photo of him she'd taken three years ago. One photo in thousands she'd taken that month, but the one everyone remembered most. The one that had made her name. Kick-started her career, when The Swifts had hit the big time.

She'd been assigned to the up-and-coming band by a magazine she'd done some work for before, asked to follow them on tour for an in-depth photo piece with some interviews. Someone high up at the magazine had a feeling about them, she'd been told, and they wanted to get in there first, before anyone else.

Whoever that person was, they'd been right. And they'd changed Rosa's world with that one commission, in too many ways to count.

If she hadn't taken the job, she'd never have taken the photo that started her rise to the top of her profession, that gave her the luxury of picking and choosing jobs wherever she wanted in the world.

If she hadn't taken the job, she'd never have met Jude. And if she hadn't met Jude, she wouldn't have spent three years taking any job that kept her away from England, Spain and New York.

'Three years.' As if he didn't already know.

'You look good.'

'You look pale.'

Jude laughed, the first true emotion she'd seen from him since she arrived. 'You never were very good for my ego, were you?'

'You never needed me for that.' He'd always had plenty of hangers-on and groupies, ready to tell him how wonderful he was, even back then, before The Swifts took over the music world. Gareth might have been the lead singer, but Jude was the mysterious lead guitarist, and that had its own appeal.

And he'd had Gareth to keep him optimistic. To keep him humble.

How had he coped without him?

She should have called. It was three years too late to be asking these questions. But back then…she couldn't.

Rosa shoved the last of the Scrabble tiles aside and got to her feet. 'I really should go and find my mother. Let her know I'm here.'

Jude inclined his head in a small nod. 'Of course.'

She waited, just a moment, in case he was going to say anything more, but he was already studying his letters again. If those groupies could see him now—wild-child rock-and-roll star plays Scrabble. Wouldn't they be disappointed?

Was *she*, though? Rosa wasn't even sure. Already this trip home was nothing like she'd expected.

But she couldn't be certain if that was a bad thing or not. Not yet.

She paused as she reached the archway leading into the villa.

'Jude?'

He looked up. 'Yeah?'

'Did you really not know I'd be here?'

'Honestly?' Jude gave her a sardonic smile. 'I would never have come if I did.'

Rosa looked away. Well. That told her.

And really, what else was she hoping for?

Shaking away the conversation with Jude, Rosa headed inside to find her mother. And some answers.

Jude watched Rosa go, then realised she'd stopped, just inside the archway to the villa.

Not that he cared.

He shouldn't care.

He absolutely shouldn't care enough to want to watch her every move.

Except…he did. Even after everything.

Trying not to be obvious about it, Jude tilted his chair just enough for him to see inside the villa, to where Rosa had found her mother. Both women seemed far too preoccupied with each other to be worrying about him, so he took advantage of their distraction to shift his chair around a bit more, so he could watch them properly.

It wasn't his place to spy on a reunion, he knew. But since his own with Rosa had been so anticlimactic, he wanted to know what a real one would look like.

Inside, Sancia threw her arms around Rosa and held her tight, swaying her back and forth with her outpouring of affection.

Once, Jude had imagined that his and Rosa's reunion might be full of love, like that. Filled with passion, at least—the same kind of passion they'd shown each other during their brief time together.

Sometimes, late at night, he'd allowed himself to picture it. Rosa coming back, finding him backstage, just as he was finishing a gig. He'd be on a performance high, anyway, and when he saw her…everything would crystallise, fall into place. He'd sweep her up into his arms and never let her go again.

Except she'd never come back, had she?

And then Gareth had died, and he'd been so lost. So hopeless, without his best friend. He'd needed Rosa, then.

But she was long gone. And even if she hadn't been… how could he let himself love her again, knowing what that love had cost him?

From the moment they'd met, when Rosa had arrived on the tour bus and introduced herself as the person who'd be documenting their every move for the next month, her presence had filled his whole world, pushing everything else to the edges. The connection had been instantaneous, even if the physical side of their relationship had developed more slowly. Rosa had spoken to them all, of course, taking notes, filming them, her camera always to hand. But somehow, when it had been just the two of them, Jude had found himself giving up far more than she'd asked for—details about his life, his mind, his friendships, his heart. Details she'd never used in the article, because they were just for her.

Whenever the music was done, they'd gravitate towards each other, letting the others head out to party while they headed back to the bus or a hotel room. And soon, all those late-night talks had become midnight kisses, and more, as Jude had lost himself in the wonder of Rosa.

Unbidden, memories of their last night came back to him, filling his brain with the images of them together. The hotel room, the champagne, the post-gig euphoria that always came over him—and Rosa. Rosa's eyes, bright with excitement. Her hair, loose and soft and dark as it hung over her bare shoulders. Her olive skin, so smooth and welcoming under his hands.

The feel of her against him, both of them mindless

with the kind of passion Jude knew didn't come around all that often.

Or ever, for him, it seemed, unless it was with Rosa.

It was crazy. He'd been with supermodels, Hollywood actresses—some of the widely acknowledged most beautiful women in the world.

And they'd never made him feel an iota of what he felt in one night with Rosa.

He pushed the memories aside. It was that passion, that uncontrolled connection, that had made him forget the promise he'd made to Gareth after his first close call. Jude had sat beside that hospital bed looking at his best friend—too pale, too lost, so close to being utterly ruined by the drugs and the alcohol and the life it was so easy to live as a band on the road. And he'd made the most important promise of his life—he'd promised to keep Gareth safe from then on. To be the one Gareth could rely on to steer him away from temptation, to remind him how much he had to live for.

But then he'd met Rosa and let that promise slide, too distracted by passion and infatuation to notice his best friend slipping again.

Until it was too late.

Shaking his head, he looked away as he saw Sancia putting an arm around Rosa's shoulders as she led her further into the villa. He had to stop living in his memories.

He needed to focus on what this meant for his future.

He'd made a new promise, when Gareth died—an echo of the one he'd made him a year before, except *this* one he'd kept, would keep on keeping. He'd live life for the both of them. He'd have the success that should have been theirs, chase the fame Gareth had always wanted. Live the life Gareth should be there to enjoy.

The Swifts' success wasn't his. It wasn't even Jimmy's or Lee's or Tanya's. It was all for Gareth.

And that was why he could never walk away from it. He owed his friend, for the life he got to live, without him, and for the promise he should have kept.

But even then, he couldn't stay in New York for the publication of that book.

He'd come to La Isla Marina with a very firm objective in mind—to stay out of the public eye for a few weeks, long enough for all the fuss about *The Naked Truth* to fade away again, and to give him time to think about his next move, musically.

But Rosa being here…that could change everything. He mustn't forget that he'd actually met Rosa when she was photographing the band for some British music magazine. What were the chances she was still doing that sort of work? Just because he hadn't seen her at any of his gigs since didn't mean she wasn't still in the game.

And even if she wasn't, she was a freelance photojournalist. A few shots of Jude Alexander hiding out on a remote Spanish island, when no one else had been able to get a hint of where he was…that would pay big money. Enough for a struggling freelancer to not have to worry about bills for a while, anyway.

Would she sell him out?

Three years ago, Jude could have answered that question without hesitation: never. Rosa wasn't that sort of person. He might have only known her for four weeks, but he'd learned more about her in one month than he'd known about his own parents in a lifetime.

And maybe it still meant something. After all, she hadn't used his secrets in the eventual article that had been published about that month-long tour. And there was no mention of Rosa—or any of the secrets only she knew—in That Book. There were whole chapters on Gareth, his death, Jude's guilt over it, and everything that happened next, but no mention of the part Rosa had played in everything that happened.

Of course, probably the author just hadn't known to look for Rosa. If they had...

No, she still wouldn't have talked. She wasn't that sort of person, he was sure.

But that didn't mean it wasn't worth making sure she was on the right side of his hide-and-don't-seek game with the press, before she let something slip to the wrong person.

The last thing Jude wanted was to have his hiding place uncovered now, just when his last remaining secret had walked back into his life.

CHAPTER THREE

'Mama. Mama!' Rosa interrupted her mother's non-stop flow of conversation with an impatient shout. It might be rude, but she knew from experience that if she didn't get in there quick before Sancia got lost in one of her conversational tangents, she could be stuck discussing anything but the matter in hand for hours before she got back to the point.

Sancia stopped talking, smiled, then hugged her again.

Rosa hugged her back. Maybe there were some parts of this homecoming that weren't completely awful. Hugs from her mama were definitely one of them. Whatever their family issues, Rosa knew she was lucky to still have her mother in her life. Ten years after she left, Rosa had long forgiven her for walking out on them—understood why she'd needed to, even. Rosa knew that, in her place, she'd have done the same.

If she couldn't fix a situation, couldn't get what she needed from it, she broke free. Just as her mother had done. Just ask Jude.

'I'm sorry, *querida*,' Sancia said, with a warm smile. 'I'm just so excited to have both my girls home with me again.'

Which led Rosa neatly into the first of her very many questions. 'Where *is* Anna, anyway? Jude said something

about her going to Barcelona with someone called Leo?'
Which seemed utterly unlike her sister, to be honest.

'Ah, you've already met Jude! Isn't he a delight?'
Sancia beamed. 'We were so lucky he decided to come
and stay here, you know. And he brought your father
over with him, for which we are all grateful.'

'He…brought Dad?' Rosa frowned. That made no
sense at all. But then, Sancia's ramblings often didn't.

'Well, they arrived together. They travelled over from
the mainland in the same boat.' Which was not at all the
same thing, Rosa realised.

Sancia didn't always operate on exactly the same
plane as everyone else. It wasn't worth explaining the
difference—or asking if Sancia had even realised who
Jude was. The Swifts wouldn't mean anything to her
mother. And she definitely didn't want to mention their
past acquaintance.

Which left her with her more immediate concerns.

'So, Mama. Anna. Where is she?'

'Why, Barcelona, like Jude said. With Leo.'

'And Leo is…?' Rosa pressed.

'Anna's…well, not boyfriend, exactly. At least I don't
think so. Lover, I suppose.' Sancia sounded far too happy
with that answer. Rosa tried to imagine Anna's face if she
heard their mother describing any man as her 'lover' and
bit back a laugh. 'And he's close to the bride, of course,'
Sancia went on, bringing Rosa quickly back to the matter at hand.

'Why don't you tell me more about this wedding,
Mama?' she suggested as she manoeuvred her mother
further into the villa, towards the small office that sat
behind the reception area.

'Of course! You'll need to know all about it,' Sancia

agreed, a little too readily for Rosa's liking. 'Anna has left you a list of all the things she needs you to take care of.'

'Has she?' Of course she had. St Anna always did need to be in perfect control of everything. She wouldn't let a little thing like, oh, not actually being there get in the way of that.

Sancia nodded enthusiastically. 'Oh, yes. She's thought of everything. Just look!' She rustled around on the desk until she pulled out a clipboard, with a neatly typed list that, Rosa was almost certain, would prove to contain no typos or grammatical errors.

Although it did seem to contain an awful lot of work to be done.

Rosa took the clipboard from her mother and flipped through the three pages of jobs. 'Seriously? What's *Anna* been doing since she got here?'

'Oh, everything!' Sancia clapped her hands together, pride shining from her eyes. 'She and Leo, they've re-painted all the bungalows, tamed the jungle growing out there on the island, fixed all the little things I've been meaning to get around to around here, sorted out the swimming pools for the season…everything!'

'And did she walk on water as well?' Rosa muttered as she looked through *her* list.

'Sorry?' Sancia asked, thankfully unable to make out the words.

'Did they do all that alone?' Rosa asked, instead of repeating her original question.

'Well, Anna's got a whole lot of extra staff coming in this week to help finish it off. But she's organised it all—and been out there with her paintbrush doing more than her fair share!'

Guilt gnawed at Rosa. 'I'm sorry I couldn't get here sooner, Mama.'

'It's fine.' Sancia patted her shoulder. 'You were busy. I understood. And so did your sister.'

That part, Rosa found harder to believe. Even harder than picturing pristine St Anna with a paintbrush in hand.

'Well, she's left me plenty to do to make up for it, anyway.' Rosa stared down at the list again. Then she turned it over so she didn't have to look at it any more. 'So, tell me all about this wedding.'

And why on earth it's sending this whole island into general insanity.

Twenty minutes later, Rosa had her answers. She just didn't like them very much.

'So, when you called and said that there was a wedding booking on the island, what you failed to mention was that it was a five-star, luxury, last-minute wedding for Internet sensation and supermodel Valentina, whose every move is documented online to millions of fans.' A wedding like this could make or break La Isla Marina for the foreseeable future. If they could live up to Valentina's expectations, the resort would be fully booked for years. But if they screwed it up…

That didn't bear thinking about.

Sancia smiled. 'Anna says it's a great opportunity. Apparently Valentina is very popular.'

Understatement. Even in the middle of a South American rainforest, Rosa hadn't been able to avoid Valentina's doings. 'She's about as famous as Jude is.'

Sancia's expression turned curious. 'Jude is famous?'

Oh, honestly. How was she supposed to work like this?

'Just take my word for it, Mama.' She thought about Jude, unrecognised and playing Scrabble with her father. He was hiding. Even if he hadn't fully admitted it yet. 'And maybe don't mention the fact that he's here to anyone, okay?'

'Of course. But Rosa…can you do all these things Anna has asked?' Sancia chewed on her lip, nervously. Because only St Anna could be useful and take care of the family business, right? Only Anna was reliable and dependable—never mind that Sancia had no time at all for those traits usually. Now that she was in trouble, of course it was *Anna* that she needed. Not Rosa.

'I think I can manage a little bit of organisation, for once,' she said, drily. 'Don't worry about it, Mama. I've got you covered.'

She resisted the impulse to look back down at the list and wince. How hard could it be, really? Arranging hotel rooms and putting up decorations was hardly the same as trekking miles through war zones or eluding border patrols, now, was it?

'Oh, good.' Sancia's face relaxed into its usual smiling countenance. 'Then how about I go and fetch you some wine? And some dinner—you must be starving after your journey!'

Rosa knew it wouldn't have mattered what time of day she'd arrived, Sancia would still assume she needed feeding. And a glass of wine. Today though, she wasn't wrong. However, there were a few other things she needed to get straight first.

'In a moment, Mama. You never explained what Dad is doing here.' Rosa remembered what life had been like with both her parents in the same house as a child, and she wasn't sure she wanted to experience it again. For years, Sancia had lived life her way—ignoring her husband's requests for more order in their lives. She'd picked up new creative hobbies that had covered the house in paint or pottery, and brought new friends home to open their lounge up for art classes or book groups. And through it all, Ernest's only comments would be to stay out of his study and clear up after themselves. Rosa wondered, sometimes, if some of the crazier ideas Sancia had come up with—like the midnight picnic in the garden, with fairy lights and music, or the time she'd repainted the whole house yellow, or the last-minute road trip across the country with no preparation or, as it turned out after the first fifty miles, petrol—had just been attempts to get her husband to pay attention to her, for once.

If they had been, they hadn't worked. Even when she'd left, Rosa's father had just increased the time he'd spent at his college, and let Anna take over.

So why was he here, now? And…was Sancia blushing? Really? Rosa was fairly sure her mother had never been embarrassed by anything ever—she just wasn't that sort of person.

Yeah, there was definitely something odd going on here.

'Is it something to do with the wedding?' Rosa pressed. 'Or the island? Is the resort in trouble?' If things were really bad, maybe Sancia had needed to call in the big guns—not just the responsible daughter, but also the ex-husband who'd tried to structure their family lives together to the point of insanity, while Sancia had fought to keep them spontaneous and freeform, until the day she'd left.

Of course, then Anna had taken over organising Rosa's life, so it wasn't as if it had made all that much difference.

But for Mama to call Dad now…

'That's not it at all,' Sancia replied, sounding affronted. Rosa had never been very good at treading carefully around other people's feelings. She suspected it might be a family trait.

'Then why is he here? I mean, now, after all this time?' It had been a full decade since Sancia had left the family home in Oxford. Of course, that was supposed to just be for a holiday—at least, that was what she had told them. And knowing Sancia as Rosa did, she'd probably believed it herself, at the time.

But a holiday had turned into an extended stay—to help her parents out with the resort, all perfectly understandable.

Except for the part where she'd never come home again.

Rosa wasn't even sure her parents had ever officially divorced. It would be just like her mother to leave things completely up in the air as far as officialdom was concerned. And just like her father to refuse to do anything to agree to a situation he hadn't planned for.

They were both as bad as each other, in some ways.

'Your father knew that Anna was here helping me, and he was worried about me,' Sancia said, in such a defensive way that Rosa knew it couldn't be the whole truth.

'And?' she pressed.

'And apparently his cardiologist might have suggested that it was a good idea, too,' Sancia admitted.

'His cardiologist?' That horrible, guilty feeling was back, clenching around her own heart, as she remembered that last argument with Anna. The one that had started out being about their father's health, and ended up being about *them*, and all the ways they were just too different to ever have that sisterly relationship Rosa had once believed just came from having the same parents.

Of course, since their parents were complete opposites, perhaps it stood to reason that their daughters would be, too.

'Apparently some sun, sea and relaxation are just what

he needs—and, of course, La Isla Marina is perfect for that!'

Sun and sea Rosa could agree with. Relaxation seemed an awful long way off right now.

'And you look like you could use some of the same.' Sancia frowned at her youngest daughter, before giving her a little shove towards the door. 'Go on. You go and be nice to our guests, and I'll bring out some food and wine for you all. It'll be a party!'

The headache forming behind Rosa's eyes told her that the last thing she needed was wine, or to spend any more time with the father who had never understood her, or the one man who maybe could have, if she hadn't walked out on him.

But Sancia in hospitality mode was a force to be reckoned with, so it appeared that Rosa didn't have any other choice.

Jude was instantly aware, the moment that Rosa appeared on the patio again. Once, he'd have believed that was a sign of their cosmic connection. Now, he knew it was merely a sign that Rosa was unhappy, and her stamping feet made her flip-flops slap against the tiled floor noisily.

Apparently, questioning her mother hadn't gone well.

'Mama's bringing out food and wine.' Rosa threw herself back into the chair opposite him, the one her father hadn't come back to claim, and tossed a clipboard on top of the Scrabble board between them. 'I couldn't stop her.'

Apparently they were ignoring the tension and difficulties their first conversation in three years had raised, forgetting all about their past connection, and moving on. Well, Rosa always did like to run away from things; maybe he shouldn't be surprised.

And really, it was probably for the best.

'Why would you want to?' Jude asked, following her lead and focussing on the present instead of the past. 'Sancia showing up with food and wine periodically is basically my favourite thing about the island.'

Rosa shrugged. 'Principle, mostly.' He gave her a confused look, and she laughed. 'Let's just call it my contrary nature. Someone tells me I have to go and sit down and make nice with *Melody Magazine*'s Most Gorgeous Man of the Year, while drinking good wine and eating delicious food, and I instantly want to do anything but that.''

'That must make life interesting,' Jude said, drily. But a part of him couldn't help wondering if that 'contrary nature' of hers explained a little of their history.

He'd always felt, right from the first, that Rosa was a bit like a wild animal—not one to be tamed, exactly, but one he needed to avoid spooking if he wanted to keep her near.

He just wasn't at all sure what he'd done that had scared her off so much that she'd run away without leaving a forwarding address—and stayed as far away as possible thereafter. His ex, Sylvie, had regularly told him that he was a disaster with women, and she didn't even know about Rosa. He just wished that someone would explain to him what he was supposed to be doing differently.

Except, maybe it wasn't him. Jude leant back in his chair and surveyed Rosa as her gaze flickered from the clipboard on the table, to the archway where Sancia would probably appear from, to him—ever so briefly— then back to the clipboard again. She chewed on the edge of a nail as she did so, and her knee didn't stop jiggling as she sat, sprawled across the chair.

Anyone not watching her carefully might think, from

her posture, that she was as laid-back as it was possible to be. But Jude, looking closer, saw more.

Rosa was coiled as tight as a spring, and he was pretty sure that wasn't his doing. Maybe her running away that night wasn't entirely his fault, either.

But right now, whatever was eating her up was making *him* tense just watching.

'So, what's got you wanting to flee in the opposite direction right now?' He regretted his turn of phrase the moment he said it, and he could tell from the way that Rosa's gaze flew to his that she had the same, instinctive memory at the words—of her, disappearing from his bed and running off into the night, without so much as a goodbye.

She didn't mention it, though. Jude couldn't quite decide if he was glad about that or not.

'This wedding Mama has agreed to hold on the island.' Rosa waved a hand towards the clipboard. 'Apparently Anna has run off with her new *lover*, and left me with all the grunt work.' She dragged out the word 'lover', as if she didn't really believe that was what Leo was.

Jude had seen Anna and Leo together—not intentionally, but they weren't exactly subtle—and he had absolutely no doubt that 'lover' was the right term.

'Who's the wedding for?' he asked, idly. Sancia had mentioned it in passing, when he'd checked in, and he knew Anna had been stressing about it. He'd assumed a family member, or something, but that clipboard had an awful lot of names on it. How big was this thing?

He looked a little closer, and froze as a familiar name caught his eye. *Sylvie Rockwell-Smythe.*

'Valentina.' Rosa sighed. 'Internet sensation, supermodel, millionaire and all-round beautiful person, by all accounts. God only knows why she wanted to hold her wedding *here*.'

Jude knew why. Because he suddenly remembered who told him about La Isla Marina in the first place. Who was responsible for his late-night Internet-searching and his decision to escape to the island.

He'd only met Valentina a handful of times, usually at the sort of event his label loved for him to attend and he tried everything in his power to get out of. But she was a friend of Sylvie's, so when they were in the same place they tended to spend time together. Valentina hadn't been anything like he'd expected her to be—of course, she was beautiful, but so were all the other women at these events. And of course, she was successful, but any suspicion that her fame had been acquired by chance or luck had been dispelled within a few minutes of talking to her.

Valentina was a shrewd businesswoman with a good eye for opportunity. She was curvier and shorter than supermodels were expected to be, but by building her brand online, and tapping into the hashtag, instant-photo-update world, she'd gathered a following that businesses would spend a fortune to access. And they did.

But what had surprised him most, he remembered now, was the night he'd ended up alone at some party with Valentina, late on, when most of the other partygoers had passed out or given up. And she'd spoken, for the first and only time—to him at least—about her childhood in Spain. Growing up as the illegitimate and unacknowledged daughter of a Spanish aristocrat, watching her mother trying to scrape together a life for them both, any way she could.

'My favourite time was when Mama worked as a cook on this fantastic island resort—La Isla Marina,' Valentina had said. 'I thought it was the most magical place in the world.' The name had stuck in his head, and when he'd been looking to escape for a while, he'd plugged it into a search engine and been on a plane less than twenty-four hours later.

Why hadn't he remembered that sooner? And if he had, would it even have made any difference?

He hadn't thought for a moment that Valentina would plan a trip here, too. Yes, she had fond memories of the place, but that wasn't the same as relocating her entire wedding there—especially since, last time he'd had an update on the wedding planning from Sylvie, when they were still together, Valentina and Todd were getting married in some top-notch, luxury villa somewhere. Between them, Todd and Valentina could afford any wedding venue in the world. So why were they coming *here*?

Maybe this was fate. Destiny's way of making him deal with all the things about his life, his future, his whole existence that he'd been putting off for too long. The breakup with Sylvie and the book's release had lit the fire under him, and now look where he was—stuck in the middle of nowhere with the one woman he'd thought he could love, and the one he knew he couldn't arriving imminently. That definitely felt as if the universe was sending him a message about dealing with his issues.

Except, just in case some more earthly powers were behind this unlikely coincidence, Jude decided it was worth asking at least one practical follow-up question. Especially since he knew La Isla Marina wasn't Valentina's first wedding venue choice—however nostalgic she was for the place.

'I thought Valentina was getting married out in some incredible luxury villa somewhere?' Somewhere very much else.

'Apparently it burnt down.' Rosa sighed. 'Which is

very sad, obviously, but she seems to have decided to move the whole shebang here, decorations and all, despite never even doing a site visit.'

Because she had it all in her memory, of course. But Jude wasn't going to spill Valentina's secrets for her.

'Well, I'm sure she'll love it here,' Jude said, trying not to look around him for evidence to the contrary. He knew what sort of luxury Valentina and her friends were used to and, despite all the hard work Anna and Leo seemed to be putting in to get the bungalows up to scratch, Jude had to admit that La Isla Marina wasn't quite the magical paradise that Valentina seemed to remember. Yet, anyway.

'Not right now, she wouldn't,' Rosa said bluntly. She'd worked around celebrities, of course. She knew the expectations, too. 'Mama says that Anna's arranged for an army of seasonal staff—including a plumber, joiner and builder—to arrive tomorrow and finish off the work of making the accommodation decent.'

'Well, that's good, isn't it?' The way Rosa said it, he suspected not.

'I suppose. Except it means that I'm left with all the wedding stuff. Allocating accommodation for the guests, decorating the pagoda, working out seating plans, dealing with what is sure to be their many, many issues when they arrive.'

'And you'd rather be painting?' Jude guessed.

'I'd rather be thousands of miles away with my camera, chasing a good story.' She gave him a half-smile, as if to indicate that she was joking—which Jude was pretty sure she wasn't. 'It's just that this sort of thing—admin and paperwork and people—it's not really playing to my strengths. I'm better with a paintbrush in hand.'

'So why has Anna given these jobs to you?'

'Punishment, I reckon. For showing up two weeks

after she did.' Rosa sighed, and pulled the clipboard towards her. 'I mean, look at some of these names. Tyrana Lichfield-Burrows. Ursula Pennington. Isadora-Marie Woodford-Williams, for heaven's sake. Do they sound like my sort of people?'

'Actually, Isadora-Marie is nice. And funny. But I can tell you now you're going to hate Ursula.' It was a flippant remark, but Jude realised his mistake almost instantly.

Rosa's gaze sharpened, fastened on his face as she leant across the table towards him. 'You know these people,' she said, in the sort of voice he'd never been able to lie to.

Wincing, Jude nodded, reluctantly. 'Yes.'

CHAPTER FOUR

ROSA SMILED. This guest list featured some of New York's most celebrated and fabulous citizens—*of course* Jude, rock-star celebrity, would know them. And probably know them well enough to be able to tell her who shouldn't be sat next to whom, and which of them were likely to cause the most trouble. She might not like doing the admin and organising side of things—she'd always been more of the 'make it up as you go along' type, like her mother—but if she *had* to do it, then some insider knowledge would most definitely prove helpful.

'You can help me, then,' she said, and saw Jude wince again. What was the problem? These were his friends—he should be looking forward to seeing them. Except… she flipped through the guest list. 'Hang on, why aren't you invited to this shindig?'

Jude sighed. 'Probably because one of the bridesmaids broke up with me six weeks ago.'

'Sylvie. Right.' That might explain all the wincing. 'So, was it her or the book that you ran all the way to Spain to escape from?'

'Bit of both,' Jude murmured, but didn't elaborate.

'I guess you won't be staying for the wedding, then?' At least his answer had proved her right about one thing—Jude *was* hiding. But how bad an ex-girlfriend were they talking about that he had to run away to a decrepit Spanish island to escape her?

Mind you, she'd run to the other end of the earth to escape him, and he'd been pretty much perfect.

Of course, that was why she'd run. Perfection was terrifying—especially in the face of all her faults.

'Depends, I guess,' Jude said. Then he shook his head. 'I honestly don't know. I came here to get away from everything, but now…maybe this is meant to be. Maybe it's time to face some demons from my past.'

His gaze caught hers as he said it, and suddenly Rosa felt the knowledge that they weren't just talking about his ex, or some book any more weighing heavy on her heart.

She'd tried not to think too much about Jude after she left—that way, she was pretty sure, madness lay. Or at best, running back to him, just when she'd escaped his thrall. Rosa wasn't the sort to dwell. She moved on, got over it and kept going. That was all she knew.

He talked about being here to face his demons as if it were a good thing. If Rosa had the choice, she'd be running as fast as she could in the opposite direction from everything and everyone on La Isla Marina.

'So…you're planning on staying?' Rosa asked, surprised. 'And I kind of have to stay.' At least, if she wanted her family to speak to her ever again. Although she'd gone three years without that from Anna and her father already… No. Rosa didn't have so much family that she could be *quite* that cavalier about losing them.

'So we're both here. On the island. For the duration.' Jude's gaze was heavy and meaningful, and Rosa had an awful feeling she knew exactly where he wanted this conversation to go: back to the night she left, and searching for explanations why.

Yeah, she really wasn't ready to have that talk yet. Let

him deal with his other demons—whatever they were—first, and come back to her last. Like when someone was taking for ever to make up their mind choosing from the menu in a restaurant, and asked the waiter to ask them again at the end.

But Jude wasn't a waiter. And if she couldn't avoid Jude any longer, she might as well take advantage of the fact he was there. Apart from anything else, giving him something else to focus on—like the impending arrival of his ex—might distract him from their own past. And honestly? She could use the help.

Pasting on a bright smile, she ignored the vibes and merrily changed the subject. 'Great! Well, in that case, you can definitely help me out with all these tasks Anna's left for me. I'm sure your insider knowledge will be invaluable.'

Jude didn't seem particularly excited at the prospect. In fact, he didn't look as if he wanted to change the subject at all.

'Rosa. Don't you think we need to talk—?'

'Not really,' she said, honestly. 'I think we were friends, three years ago, before anything else. Maybe we can be that again. I have too much to focus on here for this wedding to even think about anything else right now.'

He didn't agree with her; she could see it in his face. Jude was the talking sort, and she, well, wasn't. Not unless she had to be.

But then, just as Jude opened his mouth to argue, Sancia appeared in the doorway, holding a tray of tapas and flanked by Rosa's father, carrying wine.

She had, quite seriously, never been so pleased to see her parents in her whole life.

'Mama! Dad!' She jumped up from her chair and bounced across the courtyard to help them with the plates. Her father in particular looked surprised at the welcome. Understandably, she supposed. They'd never been affectionate, the two of them. Professor Gray kept even people he loved and liked, like Sancia or Anna, at arm's length, and he'd never known what to make of his younger, wilder daughter. It was as if blood was the only thing they'd ever had in common.

Until now. Now, they all had the future of La Isla Marina in common. And she and her father had the added connection of Jude's friendship.

Now, they were all going to have to try and get along for a while.

And they could start by getting her out of a very awkward conversation with Jude. 'Why don't you come and join us? Jude has lots of questions about the island.'

Once Sancia got talking about La Isla Marina, it would be impossible for anyone to get a word in edgeways. Especially if that word was the one question Rosa really didn't want to answer. *Why?*

Because, seeing Jude again, all of her reasons had already started to fade away. And she couldn't afford to let that happen. Not when she knew she was leaving again, as soon as this wedding was over.

Jude awoke the next morning to the sound of the sea lapping against the rocks outside his bungalow window, the sun already shining through the thin gauze curtains. He lay for a moment just enjoying the peace, the solitude and the beauty of La Isla Marina.

And then his brain caught up with his body.

Rosa was here. Sylvie was coming here. And he'd promised to spend his day helping Rosa prepare for the socialite wedding of the year.

Just perfect.

His head suddenly aching, Jude forced himself out of bed and into the shower. So much for his idyllic secret getaway. From the look of Rosa's clipboard, half of Manhattan was now following him there. And it wasn't even the half he really *liked*.

Letting the water sluice over his skin, Jude thought back over the strange events of the day before. Had he been imagining it, or had Rosa been trying to avoid talking about their history together? She certainly hadn't let on to her parents how close they'd been, once. Instead, she'd talked about him as just one more subject she'd photographed and written about.

Maybe that was all he was, to her.

Could he have imagined that connection between them? That instantaneous, shocking attraction?

Had she just been patiently listening three years ago, as he'd poured out his heart to her, in the hope that she'd find a good story?

No.

He shook water droplets from his hair as he stepped out of the shower, letting the warm Spanish air dry his skin.

He'd seen the same confusion and amazement in Rosa's eyes, that first night they'd been together. That overwhelmed, overtaken look that had echoed exactly how he'd felt.

She'd been as rocked by their connection as he had. She'd just reacted differently.

And maybe now the universe was giving him the chance to find out why—whether she wanted to tell him or not.

Rosa might have distracted him last night with Sancia's tales of the island, and the truly excellent wine and tapas she provided. But today was another day—and they'd already arranged to meet at the villa to go over the guest list and arrangements.

Jude smiled to himself as he pulled on his dark linen trousers and a crisp white linen shirt. If Rosa wanted his help, she'd better be prepared to pay in her secrets.

Especially since she already knew all of his.

The villa was deserted when he reached Reception, so Jude loitered in the cool shade of the tiled reception hall. The white painted arches overhead and the cool vistas reminded him more of a Middle Eastern palace than a Spanish villa, but he liked the feel of the place. It felt as if time had stopped, or at least slowed to a lazy, honey-slow meander. After the bustle of New York City, Jude was enjoying the change of pace.

Sancia had told him the romantic tale of how the island came to her in her family the night before: how Sancia's grandparents had built the villa as their retreat from the world when they married, and how Sancia's parents had built the resort around it when they inherited it. At one time, it was supposed to have been a jewel in the Med, *the* place for the movers and shakers of the time to be seen.

He supposed it would be again, soon. If they got all the necessary work done on time.

Jude was about to reach across the reception desk to pick up the phone and see if there was a direct line to the office, or someone—anyone—who might know where Rosa was, when she suddenly appeared before him.

He blinked. 'Where did you come from?'

'Mama didn't show you the secret door, then, when she gave you the tour?' Rosa grinned. 'Good. A girl has to have some secrets.'

'Secret door?' Jude honestly couldn't tell if she was teasing him or not. 'Are you kidding?'

Rosa shook her head. 'Nope! There's a secret door somewhere in this reception hall that leads to the family quarters. How else are we poor staff supposed to get some peace and quiet from all you demanding guests?'

'I'm going to spend my entire stay trying to figure out whether you're making this up or not,' Jude admitted, which made Rosa's grin grow even wider.

'I'm okay with that,' she answered.

'So, where do we start today?' Jude nodded at the clipboard in Rosa's hands. 'Want to go through and see how many names I recognise? Or how about you run me through the schedule for the week, see if I can highlight any potential danger zones.' If he was here to be useful, he might as well make an effort. And by pure osmosis—and listening to Sylvie gossip—he thought he could probably offer some pretty good insights. Who was likely to abuse the free bar and might need to be kept away from the sea afterwards. Who would find something to complain about regardless, so it was worth giving them a tiny flaw in their bungalow that was easily fixed, just so they'd feel happy. Hell, he even knew one of the bridesmaids was allergic to fresh-cut flowers!

How much of his brain had been taken over by this world—Sylvie's world? The world of celebrity that his label wanted him to be seen in.

What had happened to the music being the most important thing?

'All of those sound like great ideas,' Rosa said. 'But actually… I thought we might take a walk around the island, first. I kind of want to see what Anna's been doing here for the last two weeks, and get an idea of what shape we're in, before I get down to the nitty-gritty stuff.'

'Makes sense,' Jude said. 'Of course, it also sounds

like a total procrastination attempt to avoid doing the *actual* work Anna left you…'

Rosa hit him in the arm with her clipboard, not hard enough to hurt, but enough to make him shut up and grin at her.

This was interesting. Last time they'd met, they'd been on his home turf—as much as a band tour bus could be called anyone's home. They'd been in his world, before The Swifts had really hit the mainstream and started playing stadiums instead of pubs and tiny music venues. He'd known his place there, in a way he didn't quite, these days.

But this time, they were on Rosa's patch—her family home, even, for all that it was also an island resort. This was the place she ran to when they called—rather than running away.

And that meant he got to see a whole other side of Rosa, this time. Maybe he'd even see enough to understand why she left.

Rosa led them out of the villa, down the long, straight path that led back to the jetty and escape from the island. But before they reached the sea, she took a sharp right down a narrower path, through recently cut-back lush greenery. It was the opposite direction from Jude's own bungalow, but, still, things looked familiar.

The bungalows they passed were just like the one he was staying in—low and white, half hidden between the plants and brightly coloured flowers. The smell of fresh paint lingered as they got closer to one; Jude knew that even a few days ago many of them had been grey and dingy. One or two he'd seen on his rambles across the island had displayed broken roof tiles and wooden shutters that hung from their hinges.

Not now, though.

Now, every bungalow gleamed in the sunlight, the freshly painted shutters giving a splash of colour against the white walls. The jungle Jude had fought his way through on arrival had been tamed, so the island looked lush, fresh and green, rather than overtaken by plants. Even the patios outside the bungalows had been swept, scrubbed, and the iron patio furniture cleaned and looking ready for use.

It was quite the transformation. If Jude had been paying more attention to the island, rather than his own thoughts—and Scrabble games—he would have noticed sooner. As it was, suddenly he could see what had drawn Valentina to the island.

Rosa was surveying it with a more critical eye. 'How bad was it? Before the work started, I mean.'

Jude shrugged. 'It was already pretty far under way when I arrived.'

'But some parts weren't done yet, right? What did they look like?'

'They were…' He winced as he tried to find the words to describe how run-down and derelict parts of the island had looked, just a week or so ago.

'That bad, huh?'

'Worse,' he admitted. 'Anna and Leo—and their crew—have done an incredible job around here.'

Rosa let out a long sigh. 'Then she's going to be even more unbearable when she gets back.'

'What do you mean?' Jude dropped to sit on the cast-iron chair on the patio of the nearest bungalow. Motioning across the table, he indicated for Rosa to take the other seat.

'We should have brought coffee with us,' she grumbled as she sat.

Having tasted Sancia's coffee, Jude definitely agreed. But getting Rosa to talk about herself, that was good, too.

Part of him wondered why he still cared—why it still mattered to him at all. It had been three years since she'd left him, and it wasn't as if they'd had a lengthy relationship before that. It had been a short, hot fling—and if he had any sense at all, he'd just keep the memory of that and move on.

Why had he expected anything else, anything more? Because it had felt so real, while it was happening. And like a dream once it was over.

There'd been women since, of course—short-term and long-term. And his life had changed beyond all measure—the tour bus replaced with a private jet, and the grim pubs they'd played with hundred-thousand-seater stadiums. His music was recognised, loved, had gone double platinum—twice. The band had grown closer still, as they'd gone through all the changes together. Especially after they'd lost Gareth. They all knew they had to take care of each other, in a way they hadn't been able to take care of Gareth. In the way he *should* have taken care of Gareth.

But somehow, Jude had become the star—more recognisable than his bandmates, the one the papers and magazines wanted to interview, to photograph. The one who drew the rumours and the stories and the lies.

Still. He had so many people in his life now—from bandmates to friends to acquaintances to his agent to the people at the label to the *über*-fans—that Rosa should have faded from his consciousness completely. He shouldn't even have *recognised* her when she walked in last night.

But he'd known her voice in an instant.

Maybe it was just that he knew what had gone wrong

with every other relationship in his life—but Rosa's motives for leaving remained a mystery. But deep down, Jude knew it was more than that.

He'd opened his heart and his soul to this woman, let her see everything that he was. She was the only person he'd ever done anything close to that for—besides Gareth. But Gareth had been his best friend since they were three. He'd known Rosa less than a month. And still, she was the only person in the world that had seen every inch of the real him. The only one to know him at all, once Gareth died.

And she'd run away. What did that say about the real him?

No wonder he hadn't let anyone else so close since.

He wanted to know her as well as she'd known him, then. Wanted to understand her—find what was wrong with him, or with her, that she'd left and never looked back.

Starting with her obviously acrimonious relationship with her sister.

'So. What's the deal with you and your sister?'

Rosa stared mutinously at him. 'We're sisters. What do you expect?'

Jude thought about his cousins—three sisters who were so close they could practically read each other's mind. 'I guess all sibling relationships are different.'

'You're an only child,' she pointed out, and Jude felt a small jolt as he realised she'd remembered that small fact about him. 'What would you know?'

She was right, he supposed. He'd had Gareth, but that wasn't the same. They'd grown up together, sure, but they hadn't had the same parents, lived the same life in the same place, not until they were eighteen.

'So tell me,' he suggested.

Rosa sighed. 'Anna and I…there's only two years between us, but sometimes it feels more like decades.'

'You're not very alike?'

'Physically? Sure—we both look like Mama, in case you hadn't noticed.'

He tried to remember what Anna looked like; he'd only met her briefly a couple of times since he arrived. Obviously she couldn't look too like Rosa or he might have noticed sooner. 'I suppose…' he said, slowly. 'I mean, yes, you look like Sancia. And so does Anna. And yet, I never looked at Anna and thought she looked like you.' And he would have done. He'd spent three years looking for Rosa in strangers.

'Dad used to say that when you looked at the two of us in photos we could be twins,' Rosa said, sounding a little wistful. 'It was only when you saw us in motion that it became clear we were completely different people.'

Jude tilted his head to look at Rosa, taking in her slouched posture, one ankle resting on her knee. Her long, dark hair hung over one shoulder in some sort of complicated braid, and she was watching him from under long, dark lashes.

She was trying to look relaxed, he realised. And maybe to other people she'd look that way. But Jude could almost feel the tension coming off her in waves—the same as last night.

With another sigh, she sat upright again, leaning her elbows forward onto the patio table. 'The thing is, Anna was always Dad's favourite. She's just like him, really— all academic and serious and organised and stuff. And me, I'm more like Mama. A free spirit.'

'That's why you don't get on?' Jude asked. 'Too different?'

'Partly.' She bit her lip, bright white teeth sharp against

the lushness of her mouth. Jude felt a jolt of lust rush through him as he remembered the last time he'd seen her do that. She'd been sitting astride him at the time...

He swallowed. Hard. 'What else?' Focussing on the facts, that was what mattered now.

He was going to learn why Rosa left him. He was going to understand, finally, the terrible string of events that led to Gareth's death. And then he was going to turn around and leave her, and any influence she had on his life, behind. Move on himself, at last. That was the plan and he was sticking to it. Memories be damned.

'My mother left us. I must have told you that?' She looked at him, waited for him to nod a confirmation before she carried on. 'Before then life was...balanced, I guess. Dad would spend all his time at the university, or in his study, only appearing to complain about the state of the house, or to try and install some sort of order into our lives. And Mama...she just concentrated on us all being happy. She didn't care if we arrived at the beach without the picnic, or our swimming costumes. We'd have ice cream for lunch and swim in our knickers.'

'They were the ultimate in opposites attracting, then?' Jude guessed.

'Pretty much.' Rosa gave him a lopsided smile. 'But it worked, you know? At least, until it didn't.'

'What happened?'

Rosa sighed. 'Can we walk while I tell this story? I talk better when I'm moving.'

He remembered that, Jude realised. All those nights cramped on the tour bus, and it was always him whispering secrets and telling his soul. Rosa only started to talk when they escaped—when they ran down Southend pier at night together, or explored the streets of London, just the two of them. That was when he got to hear the inner workings of Rosa's heart.

'Where do you want to go?' he asked, getting to his feet.

Rosa had already jumped up, and was halfway down the track. 'To the sea, of course,' she said, the words tossed back over her shoulder.

Jude didn't mention that he'd had enough of the sea on his crossing from the mainland, or that his bungalow was right next to the shore. Why wasn't he surprised that Rosa—shiftless, always moving Rosa—was drawn to the ocean, with all its ebbs and flows and tides?

At least the sea was predictable, to a point. Except for tsunamis and stuff.

Even they seemed more predictable than Rosa.

Jude kept quiet and waited for her to start talking again as they walked. He caught up easily, and walked beside her on the narrow path that wound across the island, down to the shore.

Eventually, she spoke.

'When Mama left…she didn't exactly walk out. That's not Mama's style, really—a monumental decision and a fight and a definite end.'

'So what did she do?' Jude couldn't quite quash the hope that somewhere in the story of why Sancia left Ernest Gray would be the explanation for her daughter's hit-and-run attitude.

'She came here, to La Isla Marina, for a holiday.' Rosa's smile was too tight, too fixed. 'It was only supposed to be for a week or two. She left Anna and me with Dad.'

'How old were you?'

'Sixteen. Anna was eighteen. About to sit her A-levels.'

'And you must have had your GCSEs,' Jude pointed out.

'Yeah. But they didn't matter in the same way. Anna

was always the academic one.' Rosa shook her head. 'Anyway. Two weeks turned into a month. Mama said that our grandparents needed her help—that running the resort was too much for them now they were getting older. And it wasn't a lie—I mean, you saw this place when you arrived. But…somehow, she just never came home again.'

Jude's heart ached for this girl who'd lost the only family member who made her feel as if she belonged. 'I can't imagine how that must have hurt.'

Rosa shrugged. 'It wasn't so much Mama leaving, I don't think. I mean, I visited her out here every holiday and, to be honest, the weeks I spent here on the island were the happiest I remember. And *she* was so much happier here. It wasn't until she left that I saw the truth—how unhappy, how stifled she'd been in Oxford, surrounded by people who needed academic proofs and publications to back up their every feeling.'

'People like Anna and your dad.'

'Exactly! Mama was never like that. She was all impulse and fun and living life in colour. She needed to be free.'

'Like you.' Because that was always how he'd remembered Rosa. Full colour. Even when he felt stuck in black-and-white noir.

'Maybe.' She gave him a sidelong look. 'Anyway, with Mama gone, it was just Dad and Anna. And Dad retreated back into his office again, so Anna took over everything else. Running the household, organising Dad, and ordering me around.'

Jude winced. 'I'm guessing that didn't go down so well with you.'

'You guess right.' Rosa sighed. 'The worst thing is, now, with ten years of hindsight, I can't even blame her completely. We were both trying to cope with a monumental change in our lives, and I guess we each did it differently. But then… I just felt so hemmed in and frustrated. Before then, we'd always got on well. Yes, we were different, but we were sisters and we were close. It was us against the parents, you know? But when Mama left…'

'It was you against Anna.'

'And it has been ever since.' Rosa pushed a last, stray branch out of their path, then moved ahead of him, her long braid swaying in time to her hips. It was almost hypnotising. As if she could take over his mind just in the way she moved. Which, on past evidence, wasn't entirely untrue. 'We haven't spoken in three years, now.'

Then she stopped in front of him, so suddenly he almost crashed into her. Jude's hands came up, ready to grab her hips for balance, but at the last moment he realised the insanity of that plan and held onto the nearest tree, instead.

Rosa breathed in deeply, her shoulders moving with the motion. 'I miss the sea, when I'm away. Other oceans don't smell quite the same.'

'It must be strange to be home, with your whole family here.' Jude let Rosa step out onto the small beach in the cove they'd arrived at. It was secluded, idyllic and, under other circumstances, wildly romantic.

'Very,' Rosa admitted. 'There are so many memories tied up in this place…' She trailed off, then gave a low laugh.

'What?'

'Talking of memories, I just realised where we are,' she said. 'This is the beach where I lost my virginity.'

CHAPTER FIVE

ROSA REGRETTED IT the moment she said it. *When* would she learn to think before she spoke? When she was little, her father had always told her she needed to learn that lesson more than any other, before she grew up. Now she was twenty-six, she was starting to think that it might be a permanent condition.

What else could explain her impulse to mention sex in front of the one man she was busy pretending she had never slept with?

She glanced quickly at Jude's face, looking away almost instantly to stare out over the sea. This was one of her favourite spots on the island—always had been. That was why she'd chosen it for what she'd imagined would be a memorable night—her first time.

It was memorable, she supposed, if not entirely for the right reasons. It had basically been a disaster.

Much like the conversation she felt coming.

Jude came to stand beside her, close enough that his arm brushed against hers. His skin was too pale, Rosa thought, looking at it next to her own. As if he'd been locked away somewhere, forced to make music and never see sunlight.

No wonder he'd felt he needed to run away to a sunny island in the middle of nowhere.

'Talking about sex,' Jude said, his voice soft, his gaze fixed on the horizon. 'Are we ever going to?'

'Have sex?' Rosa's voice came out squeaky, even as she realised that *of course* that wasn't what he meant.

'Talk about it. What happened between us.' He turned his head to look at her, and his bright blue gaze seemed to see right through her clothes, her skin, deep into the heart of her.

That was the problem with Jude. He always saw too deep.

'Why you left,' he added, and Rosa broke away from his gaze.

'Do we have to?' she asked, kicking at the sand with the front of her flip-flop.

Jude's cool fingers came under her chin, lifting her face so she had to look at him again. 'Rosa... I can't help but think that I'm here on this island for a reason. To find closure, on all kinds of things—starting with what happened between us, and everything that happened afterwards. And if you want us to work together on this wedding, I think we're going to have to, you know...'

'Have the talk.' Rosa sighed. Why couldn't she have fallen for one of the roadies, or even one of his bandmates like Jimmy, three years ago? Most men she met would run a thousand miles rather than talk about their feelings—which suited Rosa just fine, thanks.

But no, she had to go and fall for the sensitive artist. The one person who wanted to *understand* her.

Even if she didn't want to be understood. Even if she didn't understand herself, sometimes.

'I'll do you a deal,' Jude said, his voice more normal suddenly—as if they weren't talking about sex and love any more. 'You tell me what happened that night—why you left, and why you never came back. You help me understand that, and we never have to talk about it again, okay? We can just be acquaintances—friends, even—spending time together on a holiday island. Okay?'

'Okay,' Rosa said, slowly. It sounded good, she had to admit.

The only problem was, for all her brave words, she couldn't imagine ever being friends with Jude Alexander. Not after what they'd shared.

But she was willing to try if he was.

Taking a few steps forward towards the sea, she kicked off her flip-flops and sat on the edge of the sand, letting the waves lap over her toes.

Leaning back on her hands, Rosa shut her eyes. The warm sun on her skin felt like home. Like love.

'So,' she asked, her eyes still closed. 'What do you want to know?'

She felt rather than saw Jude settle beside her, and wondered if he'd taken off his shoes, too. Maybe even rolled up those dark linen trousers. He might have a slender, rock-star frame, but his shoulders were broader than you'd think, and there were muscles on that frame, too, she remembered. Could almost see through his thin white shirt if she didn't concentrate on not looking…

She opened her eyes. Jude had his bare feet in the water, just like her. Rosa smiled. Good. He needed to relax more.

'Was it something I did?' he asked, staring out at the sea. 'Or did you just not feel the same way I did?'

Rosa swallowed, tasting regret in her mouth. 'How did you feel?'

'Like magic had walked into my life, the moment I met you,' Jude said, simply. 'Like I'd been waiting for you for centuries.'

Guilt pierced through Rosa's heart. She knew exactly what he meant, and *of course* she'd felt it, too. But how could she tell him that was the whole problem? That sort of perfection wasn't meant for the mess that was her. She'd screw it up sooner or later, and sooner was better, in her experience.

'And that's why you're the songwriter of the two of us,' she joked, her heart breaking as she said it. 'You can take a tour-bus fling and make it into poetry.'

'Is that all we were?' Jude shifted on the sand so he could look at her, almost lying down on his side as he spoke. 'A tour-bus fling?'

God, but it was so tempting to curl up there with him, safe in his arms. But Rosa knew she might not have the strength to leave them twice.

'We knew each other for four weeks, Jude,' she reminded him, gently.

'I knew all I needed to in the first day.'

She remembered. Remembered the way their eyes had met and she'd just *known*. Known that this man was going to be important.

Rosa didn't believe in love at first sight, but if she had…

She shook her head. What difference did it make if it was love or not? That didn't change everything else that it was.

A burden. A chain. A prison.

She'd seen what happened when a woman fell in love—so deeply in love that she gave up all her own dreams and moved to Oxford to live his life, instead of hers. She'd seen her mother live it, so she didn't have to. Twenty years of frustration and bitterness, followed by her finally leaving for her island refuge.

Rosa had known, even then, that she wasn't willing to live that life. Wasn't willing to compromise her own dreams one bit to live someone else's.

She needed to end this now. She needed to tell Jude enough to get him to stop asking—to give him his closure. Then they could both move on, and she'd be as free of him as he was of her.

That was what she wanted. It was all she ever wanted: freedom.

'I told you why at the time,' she said. 'I had to come home for my *abuelo*—for my grandfather's—funeral.'

'Except you didn't tell me where home was,' Jude reminded her. 'Or that you weren't coming back.'

And there was the sticking point. She hadn't really known that, at the time. It was only once she was out of Jude's sphere, without his smile or his hands or his eyes influencing her decisions, that she realised the risk. When she knew that she had to stay away.

That, and a terrifying two weeks when her body told her she might have made a monumental, life-changing mistake, that first, impulsive night she'd spent with him.

As she'd waited, too scared to even buy a pregnancy test and know for sure, too distraught dealing with all the funeral stuff to even really think about it, one thing had been abundantly clear to her.

If she went back to Jude when she left La Isla Marina, that would be it. If four weeks in each other's company, in his bed, could have this kind of impact on her life, her heart, then going back would be a life sentence.

She'd fall irrevocably in love with him, and never be able to break away. She'd live her mother's life— following him around the world as he toured, always being his plus one, and never finding her own life, her own self. Her own happiness.

Or worse, she'd be Anna—managing Jude's personal life as Anna managed Dad's, giving up her own opportunities and possibilities to him.

She couldn't do that. Couldn't sacrifice all her dreams for his dream of stardom.

And she'd had no doubt that Jude would be a star—anyone who'd heard The Swifts play had known that it was only a matter of time before they made it big. And Jude and Gareth, they'd made a pact, when they were barely teenagers, that one day they'd be famous together. They'd escape all the people who told them they'd never make anything of themselves, the families and schools who told them it was impossible. They were going to conquer the world together—and they'd already been so close, when Rosa met them. She knew it wouldn't be long until the name Jude Alexander was on everyone's lips.

Would he even want her around, then? When beautiful women were throwing themselves at him, and every door was open to him?

By the time her cycle had returned—delayed by stress, rather than her carelessness in bed with Jude, it seemed—the funeral was long over and Rosa had made a decision.

She needed to find her own life, her own happiness. She wouldn't make her mother's mistakes all over again, falling for a man whose career would always come first, who would forget she existed for weeks at a time.

And so she'd run as far away as she could—and ended up back here with him three years later, anyway.

Looking at him, Rosa knew the risk was still there. If she let herself get too close to Jude, let herself hope, she could fall anyway, despite all the distance she'd put between them. And if she gave him a hint that she still felt that way…

So she had to lie. Or at least, not tell the whole truth.

'Honestly?' she said, knowing she was being anything but honest. 'I hadn't decided when I left what I was going to do next. But then an opportunity came up for a new commission out in the Middle East, and it sounded interesting so…' She shrugged. 'You know me. I like to keep moving, finding new experiences, seeking out the next big thing.'

Jude grabbed her hand suddenly, making her turn to face him, staring into her eyes as if he could see the truth behind them. Rosa held her nerve, ignoring her heart beating too fast in her chest, and let him look. Nothing she had said was *technically* untrue, after all.

'So, is that what I was?' Jude asked, after a moment. 'Just another new experience?'

No. He'd been *the* experience. The one she judged every other moment of her life against. And all too often found them lacking.

No other man had ever lived up to four weeks with Jude. And yes, she'd had regrets, had imagined what could have been.

And he couldn't know that. Because regrets didn't change anything. The only way she knew how to move was forward.

Rosa gave an apologetic shrug, and Jude dropped her hand.

'So, does every experience have to be new?' He'd gone back to staring at the sea again now, and Rosa's heart had started to settle back down to a normal rhythm. Maybe that was why she didn't think carefully enough about her response. As usual.

'Some are worth experiencing twice,' she admitted, her words coming out soft and husky.

Jude's gaze snapped back to hers, and she saw the lust there. The want. The *need*.

And the worst thing was she was almost sure her eyes were reflecting the same feelings right back at him.

Rosa leapt to her feet. 'Right! We should get back to work.'

'Work.' Jude shook his head. 'Sure.'

She'd given him the answers he wanted, and now he owed her his help with this damn wedding.

And if Rosa wished she could have told him the truth? She'd get over it. She'd move on.

She always did.

Jude stared at the room full of boxes, all with comprehensive shipping labels stuck on them.

Somehow, the resolution he'd made to be all business with Rosa was coming back to bite him. He'd *almost* rather live through that soul-crushing conversation with Rosa on the beach all over again than sort through fifty boxes of wedding decorations and accessories.

But only almost. He wasn't sure he could take hearing Rosa tell him how he was just one more experience again.

It wasn't as if he hadn't known she was a free spirit back then—it was one of the things he liked most about her, the way she surged forward after her own life, not caring about schedules or plans or what other people thought.

She was the way he'd always thought *he* was, until he realised how much of his life was organised by other people.

Music—that was supposed to be the ultimate freedom, wasn't it? Creating something from nothing, something from inside the soul, something that touched millions of others. It was supposed to be his escape—from a town with no work, a father who told him he was a waste of space and a school that told him he had no future. He and Gareth had dreamed of the day they'd prove them all wrong—and they'd never doubted they could do it, together.

Music was *their* thing. The one thing in the world that no one could take away from them. But then the world, and addiction, had taken Gareth away from him. Maybe that was why he felt sometimes as if it wasn't his at all, any more.

That was why he'd come to La Isla Marina—to find his freedom again. The fact that he'd found the one person chaining him to his memories of the past was beside the point.

Jude knew it all came down to what happened with Gareth. It was all tangled together in his head—the promise he'd made, and broken. If Rosa hadn't been there, he'd have seen the signs sooner. He'd have been at whichever party it was when Gareth decided just one more hit wouldn't hurt. He'd have noticed one becoming two becoming every night again.

Gareth had overdosed less than a month after Rosa left, and Jude knew that if he hadn't been so focussed on his own pain during that month he would have noticed Gareth's. The events were all tied up together, running together like two melodies in his head, twisting together to make a new song. However much he told himself that Gareth's addiction wasn't his fault, wasn't Rosa's fault for leaving, he knew he was the only person in the world who could have stopped it.

He knew he'd always blame himself for his friend's death, more than the drugs that had caused it. Because when Gareth had needed him, Jude had been too caught up in Rosa to even notice. He'd broken the most important promise he'd ever made—the promise he'd made in that hospital room, a year before Gareth died, that he'd be there for him. That he'd keep his friend safe.

He shook his head, and tried to focus on the task in hand. Gareth was gone. All Jude could do now was live their dream for both of them. Enjoy the success Gareth had craved, and the high life he'd looked forward to so much. Show the world that had dismissed them that they could do anything—even if the price they had to pay seemed far, far too high.

And as for Rosa… He had the closure he'd asked for, at last. He knew why she left—however much he didn't like it.

Now he had to keep up his end of the bargain. Which apparently involved wedding decorations and accessories.

'Did you count them yet?' Rosa asked, clipboard in hand. 'Anna's notes say there should be fifty.'

'What could Valentina possibly need for her wedding that requires fifty boxes?' Jude asked as he started counting again. Just the sight of Rosa in her tight jeans, rolled up to show off slim ankles, and her close-fitting white T-shirt was enough to make him lose count.

'Everything, according to these lists.' Rosa stared at the clipboard with disgust. 'My sister and her bloody lists.'

'When is Anna getting back? And it's definitely fifty, by the way.' Jude pointed to the boxes when she looked confused.

'Of course it is. Just like on the list.' Rosa ticked something off, and scowled at it again. 'Mama says she and Leo should be back this afternoon. With a full report of the catering staff that Valentina's flying in from Barcelona.' Perhaps her sister's imminent return explained Rosa's bad mood.

'This is going to be quite the wedding, huh?'

Jude opened the first box to find string after string of fairy lights, all neatly wrapped around pieces of card. The next box revealed larger lanterns to house candles, and the one after that the candles themselves.

'Is Valentina expecting some sort of power cut?' he asked, motioning towards the boxes.

Rosa laughed. 'Sort of. She wants a very traditional

Spanish wedding, apparently—which means it doesn't start until the evening and it goes on all night long. And since it's all taking place outside...'

'Hence the candles.'

'Exactly.'

Rosa perched herself on the edge of the nearest box, sitting gingerly until she was certain it could take her weight. She'd pushed her sunglasses onto the top of her head, and her usual heavy plait hung over her shoulder. Jude couldn't help but watch her. What was it about her that drew his eye, even after everything? Even now he knew the risk of getting caught up in Rosa again?

She was beautiful, of course. Maybe even more beautiful than she'd been three years ago. She'd been fresher then, he supposed, but there was a new worldliness about her now that he liked.

The tension he'd noticed on the first day was still there, tight in the lines of her shoulders and her mouth, for all that she kicked her feet casually back and forth. She chewed a pencil as she stared down at her clipboard.

'Okay, so as far as I can tell, this is what's happening. The bridal party arrive on the Wednesday, for general wedding prep and whatever it is bridesmaids do before a wedding.'

'Drink, mostly, I think,' Jude said. 'Have you never been a bridesmaid?'

Rosa looked at him as if he were crazy. 'Aren't they supposed to organise things and commit to being in the country on the right day and stuff? Who on earth would ask me to do that?'

'Good point,' he allowed. Rosa wasn't the woman you went to for commitment. He had the heartbreak to prove it.

'Anyway, the groom and his family and groomsmen arrive on Friday night, then the wedding is on the Saturday evening, so that whole day will probably be pretty hellish with last-minute traumas. If you wanted to run, I'd suggest you do it then.'

She was watching him from under her lashes, Jude realised. Waiting to see what his reaction to the idea of leaving was.

Did that mean she wanted him to stay? What had she said last night? *Some are worth experiencing twice.* Well. If that wasn't a hint...

'I'm not going anywhere,' he said, cursing himself a little as he did so. What was he doing, promising to stay for the woman who'd been running from him for three years?

'Want to stay and see the ex-girlfriend, huh?' Rosa asked, and Jude realised he'd actually forgotten for a moment that staying would mean seeing Sylvie.

'Not really.' Especially since thinking about her still made his blood boil.

'You said it was a bad breakup?'

'She fabricated stories about me to sell for the stupid kiss-and-tell book about me.' Of course, the made-up ones were easier to laugh off than the true, private ones she'd also sold. The ones where she'd talked about Gareth, and his remorse and guilt over his death. The broken promise. Those were the ones that hurt the most.

Gareth was no one's business except his.

'*The Naked Truth* thing?' Rosa winced. 'Ouch.'

'Yeah. The book came out this week.'

'Which is why you decided to be on a remote Spanish island at the time.'

'Exactly.'

'Except now your fantastically twisted love life is following you here,' Rosa commented.

Jude shot her a look. 'In more ways than one.'

'Well, you said you wanted closure.' Jumping down from the box she was sitting on, Rosa busied herself with sorting through a box full of orders of service and menus and such, sending them flying into haphazard piles on the other boxes. Jude foresaw a lot of resorting them in his future.

A figure appeared across the courtyard: Anna. Rosa's sister picked her way carefully past the reflecting pool towards them.

'Looks like you have some closure coming your way, too,' Jude said, nodding towards her.

Rosa spun round, then froze as she spotted Anna. The tension that had been hidden under casual, forced relaxation was suddenly obvious to all—but only for a moment. As Jude watched he could see Rosa purposefully relaxing her shoulders, her arms, as Anna grew closer. She took a few lazy steps towards her sister, then hopped up to sit on the large wooden table Sancia used for breakfasts, leaning back on her hands and waiting, letting Anna come the rest of the way to her.

Jude busied himself with the boxes, hoping it wasn't too obvious that he was eavesdropping.

They didn't hug. That was the first thing he noticed as the sisters greeted each other. What had Rosa said? That it had been three years since they'd last spoken.

He wondered if it was a coincidence that her last conversation with Anna must have been around the same time as she left him. Or was there more to the story than she'd told him before?

'You made it back, then,' Rosa said. 'I thought you might decide to just stay in Barcelona with this Leo I've heard so much about from Mama.'

'Not really my style, abandoning the family when they

need me.' Anna's tone was mild, but Jude could hear a bite behind it.

'Right.' Rosa heard it, too, judging by the tightness of her reply. 'Mama gave me my chore list, by the way.'

'Good. Any problems?'

'Other than the fact I'd be much more use to Mama out on the island, dealing with stuff, than stuck going through lists of bungalow allocations and boxes of fairy lights.'

Anna looked past her and her gaze alighted on Jude, who looked away quickly. He did *not* want to get drawn into a sibling squabble. It was the only advantage he'd found to being an only child—and besides, bandmate squabbles were bad enough for him.

'Looks like you've found someone to palm some of the work off onto already, anyway,' Anna said, drily. 'Why am I not surprised?'

'Well, since you were off gallivanting with your Latin lover, I had to work with what I had.' Jude hadn't expected Rosa to go into the details of their complicated history, but hearing himself resigned to leftover help stung a little all the same.

'As long as it all gets done.' Anna turned away. 'Let me know if you can't manage any of it.' She tossed the words back over her shoulder as she walked away, and Jude saw Rosa's hands clench up into fists before they relaxed again.

'You okay?' he asked softly, once they were alone again.

Rosa spun round so fast he wondered if she'd forgotten he was there. Again.

'I'm fine.' Her clipped words said otherwise, but Jude didn't call her on it. Not yet, anyway. 'Come on. Leave this. We're going sailing.'

CHAPTER SIX

Rosa didn't wait for Jude as she stormed down to the jetty. He'd catch her up if he wanted to come with her, and if he didn't she'd go alone.

So, it seemed that regular sex with a man Sancia had described as a hunky pirate hadn't mellowed Anna out any—which probably meant nothing could. She was still the big sister who thought she could run her life, who would always highlight her perceived mistakes and ignore her successes. Rosa didn't know why she'd imagined for a moment that three years apart would have changed anything.

The hardest part was, even now Rosa could see that eighteen-year-old Anna had only been trying to hold the family together after Mama left, it seemed that twenty-eight-year-old Anna still thought Rosa was the sixteen-year-old little sister she'd got used to bossing about. She still didn't trust her to take care of anything herself, not really. She had to control and manage everything, because only *Anna* could get it right.

Of course, some of that might be more to do with their argument three years ago…

Rosa shook her head. She wasn't thinking about that now.

The small boats the resort kept for guests to borrow

to sail over to the mainland were all neatly tied up along the jetty, each looking freshly scrubbed and cleaned—which made Rosa scowl even more. Just extra evidence of all St Anna's hard work.

She squeezed her eyes tight and tried to get a grip on her temper. She was better than this. Older and if not wiser, at least more rational. She'd seen sights all over the world that others couldn't imagine, highlighted horrific situations to the public, and uncovered forgotten treasures with her work. She was *not* going to let herself get all riled up by her sister's martyr complex. That was just one of many things she'd decided to break free from when she'd left Britain, three years before.

The other main thing she'd broken free from caught her up pretty quickly, standing beside her as they stared at the boats.

'So, where are we going?' Jude asked, and Rosa realised that you couldn't leave everything behind, every time.

Sometimes you had to stand and face them.

But not Anna. Not today.

'The mainland,' she said, choosing a dinghy and starting to prep it to sail. 'There's a little seaside village, Cala del Mar, just across the way. It has the best tapas outside of Barcelona. Also, wine.'

'Then let's go,' Jude said, stepping aboard.

He let her get a little way away from the island before he started asking questions, which she appreciated.

'So, you and Anna. Any more you wanted to tell me about that?'

'Not really.' Mostly all she wanted to do was get away from the island for a while. Even a few days there had left her feeling claustrophobic, in a way living in a tent in a war zone or an unexplored rainforest never did.

'Because I realised something. If it's been three years since you last spoke to her, that must have been around the same time I last saw you.'

He was fishing. Suddenly Rosa regretted bringing Jude along. She'd hoped they were done talking about their past relationship, now she'd given him the closure he'd asked for, but apparently he wanted more.

'It was at my Grandfather's funeral, actually.' The mention of death usually shut people up.

Not Jude. 'A difficult, emotional time for you, then.'

Sighing, Rosa turned to face him. He lounged, pale and beautiful, against the back of the boat. His sharp cheekbones and brooding eyes that looked so perfect on album covers looked oddly out of place here on the water, as if he were a being from another world.

In a way, he was, she supposed. The world of celebrity, a million miles away from La Isla Marina, before this week. Now it looked as if it was going to be packed with them.

Hopefully none of the others would be so interested in her past.

'Look, why don't you just ask whatever it is you want to know?' Rip the plaster off and get it over with, that was her way of dealing with difficult things. Anna, as always, disagreed, most of the time.

'I just thought you might like to talk about it,' Jude said, mildly. 'I mean, whatever that last conversation was, it was clearly a corker.'

It had been. Fireworks and hateful words and dramatics all together. The culmination of seven years of frustration and lack of understanding. Of Anna never listening to Rosa's feelings, Anna always knowing best and Rosa always screwing up.

Rosa sank down to sit on the little bench at the front

of the boat, where she could keep steering, but slowed them to an almost stop so they just bobbed in the water. She needed her full attention for this conversation.

Maybe it would help to talk about it. If she could explain her side of the story, and have someone understand, maybe she'd stop feeling so damn guilty about it.

'Like I said, Anna and I had both come to the island for our *abuelo*'s funeral. Anna was fretting about leaving Dad home alone, which was ridiculous, because he's a grown, intelligent man who should be able to take care of himself.'

'But she thinks he can't?' Jude asked.

'Apparently. But it seems to me that if he can run his department, organise his research and make a career as a semi-famous Oxford academic, then he is perfectly capable of arranging his own meals and remembering to take his pills.'

'Pills?'

Rosa waved a hand. 'A preventative measure. He has a heart condition—has had it for years—so he has to take a few tablets to keep it under control.'

'And Anna makes sure he does?'

'Well, yes. Because she's St Anna and she wants to have everyone rely on her and say how wonderful she is.'

Jude tilted his head as he watched her, and Rosa looked away. She didn't like that knowing look in his eye. 'Do you really believe that?'

'No,' Rosa admitted, talking down to the bottom of the boat. 'I don't. But I think she's got so used to controlling everyone and everything she doesn't know how to stop. And I think Dad takes advantage of that. He likes having her to deal with all the boring things he doesn't want to have to think about—like how food gets in the cupboard, or how the house gets clean. He likes having his pills waiting for him by his breakfast plate in the morning, so he can pretend they're just vitamins and that he's fine. He likes Anna looking after him because it means he doesn't have to look after himself. You know, his cardiologist told him four years ago that if he changed his diet, exercised more and started cutting down his hours at work, he might be able to reduce the amount of medication he's on. But he wouldn't do it. Anna managed to sneak in some more healthy meals—although he still eats nothing but red meat and red wine when he dines at the college, I'm sure. And she bullies him into taking a walk now and then. But he won't even *talk* about retiring.'

'I've only known your father a week or so, but from playing Scrabble with him I can confirm that he is a very stubborn man.' Jude shifted, leaning forward with his elbows resting on his knees as he looked at her. 'So you were mad with Anna for letting your dad take advantage of her?'

'Sort of.' Rosa looked out over the water, back towards La Isla Marina, and thought of the real reason Anna hated her.

'Something else happened,' Jude guessed.

'Yeah.' Taking a deep breath, Rosa let herself remember that horrible night. 'She'd been offered a visiting professorship at Harvard, just for the semester, starting the term after the funeral. She wanted to take it, of course, but she—' She cut herself off.

'She didn't want to leave your dad alone,' Jude said. Rosa nodded. 'She asked you to stay with him?'

'She said that if I was there to take care of him, she'd feel like she could go. And it just made me so mad—not that she wanted me to stay home, but that she was putting her whole life on hold for a man who just saw her as a combination of nursemaid, housekeeper, chef and occasional replacement for the wife who'd left him at college functions. He always said how proud he was of her career, but he was holding her back—by not taking responsibility for his own health and well-being.'

A niggling whisper in the back of her brain reminded Rosa that their father had been abandoned when Sancia left, too. That he'd been trying to cope, just as Anna had, just as she had. That he'd wanted to keep the family he had left close.

But that wasn't enough of an excuse for stifling Anna's whole life, was it?

'What did you say?'

'I told her that she should go anyway. That I couldn't stay with him—let's be honest, I wouldn't have been any good at doing all the stuff Anna did for him, anyhow.' Rosa knew her limitations. If she'd been forced to babysit her father for three months, one of them would have moved out within the first few days for sure. 'But that she shouldn't feel tied down by him. He's a grown man, not her responsibility any more.'

'She didn't go to Harvard, did she?'

Rosa shook her head, deflating from her righteous indignation. 'No. She stayed there and put her life on hold for him, like always. And I...'

'Ran to the other side of the world to get away from me.'

'Not just you,' Rosa admitted, meeting his gaze for the first time since the conversation started. To her amazement, she saw understanding there, rather than judgement. 'Like you said, it was an emotional time.'

'It sounds it.' Cautiously—he obviously wasn't used to being on the water—Jude crossed the boat towards her, crouching in front of her and taking her hand. 'I can understand why Anna would be mad and disappointed, but that doesn't mean you were wrong. If anything, it seems to me like you were trying to help her.'

'Not very well, it seems.' She blinked, hard, to try and stop the prickling behind her eyes. She was *not* going to cry about this. Especially in front of Jude.

'Oh, I don't know,' Jude said, giving her a small smile. 'I mean, it might have taken her a while, but she came here, didn't she? She left Oxford to come and help out your mum.'

'Dragging Dad after her for the good of his health,' Rosa pointed out. 'But maybe you're right. It's a start.'

And maybe Leo could be the next step for Anna. She should find out some more about him. Make sure he wasn't just going to take over Anna's life in their father's place.

But for now… Rosa looked down at Jude. He had the same look Anna had sometimes—the tightness around the eyes and the tenseness of the shoulders that told her he was trying too hard for the wrong things. He'd never looked like that three years ago. Then he'd been all enthusiasm and excitement—and loose-limbed, bone-deep satisfaction in bed afterwards.

No. She wasn't thinking about that. She was thinking as a friend, not an ex-lover.

And as a friend, she could see that Jude needed to cut loose a bit. Maybe she was the one who could help him lighten up.

'You know, you're far too pale for this place. Come on. Let's go get tapas and wine and sit in the sunshine for a while.'

Cala del Mar was a perfect, sleepy seaside fishing village. Jude strolled along the seafront with Rosa at his side and wondered if he'd be happier somewhere like this, than in

New York City. Rosa certainly seemed content enough—but he suspected that, like everything else in Rosa's life, would only last until she got bored.

And he had promises to keep. Music to make. And Gareth's memory to preserve, out there in the real world.

Fishing boats still bobbed out on the waves, under the slowly fading sunlight that sparkled and shone on the water. The air was warm around them and, for a moment, Jude could almost let himself believe that he was here with Rosa, celebrating their three-year anniversary or something—instead of as wary acquaintances working together on a celebrity wedding.

'The place I wanted to show you is up here,' Rosa said, leading him to a narrow flight of steep stone steps that wound up between the tiny painted cottages and shops into the heart of the village. The walls either side of the stairs were cold and damp, their location meaning they were permanently in shadow. Jude kept his gaze firmly on Rosa's swaying plait as they climbed, refusing to look lower, or let him think about all the things this evening wasn't.

It wasn't a date, however it felt. It wasn't even an opportunity. He'd learned that lesson too well the first time.

The tapas place Rosa led him to barely even qualified as a restaurant. It had two tables inside by the bar, and another three out on the balcony, looking out over the seafront. Rosa chatted happily in Spanish to the elderly man behind the bar, who welcomed her warmly, and moments later they were seated out at the best balcony table, olives, breads, oil, vinegar and a carafe of red wine between them.

Rosa filled up their glasses. 'Doesn't this feel better already?'

'Much.' It wasn't a lie, not exactly. It *did* feel wonderful to be relaxing in the sunshine with a beautiful woman, with good food and better wine. He just wished he could shake the feeling that it wasn't enough, just being with Rosa this way, unable to take her in his arms and kiss her whenever he wanted.

But then…the story she'd told him about her argument with Anna still pulsed around his head. And he couldn't help wondering, if she hadn't argued with her sister, might Rosa have come back to him? Had she felt that returning to him, to the tour, to his life, would be the same as Anna sticking with their father's life even though she wanted more?

It wouldn't have made any difference, in the long run, he supposed. Rosa there was as distracting as Rosa gone; he still might have missed the signs with Gareth. It was *his* obsession that was to blame there, not Rosa.

But if the argument with Anna *was* why she had left… maybe he could convince her that things were different, now.

Jude leant back in his chair and watched Rosa watch the sea. He didn't dream of for ever with her, not the way his younger self had. He knew she wasn't a for ever kind of girl. Rosa would never stay in one place long enough to be tied down by love—she was too full of life, a free spirit. He wouldn't *want* to contain her that way and make her unhappy.

And like it or not, his real life was waiting for him back in New York, once the furore over the book had died down. He'd go back to the band, to making music he loved, and doing all the things the label expected him to do to keep The Swifts in the public eye and their music selling.

But right now, while they were both here together… could there be a chance for something more between them? An island fling, perhaps, with none of the expectations and hopes he'd placed on them before.

If he could convince Rosa that all he wanted was right now, maybe he could have her in his arms again.

And maybe that would be worth the potential pain of watching her walk away once more. At least this time, he knew it was coming, and could prepare himself for it.

He wasn't angry at her for leaving him, not any more. He understood, even if he didn't like it. But Jude was starting to think that the closure he needed to *truly* move on didn't come in words. It wasn't explanations he needed.

It was touch.

'It's hard to stay mad too long in a place like this, isn't it?' Rosa said, looking back from the sea.

'Yeah,' Jude agreed. 'It is.' Only he wasn't talking about her argument with Anna.

He was imagining how the next two weeks might cure him of that anger and resentment for good.

Rosa had been staring at the guest list so long it had given her a headache. Over the handful of days she and Jude had made good progress with all things organisational for the wedding, but the bungalow allocations were still causing her trouble. Every time she thought she had it sorted, she found another name, or another couple who couldn't be near someone else, or who needed something specific that the bungalow she'd assigned them didn't have. When she added in the constant phone calls from guests to add extra requirements to their bookings, she wanted to throw the stupid clipboard into the sea and head for the airport.

It was, quite frankly, an impossible task. One even

Jude had given up on and disappeared off with his guitar after taking a call from his agent.

Rosa would be ready to admit defeat if doing so didn't mean telling Anna she wasn't up to the job.

And speaking of Anna…after her talk with Jude on the boat, Rosa had been doing a lot of thinking about her sister. And more specifically, about Anna and her new beau. Rosa had done some research, and what she'd learned hadn't made her any more comfortable with Anna's relationship. Leo di Marquez had *quite* the reputation—and it wasn't the good sort. International playboy, gambler and general debauched human being by all accounts, he was most definitely not Anna's usual type. In fact, she could only remember Anna dating anyone vaguely like that once before—and given how that had ended, Rosa didn't look forward to a repeat of the experience.

In the end, she realised she was going to have to talk to her sister. About Leo, and about the room bookings.

What the hell. She needed a walk anyway.

As it turned out, though, she didn't have to go far to find her sister—she was already in the villa reception area. Leaning against the office doorway, Rosa watched Anna staring out towards the courtyard, a soft smile on her face, and wished that she could just let Anna enjoy the fun and relaxation of no-strings sex with a gorgeous man. Except Anna didn't do casual, and the way things were going Rosa was pretty sure her sister was going to end up with a broken heart. Again.

'You're looking all doe-eyed. Does Señor Tall, Dark and Handsome have anything to do with that?' As an opening gambit, it wasn't great, but it got Anna's attention at least. She spun round and glared at Rosa.

Then she replaced the glare with an overly sweet smile. 'None of your business.'

Right. Of course.

'How's the paperwork?' Anna asked. 'Sorted out the wedding guests into rooms yet?'

Rosa's jaw clenched at the reminder. 'I don't understand why you're being so stubborn. You love spreadsheets and solving problems. I love being outside and fixing things. We should just swap...'

'If you'd hadn't arrived over two weeks late then you could have had your pick of jobs. As it was I had to get on and do what needed doing most. You keep going with the wedding planning and helping Mama with the office. It'll do you good to stretch yourself.'

Still trying to control things for my own good, huh, St Anna?

Rosa's good intentions faded away as her ire rose at the condemnation in Anna's voice. 'Of course you dropped everything and rushed straight here.'

'It's a good thing I did, look at what your *"stand back and let them make their own mistakes"* plan has achieved. This place was chaos...'

'Chaos until St Anna turned up and fixed it all?' Like always. She had to be the saviour, didn't she?

'Yes. Actually.'

'Dragging Dad with you? Couldn't trust him on his own for a month?' God forbid that anyone be allowed to take control of their own lives for a change.

'Dad turned up on his own.' Anna folded her arms over her T-shirt. 'You do know he nearly died?' she said almost conversationally.

'What?' Rosa's chest tightened. Then she realised Anna had to be exaggerating. 'Nonsense, he looks fine.'

'He looks fine now. He looks fine because he has no stress outside work, his meals are prepared, he takes his pills, he gets reminded to take regular walks. Not because I'm a saint, not because I'm a martyr, but because someone has to do it—and no.' Anna raised her hand as Rosa tried to interrupt. 'Don't tell me he's an adult. I know that. I also know that when he wants to be he's the most organised man alive. But his health isn't a priority, work is. And he would forget, just like Mama forgot to take care of the basics here. So what do I do, Rosa? Swan off to Harvard and let him get ill and Mama sink? Is that your answer?'

Yes. Yes, it was. Because it might not be the perfect answer, but what else was there? How could Anna mortgage her life to their father when he couldn't be bothered to even look after himself?

'I don't understand.' She never had. It didn't make any *sense*. But Anna's words—*nearly died*—echoed through her head again and again. 'I was ten before I realised other families didn't get given their own individual holiday itineraries and checklists two weeks before they went on holiday, and most families didn't stock check their cupboards monthly. How can he not remember to take his pills?' He could, if he wanted to. It was just easier to let Anna do it. That was all. And until she left him to take care of himself, it always would be.

'Things changed after Mama left.' Anna blew a frustrated breath. 'You were still at home then, Rosa. I know how self-centred you are, but surely even you noticed?'

She just couldn't resist getting another jibe in there, could she? Another complaint about how Rosa wasn't as perfect as Anna, and never would be. Really, when you knew you could never live up to expectations, why even try?

'I know you got bossier and more self-righteous than ever. I know you refused to move into halls during term time, staying at home to prove what a good daughter you are. At least until you started seeing that guy, then suddenly we saw another side of Anna…until he dumped you, that is. Then you got even more boring than before.' Rosa ignored the pang of guilt in her chest. This wasn't how she'd meant this conversation to go. But somehow, whenever she was faced with Anna and her perfection, she just lost any cool rationality she'd ever possessed. Why did the people closest to you sometimes bring out your worst side?

'It's always lovely catching up with you, Rosa, but I have a lot to do. Good luck with those spreadsheets.' Anna turned away, and Rosa realised she'd missed her chance. She'd screwed it up again, just as she always did with her sister.

No. This time, she was going to give it one more try.

'I'm just worried about you, Anna,' she said, and her voice stopped Anna in her tracks. 'Leo di Marquez isn't the kind of man you're used to…'

'I'm more than capable of handling Leo, thank you,' Anna said, dismissively.

'I just don't want a repeat of the Sebastian situation. I mean, he was an utter idiot, and Leo doesn't appear to be quite so arrogant, or as sleazy, but he broke you, Anna. I don't want that to happen again.'

Was Anna crying? No. Rosa couldn't remember the last time she'd seen her sister do that. 'Sebastian didn't break me, Rosa. I did that all by myself.' And with that, Anna walked away, leaving Rosa alone with her clipboard, and the feeling she might have just made things worse between her and her sister.

'I didn't even know that was possible,' she muttered.

CHAPTER SEVEN

WITH ONE MORE day to go until Valentina and her bridal party arrived, it seemed that La Isla Marina was almost ready for its sudden brush with celebrity. Jude had to admit, the place was looking a lot better than when he'd arrived. And last time he'd checked, Rosa had *almost* finished the room allocations, which were proving more of a nightmare than either of them had predicted.

He was almost glad of his agent's call as an excuse to get away from helping for a while. Almost.

'What's up, Robyn?' he said, sauntering towards his bungalow and his guitar as he answered.

'When are you coming back?' Robyn asked, bluntly. 'With all the publicity about the book, we need you here, capitalising on that.'

'I think people are perfectly capable of talking about me without me actually being there to hear it.' God knew, they managed it often enough normally.

'Look, Jude, I know you're not happy about some of the things they say in the book—'

'I'm not happy that the book exists at all.'

'But it does. You can't unprint it now, or stop people from reading it.'

'I could sue for defamation,' Jude suggested, although he knew he wouldn't.

'Do you really want to have to go to court and prove which of those stories are lies?' Robyn asked, gently.

Jude sighed. 'No.' Because in doing so, he'd only be confirming that all the others were true. And all the worst ones were, unfortunately. 'I just wish they hadn't written so much about Gareth.' And how Jude had let him down.

His mind flashed back to that day in the hospital, almost a year to the day before Gareth died.

He could still hear Gareth's raspy, exhausted voice saying, *'I know. I know I have to stop. But I need help.'*

And his own reply. *'I'll help. I'll be there every day, reminding you of everything you have to live for. Keeping you out of trouble just like I've always done. I promise.'*

It wasn't the idea of the whole world knowing how he'd betrayed his best friend's trust that upset him. It was seeing that betrayal in black-and-white and knowing that there was nothing he could do about it. No way to change the past, however much he wished he could.

Somehow, the book made it all real, all over again. Just like seeing Rosa again transported him back three years to a time when the only place he could be happy was in her arms.

'I never met him, but from what you've told me about him? Gareth would have loved being the centre of attention in a bestselling book.' Robyn had only become their agent after The Swifts hit the big time. But Gareth was part of the band's legacy, its history, and it had been important to Jude that she know all about him.

Apparently she'd got a pretty good handle on him, after all. 'He'd have been mad the book wasn't all about him.'

'Do you wish it was?'

'If it meant he was still here with us? Definitely. As it is…no.' Bad enough to have his memory raked over the coals in a few early chapters of this book. But a whole book trashing Gareth's memory? Jude couldn't have lived with that.

'Jude…these books don't mean anything. Not really. You know that.'

'I know. I just… Sylvie gave them a lot of those stories, you know?'

'I suspected.' Jude was pretty sure Robyn was wincing on the other end of the line. 'She knows how to play the game, that one.'

'Yeah.' Rosa didn't. Rosa had no idea of the rules of any game but her own. 'Look, Robyn, I've got to go. But if you get lucky, you might get some photos of me online sooner rather than later.'

'Really?' Robyn perked up at the idea. 'Why? Where are you? And who are you with, more to the point? Because if it's a woman, a nice, juicy, romantic scandal would definitely distract from the book…'

Jude laughed, and thought of Rosa. 'I'll see what I can do.'

But not for the publicity. For himself.

To celebrate actually managing to get ready on time, beating all the odds, Sancia had insisted on a family dinner that night—a proper, five-course banquet with matching wines, by all accounts. Jude wasn't exactly sure what he'd done to make Sancia think he was family and issue an invite, but he wasn't about to turn down the spectacular catering at the villa, either. Besides, Rosa would be there, and that was enough for him.

Things had been so busy since their trip to the mainland that the time simply hadn't been right for him to propose any sort of rekindling of their relationship to her. But now, with everything almost sorted, perhaps tonight could be the night. And just because they hadn't been physically intimate, that didn't mean they hadn't grown closer. Working together, seeing each other every day, talking about their lives and families—sometimes, Jude felt closer to Rosa now than when they'd been in the midst of their passionate affair three years ago.

He'd been at a bit of a loss for a hostess gift for the dinner, since Sancia technically already owned everything on the island, but he had brought his guitar, in case he could offer some background entertainment later. He'd been listening to a lot of classical Spanish guitar music since he arrived, playing around with some ideas on the theme, coming up with new threads and melodies that might one day become actual songs. It was kind of exciting, to be working on new music again—just him, messing around with tunes that appealed to him, rather than arguing with the rest of the band about what direction The Swifts should be moving in, musically, and what fitted best with their brand.

Jude didn't want to be a brand. He wanted to be a musician. And here, on La Isla Marina, he almost felt as if he could be, again.

So, anyway, he was looking forward to dinner that evening. At least, until he sat down at the table.

Professor Gray sat at the head of the table on one end, with Sancia at the other. Jude found himself sitting opposite Rosa, either side of her father, with Anna on his left, and Leo opposite her. Straight away, he could feel the tension strung out across the table like the fairy lights hanging overhead.

Rosa didn't look at her dad, he realised. In fact, he wasn't sure he'd seen her talk to him at all since the day she first arrived on the island. He'd been so focussed on her relationship with her sister, he hadn't noticed the fissure between her and her father. But from everything she'd said about him, Jude wasn't really surprised. It was hard to imagine the buttoned-up and structured Professor Gray appreciating the wildness of his younger daughter.

Unfortunately, the situation with Anna didn't look much brighter, given the way she and Rosa were both avoiding each other's gaze.

Anna and Leo spoke quietly across the table, intimate and happy, as they worked their way through the first course. Jude tried to strike up a conversation with Rosa, of the sort they'd been having more often of late, but she was distracted, and he couldn't seem to connect with her. Eventually, he gave up and chatted amiably with Professor Gray about his latest research. As ever, the professor was happy enough to carry on a monologue for most of the meal, so it wasn't as if Jude needed to contribute a lot.

'So, Leo,' Rosa said suddenly, cutting across the other chatter at the table. 'Why *are* you helping out so much for Valentina's wedding?'

The hint was there, Jude realised, behind the question—the idea that Leo must have a prior relationship with the star, or something. What was Rosa trying to do? Drive a wedge between Anna and Leo? He knew she was concerned about Leo's reputation, but watching them together Jude couldn't help but think that Rosa had judged this one wrong. He'd never seen a man so obviously in love as Leo di Marquez.

'Valentina is Leo's half-sister,' Anna said, after a quick glance across the table to confirm it was okay to do so.

Rosa's eyebrows rose up towards her hairline. 'I didn't know she had a brother.'

'Not many people do.' Leo sounded obviously uncomfortable with the situation. 'We didn't grow up together.'

'Do you think she'll be pleased with the island?' Jude asked, trying to get back onto safer topics.

Leo's expression warmed. 'I think she'll love it,' he said, smiling across at Anna as he spoke.

'Oh, it's so lovely to have all my family here once more,' Sancia said, beaming around the table. 'And to see both my girls so happy with their men.'

Jude's gaze flew to Rosa, who stared back, wide-eyed and panicked.

'Oh, we're not—' she started.

As Jude said, 'Actually, we're just friends.'

Sancia didn't reply, just smiled knowingly at them both.

Rosa was silent for the rest of the meal. Jude tried to concentrate on his conversation with Professor Gray, but by the time they finished dessert he wasn't sure he could have said for certain what they'd even been talking about. His attention kept being drawn across the table, to where Rosa sat quiet and subdued, sneaking glances at her sister from time to time.

When Sancia motioned for the coffee and liqueurs to be brought out, Rosa pushed her chair back from the table, mumbling some sort of excuse. Jude watched her go, wondering if he should follow, or if he'd only make things worse. But when he glanced up the table, he saw Sancia staring at him, eyebrows raised, and realised that Rosa's mother, at least, had a clear idea of what was best for her.

'Take these,' she murmured as he passed, and Jude accepted the two wine glasses and the rest of the bottle of red gratefully. He'd take whatever help he could get in trying to understand Rosa.

He found her out on the back veranda, looking out over the far side of the island towards the sea.

'Thinking about escaping?' he asked, handing her a full glass of wine, and placing the bottle on the nearest table.

'Always,' Rosa replied, and Jude thought it might have been the most honest thing she'd ever said to him.

'I'd like it if you'd stay, for a while at least.' He perched on the edge of the table, looking up at her in the shadows of the night. Overhead, the moon was almost full, and he could make out every contour of her face, every uncertainty in her eyes, even in the darkness.

'You know they all think we're sleeping together,' Rosa said, bluntly. 'Mama is probably planning some sort of huge double wedding for me and Anna, even though we're not a couple and Leo is going to walk out and break Anna's heart any day now.'

'You don't know that for sure,' Jude said. Although, given what he'd heard about Leo's reputation, he could see Rosa's point.

'Ah, but you see, I do.' Rosa's smile was sad. 'Leo and me, we're cut from the same cloth, I reckon. Not made to stay. We have to keep moving to keep living.'

'Like sharks,' Jude said, absently remembering a nature documentary he'd watched on some flight to a gig, somewhere or another.

'I bite, too,' Rosa joked.

'I remember.' The words were out before he could even think about them, and instantly the image they conjured up heated his blood.

No wonder her family thought they were together. If his gaze was half as heated as the one she had trained on him, then they must look as if they'd been lovers for years.

Rosa licked her lips, and Jude felt the pressure building inside him. He had to say something. Do something.

He had to have her again—even if she left him to-morrow.

Just one more night with her, that was all he needed.

God, he sounded like Gareth, at the end.

'Just one more hit. I'll quit tomorrow, Jude, I promise. Just one more. One more for the road...'

Was he every bit an addict as his friend had been? And while his addiction might not be so deadly, could Jude really say it wouldn't destroy him, all the same?

But then Rosa said, 'Let's go for a swim,' and he stopped thinking altogether.

If he was an addict, maybe he didn't care any more. He needed one more night with Rosa Gray.

She didn't have to ask Jude twice. Whether he'd read her mind, or their mutual lust had just taken over his brain as it seemed to have taken over hers, he abandoned the wine and followed her down to the beach without question.

Rosa didn't think too much about what she was doing. Overthinking wasn't her style—she was more of an impulse person. She went with what her instincts told her were right and, if it went wrong, well, at least she'd been true to herself.

Tonight, she felt as if she was being true to an impulse she'd been denying for three long years. And the relief of it was almost overwhelming.

'There's a cove, just around here,' she said, picking her way over the rocks and out of sight of the villa. She really didn't want any of her family members coming looking for them tonight.

Tonight was about her and Jude. Not them.

She could feel him behind her, feel the heat of him jumping the inch or two of space between them.

Maybe this was inevitable. Maybe, from the moment

she'd first seen him sitting there in the courtyard, as if he'd been waiting for her, they'd been leading to this.

Maybe this was the *real* closure Jude had been looking for.

One more night together. Maybe that was what they both needed to be able to move on.

All Rosa knew was she couldn't have sat at that dinner table any longer, with everyone playing perfect happy families, when she knew what a lie it was. They were all pretending that they were settled, stable, that this was how things would be for ever. But none of that was true. Her parents hadn't been together in ten years—and if she knew them at all, she doubted they'd even talked about why Sancia had left, all those years ago. Nothing had been resolved. Anna and Leo weren't going to live happily ever after, whatever fairy tales Anna was telling herself. Things would get hard and Leo would run, and so would Sancia.

And as for Rosa and Jude...they weren't even ever a couple. Not really.

And they weren't about to start now.

But there was something between them, that much was true. And if she had to stay here on the island and witness all this hypocrisy, at least she could get to explore the fun side of it, too.

Jude knew who she was now. He wouldn't be fooled into thinking she'd stay, this time.

This time, it was all about transient fun. About freedom and enjoyment and letting the wildness inside loose again.

And what was more wild and free than swimming naked in the ocean?

The cove was just as she remembered: tucked away at the back of the island, protected by rocks and cliffs on either side, but with a small crescent-shaped beach in the centre. Rosa hopped down onto the sand, the sea already calling her. Even in the dark, it glistened in the moonlight, open and wide and free.

Without pausing in her stride, Rosa pulled off her top, and heard a sharp intake of breath behind her.

She spun to face Jude, still walking backwards as she fumbled with the clasp of her bra, letting it fall to the sand at her feet.

'Is this safe?' Jude asked, his eyes nowhere near her face.

'Do you care?' she asked, grinning.

'No.'

Rosa pushed her skirt and her underwear down her legs at the same time, stepped out of them and ran for the water, knowing that Jude wouldn't be far behind her.

The sea flowed cool and fresh against her hot skin, the salt stinging and sharp. Rosa welcomed every sensation— the rocks and sand under her feet, the water lapping against her, the breeze that blew loose strands of hair around her face. She stayed, treading water, just far enough out to be out of her depth—just where she liked to be—and watched Jude as he stripped off on the shoreline.

His skin was pale in the moonlight, his hair so dark it was almost lost in the night. But his body...oh, there were those lean, strong muscles she remembered. Those powerful legs, those well-defined arms and abs. That trail of hair that led down his body...

She remembered every inch of him. And she wanted him again.

He didn't flinch as he stepped into the cool water; she admired that. Throwing him a reckless grin, she flipped in the waves, diving underneath and kicking hard until she was further out. Let him chase her, the way he never had when she left.

That thought tugged at something in her mind, but she pushed it away to worry about another day.

Right now, all she wanted to do was enjoy the water on her skin, and Jude—when he caught her.

It didn't take him long.

She surfaced, a short way from where she'd watched him enter the water, and already she could see his powerful arms scything through the waves, propelling him towards her. He was barely even out of breath when he reached her side, treading water next to her as his arms reached out to slide around her waist.

His hands glided over her skin, under the water, pulling her close against him. Her whole body vibrated with the surety that this was right. This was meant to be. Here, now, like this. Wild and free and passionate—just the way they'd been together three years before.

She knew he was going to kiss her before his lips even lowered to hers, knew the surge of need that would pulse through her at the feel of his mouth, his tongue.

'Rosa.' He murmured her name like a wish.

'Let's take this to the shallows,' she whispered, pushing away from him and swimming for the shore.

Soon, Jude Alexander would make love to her again. And then maybe the island would feel like where she belonged.

CHAPTER EIGHT

LATER—MUCH LATER—they lay in each other's arms on the beach and watched the stars overhead.

'Planning on running away yet?' Jude asked, pressing a kiss to Rosa's bare shoulder. Her olive skin felt smooth and soft under his lips, the clothes they'd abandoned on the beach protecting them both from the sand.

'Not *just* yet.' Rosa stretched out against him, her body pressing closer to his. 'I might need to do that a few more times first.'

A few more times. At least he had some idea of a time-table now, then.

So much for one more night. He should have known—having Rosa again only made him want her more. For as long as they had together, anyway.

'You don't need to, this time,' he said, trying to keep his tone light. He wasn't usually one for serious relationship talk straight after sex, but if he'd learned one thing about Rosa it was that if he didn't get in there fast she'd be gone before he ever got the chance to say anything. 'Run, I mean.'

'Oh?' Propping herself up on one elbow, Rosa looked down at him, her damp hair curling around her face where it had escaped her braid. 'Why's that?'

'Because I know the deal, this time.' Jude swept his

hands up her back, under her heavy plait, enjoying the opportunity to explore all that beautiful skin. 'No strings, no expectations, right? Just you and me, enjoying the time we have together on the island.'

'A fling,' Rosa said, her mouth twitching up into a lopsided smile. 'An island romance.'

'Exactly.'

'Sounds perfect.'

She kissed him again, then, and Jude forgot for a moment how much it had hurt when she left, before.

Not this time, though. This time, he was prepared, he knew what he was getting into. He could steel his heart against falling for Rosa Gray all over again. Right?

'Besides,' Rosa said, sliding down to nestle in the crook of his arm again, her head resting against his shoulder, 'you'll be running back to New York again yourself any time soon, right?'

'Yeah.' New York. The city for dreamers. The place he'd wanted to get to his whole life. Except now, it felt like the last place he belonged. Especially without Gareth there to share it.

'There's a considerable lack of enthusiasm in that "yeah",' Rosa pointed out. 'Want to talk about it?'

Jude sighed. Did he? Maybe it would help. And Rosa… Rosa was one of the few people, other than his bandmates, who knew him well enough to understand. She knew what he'd been looking for in his music, in his career. What he'd hoped for from fame.

She might understand why he was disappointed with what he'd found instead.

'I am aware that this could be considered as being ungrateful,' he said, as an opening disclaimer.

Rosa laughed. 'Remember who you're talking to here. Just ask Anna how well I know ungrateful.'

Jude hugged her a little closer to him. Whatever had been bothering her at dinner still rankled, it seemed. He'd hoped that the last hour or so of being naked in his arms might have cured it. Maybe he'd have to try again…

'You've stopped talking,' Rosa pointed out as he started kissing along her hairline again.

Talking. Right.

Jude sighed, and dropped his head back down to his shirt on the sand. 'Do you remember, on the tour bus, how we talked about music and fame and everything that went with it?'

'Yes.' He hadn't expected her to sound so definite. It was three years ago, after all. 'I remember it all, Jude.'

His heart contracted at that. He'd always assumed she'd cared less than him, to be able to leave so easily. But there was something in her voice, a weight he hadn't expected. Maybe he'd misjudged her.

Except that she'd still left. Nothing she said now could change that simple fact.

'I thought that making music and getting paid for it would be enough. Gareth always wanted more, of course—he was the one who wanted the stardom, really. Wanted to show them all. He needed the riches and the success and his face in every magazine… I just wanted… I wanted to create something new and share it with the world. It was as simple—and as naive—as that.' He almost pitied the younger man he'd been. The Jude who'd thought that music was enough and that Rosa would stay. That Gareth's star, burning so bright, wouldn't consume him in the end. That he could hold the world together the way he wanted it through sheer force of will.

Thank goodness he grew up.

'And now?'

'Now I know it doesn't work like that.'

Rosa pressed a kiss to his bare chest, right above his heart. 'Maybe it should.'

He huffed a laugh. 'Maybe. But instead… I shouldn't complain. I get to do a job others would do for free and I get paid obscene amounts of money for it. And normally I'm fine with what that means.'

'What *does* it mean?'

'It means…' Jude sighed as he trailed off. 'It means being Jude Alexander the brand, rather than the man. It means deciding if the songs I write fit the band's direction, rather than if I like them. It means considering the label, the fans, the advertisers before the music.' It meant being the person Gareth had always been, the one who thought about how to be a success first.

'Putting them all before yourself,' Rosa added.

'Sometimes.' The truth was, he'd got so used to being led to the decisions others wanted him to make, to automatically defaulting to the best business decision, he wasn't sure if he even knew what *he* wanted any more.

Except for one thing: he knew he wanted to live Gareth's dreams for him, now he was no longer there to live them himself.

That was what mattered. Gareth's memory, and the music.

He owed Gareth that much, at least, if that was all there was left to give.

'And then there was the book…' Rosa lifted her head to look him in the eye. 'I guess that didn't go down well with the label?'

Jude laughed. 'The opposite, actually. They loved it. It made me sound like a real rock star—affairs and parties and wild behaviour. Add in Gareth's addiction and everything that came after and it was exactly what people imagine rock-star life to be.'

'Was it true, though?'

'Some of it,' Jude admitted. 'Some of it was exaggerated, and some just plain fantasy. But it didn't seem to matter. The publicity around it, even before it came out, was enough to bump our latest album a bit further up the charts.'

'All publicity is good publicity, huh?'

'It seems so.'

'Not for you, though.'

Jude closed his eyes, shutting out the stars above. 'No.'

'Tell me?' He felt Rosa inch closer, her leg over his, her arm around his waist. She was wrapping herself around him like a protective blanket, as if she could ward off the dark or the bad memories or both. He smiled, involuntarily. For someone who never stayed, while she was there, Rosa could make a man feel as if he were the whole world.

Fame had done that for a while, too. He'd felt important, the big man in the city, just as he and Gareth had dreamed when they were poor schoolboys with no future. And yes, he'd taken advantage of it. He'd done things he looked back on and winced. He'd treated people badly, tossed his fame around like confetti.

But that wasn't who he really was. He knew that, now, even if the readers of *Jude: The Naked Truth* never would.

'Imagine someone printed a book that detailed every screw-up you'd ever made, every bad choice, every awful day, every time you were an idiot or just plain rude. And now imagine that anyone who ever thought anything of you is going to read that.'

Rosa squeezed him a little tighter around the middle. 'I don't think there's a book long enough for all my screw-ups.'

'Mine appears to be pretty lengthy, too.' He sighed. 'The worst part was realising all the people I'd trusted who must have contributed to it. There are stories in there that only a few people knew. The author—who has never actually met me, by the way—couldn't have got them from anyone else.'

Suddenly the warmth of Rosa's body next to him was gone, and when he opened his eyes she was sitting up over him, her arm across her bare breasts. 'I'm not in there, right? Because, Jude—you know I didn't talk to anyone, don't you? I wouldn't—'

'You're not in the book,' Jude told her, grabbing her hands and pulling her back down to him. 'You…that's one screw-up I know you'd never make.' She'd break his heart, leave without a backward glance, but Rosa would never sell him out. He'd doubted, for a time, but now he was sure.

'Okay. Good.'

'My ex-girlfriend, however, had no such restraint.' And that still hurt. Yes, maybe he and Sylvie were never going to make it long-term, but still.

Rosa winced on his behalf. 'You said she sold her story after you broke up?'

'Worse. She sold it when we were still dating. I only found out *after* we broke up.'

'Ouch.'

'Yeah.'

'So…not really looking forward to seeing her tomorrow, then?' Rosa asked.

Jude hauled her further up his body so he could kiss her thoroughly. 'I'm really not thinking about my ex-girlfriend right now.'

'Mmm, good.' Rosa returned the kiss. Then she pulled a little way away, her gaze uncertain. As if she didn't want to know the answer to the question she was about to ask. 'Jude. What happened with Gareth?'

In a way, he was surprised she'd waited so long to ask.

Gareth had adored Rosa, and she'd returned the feeling. Jude had loved that—seeing the two people who knew him best getting along so well. Of course she needed to know the full, awful story.

But her question still hit him in the gut. Was he afraid of his own guilt, or passing some of it on to her by association? He wasn't sure any more.

'You read the newspaper reports, I'm sure,' Jude said, no emotion in his voice. 'They were very…comprehensive.'

Every single detail, spelled out in black-and-white print. They'd only just started making a noise on the scene, but Gareth was a big part of that noise. He was the one people had heard of, the one they wanted to see perform, back then. Jude had just been the guitarist, the accompanying vocals, not the frontman.

Not while Gareth was there to sing for both of them.

And when he had gone…of course, he'd blazed out in the most sensational way he could. Gareth wouldn't have known any other way.

'I read…it was at the awards show, wasn't it?'

Their first awards show. Their first award—best up-and-coming band, as voted for by *Melody Magazine*. The first sign that they were getting where they needed to go.

'He wanted to celebrate, of course.' Jude swallowed around the lump in his throat.

'Gareth always did.' Rosa's smile was soft, and he knew she was remembering. 'He celebrated everything, didn't he? A birthday, a gig, a sunrise. Hell, he threw a party the night we first slept together.'

'He said me getting laid was a rare enough occurrence that it deserved marking,' Jude said, drily.

'So. He went to the after-party to celebrate?' Rosa asked.

Jude's laugh felt so sharp it hurt his throat. 'Oh, Gareth

couldn't wait that long. He went straight to the gents and shot up there. With a little celebratory extra, of course.' And he should have gone with him, been with him to stop him, to keep an eye on him. Should have stopped it before it even got that far. As he'd promised. 'It was that extra that killed him.'

But he'd been at the bar, drinking away the knowledge that Rosa wasn't coming back to him.

'They found him an hour or so later, when someone got suspicious about why the stall was still locked.' That was the worst part. It hadn't even been Jude who realised he was missing. He'd just assumed he was off chatting up some woman, or partying with his other friends. He hadn't even realised Gareth was using again, he'd been so self-absorbed. 'He was already gone, but they called the ambulance anyway. The paramedics stormed through just as they were announcing the winner of Artist of the Year.'

And so, of course, it made all the papers. Every gossip rag and website had the story—and the photos. Jude, pale and gaunt beside the stretcher, holding onto the closest thing to a brother he'd ever had.

'I made him a promise, you know,' he said, squeezing his eyes tight shut. 'A year before he died, he had a close call. Ended up in hospital after an accidental overdose, and it was touch-and-go for a while. When he woke up, I swore to him that I wouldn't let it happen again. I would keep him clean and straight and away from temptation. I'd be the angel on his shoulder. I promised I'd keep him alive. He had so much to live for...'

'Jude.' Rosa's cool hand pressed against his face, followed by her kiss. 'That wasn't a promise you could keep. No one could keep that promise. Gareth's addiction...you couldn't beat it with words.'

'Why not?' Jude cried out, into the night. 'Everything

else in my life, it's all been words and music. That's what I have. I've fought everything else in the world with those two things. Why weren't they enough to save Gareth?'

'I don't know,' Rosa said, her voice small.

But Jude knew. He knew exactly why. 'It *was* working. Until I met you. It was like you took over my whole world, in that instant. And I stopped keeping my promise because I needed to be with you.' Rosa started to speak, but he cut across her. 'Oh, I know you weren't there when he died. But I was so caught up in my own misery about you leaving that I *still* didn't see what was right in front of my face.'

Rosa pulled away. 'So, you blame me for Gareth's death?'

Jude looked up at her, beautiful in the moonlight, and knew how unfair he was being. Reaching up, he pulled her back down to him. 'No. No, I don't blame you. I blame myself.' And he always would, whenever he remembered that image of Gareth being wheeled out of the awards ceremony in a body bag.

The next day, the calls had started, asking about what happened next for the band, and the others had nominated him as the new frontman without his even being there.

'I wanted to stop,' he said, softly. 'Afterwards. I wanted to walk away from it all. The band, music, everything.'

'What changed your mind?' Rosa's voice was still quiet, as if she didn't fully believe him about where the blame lay.

'The rest of the band. They told me…' He swallowed. 'They told me that I had to carry on. For Gareth. To achieve all the dreams he never would, now. It took me a while to believe them. But then one morning, about four months afterwards, I just woke up and knew they were right. Gareth and I had talked about making our band a success our whole lives, it seemed. I couldn't give up on that now. He'd never forgive me. I'd let him down so badly… I had to do anything I could to keep his memory and his dreams alive.'

Rosa's eyes were sad, and she kissed him so sweetly he knew that it had to be pity.

'Gareth loved you,' she said, and he believed her. 'He'd want you to be happy, more than anything else.'

'I know that.'

'Then why are you going back to New York?'

It shouldn't be so hard to think of an answer to that question that she'd accept. 'Because it's my home, now. The band are there. I couldn't leave them—or the music— now. I have an obligation—to them, and to Gareth's memory. And there are the contracts with the label, of course. I owe them all.'

'You sound like Anna,' Rosa said, softly.

Jude shook his head. 'This is different. This is my dream.' His and Gareth's dream. And he would live it for both of them.

'Then why do you look like you've been caged?'

There wasn't an answer at all for that one. 'Go on, then. What do *you* think I should do?'

'I don't know.' Rosa gave a one-shouldered shrug. 'I've spent pretty much my whole adult life avoiding getting trapped that way.'

And she'd keep avoiding it, he knew. Once the wedding was over she'd leave him again.

But this time, he knew that ahead of time. Which meant he wasn't going to waste a moment of the time they had together.

'I don't want to talk about New York any more,' he said. 'Or the past.'

Rosa raised an eyebrow. 'Oh? What do you want to talk about?'

'Honestly?' Jude ran his hands up the side of her naked body. 'I don't want to talk at all.'

'Works for me,' Rosa said, and kissed him.

The bridal party were due to arrive after lunch, so Rosa and Jude spent the following morning putting the finishing touches to the bridal bungalow, and hanging the more delicate decorations for the main function areas that had been left until the last moment, just in case. Basically making sure everything was hashtag perfect for Valentina's arrival.

Anna had already stopped by three times to check on their work, but even that couldn't dim Rosa's mood today. Every action, every moment seemed to remind her of the night before—of being wild and free, first in the sea, and then in Jude's arms. Even the darker turn the conversation had taken…as upsetting as it was to hear about Gareth's death from Jude's own lips, to hear how he blamed himself, she was glad that she knew, now. And if anything, it had only made her feel closer to him again. As if they were finding their way back to how they'd been three years ago, before she walked away.

He said he didn't blame her for distracting him from Gareth's slide into addiction again, and she wanted to believe him. And for now, that would have to be enough. It wasn't as if they had for ever for him to throw blame back at her. They had another week or two at most, and Rosa had very firm ideas about how they should spend that time.

She stretched up to secure a string of tiny lights, and felt a muscle ache, a physical reminder of her actions the night before, and smiled.

'You're doing it again,' Jude said, from across the way.

'Doing what?'

'Distracting me.'

Rosa laughed, just a little uneasily, given her earlier thoughts. 'I can't help that, I'm afraid.'

But Jude grinned back, and she knew he wasn't thinking about Gareth at all. That was good. As much as he'd loved his friend, he couldn't spend the rest of his life in mortgage to his memory.

It all felt so different this time, she realised, for all that it was the same. This time she was older and, yes, maybe even wiser. She didn't have to be afraid of getting drawn in and tied down to Jude. They both knew what this was—an island fling. When it was over they'd go their own ways, still friends, she hoped. It was a better ending than she'd ever hoped for, after she'd left him in London three years before.

And in the meantime…she intended to enjoy every moment they had together. The time limit made everything more intense, in her experience. That was why she kept reliving the night before over and over in her head. Why she couldn't wait for night to fall again so she could take him to bed…

'Right. Is that it?' Jude jumped down from the chair he was standing on and Rosa bit her lip as his loose shirt rode up displaying those tight abs again. Tonight… 'Are we done?' Jude asked, dragging her back to the present.

Rosa checked her clipboard for the list Anna had given her, and scanned the area they'd been working on. 'Believe it or not, I think we are.'

'In that case, I'm off to take a shower.' Jude tossed her a smile as he started unbuttoning his shirt halfway to the path. 'I'd invite you to join me, but there's no way you'd ever be ready to meet the bridal party then.'

'Mmm, probably not,' Rosa agreed, her eyes still fixed on his chest. 'Tonight, though?'

'Definitely tonight,' Jude agreed. 'I'm hoping you might even show me where that secret door that leads to your bedroom is…'

'Ha! You should be so lucky.'

In two swift strides, Jude headed back into the courtyard and kissed her. Thoroughly. 'Oh, I am.'

Rosa smiled after him as he finally left. Then she ran into the villa, through the secret door, and up the twisting wooden stairs to her childhood bedroom in the turret to get ready herself.

'It looks good down here,' Anna said as Rosa appeared. 'And you look nice, too, actually.'

'Thanks,' Rosa said, surprised by the unexpected compliment. She'd dressed in a hot-pink sundress she had a feeling that Jude might enjoy stripping off her later. Her wet hair was piled up in a messy bun, and her make-up was minimal, but she felt beautiful all the same. As if she was glowing.

And she knew that was all down to Jude.

'Their boat arrived a few minutes ago,' Anna said, all business again. 'I've got four staff members down there taking their stuff to the bungalows, and another one bringing them straight here for welcome drinks.' She indicated the table set up with pink champagne in flutes, just inside the courtyard.

Rosa heard a noise further down the path from the villa and stepped forward to the open doorway. 'Here they come.'

'Okay.' Anna took an audible breath.

'Are you *nervous*?' Rosa asked. She wasn't sure she'd ever seen that emotion in her sister before.

'Of course not.'

And then it was too late to press the issue, because the bride—instantly recognised from a million online photos—and her bridesmaids were there, all giggling and talking over each other.

Anna stepped forward and introduced herself to Valentina, who took her hand and pulled her into a hug. 'The island looks so beautiful! Thank you so much for managing to fit us in here for the wedding. It means so much to me and Todd!'

'It's our pleasure,' Anna said, sidestepping the weeks and weeks of work it had taken to be ready for the wedding.

Mind you, given how much Valentina was paying for the privilege, Rosa supposed that was only fair.

'This is my sister, Rosa,' Anna said, and Rosa braced herself for the over-enthusiastic welcome hug from the Internet sensation. 'Now, if you'd like to come through to the courtyard we have welcome drinks for you all, before we take you down to get settled into your accommodation before tonight's dinner.'

'It seems to be going okay,' Rosa murmured to her sister half an hour later, as waiters topped up the glasses of the bridal party—all except Valentina, who was far too busy opening last-minute wedding-week presents from her friends to hold a glass. So far she'd opened monogrammed slippers, robe, nightdress and underwear. Rosa was almost afraid to see what was in the last packages.

'It does.' Anna sounded relieved. 'And here come our men,' she added, nodding in the direction of the arch from the villa.

Rosa didn't correct her. Just the sight of Jude standing beside Leo on the edge of the courtyard, pale where the other man was tan, but both tall and broad and gorgeous.

Except neither of them were looking at her or Anna.

Leo, understandably, headed straight for his sister, embracing her warmly. Seeing them together actually made Rosa feel a little brighter about the possibilities for her own sister's relationship. Maybe there was more to Leo than the gossip websites would have her believe.

But when she watched Jude, her optimism for their own fling took a little knock.

How had she forgotten, even in her happy haze of lust, that his ex-girlfriend would be here? She scanned the gaggle of bridesmaids and picked out the only redhead. Sylvie Rockwell-Smythe, even more beautiful in real life than she was in her photos.

Why hadn't she prepared herself better for this? Because she didn't want to imagine it, Rosa admitted to herself. And because her time together with Jude here felt like such an escape from the real world, she didn't want any of it to intrude on it.

But when the tall, willowy redhead squealed with delight and ran across to embrace Jude, Rosa was pretty sure reality had come to find them.

'Jude!' Valentina broke off from opening presents to welcome him, too, the redhead still hanging off his arm. 'Sylvie didn't tell me you were coming! How wonderful!'

'I didn't know!' Sylvie gushed. She batted Jude on the arm. 'He must have flown out here to surprise me.'

Rosa winced, thankful that Anna had headed inside to deal with the catering staff and wasn't there to see this.

'Not exactly,' Jude said, his voice cool.

'Sorry?' Sylvie's brows knitted together without wrinkling her forehead at all.

Suddenly Rosa looked up to find Jude's gaze on her, his eyes beckoning her over as he disentangled himself from Sylvie's hands. 'Sylvie, Valentina, have you met Rosa Gray?'

CHAPTER NINE

THE FIRST THING that struck Jude as he reached the court-yard was the noise—the high, excited voices of Valentina and her bridesmaids, so different from Rosa's warm, low, laughing tones. And then he saw her—Sylvie—her bright red hair and perfect body shining in the Spanish sunlight.

He'd thought he might love her, once, he remembered, but somehow it no longer felt real. Nothing from that world did—not when compared to swimming naked in the ocean with Rosa, with holding Rosa in his arms.

That was real. *Rosa* was real.

But it was Sylvie throwing herself into his arms, be-lieving he'd arrived on the island just to surprise her.

Well, that was a misunderstanding he could clear up right away.

'Sylvie, Valentina, have you met Rosa Gray?' He gazed at Rosa, loving how she knew what he wanted, was almost halfway across the courtyard before he said her name.

He just hoped she'd play along a little longer.

'We have,' Valentina said, smiling happily, as a bride-to-be should. 'So, is she what brought you to this beauti-ful island—if you're not here for my wedding?'

'Jude and I are old friends,' Rosa said, returning an equally warm smile as she took his arm, pressing close in a way that showed everyone exactly what sort of *friends* they were. Jude's heart seemed to settle back into a rhythm he hadn't known it had lost as she touched him.

'I thought I'd come spend a few weeks here visiting with Rosa this summer,' Jude said, lightly. 'It seemed like a good time to be out of New York.'

Sylvie's cheeks flushed a little at that, and Valentina gave them both a knowing look.

'I heard about the book,' she said. 'I didn't read it, of course. But it does seem to be everywhere at the moment.'

Strange to think that Valentina had built an entire career out of letting people see into her life—every moment, photographed and filtered and shared.

'How do you cope with it?' he asked, suddenly. 'Everyone knowing every single thing that happens in your life, I mean?'

Valentina laughed. 'Oh, Jude. They know what I *want* them to know. That's the joy of controlling your own brand, the way I do. They never see more than I'm willing to show them.'

'You show them a lot, though,' Rosa pointed out.

Valentina shrugged her slim shoulders. 'I owe them a lot. It's only fair that I share plenty in return. But that doesn't mean I don't get to keep a few of my own secrets.'

Jude was glad, he realised. He'd hate for Valentina to feel the way he did—as if every inch of his personal space had been invaded, every precious memory passed from person to person to examine.

Rosa squeezed his arm, and he found himself grateful again that the author of *The Naked Truth* had never found out about her. Maybe he still had a few secrets left, too.

'Now, I hope you'll join us for the wedding anyway, since you're here?' Valentina asked.

'I'd hate to intrude,' Jude started, but Valentina laughed.

'Don't be silly! The more the merrier. And of course, if you'd like to bring a plus-one, I'm sure that would be fine…'

'Then thank you,' Jude said, already calculating in his mind how happy Robyn would be about this one.

Being seen at the wedding of the year could never be a bad thing. And having a beautiful woman like Rosa on his arm had to look good, too.

The fact it would rub Sylvie's nose in it a bit felt pretty great, too, if he was brutally honest.

Leaving Valentina and her bridesmaids to the presents, Jude led Rosa off to the shadows of the villa.

'So, that's the ex, huh?' she asked, glancing back out at them. 'She's beautiful. Like, absurdly so. Even more than the photos.'

'She's nothing compared to you,' Jude said, making her laugh, although he couldn't figure out why.

'She's a model, Jude. A six-foot-tall, beautiful, willowy redhead with perfect hair and a dozen modelling contracts. I am under no illusions about my own charms, but they're not a patch on hers. You don't need to lie to me to make me feel good.'

'I'm not lying,' Jude said, holding her close so she had to look into his eyes and see the truth of it. 'Yes, Sylvie looks beautiful. She's stunning.'

'Not helping with the not lying part.'

'But you…' He stared down into her wide, dark eyes, her long lashes sooty against her skin, trying to find the words. 'You're *alive*. You have so much life, so much vibrancy… She could never match that. She *looks* beautiful. You live it.'

He must have said something right, from the way she kissed him.

'You're such a *poet*,' she said, fondly.

'So you'll come to the wedding with me? It won't be any fun without you.'

Rosa pulled a face. 'I'll need to check with Anna. I'm supposed to be working that day, of course.'

'But she'll be going with Leo, surely?'

'That's true. I'll ask her, I promise.'

'Tonight?'

The smile Rosa gave him reminded him they had other plans for tonight. 'Maybe tomorrow.'

'Tomorrow works for me.'

'Anna, have you got a minute?' Rosa had been looking all over the island for her sister after another day of work. Anna had been strangely absent for most of it, until Rosa finally spotted her heading down the path to the jetty.

'Not now.' Anna didn't even look back at her. Wasn't that always the way with her? She wanted to organise her life for her, but only when it suited her.

Rosa took a breath and reminded herself she was asking Anna for a favour. She needed to keep her cool. 'It's about Jude. Valentina has asked him to the wedding and he wants me to be his plus-one. Will that be a problem? I can still oversee the seating charts and things, and you'll be there with Leo anyway…'

Anna finally glanced back, pushing her hair out of her eyes. 'Leo hasn't mentioned me accompanying him to the wedding,' she said slowly. 'We're not, I mean, it's not serious.'

If Leo and Anna weren't serious, then what on earth did that make her and Jude? 'Oh, come on, I've seen the way he looks at you.'

'It's not serious,' Anna repeated, and Rosa decided to worry later about whatever games her sister was playing now.

'If you say so. So you don't mind? It turns out Jude knows Valentina quite well, he used to go out with one of the bridesmaids—the redhead who complained that the bed is too hard and that we haven't provided the right range of herbal teas—and it ended, well, horrifically. Long story short, she was involved with the book, so it's a pride thing to accept the invite and bring a date, I guess. But what with the way we left things, I think…'

Anna held up her hand to silence her, and Rosa got the feeling she was mentally counting to ten, as she used to when they were small. 'Rosa, fill me in later. I have to go over to the mainland and I hate sailing over in the dark. Yes, go to the wedding. It's fine.'

The mainland? What on earth could she be going there for? Everything for the wedding had already been delivered. Unless this wasn't to do with the wedding…

'What's so urgent?' Rosa's voice sharpened, as she took in her sister's appearance for the first time. 'Are you okay? You're very pale. Do you feel ill?'

'Rosa, don't fuss. I just have to do something.' Yeah, that wasn't very reassuring—especially if Anna didn't want to tell her what she needed to do.

'I really think you should wait till morning.' Then, as Anna shook her head, 'In that case I'm coming with you. I'll drive the boat. The way you look you won't be able to get it out of the harbour!'

Anna wanted to refuse, Rosa could tell. But she wasn't going to let her.

Not waiting for an answer, Rosa took the boat key out of Anna's hand and led her the rest of the way down to the jetty. It was pretty clear that Anna didn't want to talk about whatever was going on, so Rosa didn't press her for details, concentrating instead on steering the dinghy over the short distance as speedily as possible. She pulled up alongside the jetty on the mainland with a smooth flourish. 'Right, where next? Anna, I'm coming with you. Don't argue.'

Anna opened her mouth to protest and then shut it again. Rosa smiled. For once, she was in charge.

Sancia always kept a car in the car park near the jetty, for whenever they needed to run errands on the mainland, and Rosa was relieved to see it there waiting for them. Anna pulled the key to Sancia's ancient rusty small car from her pocket and handed it to her, not responding as Rosa's hand closed over hers with what she hoped was a reassuring squeeze.

'The town,' she said, her voice husky. 'The pharmacy. There's one on the retail park this side of town, it's not far.'

The pharmacy. Oh, that didn't sound good at all.

Now Rosa was really worried.

The roads were deserted and it didn't take long to clear the small village and head towards the town. Rosa drove at her normal speed—ten kilometres above the speed limit—more concerned by the fact that Anna wasn't issuing her usual warnings to drive carefully than by the sharp turns and corners.

Something was definitely wrong here.

Spotting the retail park, and the pharmacy, Rosa swung the car into a free space and killed the engine. 'Do you want me to come in with you?'

'No. Thanks.' Anna made no move to get out of the car, though.

'Anna, let me go.' Rosa had a feeling she knew exactly what this was. And it was bigger than any argument that had ever been between them. 'Do you need me to buy you a pregnancy test? Is that what's happening here?' What else could it be? Rosa knew that panicked, lost look on her sister's face. She'd seen it on her own, once.

Anna froze. 'Leo doesn't want a family.' Rosa had a feeling that wasn't what Anna had intended to say. 'He'll think I've betrayed him.'

'Anna, honey, it takes two to make a baby. Leo's a grown man. If you are pregnant, he'll understand.' And if he didn't, then Rosa would beat understanding into him. Not that she was going to mention that part to Anna yet.

'No, he won't. He told me from the start, no promises, no commitment. It's bad enough I've fallen in love with him. How can I be so stupid as to get pregnant, too? It's like Sebastian all over again, only much, much worse. I only *thought* I loved Sebastian.'

Okay, *that* was a surprise. But actually, it explained a lot. 'You were pregnant back then? Why didn't you tell me? Why do you never let anyone help, Anna?' The old frustrations rose up in her. If she'd known, she could have helped. She could have done *something*. 'You don't have to do it all alone. You don't have to be perfect. You can ask for help...'

'Last time I needed your help you walked away.' It was always going to come down to that between them, wasn't it?

Rosa bit her lip. Anna was never going to understand why she couldn't stay. And now really wasn't the time to confess all the other reasons—the ones that had nothing to do with Anna or their father. 'Things were compli-cated then. I'm sorry. But I'm here now and, I promise you, you're not alone. Now let me go and get the test for you and then, if you are, we'll figure out what to do. And if you're not then you and I need to have a long-overdue talk. Deal?'

'Deal.' Anna squeezed her hand tightly.

Rosa got out of the car and jogged over to the pharmacy. She might have let her sister down before, but Anna wouldn't have to worry about that this time.

And nor would her child, with Rosa as their auntie.

Something was up with Rosa.

Jude surveyed her over the rack of Scrabble tiles, ignoring the letters and potential words to consider the woman sitting across from him instead. On either side of him, Sancia and Ernest Gray were debating whether whatever obscure word the professor had come up with existed in the *Oxford English Dictionary*. Jude was fairly sure it didn't—the professor was a terrible Scrabble cheat.

The bigger mystery to him was what Rosa was thinking about.

Whatever it was, it had distracted her completely, all evening. She'd barely responded to his hand on her hip as they walked to the table, she'd had nothing to say over dinner, and now she'd barely managed more than a three-letter word all game.

Scrabble, Jude had discovered to his surprise, was the one area of the world where Professor Gray and his youngest daughter actually seemed to connect. He and Sancia usually just muddled through trying to keep up. They both fought for every tile, every triple word score, every definition.

But not tonight.

Suddenly Rosa looked up, her attention drawn by something by the darkened arch leading out of the courtyard. Jude twisted in his seat to try and see what had distracted her.

Anna. Of course. And Leo, leading her away.

Jude turned back to Rosa to see an unfamiliar look on her face. Part hope, part fear, and all uncertainty.

'I'm going to go and fetch my dictionary,' Sancia said, rising from her seat. The professor followed her, arguing that since it probably wasn't the *Oxford English Dictionary* it wouldn't count, anyway.

Jude waited until the others were safely inside the villa before he slid over to Sancia's chair and reached for Rosa's hand.

'What's up?'

'Hmm?' Rosa turned to him, blinking. 'Nothing.'

'Liar.' She'd never lied to him before, that he knew of. Let him believe things that wouldn't happen, sure, but that was his false hope, not her fault. Now he was really worried.

But Rosa looked down at the table and said, 'Sorry. You're right. It's just... I'm not sure it's my secret to tell.'

Something relaxed inside him. That he, of all people, could understand. 'That's fine. But if it'll help to talk about it...you know I'm not one to share other people's stories.'

'I do know.' Rosa gave him a warm smile, then glanced back towards the villa. 'Come on, let's go. Take a walk or something.'

'You always talk better when we're walking.'

Rosa shrugged, getting to her feet. 'You know me. I work better in action.'

'I do,' Jude said, and realised it was true.

He *knew* Rosa, in a way he wasn't sure he'd ever known anyone else. He'd thought it was just because she lived life out loud, her every action proclaiming exactly who she was. But others—her own family—still didn't seem to understand her, even with a lifetime of observing her.

So maybe it was just something about their connection.

Maybe it was just him, and just her.

She led him along the winding path that trailed around the island, through lush foliage and flowers, past the bright white bungalows and their freshly painted shutters, skirting the beaches and waterfronts. When they came too close to the bridal bungalow, Rosa tugged his hand to take a different trail, one that led them away from the laughter and the chatter.

Rosa still wasn't talking, Jude realised. The romantic walk in the moonlight was nice and all, but it wasn't getting him any closer to figuring out what was on Rosa's mind.

'Is it Sylvie?' he asked, figuring he had to start somewhere. 'Has she said anything?'

'Who?' Rosa looked up, surprised. 'Oh, no. Not her.'

Of course. Because that would mean her actually being affected by his ex-girlfriend being on the island, and they'd both been very clear that this wasn't that kind of relationship.

Then he remembered the way she'd watched Anna and Leo leaving the courtyard. 'Your sister, then?'

Rosa didn't answer that time, which was how Jude knew he'd got it right.

'What did she do?' He could feel his irritation with Rosa's sister rising. Whatever their differences, Rosa had busted a gut helping her get the island ready for the wedding, and Anna had still managed to find fault at every turn.

'She got pregnant,' Rosa said, her voice soft, and all of Jude's anger faded away in an instant.

'Are you sure?'

Rosa shook her head. 'I took her to buy the test last night. She didn't tell me the outcome but...you saw her with Leo this evening. I could tell from her face, she was going to tell him. So I guess it must have been positive.'

'Wow.' Suddenly, a terrible thought occurred to him, and he tugged her to face him. 'Wait, do we need to—?'

Rosa interrupted him with a shake of her head. 'It's fine.'

'No, but I mean, I know we've been careful since, but that first time. In the sea...'

'Jude. It's covered. Trust me. With travelling the world and all the different time zones, my body got so confused the doctor put me on a contraceptive injection anyway. There's no chance, this time.'

'Right. Okay, then.' Jude was almost certain that the feeling coursing through him was relief. Just relief. Because disappointment would have been crazy.

If Rosa got pregnant, would she stay? Or, more importantly, would she ever forgive him?

He couldn't think about those impossibilities now.

'How do you think Leo will react?' he asked, instead.

'Anna seemed pretty sure the answer to that is "badly".' She sighed, dropping down to sit on one of the brightly painted benches that studded the island path at points where the view was even more spectacular than the average La Isla Marina vista. 'But he's an idiot if he doesn't just marry her and live happily ever after.'

'I never thought I'd hear you advocating settling down and living the traditional life,' Jude observed. He sat beside her, and she took his hand in hers, absently playing with his fingers.

'Well, not for me,' Rosa admitted. 'But you've seen the two of them together. How they look at each other.

To start, I thought Leo was just playing her, but now…
I think he genuinely loves her. I just hope he realises
that, too.'

'So do I,' Jude said, although he wasn't fully thinking of Anna and Leo.

He was thinking about Rosa. How fiercely he'd fallen
for her, three years ago. How the love that had turned
to shock and anger had become an aching loss, until he
found her again. How, even now, even when he was protecting his heart the best he knew how, he knew it was
going to hurt, when she left again.

This time, he realised, he would have to leave first.
He needed to make that decision, take that control. It was
the only way he'd ever be able to live with it.

'I have to admit, though,' Rosa said, staring out at the
calm sea before them, 'I am kind of looking forward to
being an auntie.'

'You'll be the cool auntie who sends them awesome
gifts from all over the world, from places they couldn't
even imagine from their boring house in Oxford.'

'Exactly!' Rosa flashed him a grin. 'And maybe…
maybe they'll come here on holiday, and I can join them.
Like we used to when we were kids.'

'You think you'll come back to the island more often,
now?' Jude asked, surprised.

'Maybe.' Because there was never any certainty with
Rosa, was there? 'I mean, it's the only place that's ever
really felt like home.'

And suddenly, sitting in the moonlight, talking about
someone else's child, Jude realised he knew exactly how
she felt.

Only, for him, home wasn't a place.

It was a person.

CHAPTER TEN

ALMOST THERE.

Just over twenty-four hours now until the wedding, and Rosa had ticked off the last of the day's jobs on her accursed clipboard. The groom and his family had arrived, and the Spanish-style lunch they'd arranged for the whole wedding party had been a huge success. Four courses over several hours followed by much-needed siestas had made the perfect introduction to the island, and Anna and Rosa had planned for beach games and a much more informal supper to be served at the beach later that evening. The informal evening would not only be fun, but crucially it gave the island staff plenty of time to prepare for the next day, when another hundred guests were due to arrive, and for the wedding ceremony itself, which would begin at seven o'clock tomorrow night.

Rosa had to admit, Anna had pulled off a near miracle. The island looked perfect. Every bungalow was ready and—thanks to her and Jude—every tree had fairy lights threaded through it, and the pagoda and central area were set up for the ceremony and party. Anna had confirmed that Valentina's dress had arrived that day, escorted by a dressmaker who would stay until Valentina was dressed, and last time Rosa had checked in on the kitchens Sancia had been harassing the chefs from Barcelona who were setting up. Fortunately her mother was easily distracted, and the chefs seemed to be working remarkably amicably with the island's own cooks.

Valentina glowed with happiness, her groom's wealthy parents were happy, and the bridesmaids—except for Sylvie—full of nothing but praise.

In summary, they were ready. Which meant Rosa was officially free to pursue her own interests for the rest of the evening—namely, Jude.

At least, she was once she'd reported in to her lord and master, Anna.

Rosa smiled to herself as she made her way up the path to the main villa. Actually, things between her and her sister were better than they had been in years—since before their mother left, even. Rosa had managed to get Anna alone the day before and get the full story from her. Yes, she was pregnant. No, she wasn't marrying Leo and living happily ever after. But she seemed content, all the same. As if the life within her had settled her—given her a focus that mattered to *her*, rather than keeping other people satisfied, as she seemed to with her work, or looking after their father.

Part of Rosa worried that Anna was just getting tied down in a new way, but the more reasonable part of her knew that this was different. A *baby* was different, especially for Anna.

But she couldn't stop remembering those terrifying weeks when she'd believed she might be pregnant with Jude's child. Then, at twenty-three, it had felt like the end of the world—a shackle on her life before she'd even figured out how she wanted to live it.

Now, three years and an awful lot of experience on, she wondered if it might feel different.

Not that she intended to find out. She had plans, still. Life still to live, adventures still to have.

When she'd left him, and La Isla Marina, and everything else behind last time it had been to find *her* life. The one no one else in the world could live but her. The person she was meant to be, even. And, over the last three years, she'd found it. She had a career she loved, that fulfilled her—and allowed her to keep moving, to experience new places and cultures and lives. She met more people from more different walks of life in a month than many people met in their whole existence. She never had to slow down to wait for someone else to catch up, never had to modulate her expectations or her impulses to satisfy someone else. She could be exactly who she was, without judgement. Or at least, without hanging around long enough to hear or care about any judgement anyone passed on her choices.

She had exactly what she'd wanted. Yes, it could be lonely, occasionally. But the benefits outweighed the negatives, right? And if, sometimes, she wondered if it was enough, well, as long as she kept moving she could push those thoughts aside. She didn't want what Anna seemed to—to settle down in one place and live one life with one man. And even then, Leo didn't seem as if he was going to give Anna her happy ever after. If St Anna couldn't make love work, what hope was there for her screw-up little sister?

And besides, even if Rosa and Jude had that sort of relationship—the for ever kind—she couldn't live his life. She couldn't smile politely at self-important celebrities and people trying to tell her what to do. She wasn't that person.

Jude, surprisingly, seemed to be. She'd thought he'd be raging against the requirements and constraints, but it seemed that he liked the fame more than he liked the freedom. Or maybe he just stuck with it for the sake of Gareth's memory. Out of guilt for the promise he broke.

Whatever his reasons, Rosa was never going to be that way. She couldn't be that woman he needed by his side, always.

Even if she wanted to be.

The villa was lit up with tiny lanterns, bright spots in the darkness illuminating the happiness and love that filled the island for Valentina's wedding. Rosa wished some of it could spread to Anna and Leo, but she knew that if it didn't, Anna would be okay. She was strong, and she could organise her way out of any situation.

Anna would be fine.

Rosa stepped through into the courtyard, and saw her sister bending to kiss her parents, one at a time. Which was unusual on many levels. Firstly, Anna wasn't a usually demonstrative person that way, and Rosa knew she didn't intend to tell their parents about the pregnancy until after the wedding, so it couldn't be that. Add in the ongoing weirdness of their estranged parents apparently spending all their time together again, after ten years apart, and Rosa was just baffled. What had happened to her dysfunctional, tension-inducing family? At least she knew what to expect from them. The new dynamics just confused her. Where was she supposed to fit in? Or maybe she wasn't. After all, she'd be gone again soon, and they could all carry on without her, in Oxford and Spain. Rosa knew when she wasn't needed.

She raised an eyebrow at Anna. 'It all looks very cosy in here—everything all right?'

'Everything's good,' Anna said. 'I was just discussing the possibility of staying on the island. After all, it's never been one person's job to run it before.'

Rosa's eyes widened, a hundred questions jostling for

attention in her mind while she tried—and failed—to choose one. 'But… Oxford…? Book…? Dad…? Here?'

'Quite,' Anna said enigmatically. 'Did you put the volleyball net up, Rosa? Don't worry, I'll go. I could do with some fresh air.'

And then she was gone, before Rosa could confirm that, yes, actually, she had put the net up. And also, what the hell?

Anna, staying on La Isla Marina, with their mother—and possibly their father, given how things were going—and her baby.

Anna, who for the last decade had focussed on exactly the same sort of academic success that had driven their father for so long—and driven their parents apart.

Maybe this was proof that people could change, after all. And for some reason, it made Rosa incredibly uncomfortable.

If Anna could change, did that mean *she* could? More to the point, that she *should*?

No. Rosa had fought too hard to be exactly who she was to give it up now.

'I'm going to go and help her,' Rosa said, but her parents weren't even listening. They were lost in their own conversation.

Rosa walked back out onto the island proper and sucked in a deep breath. Anna didn't need her help, because there was nothing to help with. Everything was done and ready, and the staff they had in place would be running the events perfectly. If Anna was there, she didn't need Rosa's help.

So she turned away from the public areas and all the fun wedding events, and headed down the path towards Jude's bungalow by the sea, hoping she could lose herself in his arms for a while, and forget all the questions buzzing in her head.

* * *

Jude was sitting at the patio table when she arrived, his guitar resting on his knee as he noted something down in the brown leather notebook on the table.

Rosa leant against the wall of the bungalow and watched him as he picked out a melody on the strings, before stopping to write down something else. He was so handsome. Beautiful, even, in a way she'd never imagined a man could be. If she had her camera with her, she'd frame him against the night sky, the fairy lights behind him, highlighting the planes and shadows of that beautiful face.

It seemed strange now, to remember that he hadn't always been the star. The frontman of The Swifts, taking all the praise and glory. When he'd been in Gareth's shadow, others had barely even seemed to notice him.

But to Rosa, Jude had always been that bright, shining star in the darkness.

'Working?' she asked, softly, so as not to startle him.

Jude looked up and smiled. 'Playing, really.'

He strummed the melody again, carrying on for longer this time, the music almost familiar somehow.

'Do I know that one?' she asked, slipping into the seat opposite him.

'Parts of it, probably,' Jude admitted. 'It's a variation on a theme—I'm playing around with some of the local music here.'

'For the new album?'

Jude shook his head, looking down at the strings so his dark hair fell across his forehead. 'Just for me, really. I doubt the rest of the band would think this fitted with our brand.'

'Brand?' Rosa pulled a face. It always came back to that for him, it seemed. Trying to fit into a mould that he'd outgrown, even if he didn't realise it. 'Can't you just play the music you like?'

'Apparently not. At least, not back in New York. Here, however…' He strummed the strings again, making Rosa smile.

'Play me a song. One just for me.'

'Sure.' As he started to play Rosa stood up and made her way through the open patio doors into the bungalow bedroom, stripping her dress from her body as she went. The music stuttered for a second, then continued, Jude lifting his voice to join it, singing of beauty and life and water and sun.

Naked, Rosa stretched out on Jude's bed and gazed back at him, watching as he created something entirely new, something just for her. After a few lines, he looked up and met her gaze, and suddenly it wasn't her lack of clothes that made her feel exposed.

It was his eyes. The way he looked deep into the heart of her, the way no one else ever managed. She kept moving, kept talking, kept living, and no one ever kept up with her well enough to see the truth in her. But with Jude, she was frozen. Motionless. Naked—physically and emotionally.

He saw everything. And he sang it back to her.

Rosa wasn't sure if that was terrifying or wonderful. Maybe it was both.

The song came to an end, but Jude's gaze didn't leave hers. 'That what you wanted?'

'Yes,' she said, even though she wasn't sure she should have asked for it. 'At least, the first part of what I wanted.'

'Oh? What's the second part?' Jude asked, but she could tell from his smile that he already knew.

Still, she opened her arms to him to make it clear. 'You. Here. Now.'

Jude put his guitar back in its case, closing it hurriedly. 'I can do that.'

* * *

'You know, we're really, really good at that,' Jude said, running his hands over the smooth expanses of Rosa's skin, just because he could. For now, she was all his, here in his bed, in his arms. Like a song he never wanted to end.

'We really are.' Rosa twisted in his arms so she faced him, pressing a kiss against his chest.

He wanted to say it. Wanted to tell her that it didn't have to end, that she didn't have to run. That they could try a life together, for real, this time.

But he'd already said it all in his song. He'd poured his every emotion, every thought into that melody and those lyrics, sung his heart to her. She knew it all already. And if it didn't change her mind, he still needed to be able to walk away with his heart intact.

So he said nothing.

'Anna's decided to stay on the island,' Rosa said, suddenly, bringing Jude back to the here and now.

'Really? Because of the baby?'

'I guess.'

'You sound confused.' Was it just the idea of voluntarily staying on one sleepy island for ever that confused her? Or was there something more to this?

'No… I get it. I think.' Rosa sighed, and pulled away, sitting up and tugging the sheet up over her body, which Jude thought was a crying shame. 'No, I don't. As long as I can remember, Anna wanted to be an academic like Dad, living in Oxford, researching, writing her books and teaching her students. And now…she's changing her whole life.'

'Love makes us do strange things.' Jude's throat felt tight as he said it.

Rosa gave him a strange look. 'Leo's not staying with her.'

'I meant the love of her baby,' Jude explained. 'Although…she's heartbroken, remember. She probably imagined a whole future with Leo and now she's reassessing. She's finding a new future for a new her.'

'You sound like you know what she's going through,' Rosa said, curiously. 'Who did you love?'

'You.' He'd said it before he even realised he was going to. The horror in Rosa's eyes made it clear he had to take it back, though. And fast. 'Once, anyway. I mean, when you left last time. But that was a long time ago now.' He kept his voice as casual as he could, a careful eye on Rosa's face to watch the shock and fear subsiding.

'Yes. A long time ago.' Something flashed across her face though, something deeper than the horror.

'What?' Sitting up, he pulled her close again, needing her touch. 'What is it?'

'When I left… I did it badly, I know that.'

'It was a long time ago, Rosa. It doesn't matter now.' Even if she'd stayed, what would it have changed, really? Gareth would still have died, that much he realised now, seeing her again. She'd given him some peace with that, at least. But if she'd come back, how long would it have lasted? Another month? A year, if he was lucky? The axe would have fallen sooner or later, and later would have only hurt more.

'But that's the thing—it does.' She looked up into his eyes. 'I need to explain.'

'You already have,' Jude pointed out. 'You told me exactly why you left.' And to be honest, he wasn't sure he could hear it again—listen to her say how little he'd meant to her that she moved on without a backward glance, just because she didn't like to stay in one place too long.

'I didn't tell you everything.'

Her quiet words stopped his brain in its tracks. Leaning back against the pillows, he pulled her down with him, holding her tight against his shoulder. 'Tell me now?' He wasn't sure he wanted to hear it, but he knew he needed to know it.

Rosa nodded, her hair brushing his skin. And Jude waited to hear the truth.

'When I left, for my *abuelo*'s funeral… I planned to come back. I was going to come back to you.'

It was as if the world starting falling into place. As a discordant tune became a melody as the right notes were played instead.

He'd known it wasn't right. Known there was something wrong about her leaving like that. Their connection had been too strong for her to sever it so thoughtlessly.

Yes, he'd known that Rosa wouldn't stay for ever. She wasn't the sort of woman to settle down, and he'd accepted that. But he'd expected more from her than for her to just drop out of his life—that was the part that had haunted him for the past three years.

And now, it seemed, he was about to learn the truth about why.

'Why didn't you?' he asked, dreading and needing the answer in equal measure.

'Because I was scared,' Rosa admitted. 'What I felt for you…it was all-encompassing, and it scared me. When I was with you, I couldn't think about anything else. Couldn't remember who I was, what *I* wanted out of life. I was afraid that if I came back to you I wouldn't be able to leave again, and I knew I needed to, if I wanted to follow my dreams. And then—' She broke off.

'What?' He needed it all. Every detail. Even as his body buzzed with the knowledge that it wasn't just him. She'd felt it, too.

Whether she admitted it or not, Rosa had loved him, too. And it still hadn't been enough for her to stay.

'I was late. My body…all the stress of the funeral, and the fight with Anna, I guess it got to it. I was two weeks late and I thought…'

'You thought you were pregnant.' For a moment, the image of a tiny little girl with Rosa's dark eyes and hair flashed through his head. *There's no chance, this time.* That was what she'd said, when he'd asked if they needed to be concerned. And this was what she'd meant.

How could he not have seen that?

'I wasn't,' Rosa said, quickly dispelling the image. 'But the thought that I could have been… I realised how careless we'd been. How when I was with you I set aside everything I wanted for myself, every dream I had, every promise I'd made to myself that I wouldn't get tied down to a life of someone else's choosing, like Mama and Anna did. I forgot everything that made me Rosa, and that terrified me. So I ran.'

The worst part was, it all made perfect sense, in a Rosa sort of way. Of course she had run.

'I wish you'd been able to tell me, back then.' Jude's head was still spinning, imagining a world in which she might have done.

How could things have been different? Was there any way this could have ended differently?

Knowing Rosa, and knowing himself, he suspected not.

He'd been chasing fame, and she'd been chasing freedom. They couldn't have done that together, not really. He could never have asked Rosa to chase his dreams with him instead of hers, and she could never have asked him to abandon his, either. Especially not after Gareth died, and he had two people's dreams to chase already.

The worst part was, nothing had changed. They were the same people they'd been three years ago.

There was still only one way this could all end.

'I wish I had, too,' Rosa said. 'I know it wouldn't have changed anything, but still… I wish I hadn't left things the way I did.'

Jude rolled over so she was lying underneath him. 'I think we've more than made up for it, the last couple of weeks. Don't you think?'

'Definitely.' Rosa smiled up at him, so sweetly that he had to kiss her. 'But we could probably stand to make up a few more times, before we leave. Don't you think?'

That, Jude decided, was a question better answered with action, than words.

CHAPTER ELEVEN

THE WEDDING WAS PERFECT.

The sun shone down on the evening service, while Valentina and Todd took their vows with laughter and joy in between the serious moments. The actual, legal part of the ceremony, Rosa knew, had been completed in New York a week or so ago. So technically, Valentina and Todd were already tied to each other for life. But today was the day that mattered most to them—the day where they confirmed that commitment to everyone who mattered to them. When they stood proud and said, 'I've made my decision. It's this person for me. For ever.'

Rosa tried to imagine being that sure of anything, but the only thing that came to mind was Jude. And they both already knew that wasn't an option. So instead, she decided to just enjoy the day.

Valentina looked more beautiful than ever, Rosa thought, in her designer dress. The white bodice clung to her curves before flaring out into a full, knee-length skirt. But it was the sheer overdress with its embroidered flowers, bold and beautiful in a red that matched the bridesmaids' dresses, that really made it something special.

Rosa took a perverse pleasure in the fact that Sylvie's dress clashed horribly with her hair.

Her own lemon-yellow sundress was maybe a little casual for such a celebrity wedding, but she hadn't exactly packed for the occasion. She'd made an extra effort with her hair, though, braiding it carefully and threading tiny white flowers through it. If she was here as Jude's date, even just for the day, she wanted to look as if she belonged with him.

And Jude was, quite frankly, breathtaking. While the groom's party were all in pale linen suits, Jude wore a darker charcoal suit in the same light material. His white shirt was open at the collar and his skin, while darkened a little by his time on the island, was still pale enough to make his blue eyes blaze against it, and the darkness of his hair.

It was strange, being at the wedding as a guest instead of an employee of the island. Stranger still to see Anna in her uniform of dark skirt and white blouse, her dark hair pulled severely back. Rosa kept wanting to go and help—to fetch more ice, or fix a torn hem, or mop up a spill. But instead, her job for the day was to hang off Jude's arm, look pretty and annoy his ex.

She could do that. For one day, anyway. For one day, it was a novelty. Any more, though, and she knew she'd be bored rigid.

As the sky darkened, the party went on. Food was served, music was played, speeches made. Valentina and Todd had already performed their first dance—a very location-appropriate tango, with enough heat in it that Rosa had caught Jude's eye and made a mental promise for later.

'Jude!' Valentina approached them, her hand still tightly clutching Todd's. She was beaming, happiness glowing from every inch of her. 'Isn't everything going wonderfully?'

'It's been a beautiful day,' Jude agreed, his hand resting on Rosa's thigh.

'And it's not over yet! Speaking of which... Since you're here, do you think you might be able to treat us to a song or two? Since it *is* my wedding day...'

Jude laughed. 'How can I refuse a request from the bride? Especially since I gatecrashed your wedding in the first place.' He smiled at Rosa. 'As long as you're okay here alone?'

'Absolutely.' Rosa relaxed further back into her chair. 'I'm going to sit here and keep eating these dessert canapés. You can come roll me into bed when you're done.'

'It's a deal.' Jude pressed a kiss to her lips, and disappeared off to fetch his guitar.

'You realise that when he goes back to New York he'll forget all about you.' Rosa's spine stiffened as Sylvie slipped into Jude's abandoned chair. 'When he's deep in his music he forgets almost everything.'

Rosa shrugged. 'That's not a problem for us.'

'Because you're *so* different?' Sylvie's laughter was sharp and ugly. 'Trust me, every woman thinks that.'

'No,' Rosa said, patiently. 'Because when he goes back to New York I'll be heading off somewhere else, on my next assignment. Russia, I think, this time.'

That, at least, seemed to surprise her. 'You're not planning on coming to New York with him if he asks?'

'He won't ask,' Rosa said, with certainty. 'Mostly because he knows I won't go. I have my life and he has his. It just so happens that they both intersected here for a while. That's all.'

'Do you honestly believe that you'll walk away from here and forget all about him?'

'Maybe not forget,' Rosa admitted. After all, she'd never forgotten him in the three years they were apart.

There was no reason to imagine she would this time. 'But I have plenty of other things in my life to focus on. I can't see me having time to pine, if that's what you're worried about.'

Except for all those nights, alone in a hotel room or a tent, remembering. Those were always the hardest.

'Worried? No.' Sylvie gave her a shark-bright smile. 'Relieved. If you're out of the picture in New York that gives me an opening.'

'Even if he forgets you for his music?' Rosa ignored the burning feeling in her chest that started when she imagined Jude and Sylvie together in New York. He wouldn't go back to her, would he? Not after everything she'd done. 'Do you think he'll even want to see you, after all the stories you sold about him?'

Sylvie dismissed both concerns with a wave of her hand. 'Honestly, it's more about the picture than the truth. As long as he's seen with me enough to get our photo everywhere it's good for both of us. The rest is almost beside the point.'

Beside the point. All the wonderful things she'd shared with Jude were, to Sylvie, unimportant beside his fame.

How could she ever explain to someone like that how Jude's fame was the least attractive thing about him, to her? Because it was his celebrity, his success, that meant he was tied to a life that would mean she would always have to follow. To be Jude Alexander's partner, instead of her own person.

And she couldn't do that.

A cheer went up around the crowd as Jude stepped onto the small makeshift stage the traditional Spanish band had used earlier. Sylvie disappeared, off into the crowd, presumably to be seen with someone more deserving. And Rosa settled back down to listen to Jude play.

He started with a familiar song—one of The Swifts' most classic numbers, but played in an acoustic style that rendered it almost something different altogether. Rosa had listened to plenty of Jude's band's music—it was hard to avoid anywhere where music was played, like hotel bars and supermarkets, not to mention the car radio. Sometimes, when she really wanted to torture herself, she'd even look him up online and read interviews with him, looking for the man she'd once known. The photos she'd taken on tour with them, what seemed like a lifetime ago now, showed a different man altogether, she always thought. Before fame hit, and the Jude the public saw became more polished, more careful.

But she'd never heard the songs this way before—just Jude and his guitar. There was so much more emotion in the music, she thought. They felt raw, but real, without all the production and effects added to the finished pieces.

She preferred them this way, she decided. But maybe that wasn't surprising. She preferred the man playing them to the one Sylvie described as Jude in New York.

The next song he played, though, sounded different again. Mostly because the last time she'd heard it, Gareth had been the one singing it. Rosa caught Jude's eye and saw all the emotions there. Had he ever even played this song since Gareth's death? Probably not, knowing Jude.

But maybe it was time. He'd said he wanted to find closure on the island, to face his demons. Coming to terms with what had happened to Gareth had to be a big part of that.

Rosa hoped it was helping. She wanted Jude happy, even if she wouldn't be there to see it.

Suddenly, Leo pulled a chair up next to her. 'Where's Anna?'

'I thought you were leaving.' Rosa stared at her sister's ex with loathing. Hadn't he told Anna he'd be leaving the island the minute the speeches were over? If he had nothing more to offer, then as far as Rosa was concerned, the sooner he left, the better.

'I need to speak to Anna.'

'Maybe she doesn't want to speak to you.' And even if she did, maybe she shouldn't.

'Maybe,' Leo acknowledged. 'It's important, Rosa, please.'

Rosa sat staring at the stage, at Jude. She didn't want Anna to have to wait three years for closure, as they had. 'She'll be back at the villa. She's overseeing the clean-up and packing.'

'Packing?'

'She's heading back to Oxford tomorrow.' Leaving Rosa to manage the week of post-wedding festivities Valentina had requested. Yay. Except, right now, Rosa couldn't deny her sister anything. Not if it meant Anna finally finding the life she wanted.

'I thought she was staying here?' Leo sounded surprised.

'Mama wants her to go back and think about it. It's a huge change. Everyone just wants her to be sure. To make sure she's doing it for the right reasons.' She gave him a sidelong glance.

'Thanks.' Leo got to his feet.

Rosa tried to resist the urge to say anything more, and failed.

'Leo? She's actually doing really well. If you are going to make matters worse then stay away or I'll make you sorry you ever messed with my sister.' Threat made, she turned her attention back to the stage, clearly dismissing him.

'Warning understood,' Leo said and walked away.

'It better be,' Rosa muttered, under her breath. But then Jude, still up on stage, started speaking, and she forgot all about her sister's problems for a moment.

'This is my last song tonight,' Jude said, to a chorus of groans and calls for more. He held up a hand. 'No, really. But I just wanted to say, before I play it, that I wrote this one here, on La Isla Marina. I think this island has romance woven into its soil and stone and sand, because I've never felt as inspired as I do here. Although, that might be down to a certain muse re-entering my life, too.' He looked straight at Rosa as he said it, and her heart stuttered at everything she saw in his eyes. 'I'll be leaving the island soon, but I know my memories of this place will live on. And, Valentina, Todd…if your marriage is half as happy as I've been here on the island, you'll be very fortunate indeed. And I hope that it's twice as happy as that. So, this one is for the bride and groom.'

But it wasn't, Rosa realised as he started to pluck the strings, in the traditional Spanish style. It was *her* song. The one he'd written for her as she'd lain naked in his bed the night before.

She watched his face as he sang, saw all the emotion that was bursting to escape from her heart echoed there. And as his bright blue gaze met hers as he sang of water on skin and moonlight overhead, a bone-deep truth resounded through her.

She was in love with Jude Alexander.

And there was nothing she could do about it, because he was going to leave her, this time.

For good.

The week that followed the wedding had been planned as five days of non-stop entertainment for the wedding guests. Since Anna had left for Oxford (with Leo in tow, after what must have been a lot of grovelling on Leo's part, Jude imagined) Rosa was in charge, which meant she was rather busier than Jude would have liked. Given that it was their last week on the island together, he'd have preferred she had nothing to concentrate on but him, but apparently that wasn't how this worked.

'Sorry,' she'd murmur against his skin as she slipped out of his bed in the morning. 'There's cookery lessons at the villa today.' Or, 'I'm taking a group horse-riding over on the mainland.'

'Can't you skive off, just for one day?' he'd asked, on the second morning. 'Stay here with me. We can go skinny-dipping again. Or you could finally show me the secret door to your bedroom…'

'Sorry,' she'd said again, smiling sadly. 'Anna left me in charge. And for once, I'm actually trying to live up to my obligations.'

And how was he supposed to argue with that?

There were a few trips he joined in with, though—namely the tapas tour of Cala del Mar, and the wine tasting at a local vineyard on the mainland. Rosa was too busy to dedicate all her time to him on those trips, but just the shared smiles across the room or a moment enjoying a plate of *gambas* together was enough to keep him going until the evening.

And the evenings, once all the entertainment was over, were magical.

It was as if, with their limited time together shrinking by the hour, they'd both been possessed with a sense of urgency that outshone even their previous passion. Jude didn't know how Rosa was coping on so little sleep, but she never seemed tired when she arrived at his bungalow in the evening. They'd fall asleep in each other's arms hours later, and then, before he knew it, Rosa would be slipping away, murmuring her apologies.

The coldness she left behind only made him more intent on enjoying every last second they had together.

But if their nights brought them closer than ever, the days seemed to put a strange barrier between them. He was a guest, no longer helping Rosa with the arrangements, but dancing attendance on Valentina and the others instead. Just being surrounded by the sort of people he was used to partying with in New York made him feel hemmed in again, and he seemed to spend his time dodging conversations about life in the city, or his plans for after the week was up. Most of all, he seemed to be avoiding Sylvie, who never had been very good at reading when a person didn't want to spend time with her.

Rosa, of course, charmed everyone she spoke to. She swept through the events and the days with a smile and a ready hand, fixing whatever needed fixing, keeping everything running so smoothly even Anna would be proud of her, Jude thought. But he was sure the only reason her easy charm never failed was because she knew this was only temporary. Five days of making nice with celebrities and rich folk and she'd be back to her real life.

Except this *was* his real life, to a point. He would be going back to this soon enough.

Was it so wrong of him to want to spend his last few days on the island with Rosa?

But she had work to do, so he let her get on with it, smiling at her across rooms and waiting for night to fall so she could be just his again.

For their last night on the island, Rosa had arranged a moonlight picnic on the beach for everyone. Given how late the sun set, quite apart from his objections to spending his last evening with Rosa with a crowd of people,

Jude thought this was kind of stupid, but Valentina had assured him it was romantic.

'You should definitely come,' she'd said, with a sly smile. 'You need more romance in your life.'

'I have plenty of romance,' Jude had replied, thinking of Rosa naked in his arms.

Valentina, seemingly reading his mind, had slapped his arm. 'That's not romance, Jude. Come on, join us tonight. And bring your guitar.'

'Now the truth comes out. I knew you only wanted me for my music.'

Valentina had laughed. 'I think Rosa and Todd would object to me wanting anything more, don't you?'

So that was how he came to be playing all the usual songs in an unusual place, sitting on a piece of driftwood on the beach, watching the moon play on the water. They'd lit a bonfire a little way away, and the staff were providing marshmallows and sticks to toast them on. They also had a full barbecue set up a little further away, as well as the picnic buffet. By the look of the amount of food and alcohol laid on, they were expecting this thing to go on all night. In which case there'd be a lot of hung-over guests staggering to the boats to catch their flights home tomorrow.

Maybe he and Rosa could escape early, though, once everyone was suitably sloshed.

At least it wasn't the same beach where he and Rosa had gone for their fateful swim. He wasn't sure he'd have been able to keep his mind on the music if his brain had been reliving that night over and over. As it was, it was hard not to remember Rosa emerging from the sea, naked and glistening like a water goddess.

A discordant twanging sound came from his guitar, and he realised he'd managed to break a string, just imagining

Rosa naked. Thankfully, everyone was so busy talking, eating and drinking no one was even paying all that much attention to his playing, so he retrieved a spare string from his case and set about restringing the instrument.

'You okay there?' Rosa sank to the sand in front of him, her legs folded under her, as he finished fixing his guitar. Her eyes shone in the firelight, her dark hair curling loose over her shoulders for once, just as it was in bed at night.

'Depends,' he said, tuning up. 'Do you think we can get out of here soon?'

Rosa gave him a cheeky grin. 'You're just never going to see the ocean the same way again, are you?'

'Apparently not.' No point denying what he'd been thinking about. Not with Rosa. Especially since he was almost certain she'd been thinking the same.

'Play me my song again,' she said, softly. 'One more time, and then I'll take you to bed.'

'Your wish is my command,' Jude said, and started to play.

They only had one more night together. He'd give her anything she asked.

CHAPTER TWELVE

THE FAMILIAR NOTES rose up into the night, circling above
the fire, the beach, the crowd, the sea. Rosa closed her
eyes and let them wash over her. She couldn't look at
Jude as he played, even less so when he sang. The words
cut too close, piercing her chest and brushing up against
her heart.

She'd spent so long keeping everything away from
there, ensuring that no one could lasso her heart and use it
to keep her tied down. But it seemed that Jude had snuck
in there against her best defences, anyway.

She was in love with Jude Alexander. She'd hoped that
sudden truth of feeling might pass, but the week since the
wedding had only confirmed it for her. She'd spent her
days running events for the wedding guests, her brain
only half functioning—because the other half was still
thinking about Jude. And her nights…nothing about her
nights with him had gone any way at all to persuading
her to fall *out* of love with him.

The worst part was, she was starting to think nothing would.

She was irrevocably in love with Jude Alexander, and
it was entirely possible she had been for the last three
years and was only now coming out of denial.

She'd tried to tell herself that it didn't matter. It didn't change anything. Their situations were still exactly as they had been, so what difference did her feelings make? She'd vowed to make the most of their last week together, and then she'd move on. Just as she had a hundred times before. Easy.

But now she was down to counting in hours, and he was singing her song, and nothing about it felt easy at all.

How had she let this happen? She'd been so careful, always, not to let anything trap her with obligations and expectations. She'd rebelled against her father's academic expectations, lived down to Anna's expectations for her family life, run away from Jude's hopes for love and a future for them…and she'd ended up here, anyway.

Maybe Jude was right. Maybe them both being on the island at the same time was fate, or destiny. A way of making them face up to their demons.

But when her demons were as good-looking as Jude, it was so damn hard not to be tempted by them.

'I'll always see you in the moonlight,' Jude sang, the song coming to a close with a few more notes, and when Rosa opened her eyes he was staring right down into them.

She could stay lost in those blue eyes for eternity. And that terrified her almost as much as it excited her.

'Let's go,' she whispered. 'Now.'

Jude's slow smile was all the agreement she needed.

Rosa's body thrummed with anticipation as they slipped away from the beach, treading the familiar path back to Jude's bungalow. But for once, it wasn't the expectation of his hands on her body that made her blood buzz. This was something entirely new.

This wasn't sex. This was love.

Because she had to tell him. She couldn't let him leave without knowing how she felt.

Maybe it would change nothing, but she knew she'd

never forgive herself if she didn't try. And as her family well knew, Rosa didn't know how to *not* say whatever was on her mind.

The moment the bungalow door closed behind them, Jude dropped his guitar case to the floor and his hands were at her waist, his mouth at her neck, and it took all her mental strength to say, 'Wait.'

If they started this, she wouldn't be able to stop it. And they needed to talk first.

Jude pulled back, just enough to look into her eyes. 'What's the matter?' The concern in his voice was a warm comfort around her heart.

He'd loved her once. Maybe he could again.

Maybe even enough to give her what she needed to be able to have this.

'I need to…can we talk? Just for a moment?'

If he said no, this wouldn't last any longer, anyway. And if he said yes…then there was no rush any more. They could take all the time in the world.

The expanse of for ever stretching out before them, together, for the first time didn't feel like a life sentence. Like a punishment.

It felt like the ultimate in opportunity.

As long as it could happen her way.

'Sure.' Frowning, Jude led her to the small seating area, pouring them each a glass of wine from the carafe on the counter. 'What is it?'

Rosa bit her lip. She wasn't good at subtle; she never had been. And she couldn't twist words and make a fancy argument as Anna could. She relied on her pictures, an image to tell a hundred stories, with just a few words where necessary to illuminate the subject.

She wasn't a poet, like Jude. She couldn't express her emotions in clever rhyme and melody.

All she had was her truths.

What she knew to be true. So she started there.

'You need to leave New York.' Okay, so it wasn't the most romantic opening, but it was true.

Jude looked taken aback. 'Okay…why, exactly?'

'Because it's dragging you down. Your guilt for Gareth, your promises…and that place. When I met you three years ago, you were full of music, of life. And now…now it's all about the brand and the label and negotiations with the rest of the band and…don't you want to be free of that?'

'Maybe.' Jude put his glass down on the counter. 'But I owe it to Gareth's memory—'

'No! No, you don't.' That was what was keeping him back. The memory of a friend who couldn't ever be satisfied when he was alive, let alone now he was dead.

'You don't understand,' Jude started, but Rosa interrupted him again.

'Yes, I do. I understand that you made Gareth a promise to keep him alive. But you couldn't save him. No one could. It wasn't me being there, or even me leaving that made you break that promise. Gareth was an addict. He was sick, and he needed more help than one best friend saying, "That's a bad idea." And he needed to want that help. He needed to seek it out and find a way to break that addiction and he didn't. If he'd been ready to be helped, it wouldn't matter what was going on in your life. And even then…you couldn't give up your life to save his. He wouldn't want that, and you know it.' She felt breathless, saying all the words she knew he needed to hear but wouldn't want to.

'Maybe,' he acknowledged. 'But even if you're right, I still owe him. I made another promise, when he died, remember?'

'And you've fulfilled it! You found the fame you swore you'd both fight for. You've lived his success for him.' When would he see that he'd done everything he could? It was time to live his own life, his own choices now.

But Jude looked away. 'It's not enough.'

'It'll never be enough.' Rosa grabbed his hand where he stood beside her, willing him to understand. 'Nothing ever was, for Gareth. Even now…when does it stop? When do you say, I've gone as far as I can go?'

'I don't know.'

'Because that point doesn't exist!' She'd seen it before. And he *had* to believe her. 'You'll keep living your life for someone else—someone who isn't even here to see it—for ever. And you'll never be happy. And he'll never be satisfied.'

Jude shook his head, and Rosa knew he wasn't hearing her. 'It's not just about Gareth's memory, anyway. I also want to keep having a career, you know. Music was my life long before you came into it.'

'You'll always have that,' Rosa replied. 'Your music is iconic now. You could write advertising jingles for the rest of your life and it wouldn't take away from what you'd already accomplished.'

'Thanks for that vote of confidence in my musical future,' Jude said, drily.

Rosa waved a hand vaguely. 'You know what I mean.'

'I really don't.' His eyes serious, Jude moved to sit opposite her. 'Rosa. What, exactly, are you asking me to do?'

This was it. This was her last chance to put everything out on the line, and have him take it or leave it.

Take her or leave her.

And Rosa had never been more scared in her life.

She took a deep breath.

'Run away with me.'

* * *

Run away with me.

How many times over the years had he dreamt of hearing that from her? Of knowing Rosa wanted him with her, as she explored this wide world? Of having her choose him, for once, over her freedom?

Except she wasn't, was she? That was what it came down to.

She wasn't ready to give up what they had, but she wouldn't give up anything else, either.

Rosa didn't just want to have her cake and eat it, too. She wanted the damn bakery to deliver.

'You want me to give up everything I have—my band, my career, my life in New York, my future—to travel around the world at your beck and call until you get bored of me again?' Anger rose up in him, hot and furious, as he realised the truth of this.

This wasn't love. This wasn't for ever—because they both knew Rosa couldn't offer that. She never had been able to.

This was convenience. It was using his unsettled feelings, his vulnerabilities after the book's release, after Gareth, to get what she wanted.

If she'd approached it differently—suggested he extend his sabbatical away from the city until the buzz about the book died down—maybe he'd have considered it. But it was always all or nothing with Rosa. No compromise, no middle path. She didn't know how, and she wasn't willing to learn.

He looked down into her wide, dark eyes, and realised the truth.

He loved her. Of course he did. But that simply wasn't going to be enough.

'That's not what I was saying,' Rosa started.

Jude shook his head. 'Yes. It is.'

'No! Jude… I—'

'Don't say it.' If she was even *thinking* what he thought she was about to say, he couldn't hear it. He couldn't risk it. If she told him she loved him, there was no way he could walk away again, not knowing that. He'd give up everything to trail her around the world, and he'd end up resenting her for it.

A shocked laugh bubbled up from somewhere inside him.

'What's so funny?' Rosa asked, scowling.

'I just realised,' Jude said. 'This must be exactly how you felt, three years ago.' How Sancia felt in Oxford with the professor. How Gareth felt sometimes when Jude kept him safe, back at the hotel instead of out at the party where he wanted to be, blazing bright.

Maybe Rosa was right. Maybe he never could have saved Gareth. But he could decide to save himself from any more heartbreak.

It wasn't much. But it was what he had left.

'So you're punishing me. Is that it?' Rosa jumped to her feet, her colour high and her eyes blazing. 'I left you three years ago, so you won't even consider staying now? I know I hurt you, but, Jude, this is just petty.'

'Petty! Rosa, you tore my heart out and stamped on it, then breezed back into my life and told me you'd just been ready for something new!'

'I explained—' Rosa started, but Jude was in no mood to hear it. All he'd wanted was one last night with Rosa, one perfect memory to say goodbye on.

Instead he got this. Everything he ever wanted on a plate, except he knew it was laced with poison.

'You explained. Right. But what it came down to was the same thing it will always come down to with you. You value your own freedom, your own choices, above every-one else's. And that might work for you with the rest of the world. But for the people who love you? It's horrible.'

The colour faded from Rosa's face as she stumbled back-wards, grabbing a chair for support. 'What do you mean? Is it so wrong for me to want to pursue my own dreams?'

'No,' Jude allowed. 'But is it wrong of me to want to stay and look for my own?' New York might not be ev-erything he'd ever dreamed of, but he knew the rules there. He knew he was as safe as it was possible to get, knew he could look himself in the mirror and know he was living out his promise. New York had always been their dream—and Rosa was asking him to give it up.

'But you're not!' Frustration leaked out of Rosa's voice. 'You're doing what the label says you should, or the rest of the band. You're not making new music, you're just remaking the old stuff! Living for a memory. Does fame really mean so much to you that you can't give it up to pursue the music that really makes you come alive again? Like the song you wrote here, for me?'

Did she really not see? Did she really not understand? One look at her face told Jude she didn't.

'That wasn't the music, Rosa. That was you.'

'What?'

Scrubbing a hand through his hair, Jude sighed. 'I wrote that song—found the passion and the music—because I found you again. For three years, it didn't much matter what I wrote or played because you weren't there to hear it.'

'Then why didn't you come after me?' From the way her eyes widened, and her hand went to her mouth, Rosa was as shocked by her words as he was.

'How could I? You didn't tell me where you were going.'

'And in this day and age, with the Internet and every-

thing, there was absolutely no way you could find out?'
She was right, Jude knew. He *could* have found her if
he'd wanted to.

But he hadn't.

'Gareth had just died. Forgive me if—' But she could
always tell when he was lying.

'That's not why, is it? Tell me the truth, Jude. We owe
each other that much.'

'I didn't come after you because I knew I couldn't take
it if you turned me away again. You knew me, Rosa. You
knew every depth of me, more than any other person in
the world. And you turned your back on it and walked
away. No, I didn't come after you. Because I loved you,
and I knew I could never, ever be enough for you.'

'But you are!' Rosa surged forward, grabbing his
hands to her chest. 'You are. You're everything I need.
That's why I'm here, asking you. Come with me! I don't
see what the problem is. We can run together, keep having the same fun we've been having here on the island.
It doesn't have to end yet.'

'Yet.' That was what it came down to, wasn't it? With
Rosa, there was always a time limit—and only she knew
what that might be. And Jude couldn't live like that.

He'd known, deep down, that Gareth had a time limit,
too. That however hard he tried, Gareth lived too hard,
too fast, to live for ever, or even to old age. He just hadn't
expected it to be so soon. He'd thought he could buy
more time—just as he'd tried to do again on the island
with Rosa.

God, he was an idiot. Trying to control time, and other
people. Both were equally impossible.

The only thing he could control was himself. He could
keep *himself* safe, even if he couldn't ever have done the
same for Gareth.

Rosa would leave, sooner or later. It was all there in that tiny three-letter word: *yet*.

Rosa stilled as she finally caught his meaning. 'Nothing lasts for ever, Jude. Can't we just enjoy this while it *does* last?'

Jude shook his head.

'Why not?' Rosa slammed her hand down on the counter. 'Jude, I love you. Whether you want to hear it or not. And right now, I can't imagine ever loving another person my whole life—I haven't before, and I can't see that changing.'

The words pierced him straight through his body. She loved him. This was what he had always wanted.

And he was going to send it away. His choice, this time.

'So you'd marry me? Promise me for ever? Go with me wherever life took me?'

He didn't need to hear her answer. He could see it in the fear on her face.

'Why couldn't you come wherever I went?' she asked.

'Because I won't give up everything I have when I know that one day—sooner or later—you'll walk out on me again,' he said, simply. 'It almost broke me last time, Rosa. I can't risk it twice.'

'You can't trust me.'

'Can you tell me I should?'

She looked away. 'No.'

'Then I don't think there's anything more to say. Do you?'

She didn't answer.

Grabbing his guitar, Jude walked out on the love of his life.

He didn't look back.

CHAPTER THIRTEEN

TEARS BLINDED HER as Rosa raced up the path back to the villa. Thank goodness everyone was leaving tomorrow. She could be packed and on a boat with them first thing, and on a plane to Russia, or Australia—anywhere—before breakfast. She needed to get as far away from La Isla Marina, and Jude Alexander, as possible—and fast.

What had she been thinking? Of course he wouldn't give up all his successes and fame to run away with her. Who would? Rosa had always been the screw-up, the wild and free one who couldn't settle for anything. Now it seemed she couldn't live up to Jude's expectations any more than she'd lived up to her father's or her sister's. She couldn't live up to his life in New York, or the memory of the best friend he'd lost. Especially when she couldn't promise him for ever.

Except…she'd wanted to. For a heartbeat of a moment, when he'd asked if she'd marry him, she'd wanted to say yes. Wanted to fall into his arms and be his for ever.

Until he'd added 'go with me' and she'd known she couldn't promise that.

She wasn't a follower. And neither was Jude. Neither of them would ever be happy trailing around after the other.

It was an impossibility. *They* were an impossibility.

It had been fun while it lasted, but she should never have expected anything more. She wasn't good at compromise, or giving, or other people's feelings. Hadn't Anna made that clear enough?

Her sister could change her path, change her mind, her life. But Rosa never had been able to live up to Anna's example.

For one, sharp moment Rosa missed her sister so much that it ached. They might not have always—okay, often—got along, but Anna was still family. She'd turned to Rosa when she'd found out she was pregnant, eventually, and now Rosa wished that she could do the same.

But Anna was far away in Oxford with Leo, and all Rosa had left were her parents. The mother who'd taught her that the best way to deal with difficulties was to run away, and the father who'd always wanted her to be someone she wasn't.

Somehow, she couldn't see either of them fixing this mess.

Wiping her tears away, Rosa stepped into the main villa, the place she'd spent so many childhood holidays, that held so many memories.

Then she stopped.

And she stared.

'Mama?' she whispered. Sancia didn't hear her. *'Dad?'* Louder this time. 'What are you doing?'

Sancia and Ernest broke apart, and Rosa regretted her question. It was pretty obvious what they were doing.

Kissing.

Her parents.

After ten years apart. Estranged. Not speaking. Now suddenly they were…

Kissing. Passionately.

'Rosa!' Sancia patted her hair as she smiled at her daughter. 'Um, we have some news!'

'So I can see.' Rosa crossed her arms over her chest. Was *everyone* else finding their happy ever after on this island? Or, more likely, was this sudden reconciliation going to end in disaster—just as Jude and hers had?

Sancia's brow furrowed. 'Are you okay, *querida*? Did something happen?'

'I just caught my parents making out. Other than that…' She didn't want anyone to know about Jude. Not yet.

Not when his words still hurt so much.

Her father pulled a face. 'Making out? Really, Rosa. Is it so wrong for two people in love to express their affection for each other?'

'When they're *my* parents…' Rosa shook her head. 'Never mind. Just…what's going on? What's your news?' In love? Had she really heard those words from her buttoned-up father's mouth?

'Your father is moving here to the island!' Sancia practically vibrated with excitement.

Rosa blinked. And she'd thought Anna's decision to stay on La Isla Marina was the about-turn of the century.

'Here? You're staying here?' she asked her father.

Ernest put his arm around Sancia and nodded. 'I think it's about time. Don't you?'

Time? Was that all it took? If she waited another decade would she be able to make things work with Jude? Somehow, she doubted he'd be willing to wait that long.

'But…how can you just give up everything you've worked for in Oxford? All your old dreams?' His career at the university, his professional reputation—they'd been all that mattered to him, when she was growing up. Everything in their lives had been arranged around them.

And now he was just throwing them away? It didn't make any sense.

'Your mother needs support here on the island. And Anna will be here, too, so I'd be alone in Oxford.'

So that was it. Of course. 'You mean, your nursemaid is moving here so you better had, too?'

'No.' Ernest's voice was sharp. 'I'm moving here for many reasons. Not least, my health and well-being. Rosa, you've told me often enough over the years that I need to take responsibility for my health. I'd think you'd be glad I'm finally retiring to do that.'

'I am,' Rosa said, quickly. 'I just…'

Sancia pulled away to put an arm around Rosa's shoulders. 'What is it, *querida*?'

Rosa looked at her mother. 'Ten years ago you got fed up of living the life Dad wanted all the time, and you left to come here. To find your own dreams again. Right?'

'I suppose,' Sancia said. 'I was tired of always coming second to his work and not being able to follow my heart. But most of all, I just missed my home, and my parents needed me more than he did.' Her smile turned sad. 'Even more than you girls did, in some ways. Your father and I were arguing more and more, and it was making me so unhappy… I knew it had to be affecting you and Anna, too. I didn't want you to grow up in an unhappy home, and I didn't want to regret staying when I should have gone…but, Rosa, leaving you girls behind, only seeing you in the holidays, that was the hardest choice I ever had to make. You know that, don't you?'

'I do,' Rosa said as Sancia hugged her close. Her mother had always made it clear that her leaving was nothing to do with the girls—even if it had taken Rosa a while to believe it when she was younger.

Perhaps that was why she'd never asked her mother

outright for all the reasons she'd left. She'd listened to what Sancia said, tried to believe it, and always just assumed it was because she was tired of life in Oxford.

But now she needed firm answers. She needed to understand. 'Dad, what if the same thing happens to you?'

'What do you mean?' Ernest asked.

'What if, living here, you get, well, bored? You're giving up everything that has always mattered to you. I don't want you to end up resenting Mama for that in a few months, or years. When you realise you're tied to her dreams and obligated to stay.'

She'd never seen the smile on her father's face before, Rosa realised. It was softer, kinder, more indulgent than any smile he'd given her before.

Professor Gray held a hand out to Sancia, who took it with a smile of her own. Rosa watched, confused.

'You're forgetting my most important reason to stay here, Rosa,' her father said. 'I'm in love with your mother.'

Love. The word caught her in the throat. Did it always have to come down to that?

'What if that isn't enough?' she asked, and the concern on Sancia's face returned.

'Rosa, did something happen with Jude?' she asked.

'I just need to know,' Rosa said desperately, her arms wrapped tight around her middle. 'What if love isn't enough?'

'Then nothing is,' Sancia said, simply.

'When it's true love, staying isn't an obligation. It's a privilege.' Professor Gray pressed a kiss to his ex-wife's head. 'I'm giving up my old dreams for new ones. Better ones.'

'We got it wrong last time,' Sancia said. 'Both of us. We thought there were more important things than love.'

'Aren't there?' Rosa felt as if the bottom were falling out of her heart.

'There are things that matter as much,' Professor Gray allowed. 'And there are circumstances that can overwhelm it, if you're not careful.'

'So if it's love, you have to give up everything?' Because that didn't sound like love to her.

'No, *querida*.' Sancia moved forward, guiding Rosa with an arm around her shoulder to one of the low, cushioned benches that were scattered around the reception area. 'Love is about accepting the other person as they are, and loving them in spite of your differences.'

'Or because of them,' her father added, sitting down beside her. 'Your mother and I...we're very different people. But those differences don't lessen our love any.'

'And in some ways they even make us stronger,' Sancia added. 'As long as we accept them and respect them.'

'You mean he has to love me for who I am?' Because in that case, there really was no hope for Jude and her.

Sancia laughed, lightly. 'That's the easy part, *querieda*. Who could not love you?'

Rosa stared at her mother in amazement. 'You *have* to love me. You're my parents. But I know I'm not easy to love. I know it's in spite of all my flaws and not because of them. I'm no Anna.'

'We never wanted you to be Anna,' Sancia said, surprised. 'We just wanted you to be happy.'

Beside her, Rosa's father was nodding his agreement. Rosa looked at him in confusion. 'But... I never could follow the schedule or plan ahead. I couldn't settle to anything, especially not studying.'

'And none of that meant we loved you any less,' Ernest said. 'Or that we were any the less proud of you than we are of Anna.'

Rosa blinked, tears burning behind her eyes again.

'Oh, Rosa.' Sancia hugged her tightly. 'How could you think you are difficult to love? You're so full of life and spirit.'

'Just like your mother. That's one of the many reasons I fell in love with her,' Ernest put in. 'And you've taken that spirit out into the world, forging your own, brilliant path. Your sister collects all your photos and articles and saves them for me, you know. I have them all catalogued in my office.' He said it so casually, as if it were obvious. An inevitability. But the knowledge lifted Rosa's heart, even in the middle of her misery.

'We're very proud of you, *querida*,' Sancia said. 'And we love you very much. And if Jude doesn't, then he's a fool.'

Rosa shook her head. 'He's not. Last time… I left him. I broke his heart.'

'I wonder where you learnt to do that,' Ernest murmured, but he was smiling fondly at Sancia as he said it.

'Then he's a coward, if he won't take the risk of loving you again.' Sancia looked outraged on Rosa's behalf.

'I don't blame him,' Rosa admitted. 'I'm not sure I would. I'm asking him to give up everything.'

'Love does take some compromise, Rosa,' her father said, gently. 'But the rewards should always be greater than whatever you have to give up.'

'In the end, love is the only thing that lasts,' Sancia said, smiling at her husband as she stood, holding her hand out to him. 'And it's worth ten times of everything else.'

'Which is why we won't make the same mistakes again.' Rosa's father got to his feet, too, taking Sancia's hand.

'I'm glad,' Rosa said, the words thick in her throat. 'I'm glad you found each other again.'

'So am I,' Sancia said, and then Ernest swept her into his arms again, and Rosa turned away.

She couldn't watch their happiness. Not tonight.

Tomorrow. Tomorrow she'd be happy for them. She'd smile and offer congratulations on her way off the island.

Tonight, she just needed to mourn her own broken heart, and think about all the compromises she hadn't been willing to make, until it was too late.

And then she'd move on.

Jude didn't trust her love. She hadn't left herself any other choices.

Jude hadn't exactly planned on heading back to the beach, but that was where he found himself, all the same.

The party was winding down, the fire burning down low. Couples were dotted around the sand in cosy embraces, talking low, and Valentina and Todd were dancing on the shoreline as if there were no one else in the world but them.

Jude looked away. He couldn't quite bear to watch that kind of happiness tonight.

Settling back onto his piece of driftwood, he pulled his guitar from its case again. Music had always been his friend, his comfort, and he needed it tonight more than ever, since the day he lost Gareth.

Rosa would be leaving as soon as she could, of course. And he'd be left behind again, with his heart in tatters. Meeting Rosa had torn his life apart the first time, but he'd honestly thought he could withstand it this time. How much worse could she do to him, after all?

It turned out, quite a lot.

She loved him. Or she thought she did. Just not enough to give up any iota of her freedom, or give him any hope that she wouldn't leave him again without a backward glance.

Rosa was right, of course. Nothing did last for ever, and there were no guarantees in this life. Gareth had taught him that.

But he needed more than she could give him. He needed...something. Some sign that she was in this as deeply as he was. That she wanted it to last as much as he did.

Was that too much to ask?

'I didn't expect to see you back here tonight.' Sylvie settled herself onto the sand in front of him, too close to where Rosa had sat for Jude to feel comfortable with it.

'You know me. Always the last at a party.'

'Yes,' Sylvie allowed. 'But that was usually because I didn't want to leave until everyone else who mattered had. You never cared for them for yourself.'

'I'll have to get used to them again, I suppose,' Jude said.

'You're definitely coming back to New York, then?' Sylvie sounded surprised. 'I know Rosa said you were, but I assumed she was just being careful. That she was hoping you'd go with her, but she didn't want to fall too deep in case you didn't feel the same. It's what I would do.'

Jude gave a low laugh. 'Trust me, Rosa is never careful. With anything.' Including his heart.

'That's why you love her, I suppose,' Sylvie said, her head tilted to her shoulder as she looked up at him. 'She's so free and open. Like you were, when you first came to the city.'

'Who said I loved her?'

Sylvie's smile was sad. 'Oh, Jude. Anyone who has seen you together this week knows that. You're not subtle, my dear.'

'I wasn't trying to be.' He hadn't been trying to be anything, here. Not a celebrity, not a star. Not a musician. Not Gareth's best friend. Not even Jude Alexander, brand.

He hadn't even tried to be enough for Rosa—he'd known there wasn't any point.

He'd been just Jude. Himself.

And Rosa had loved him. Not enough to stay, sure, but enough to tell him. For Rosa, that was a lot.

More than he'd have expected, before tonight.

'It's better this way.' Sylvie stretched her long legs out over the sand. 'I know you don't love me. I'm not sure if I love you either, to be honest. But I think love might be overrated. You don't need love—especially not if it makes you look as miserable as you do tonight.'

'What do I need, then?' Jude asked, honestly curious. Maybe there was another path. One that hurt less. That would be good.

'You need someone to look pretty next to you at awards ceremonies. Someone who doesn't object to you being away on tour for half the year, or mind when you lock yourself away to write for days on end. Someone to keep the groupies and whackos at bay, at least a little bit. Someone who gets as much from the association as you do. Someone who fits your level of stardom.'

'Someone like you?' he guessed.

'Why not?' Sylvie shrugged those elegant shoulders. 'We were good together, Jude, admit it. It might not be love, but it was enough. Satisfactory satisfaction, if you like.'

She was right, Jude realised. Sylvie had been the picture-perfect partner for him, supporting his brand, making sure he was seen at the right places, giving him—and the band—the right level of glamour. Gareth would have been jealous as all hell.

No, Gareth would have snagged Sylvie himself, and shown her off all over the world. Gareth would have lived the life Jude had now with style and flourish and excitement. He'd have loved it.

But the thought of going back to it made Jude feel as if the sea were closing in over his head and taking him down.

And Rosa was the only one that could save him, pull him out of the water he'd been treading for too long.

'I can't do it, Sylvie.' He shook his head, placing his guitar back in its case, as clarity flowed over him like the tide. 'I can't live like that again.'

Rosa was right. Well, no, she was still more wrong than right about a lot of things. But she was right about him.

He had to let Gareth's memories, the broken promises, and all the expectations go.

He needed to be free every bit as much as she did.

And the only time he ever felt free to be himself was when he was with Rosa.

Which only left him with one option.

She couldn't promise him anything, but then nobody could. Not really. He knew, better than anyone, that some promises just weren't possible to keep.

Maybe they didn't need any promises. Maybe all they needed was love.

And the willingness to risk everything for it. Because some people were worth the risk. One person, anyway.

Gareth would have. Gareth always believed a risk was worth it, if the prize was big enough. For Gareth, the prize was always fame.

For Jude, it was Rosa.

And suddenly, Jude knew he would risk it, too.

CHAPTER FOURTEEN

ROSA'S TURRET BEDROOM had always been an escape, before. A place of refuge from her family, or the guests on the island, or whatever. But now it felt like a cell, one she couldn't wait to escape.

She folded the yellow dress she'd worn for the wedding and placed it in her case, followed by the skirt she'd stripped off on the beach the night she went swimming with Jude. Tears dripped onto the fabric, and she shoved it in fast. She couldn't think about Jude. Possibly ever again, but definitely not until she'd put some considerable air miles between them.

She needed to move on. She didn't have any other choice now.

Maybe her parents were right and love could overcome, but not for her and Jude. She'd already burned that bridge. He was probably halfway off the island by now, and she wouldn't chase him. She smiled, sadly, remembering the reasons he'd given for not chasing her three years ago. Suddenly, she understood, in a way she couldn't have before. Not until she'd lived the same moment.

But things were different now. She understood herself better, and her relationship with her family. She was a different person. Maybe, in time, her dreams would shift, too. Maybe she'd even meet someone else, one day. In the distant, distant future. But even as she thought it, she couldn't believe it. Who could live up to Jude Alexander?

So, it was just her. Just like before. That was okay. She'd go to Russia. The story there sounded interesting, important. She'd get her camera out and seek truths through its lens. She'd live the life she'd always promised herself she'd have.

And she might not be happy, but she could be content. She could be herself. And that wasn't nothing.

But then the door to her room flew open and she spun to see Jude standing there, too big in the narrow doorway, his bright blue eyes wild and his black hair crazy.

Swallowing down the last of her tears, Rosa fought to keep her chin level and her voice even. It seemed absurd that, after everything they'd shared over the last few weeks, this was the first time he'd ever even been in her room. 'You found the secret door at last, then?'

'Your mother showed me.' His voice was rough, as if he was as close to tears as she was.

Damn Sancia. Wasn't her mama supposed to be on her side?

'What do you want, Jude?' Hadn't they said enough terrible, hurtful things to each other already? Rosa wasn't sure she could stand to hear any more.

But Jude looked her straight in the eye and said, 'You.'

'I think you made it very clear that you don't,' Rosa said, looking away. 'If you've come here to rub it in some more—'

'I haven't.' Jude stepped closer, taking the dress she was holding from her hands. 'Rosa, just listen? Please?'

It was the please that undid her. She never could deny him when he asked her in that voice. Why else had she had to disappear without word, last time? If he'd asked her to stay…she still wasn't sure she could have said no.

'Okay.'

She couldn't imagine what he'd have to say that could possibly make anything between them any better, though. He'd made it very clear that it was up to her to change the conversation—to change her mind, her direction.

Sancia had called him a coward. But it wasn't him, was it? *She* was the one who needed to be brave.

She needed to find the courage to make big promises. The for ever kind. And she might have to give up everything she'd ever fought for before to do that. Could she?

Would he even let her try?

Rosa thought again of the future she imagined—living her truths, being herself, being content. But never happy.

But what was her other option?

She had to make a promise she would have to keep. She had to live up to expectations for once, whatever her parents said.

She knew, deep down in her soul, that this was it for her.

This was love, and it was all she was going to get.

Anna had changed her dreams. Her life.

So had her father, and that had seemed impossible even a week ago.

Maybe she could do it, too.

She had to at least try, or she knew she'd regret it for the rest of her life.

'I've been thinking,' Jude said. 'I can't leave things as we did, not again. When you left me last time, I spent three years wondering what I did wrong, wishing I could have one more chance to put it right.'

'Or for me to do it right,' Rosa put in, and he smiled.

'So this time, let's try, yeah?'

Hope bubbled up in her chest. 'You're giving me a second chance?' This was it. This time, she wouldn't screw it up. The third time was the charm, right? She just had to stamp down on all those impulses that told her to run. She could stay.

'I'm giving us as many chances as we need to get it right,' Jude said.

But Rosa wasn't listening. Her parents' words were echoing through her mind and finally, suddenly, it seemed possible. If she had Jude with her, she could do it all. Couldn't she?

'I've been thinking… I could come to New York. There's so many stories there, so many photos. I could work there. It could work.'

'Rosa.'

'I could stay in one place.'

'No, you couldn't.'

'I could come on tour with you, then.'

'And follow me round like a groupie?'

Why was he smiling? He kept shooting down every possibility she gave him, and he was doing it with a smile on his face.

'Jude…' She was begging. She was actually going to beg. What the hell had he done to her? 'Just tell me what you need me to do and I'll do it. I'll do whatever it takes to be with you.'

Rosa's words stuck in his chest, and he caught her hands in his in their place, holding them to him. 'You don't understand. Rosa, you don't need to do anything. Except be you.'

She blinked up at him, those dark eyes he loved still wet with tears. Jude wanted to kiss away every tear on her cheek, but first he had to explain himself.

'I went back to the beach after you left. I spoke to Sylvie about New York and the more I imagined going back there, back to that same old life again…the more I knew I couldn't do it. I can't be that Jude Alexander any more. The man they wrote about in that book is gone—if he ever existed at all. And so is the best friend Gareth knew. I'm not the same, now. I can't play that part.'

'Well, I knew that,' Rosa muttered, and he smiled down at her.

'Yeah, well, you were always the expert at being true to yourself.'

'Even when it hurts others.'

'I shouldn't have said that,' Jude said.

Rosa gave a half shrug. 'It's true. I just… I don't know how to be anything else. But I'll learn. I'll figure it out if it means I get to be with you.'

'Luckily for both of us, I love you exactly the way you are,' Jude said, gratified by the sharp intake of breath his words caused in Rosa.

'You love me? Still?'

'Rosa, I've always loved you. From the moment you walked into my life three years ago, I always knew that there was no one else for me. No one else could be so full of life—or could make me feel so alive.' Jude took a breath. 'You asked me a question earlier, remember?' Rosa nodded. 'Will you ask me again?'

'Will you run away with me?' The hope in her eyes was what helped him answer. To step over the edge and give up the life he'd worked for, the fame, the proof that he was worth something, the dreams he and Gareth had dreamt together. Everything.

He'd risk everything for her.

'I'll run anywhere with you,' he said, and kissed her.

For a moment, the world seemed to tilt and turn and snap into place. For the first time in too many years, everything felt right. He didn't have to prove anything, any more. He didn't need to be anything except the man Rosa loved.

All he needed to do was love her back. And it felt as if he'd already been doing that for ever, anyway.

Rosa broke the kiss. 'Wait. How is this going to work? What about the band?'

'I'll tell them I need a break. Or I'll take some time to write—and I can do that wherever you are.' He kissed her hands. 'I can't let you give up your dreams for me, but maybe neither of us needs to give up anything. Maybe we can both just chase them together.'

'Are you sure?'

'Surer than I've ever been about anything,' Jude said. 'Think about it. We can not settle down together. We can spend time in the city when I'm recording, perhaps, and maybe you'd like to come on tour sometimes, when you're not away working.'

'And the rest of the time?'

'I'll come with you. Wherever you want to go.'

'And we'll spend our summers on La Isla Marina with Anna and Leo and the baby, and Mama and Dad?'

'Of course,' Jude replied. 'One of these days I'm going to beat your father at Scrabble.'

'No,' Rosa said fondly. 'You're not. He cheats.'

'I knew it!'

'But you'll play him anyway?'

'I will. But only because it would be rude to refuse my wife's father a game.'

'Your wife?'

'You liked how I slipped that in there?' Jude asked, grinning.

'I know I'm unconventional about these things, but I

seem to remember something about having to be asked, first.'

Jude dropped to one knee, her hands still tight in his as he looked up at her. 'Rosa Gray, will you chase your dreams with me?'

'Yes.'

'Will you love me for ever?'

'Definitely.'

'Will you let me love you and walk by your side for the rest of your life?'

'Oh, yes.'

'Then I think we might as well get married, don't you?'

Laughing, Rosa pulled him to his feet and kissed him, soundly. 'For a poet, that was incredibly unromantic.'

'I'll work on it,' Jude promised.

'Well, we do have for ever,' Rosa said, wrapping her arms around him. 'After all, I'm not going anywhere. At least, not without you.'

'That's all the promise I'll ever need from you,' Jude replied, and kissed her.

EPILOGUE

La Isla Marina was beautiful in the late-afternoon sunlight. The tiny lights strung through the trees were already lit, glowing in the fading daylight, and lanterns lit the way to the pagoda, through the rows of chairs filled with friends and family, from the island, the mainland, Britain, the States and beyond.

Rosa peered around the corner, down to the pagoda where Jude already stood, her father at his side. Then her niece squirmed in her arms, and she resumed swaying in the way the baby seemed to like best, hoping she wasn't drooling on her dress. Being an auntie seemed to involve a lot of cuddles, which she was just fine with. Uncle Jude was better for the lullabies, though.

'Are you ready?' Rosa asked Sancia, as Anna fiddled with their mother's veil.

Sancia laughed. 'Ready? *Querida*, I've been ready for more than ten years. I was just waiting for your father to come to his senses and come after me.'

The fact that Sancia and Ernest had never actually got around to divorcing should have been a clue, Rosa thought. But at least it made things easier now—a vow renewal on the island was much more special than having to go to the mainland for a formal remarriage.

Anna held out her arms for her daughter, and Rosa

handed her over, feeling a brief pang of emptiness as she did so.

It didn't last long, though. She pressed a hand to her stomach, and remembered that wherever she roamed now, she did it with company. First Jude, and, soon, their child.

Looking down at the path at her feet to hide her smile, Rosa thought how much this would have terrified her a few years ago. Not now, though.

Now, it all seemed like the biggest adventure she'd chased yet.

'Right, that's the first signal,' Anna said as the music changed. 'Everyone ready?'

They'd agreed that they'd walk their mother down the aisle together. It just felt right, since they were entrusting her to their father again. They both had their own lives to live now—Anna and Leo on the island, and Rosa and Jude wherever the mood took them.

Leo appeared to take the baby from Anna, and reclaim his seat at the front. Then Sancia linked arms with both her daughters, and they prepared to walk down the aisle, just as Anna had nine months earlier, still barely show-ing, to marry Leo. Jude and Rosa had managed to avoid the big showy wedding so far, and Rosa wasn't entirely looking forward to telling her mother that, technically, they were already married. She had a feeling that Sancia wouldn't feel the quick register office service when they were passing through London on tour would really count.

But it counted to Rosa.

Right until the moment she said yes, she'd been half afraid she'd run—and she knew Jude had, too. But when it came down to it, she knew that their love was far more binding than any piece of paper or jewellery.

Really, what more could she give Jude than her heart, anyway? And he'd had that all along.

'It's so wonderful to have both my girls together on the island again,' Sancia said, squeezing them close as they waited for that second change in the music, the one that told them it was time to start walking.

'It is nice to all be together,' Anna agreed. 'Rosa, will you come again for longer, later in the summer?'

'We'll try,' Rosa replied, as the music changed and Anna signalled for them to take their first steps. Rosa grinned as she saw Jude waiting with her father up ahead. 'But come winter we'll definitely be here for a few months,' she said, not thinking.

'Really?' Sancia stopped walking, a pace before the aisle started, and Rosa realised that the middle of her vow renewal service might not have been quite the right time to tell her mother this news.

Oh, well. Timing had never been her strong suit. Or not blurting things out the moment she thought of them.

'Why, Rosa?' Anna had a small line between her eyebrows.

Rosa shrugged. 'Well, I need you both to teach me everything you know about babies. And pretty fast.'

Sancia squealed, embracing her tightly, and Rosa saw her father rolling his eyes over her mother's shoulder.

'You made her smudge her make-up,' Anna said, with a sigh. But Rosa knew from the grin on her face that her sister was happy for her.

'Come on, Mama,' she said, disentangling herself. 'Dad's waiting.'

'Oh, he's waited this long,' Sancia said. 'A few more moments won't make a difference.'

'Besides,' Rosa agreed, smiling at Jude at the other end of the aisle, 'the best things in life are worth waiting for.'

* * * * *

COMING SOON!

We really hope you enjoyed reading this book.
If you're looking for more romance
be sure to head to the shops when
new books are available on

Thursday 15th January

To see which titles are coming soon, please visit
millsandboon.co.uk/nextmonth

MILLS & BOON

MILLS & BOON

MODERN

Power and Passion

Prepare to be swept off your feet by sophisticated, sexy and seductive heroes, in some of the world's most glamorous and romantic locations, where power and passion collide.

MILLS & BOON

MEDICAL

Pulse-Racing Passion

Set your pulse racing with delectable doctors, hot-shot surgeons and fearless first resonders. Escape to a world where life and love play out against a high-pressured medical backdrop, where emotions and passion run high.

afterglow BOOKS

Afterglow Books is a trend-led, trope-filled list of books with diverse, authentic and relatable characters, a wide array of voices and representations, plus real world trials and tribulations. Featuring all the tropes you could possibly want (think small-town settings, fake relationships, grumpy vs sunshine, enemies to lovers) and all with a generous dose of spice in every story.

♪ @millsandboonuk
⊙ @millsandboonuk
afterglowbooks.co.uk
#AfterglowBooks

For all the latest book news, exclusive content and giveaways scan the QR code below to sign up to the Afterglow newsletter:

SCAN ME

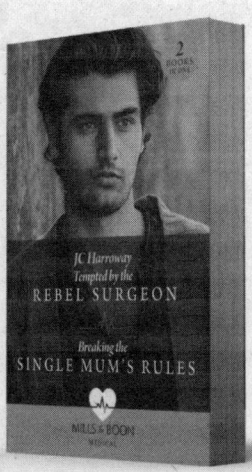

LET'S TALK
Romance

For exclusive extracts, competitions and special offers, find us online:

f MillsandBoon

X @MillsandBoon

⌾ @MillsandBoonUK

♪ @MillsandBoonUK

Get in touch on 01413 063 232